Dear Reader:

Rorik is a Viking warrior, as fierce and savage as the North Sea during the winter solstice. Mirana is a Viking woman who loves birds, is more ingenious than most men, and loyal down to her toes. Her life changes utterly one fateful day when Rorik and his men come to Clontarf, a Viking fortress on the eastern coast of Ireland, to kill her half brother. But she is the one taken as a hostage to use as a pawn against him.

Rorik is the Lord of Hawkfell, an island off the east coast of Britain. The moment he brings his captive home, it seems that everything begins to fly out of his control. The women are out to teach the men a lesson with the result that the food is rank, Rorik's family is out for Mirana's blood, a murderer is out on the loose, and a huge mongrel, Kerzog, dotes not only on his master but also on his master's captive.

Rorik and Mirana are two strong-willed people, ardent in their opinions, who will have you rooting for both of them equally.

You will also discover who really rules Hawkfell Island. Please enjoy. Do let me know what you think. Write me at P.O. Box 17, Mill Valley, CA 94942 or e-mail me at ReadMoi@aol.com.

Catherine Coulter

Catherine Coulter

The critics praise the novels of
*New York Times* bestselling author
CATHERINE COULTER

## *Pendragon*

"Coulter is excellent at portraying the romantic tension between her heroes and heroines."

—*Milwaukee Journal Sentinel*

## *The Courtship*

"This is a sexy . . . Coulter Regency-era romance . . . For readers who relish the subgenre." —*Booklist*

## *Mad Jack*

"Catherine Coulter delivers . . . straightforward, fast-paced romance." —*Minneapolis Star Tribune*

## *The Wild Baron*

"Catherine Coulter has created some of the most memorable characters in romance."

—*The Atlanta Journal-Constitution*

## *Rosehaven*

"A hot-blooded medieval romp." —*People*

"Bawdy fare, Coulter-style . . . romance, humor, and spicy sex talk." —*Kirkus Reviews*

## THE BRIDE SERIES

*The Sherbrooke Bride • The Hellion Bride •*
*The Heiress Bride • The Scottish Bride*

"A delightful romp that will surely please historical romance fans."
—*Booklist*

"Coulter manages to write explicitly but beautifully about sex as well as love."
—*Milwaukee Journal Sentinel*

## THE VIKING TRILOGY

*Lord of Hawkfell Island • Lord of Raven's Peak •*
*Lord of Falcon Ridge*

"Coulter's characters quickly come alive and draw the reader into the story. You root for the good guys and hiss for the bad guys. When you have to put the book down for a while, you can hardly wait to get back and see what's going on."
—*The Sunday Oklahoman*

## THE LEGACY TRILOGY

*The Wyndham Legacy • The Nightingale Legacy •*
*The Valentine Legacy*

"Delightful . . . brimming with drama, sex and colorful characters . . . Her witty dialogue and bawdy, eccentric characters add up to an engaging, fan-pleasing story"
—*Publishers Weekly*

*Titles by Catherine Coulter*

**The Bride Series**

THE SHERBROOKE BRIDE
THE HELLION BRIDE
THE HEIRESS BRIDE
THE SCOTTISH BRIDE
PENDRAGON
MAD JACK
THE COURTSHIP

**The Legacy Trilogy**

THE WYNDHAM LEGACY
THE NIGHTINGALE LEGACY
THE VALENTINE LEGACY

**The Baron Novels**

THE WILD BARON
THE OFFER
THE DECEPTION

**The Viking Novels**

LORD OF HAWKFELL ISLAND
LORD OF RAVEN'S PEAK
LORD OF FALCON RIDGE
SEASON OF THE SUN

**The Song Novels**

WARRIOR'S SONG
FIRE SONG
EARTH SONG
SECRET SONG
ROSEHAVEN

**The Magic Trilogy**

MIDSUMMER MAGIC
CALYPSO MAGIC
MOONSPUN MAGIC

**The Star Series**

EVENING STAR
MIDNIGHT STAR
WILD STAR
JADE STAR

**Other Regency Historical Romances**

THE COUNTESS
THE REBEL BRIDE
THE HEIR
THE DUKE
LORD HARRY

**Devil's Duology**

DEVIL'S EMBRACE
DEVIL'S DAUGHTER

**Contemporary Romantic Thrillers**

FALSE PRETENSES
IMPULSE
BEYOND EDEN

**FBI Suspense Thrillers**

THE COVE
THE MAZE
THE TARGET
THE EDGE
RIPTIDE
HEMLOCK BAY

# LORD of HAWKFELL ISLAND

CATHERINE COULTER

J

JOVE BOOKS, NEW YORK

LORD OF HAWKFELL ISLAND

A Jove Book / published by arrangement with
the author

PRINTING HISTORY
Jove edition / November 1993


For information address: The Berkley Publishing Group,
a division of Penguin Putnam Inc.,
375 Hudson Street, New York, New York 10014.

Visit our website at
www.penguinputnam.com

ISBN: 0-515-11230-5

A JOVE BOOK®
Jove Books are published by The Berkley Publishing Group,
a division of Penguin Putnam Inc.,
375 Hudson Street, New York, New York 10014.
JOVE and the "J" design
are trademarks belonging to Penguin Putnam Inc.

PRINTED IN THE UNITED STATES OF AMERICA

25 24 23 22 21 20 19 18 17 16

To My Grandmother Schatz—

She taught me to read when I
was three years old and told
me “Tricker” stories.
She was one great lady, blessed
with a beautiful soprano voice, a
wonderful imagination, and she loved me
bunches.

The halt can ride, the handless can herd,
the deaf can fight with spirit;
A blind man is better than a corpse on a pyre—
A corpse is no good to anyone.

**—The Hávamál is a ninth century compilation of earlier poems consisting of sayings attributed to Ódin.**

**Clontarf, Ireland**
**Danish Fortress, 910**

HE PLACED HIS finger to his lips as he turned to his two men. They'd crossed the plank over the deep ravine as quietly as they could, though the need for their absolute silence wasn't necessary now for lightning streaked through the night sky and with it came the booming thunder, louder and more powerful than the gods' own battles. The utter whiteness in the sky, then the shaking of the earth was as steady as the torrential rain that blanketed the sky and the earth, coming down so thickly it was difficult to see two feet ahead. But he knew exactly what he was doing. Everything was going as planned. He gave a small salute to Hafter and Sculla behind him, and he smiled, a fearsome smile.

Einar was within the fortress, he had to be. Rorik had been told that he was by his own man inside the fortress. The message Aslak had sent was only a week old. Aye, Einar had to be here, even though that witch had yelled to him from the fortress ramparts that he was in Dublin, at the king's compound, aye, that damned witch who was probably his whore, who was lying, trying to protect him.

He and his men reached the small rear door, thick and stout, able to withstand a battering ram for a very long time, but it would be open, for Aslak had sworn it would be.

It was. He eased open the door, then turned slightly to wave his men to move in closer behind him. They moved silently, pressing close.

He hunkered down, his knife drawn, and eased through the opening. Suddenly, behind him he heard a man shout, "Take him! He has nowhere to go! Don't kill him!"

Rorik lurched back to see three men coming across the wide plank still spread across the ravine, swords drawn.

He was seized with madness and blood lust. In front of him were a dozen men, armed and ready, but it didn't matter. He wouldn't retreat, not now, even though he knew he alone could kill the three men who'd crossed the ravine. No, he must go forward. One of the men in front of him was Einar, a man he'd never seen. He yelled his name, calling him a coward, a murderer, taunting him to come and fight him.

"Einar! Einar!"

The garrison warriors remained together, pressing closely, drawing nearer, their shields and swords raised. He growled his fury. He shrieked his rage to the sky. They were hiding him; they were protecting Einar.

Rorik raised his sword over his head, and like a *berserker* lunged into the mass of men. His blood pounded madly through him. His brain saw only the frenzy of killing. He hacked his way wildly through the warriors that surrounded him. Einar must be here. He was hiding, using his men as a shield to protect him, but

Rorik would find him. Aye, and he'd send his sword through his throat. He heard a scream of pain, then another and another. He paid no heed.

"Einar!"

Again, he heard that same man shout from behind him, "Don't kill him!"

Suddenly, he was grabbed by a dozen hands and jerked down to his knees on the muddy ground. He struck out with his sword, dropped his shield, and used his knife, carving a slice from one man's leg. The hands eased in that instant, and he was up, his knife in one hand, his blood-covered sword in the other. He yelled at them, cursing, his eyes demon-red in the thick sheeting rain, deadened to anything save his mad lust for revenge. Thunder shook the earth beneath their feet, and the men jumped back. Then they formed a circle around him, always moving, first to the right, then to the left, adjusting as he shifted his position, always balancing on the balls of his feet. He yelled at them, calling them cowards and worse, sons of whores.

Gunleik, the garrison commander, stood a bit behind the circle of men, studying the warrior. His two men were already prisoners, both of them wounded, but not gravely, and that through happenstance. Both men were brave and strong, one of them nearly seven feet tall, and he'd fallen like an oak tree when Ivar had struck him over the head with the blunt side of an axe. The other had gone down when he'd slipped in the mud and four men had held him down, cuffing him with his sword handle. But this man with his wild eyes and his cunning, this man wouldn't give up, nor would he be tricked with guile, but still, Gunleik refused to kill him.

Four of his own men were down, screaming in pain. He yelled out again, "Keep back! Don't kill him!"

But his men were angry. They wanted the man's blood. He couldn't let this continue. His men would kill the warrior soon and he wouldn't be able to stop it.

He drew his knife from his belt. Slowly, with great deliberation, he raised it and calmly aimed. When the warrior turned to face him, the knife flew from his fingers, a silver blur in the heavy rain. It struck him high in the fleshy part of his right shoulder. It hadn't struck bone, for it wasn't meant to, just thick muscle, which was bad enough.

Rorik heaved and jerked backward with the force of the blow.

He shuddered, but didn't fall.

He screamed and lunged at another man, but he was slower now, his mortality finally eroding his warrior's resolve, weakening the iron hold he had on his body.

He stumbled, then regained his balance, standing within the center of the circle now, still slashing his sword in a wide arc around him.

"Move away from him!" Gunleik shouted. "Nay, Emund, keep back! I order you, don't kill him!" It couldn't last much longer now. He was a man, after all, he was mortal. His eyes would blur from the pain, his powerful arm would numb, his guts would cramp, and he would fall.

Rorik felt no pain, only a sharp cold that seemed to surge through his shoulder. He didn't understand it, but it didn't bother him—yet. Oddly, he felt strangely apart from himself for a few moments. Suddenly a woman broke through the circle of men. She stared at him, at the knife stuck through his shoulder, its handle glistening in the rain, but still Rorik stood straight and swung his sword in a powerful arc, the knife in his other hand just as deadly to those who ventured close. She looked as if she were terrified. But if she was, why was she here? Why was she staring at him? Why was she coming closer?

He watched her as she slipped between two men and came to the fore. He realized it was the same woman who had lied to him, the black-haired witch, Einar's whore.

"Mirana! Get back!"

It was the man's voice, the man who'd thrown his knife into his flesh, the man who'd yelled at the warriors not to kill him, but Rorik saw that she paid the man no heed. Slowly, her hand outstretched, she walked toward him. One man tried to stop her, but she shook off his hand, paying him no attention. Was she mad? Did she believe him on the point of death? Did she believe him no longer man enough to kill?

Rorik stared at her, a witch, aye, she must be an Irish witch, her thick hair black as a man's dead heart, plastered against her head, making her face a death mask, and she had no fear of him, nothing showed in her white rain-streaked face. He stared at her outstretched hand, as white as her face. She was come to take him to Valhalla. She was a Valkyrie then. Nay, that couldn't be right. A Valkyrie was all white and blond and solid, not slight and skinny like this girl. She was mortal, she had to be—all that black hair streaming down her shoulders, over her breasts, aye, she was mortal and his enemy. He could kill her if he could but reach her.

He slowed, still staring at her, unable to look away from her, for something about her drew him, held him. He looked at her mouth, blue with cold, and heard the words she spoke, but he didn't understand them. No, all he felt was a deadening weakness that was twisting through him, and he was caught within it, as an insect would be in a spider's web. It was slowing him, holding him still now, and he hated it, knowing that it was crushing his very soul. It was defeating him, destroying what made Rorik Haraldsson a man and warrior, and alive. He couldn't breathe. He knew a knife was in his shoulder, he saw the silver of its blade sunk nearly to its hilt into his flesh, the whiteness of its bone handle. Weakness swept over him, pulled at his arms, gripped him hard, made his legs weak as a woman's.

The witch with the soft gentle voice said, "Put down the sword. You are injured. None will harm you. I swear it. Give me the sword." And she held her hands out to him, so small her hands, the wrists so slight he could break them easily, very easily.

He frowned at her for she was still there, standing in front of him, unheeding of the rain, unheeding of the fact that he could cleave her apart. Those damned hands of hers still stretched toward him. He wanted to kill her. He wanted her white throat between his hands.

"Come, put down the sword."

He shook his head, took a step toward her, his sword raised. Then, very slowly, he sank to his knees. He stared at the muddy ground and felt the cold of the pounding rain and the air settle onto his body like a heavy shroud. He fell forward on his face then lurched to his side. He felt the coldness of the sucking mud to his very soul. It was the relentless cold of failure. He'd failed, there was naught else to do but die.

THE BLACK-HAIRED WITCH was leaning over him, her white face very close to his. She was speaking to him, her words quiet, the sound of them soft, but he didn't understand. He wondered vaguely what she wanted of him, but then he didn't care. He sought death. He'd failed, not only himself but his father and mother. He eased out his breath and welcomed it. He was drawn quickly inward once again, and he saw her no more.

Mirana backed away from the bed. The man was deeply unconscious, which was just as well. She watched Gunleik lean over him, brace one hand on the post of the box bed, clutch his fingers around the ivory handle and pull the knife from his flesh. He did it quickly and cleanly. Blood gushed out in its wake, red and thick, too much blood, flowing under his arm, snaking down through the thick blond hair covering his chest. Quickly she pressed clean woolen cloths against the wound. Gunleik wiped his knife on his tunic, then slid it back in its sheath. He grunted, and moved her aside.

"I have more strength," he said, and sat down beside the man, bearing down on the wound.

"You truly don't know who he is," she said as she bathed the filth from his face.

"Nay. But I know that if he'd gotten his hands on Einar, he would have told him, aye, he would have told him who he was and watched his eyes as he killed him."

"Why do you wish him to live? Einar shows no mercy for a man who steals a chicken. What would he do to this man?"

"Kill him slowly and with great pleasure."

She was silent, drying his face now, pale and drawn in the dim rush light.

"Let him die," she said finally.

"Nay, I cannot. My loyalty is to your brother. I must grant him the choice of this man's future. Besides, we must find out who he is, we must know what he wants, why he hates Einar so much. There might be others, the man's kin. There are strong feelings here, hatred that runs very deep. Nay, we must know who he is."

"Ask his two men once they are conscious again."

"Aye, I will, but I doubt they'll tell us. No, I must speak to this man, and only he, for he is their leader and he is the one who seeks revenge." The man wouldn't speak, Gunleik knew, not until he saw Einar, and even then perhaps he wouldn't, for he had failed in his vengeance. He would probably die unknown to them and to Einar.

"Why is there such hatred for my brother?"

Gunleik pressed more firmly on the wound, frowning at the seeping blood from beneath the thick wad of wool. "You will seek your answers from Einar. I trust he will recognize the man. There is hatred here that chills the soul."

"He is a very young man," Mirana said. "With his silver helmet and its nose guard, he looked fearsome, like a demon, unknown and thus frightening. But he isn't. He's just a man and he—"

"Aye, he is just a man, Mirana, and he is well formed and strong, a warrior. I hope that Einar will allow him to die like a man."

Mirana did as well, but she doubted Einar would ever consent to forgo his pleasures, for the pain of others brought him a good deal of pleasure. This man was fine-looking as well, Mirana thought, turning away from him. When she had watched him fighting in the outer yard, his sword had gleamed as brightly as the silver arm bands that still encircled each of his upper arms. Aye, he'd looked like a demon in that helmet, but not an old devil though, for he was large, his body lean and beautiful with its golden hair, his legs thick with youth and muscle. He wore only a tunic that was belted at his waist and thick leather shoes cross-strapped to his knees.

"I will send two of the women to strip off his wet tunic and bathe the blood and mud from him."

"I will keep the pressure on the wound. The blood is slowing already."

She sent Einar's two mistresses. She'd not been honest with herself. Actually, the man was magnificent, his face all hard lines and shadowed planes, a beautiful face with arched golden brows, a deep cleft in his chin. Let them sigh over him and caress his body, the lustful fools. She wouldn't care. She refused to let herself care, for down that path lay only sorrow and pain, for her as well as for him.

The hour grew late. Mirana saw that their four wounded men were tended. None would die, thanks be to Thor. The warrior's two men were bound and locked inside a storage shed, their wounds tended as well, slight wounds really, but their heads ached terribly. She told Ivar, who was guarding the two men, to keep a sharp eye on them; perhaps, she told him, just perhaps, one of the men would tell Ivar who their leader was.

Gunleik assigned men to keep a watch on the rest of the enemy, who were now standing miserably cold and silent on the beach, huddled under their bearskins in the pounding rain. Perhaps they didn't yet know their leader had failed.

It neared midnight. She rose and stretched. Men were snoring on the benches that lined the longhouse, each wrapped in his woolen blanket or bearskin. Gunleik was standing, staring into the orange sparking embers in the fire pit in the center of the longhouse. His age-seamed face was set and hard, his pale gray eyes as calm as the core of a storm. His legs were bare but they didn't look like the warrior's legs. His legs were bowed and scarred from many battles.

She said quietly to him, "When do you think my brother will return?"

"Your half-brother, Mirana. In two days, he told me."

She smiled at that, for there was firmness in Gunleik's voice. Then she said, "I was just thinking of the warrior's trickery. Conquest wasn't his plan. He brought only two warships and no more than thirty men. He had no plan to go anywhere but here because Einar was here and he wanted him."

"Aye, I admire his mind and his guile. He knew of the small rear door all along, and he waited until the storm began and darkness had come to invade the fortress. All his taunting, his curses, and his insults, all was bluster and a sham. He came with only two men. They would come into the fortress and search out Einar and kill him at their leisure. His other men would continue their taunting on the beach, holding all my men's attention. I admire him, Mirana. He is bold and he was taking a grave risk. But his plan failed and now he will die."

"There are his men on the beach. Do you believe they now realize that he has failed and will sail away without him? Surely they won't try to storm the fortress, they would have no chance."

"Were I one of his men I would wait for him until the Christian's devil came to take me."

"I would wait too," she said, and smiled sadly into the embers of the fire pit. "You know, of course, that this means there is a spy here at Clontarf, a man who is loyal to this warrior."

"Aye, I know. I will find him. I must find him soon or lord Einar will not be pleased."

And Einar might punish Gunleik, she thought. Mirana spooned some porridge into a wooden bowl and handed it to Gunleik. "You have not eaten. It is tasty. Here is some honey. Eat. We will find the spy, fret not."

She watched him fondly, this man who was as close to her as her father had been, dead now since her twelfth year, and she'd been sent here to Clontarf to be in her brother's guardianship. Her half-brother's guardianship. And Gunleik had been here and she'd turned to this man who treated her gently yet matter-of-factly, and had taught her how to use weapons because he knew nothing else to teach her. And Einar had approved because she realized it had pleased him to know that she could sew and cook and keep his household and fight like a man. Aye, Einar was like that.

Old Halak stopped beside her and patted her arm. He wished her a good night. She nodded to him, thanking him, for nothing really, but just because he was a good man and had served her well. He had also fashioned a protective shielding around the hole in the roof so no rain poured into the longhouse. It was warm within, a bluish smoke haze hanging in the air, but not so thick that it was uncomfortable to breathe.

She watched Gunleik eat his porridge, slowly at first, then with more appetite when he realized how hungry he was. Just a few short hours ago the warrior had come with his two warships. It seemed much longer than that now. She'd known immediately he was their leader. He'd stood there on the beach, some fifty feet below the Clontarf fortress, his legs spread, his head thrown back, and taunted them from the beach, called them cowards, derided Einar for hiding behind the witch's skirts. But it had been her responsibility to speak and she had. When she'd shouted down that Einar wasn't here, he'd laughed, a deep scornful laugh that had rung out loud in the still air. Einar's men, clustered below in the yard, were furious; she could feel their tension. To have all of them taunted was one thing, but Einar's sister was another. She'd shouted again. "I am Mirana, sister of Einar. He is in Dublin at the king's fortress there." She would never forget his stance, the arrogance of him, when he'd yelled up to her, as she'd stood on the fortress ramparts, "Lady, get you below to your spinning! Prepare your evening meal and keep your tongue behind your teeth where a woman's tongue belongs." She'd known then that he wouldn't believe her, believe anything she said. And his trickery, she had admired that as much as Gunleik did. "Will he live?" she asked him now.

"He is young and strong. If he doesn't succumb to the fever, aye, I believe so. But you would know that better than I."

She left him then and walked to Einar's sleeping chamber where the man lay. The man fascinated her. She couldn't seem to stay long away from him.

There was only one rush torch lit, giving off sluggish light. The room was dim and warm. There were several thick woolen blankets covering the man. His shoulder was bound tightly with clean white wool. No blood was seeping through the bandage. He was either asleep or unconscious, she didn't know which.

She eased down to sit beside him on the box bed. She laid her palm on his forehead. He was hot as the coals in the fire pit. She fetched a cloth, dampened it in a bowl of cold water, and began to stroke it over his face and shoulders. Over and over again. He muttered something but she couldn't understand him. She wondered if he were going to awaken and, when he did, what he would think, what he would do.

Rorik thought he was dead, gone to Valhalla. Aye, surely he'd gone to Odin All-Father because he'd died as a warrior should, fighting with all his might, filled with rage and valor, and there was the soft voice of a Valkyrie above him, her cool fingers on his forehead, and she was speaking words he couldn't grasp, but it didn't matter. She was there and thus he was dead, there were no more choices for him now, no more decisions to be made, no more vengeance to take. But he couldn't see and surely that was odd. Did a man become blind when he died? Nay, that couldn't be right. A man in Valhalla felt and saw and ate and sang and took his pleasure with any woman he pleased. He didn't feel like singing. He felt a lurching of pain in his shoulder and it shook him deeply. He didn't expect pain, surely there shouldn't be pain after he'd died. The pain ebbed and flowed, and he tried to force his mind to accept it, but it was difficult. Perhaps he was close to death, and thus hadn't yet gained all that would be his. He felt cool dampness on his face, another odd thing that shouldn't be. The cool dampness was on his shoulders, his arms, his belly, but no lower.

The Valkyrie's voice grew dimmer until it faded into the blackness that drew on him. Then he felt nothing.

Mirana rose and stretched. The fever had lessened. He was nearly cool to the touch. Gunleik was right. He would live. He was young and strong. She stared down at him, wondering if she shouldn't simply feed him some poison and let him die easily. She thought of Einar and knew that he would torture this man, break him until he was naught but a shell, and enjoy himself with every moan from the man's mouth.

Men and their vengeance. He would die horribly because he'd tried to gain vengeance on Einar. Aye, she should poison him, but she knew she couldn't, it was that simple. For so long as he lived there was hope for him. A slender thread of hope, but hope nonetheless. She knew deep down that was a lie but she wouldn't release it.

She frowned down at him, then picked up the damp cloth again. She continued to wipe his face and shoulders, over and over until she was satisfied that the fever was truly gone. She pulled the woolen blanket to his chest, looked at him for a very long time, then left him.

She needed to see Gunleik. He was speaking quietly to one of his men, Kolbein the Ox, who was given the name not because of his size, but because of his droopy eyelids that made him look very foreign and stupid, which he wasn't. She paused, listening.

Gunleik scratched his head, saying, "There's a traitor amongst us, you know it and I know it. That man, whoever he is, raised the cross bar on the rear door for him to enter. He didn't know I had planned a surprise attack on his leader down on the beach, thus he isn't part of my inner circle of men. He didn't know I and my two men left by that same rear door, and thus he couldn't have foreseen that I and my men would have been behind his leader. The spy must have been rotting with fear when the man's scheme failed."

"I know not who this man is," Kolbein said low. "I do not like it, Gunleik. I do not like traitors. Not all that many men knew of your plan."

"That is true. Ah, Mirana. How is our captive? Has he survived the fever?"

"Aye, and he's resting more easily now. This traitor, Gunleik, you have no suspicions?"

He shook his head. "We will know eventually. Perhaps Einar will know when he returns."

"What about his other men?"

"Let them remain on the beach. I doubt they'll try to attack us, 'twould be suicide. There is no reason to try another attack on them, even though the storm still rages and we could possibly surprise them. There is no reason to cut their warships away now. Besides, Einar will want to capture those warships and add them to his own fleet."

Mirana walked to the fire pit and dipped a big wooden spoon into the iron pot. She filled her wooden bowl with porridge. She added butter and walked to the long benches that lined the longhouse's walls. She sat next to a snoring man. She forced herself to eat, calmly, methodically.

What had Einar done to earn this man's hatred?

He was awake and he welcomed the pain. The pain pleased him because he knew now he was alive; he also knew he could control the pain and he had, for he'd thought and thought, knowing he was in very serious trouble. He was in a dimly lit sleeping chamber, alone. Then he heard a voice coming nearer and quickly closed his eyes. It was the woman's voice, soft and quiet, and she was saying to someone, "He's been sleeping for nearly two full days. I've fed him but he hasn't acknowledged me, refuses to acknowledge me. He's just eaten broth and porridge. He should awaken soon for he has slept many hours now. Einar will be here tomorrow." She gave a short laugh that held no humor at all. "By then he should be well enough for Einar to torture before he kills him."

"It's the way of things," a man said. It was the man who'd sent the knife into his shoulder, the man who'd shouted that he wasn't to be killed. He said now, "I must go, Mirana. Take care. No matter his wound, he is still a man and a Viking and he would kill you if he could."

He heard the rustle of her skirt, felt her hand on his forehead, felt the warmth of her breath on his cheek. He wanted to open his eyes but he didn't. He would wait.

She said, "I've brought you some more porridge. You must eat more and regain your strength. I have put honey on it, 'twill give you vigor and add sweetness to your mouth. I know you're awake. You have but to lie still and open your mouth. I will feed you just as I have before."

Still, he made no move. She stood there staring down at him, wondering about him, if he had a wife, family, and where they lived. She wished she'd let him die, quickly, honorably, but she realized now that she simply couldn't. There was something about him that drew her. It was odd, but it was true. She would not be responsible for his death. She had always admired strength and courage, and he had that in abundance, but it was something more than that, something she didn't understand. She wouldn't, couldn't, have let him die, for even in the rain-sodden outer yard when he'd been surrounded with men, Gunleik's knife sticking obscenely from his shoulder, she'd had to step forward, she'd had to stop it, for she knew she couldn't let him die. And he would have died for he was too far into his rage, too deep into the battle and into himself to allow himself to withdraw, to allow himself to realize he'd lost and give up his weapons. He needed strength now and she was determined he would have it, and thus she said again, "Open your mouth and I will feed you."

He opened his eyes and looked at her. He remembered her now, the witch with all the black hair and the pale face, her hand outstretched toward him. He remembered the rain striking down her face, plastering her hair to her head, rain dripping from her lashes. She was looking at him, her expression calm, unworried. Did she believe him to be so very weak? So helpless?

She sat down beside him and put the wooden spoon to his mouth. He opened his mouth and ate. It was delicious. It focused him momentarily on his stomach instead of his shoulder. He ate all the porridge, feeling the strength flow into him, then said, "Who are you?"

"Mirana, sister to Einar." His eyes were the color of the cloudless sky in midsummer.

"Einar has no sister."

"I am his half-sister. We have different fathers. My father was Audun; his was Thorsson."

"You're keeping me alive so that he may have more pleasure in his torture of me."

She had no answer to that. It would be the result, surely, but that wasn't why she'd done it. She rose and said, "You must rest. I will feed you again soon. Do you have need to relieve yourself?"

He opened his eyes again and stared at her. "Aye," he said, and closed his eyes again.

"What is your name, Viking?"

"It matters not that you know. I am Rorik Haraldsson."

"Why did you come here? Who is your spy? Why do you wish to kill Einar?"

"I don't answer questions from foolish women. You annoy me. Leave me alone."

From beneath half-closed lids he saw her stiffen, even as she repeated his name, but she said nothing more to him. What more was there to say? He wouldn't bend and she couldn't.

She returned later, how much later he didn't know, for he'd slept again deeply. She carried another bowl of porridge. She said nothing, merely sat beside him and began spooning the thick porridge into his mouth. He turned his face away when he was full.

When he turned back to her, his look was speculative, his eyes cold. "I could strangle you," he said. "You have a skinny little neck. Aye, I could twist it with but one of my hands and you would be dead before any of your brother's men came to your rescue."

She laughed and he stiffened at that unexpected sound. He'd sounded mean and cruel, he knew well how to use his voice to bring fear, and yet she had laughed at him. He felt anger roil in his belly. His eyes narrowed on her face. "You believe me so very weak still? Too weak to kill a woman? A witch? Possibly Einar's whore?"

"You should not have said that, Viking."

SHE RAISED A very sharp knife, gently touched it to his bare throat, and pressed inward. "It is I who could kill you. Don't think me unworthy as an enemy. Don't think me soft and weak, Viking, with a woman's feeble strength. I could kill you quickly and easily, slice your throat with as little effort as I would a chicken's." Men, she thought, they were filled with bravado, even when they lay flat in their own helplessness. She admired him greatly in those moments.

"You're naught but a girl," he said, but he didn't move because the tip of her knife was sharp against his flesh. He felt it prick his skin. "You are worth naught save what you have between your legs and how well you use it."

The knife tip slid easily into his throat, not too deep, but he felt the sharp sting, felt the hot stickiness of his own blood.

"I think you should keep your tongue behind your teeth, Viking. You push me to anger. It is unwise of you. 'Tis I who have fed you and who bathed the fever from you."

"You are very young," he said abruptly, looking up at her. She was very close, the dark green of her eyes clear to him in the dimly lit chamber.

"Not so young. I am eighteen, an age most girls are wedded and suckling their own babes. Since I have no need for a husband, why then, I'm still free."

"Einar will wed, and when he does you will have naught of anything. He will be pleased to release you to any man who would pay him a large enough bride price."

She merely smiled and shook her head. "I don't think so. We will see. Until that time, I am mistress here and free to do as I please."

"No man wanted you? That is the truth, isn't it? You with your knife and your ill-fitting pride and your foolish bragging? Or perhaps you are Einar's whore and he will keep you close until he is bored with your endowments."

She laughed again and he felt the knife tip ease from his flesh. "You need to measure your words more carefully, Viking, particularly since you are flat on your back. Your tongue is as smooth as the sharp spines on an eel's back. I cannot believe you have managed to hold to your life this long. You must have a legion of enemies, all clamoring to slit your throat. I could slit it now, and it is wise of you to realize it. Do not be a fool and underestimate me. It is a mistake many men make, to their grief. Cease your insults. How old are you?"

"I'm twenty-five." For a moment, he looked surprised that he'd answered her. Then, "I spoke only the truth to you. Your hands are soft as is your voice, but you are blooded with that vile bastard. Aye, you're no whore, I'll believe you. I would rather you were his whore; then I could pity you. No, you have his blood in you. You have filth in you. It's possible I will kill you after I send him to a soulless pit."

"You may try," she said, and there was no expression

on her pale face, no hint of feeling in her voice.

He frowned. "You have healed me. It was your hands on me with the wet cloth to cool my fever. It was your voice I heard. As you said, it was you who fed me when I barely knew I was alive. Why?"

"I don't know." How could she tell him that if she'd done nothing, she wouldn't have survived it herself. She'd had no choice but to help him, but she couldn't say that to him.

She saw that he would insult her again, and said quickly, shrugging, "I dislike to see animals suffer."

She saw the cords in his neck swell with his anger. It made her smile and made the cords swell even more, made his skin flush. "You want me to strike you, lady? You want me to kill you now?"

He felt the damned knife again, caressing the flesh of his neck. He felt a slick of his blood trickle slowly over his throat. Let her feel herself in control, he thought, not moving. Let her feel superior and confident in her foolish bravado. She would learn. He wouldn't mind being the one to teach her. Ah, but she was Einar's sister. She was fouled with his blood.

"You won't kill a mouse unless I give you leave to do it," she said. "You will lie here and I will tend you unless you would prefer one of Einar's whores. They are comely, submissive as sheep, for my brother prefers women who have nothing in their heads except flattery for his prowess. They undressed and bathed you. They much enjoyed themselves. I heard them speaking of how finely you were made, how your man's rod was thick and how it swelled to a wondrous size as they bathed you. I believe they compared you to Einar and deemed you the more appealing. Of course, they are stupid."

"I have no memory of this," he said, and frowned. He

realized then that he was naked beneath the woolen blanket. "You did not touch me?"

"I bathed you, yes, but not below your waist. I have no interest in you like those other two who slavered even whilst they spoke of you later."

"No interest in men? Are you indeed a witch?"

"It doesn't matter. Now you will sleep. My brother returns tomorrow. Then you are his prisoner, no longer mine."

"I will never be a woman's prisoner," he said. She merely shook her head. The knife withdrew from his throat. He watched her pick up the damp cloth, clean the tip of the knife, then wipe his blood from his throat. She was thorough.

"You will pay for that," he said.

She laughed. She walked quickly to the opening to the chamber then turned. "Your talk is a man's bluster. It is piteous. You were stupid to come here. I was stupid to keep you alive. Now you will die for your stupidity and for mine."

He lay there unmoving for many minutes, deep in thought. How many times had she told him that Einar was returning on the morrow? Surely more than was necessary. Surely.

It was dark as a well in the sleeping chamber. He could hear no voices, no noise from the outer hall. It must be very late. He lay there, still and quiet, but his breath was coming in mewling gasps, and he cursed his body for betraying him. He would wait a few more minutes then exercise again. He was hungry, but he knew that he must pretend to sleep or unconsciousness should anyone come in. Especially to her he must appear weak and helpless. Let her gloat. Let her believe him feeble, powerless even against her and her silly little knife. Still, he had a slit in his neck from that knife. He unconsciously touched his fingertips to it. No woman had ever done such a thing to him in his life. Then he smiled, a smile that held both amusement and promise.

After some time, he gritted his teeth and swung his legs over the side of the box bed. Pain sliced through his shoulder, but he withstood it. He had no choice. He cursed softly, then stood. His legs held him. He smiled into the darkness. He walked to the entrance of the sleeping chamber and pulled the bearskin aside. He smelled smoke from the now banked fire pit. He heard men snoring. He heard one man and woman giggling, then he heard her moan in her release.

Suddenly he heard a whisper to his right. He smiled into the darkness. Aslak had not failed him.

"Lord, 'tis I, Aslak. We must be away now for Einar arrives on the morrow. I heard Gunleik speaking of it, but he didn't sound pleased. We must go now. Are you strong enough for it?"

"Aye," he said. "Where are Sculla and Hafter?"

"In the storage shed just outside the longhouse. We will escape through that rear door."

"The witch, Mirana, where is she?"

"Sleeping in her own chamber. Her brother grants her privacy."

"I want her."

Aslak paled. "It is too risky, my lord. Far too risky. There are others to use as hostage, but not Einar's own sister. She is no mealymouthed weakling to gasp and faint. Nay, my lord, she would yell and fight until you had to kill her. She would bring you low, my lord."

"I want her," he said again. "No more arguments. She is the best hostage we could take. Give me clothes and fetch rope so that I may tie her hands and feet. If you can, get my weapons and my helmet. Go quickly."

Aslak returned within minutes, his hands filled with weaponry and rope. "Here, my lord Rorik. We must hurry. Your men who are waiting below on the beach, I fear they will believe you dead and leave us. Einar will delight in killing both of us. Already Gunleik is questioning all of us to see who the traitor is. It is but a matter of time until I am discovered. Gunleik is no fool."

"We will leave shortly," Rorik said as he strapped on his wide leather belt and slipped his sword into its sheath. "Quit your plaints. As for my men, they would await me on the beach until the day of the world's death."

He dressed, gritting his teeth against the grinding pain in his shoulder. At least the bandage fit tightly, thanks to the damned witch and her strong hands. "Now," he said, "I will get her. Keep watch."

Mirana was deeply asleep one moment; the next moment she was wide awake and she knew he was there, in that brief instant, standing over her. But how was it possible? He was so very ill, so very weak. It had to be another, but it wasn't, she knew it was he, Rorik Haraldsson. But she felt his breath on her cheek. She recognized his scent. She opened her mouth, felt the stark pain of his fist against her jaw. She was unconscious, her head lolling on her bed.

Rorik saw she was wearing only a light linen shift. This small chamber wasn't a dark pit as was Einar's and for that he was grateful. He quietly opened the trunk at the foot of her box bed and rifled about until he found a gown. He jerked it over her head, smoothing it down over her hips. There were leather shoes and he quickly slipped them on her feet and tied the leather cross straps. Aslak came into the small chamber and handed him the rope. He tied her hands behind her, her ankles together. He stuffed one of her shifts into her mouth then tied it securely about her head with another shift. He wrapped her in her wool blanket and hefted her over his shoulder. The pain nearly brought him to his knees.

"So much for her conceit," he said under his breath, his teeth gritted against the pain, and he said it again, and he remained upright and he carried her.

They were quiet as the now dead coals in the fire pit. Smoke still hung thick in the air and Rorik felt it curdle in his throat. He wanted to cough. He nearly crossed his eyes with the effort to keep quiet. He didn't want to die here in the middle of this longhouse all because of a cough. A man jerked upright, stared at them, then grunted, and fell again onto his back. Rorik didn't see Gunleik, the man who'd sent the knife through his shoulder. He would like to kill him. But he would like to thank him before he did kill him. He and the witch had kept him alive—for Einar to torture—but still Rorik had lived and because of them. Because of them he was now escaping.

When Aslak managed to pull the cross bar up on the double-thick oak doors, Rorik's heart was pounding so loud he feared the enemy would hear it. In those few moments, he wasn't even aware of any pain in his shoulder. All his concentration was on escape. On not coughing. On holding the woman steady on his shoulder.

They were outside the longhouse. There were still the dogs and the other animals to get past and the half-dozen or so guards.

Suddenly, a man was standing directly in their path, his mouth open, gaping in disbelief at them. He opened his mouth at the same time Rorik dropped Mirana.

Rorik was on him in the next instant, his hands around his throat, squeezing until the man's eyes bulged and his tongue burst from his mouth. He released him and watched him gasp and heave on the ground at his feet. He pulled his sword from its sheath. He leaned down and struck the man's head with the smooth handle.

"Kill him, my lord!"

"I have no need of a stranger's blood on my hands," Rorik said. "He did not fight me. He does not deserve to die." He hefted Mirana over his shoulder again, settled her to his comfort, then motioned for Aslak to continue. He took two steps before he felt dizzy with the pain from his shoulder. He paused a moment, shaking his head, forcing himself to block off the pain. He breathed deeply and slowly and soon the pain was manageable. His father had taught him this. His father had also taught him that vengeance was more important than his life, that to live without seeking vengeance reduced a man to pitiable nothingness.

They reached the small shed where his two men were being held prisoner. There were two guards lolling on the ground in front of the shed, both of them sleeping soundly, their snores filling the night air. They were wrapped in wool blankets, their swords and knives at their sides.

Rorik again dropped Mirana to the ground. He struck each man's head, then sheathed his sword once more.

Sculla and Hafter were in better condition then he was. They weren't surprised to see him and that made him feel better. They'd trusted him to save them and he had. His small band, the still unconscious woman over his shoulder, left through the rear door of the fortress. The plank was still over the ravine, thank the gods, for Rorik had forgotten about it.

Rorik Haraldsson and his thirty men and the one

woman were rowing toward the open Irish Sea within ten minutes.

Rorik looked back at Clontarf, at Einar Thorsson's fortress. He'd lost this time. Next time he wouldn't. There would be vengeance. For now, he had her, the witch, the woman who'd dared stick her damned knife into his throat.

He looked down at her when he laid her onto the ship's planking next to his feet. She was still unconscious, still bundled in the wool blanket. Her hair was black as a Christian's sins, tangled wildly about her face. Her face shone white as the snow in the Vestfold in the deep of winter under a pale moon. Her coloring was different, intriguing, the white flesh with her black hair and eyes so green they looked like wet moss, not like the light sky-blue of so many of his countrymen. He wondered what race her mother had belonged to. It didn't matter now. She was his prisoner and he would use her as he wished. From her he would learn everything he needed to know about Einar. If she refused him anything, he would kill her.

The night was cool and clear, the sea calm, a half-moon shining overhead, no clouds to mar the purity of the sky. In three days, the seas and the gods willing, they would be home.

Home to Hawkfell Island.

Einar would know his name for he didn't doubt that she'd told everyone he was Rorik Haraldsson. But still, Einar wouldn't know where to find him. It had taken Rorik two years to find Einar.

He allowed himself to ease back against the edge of the boat. The oak was smooth against his back. The lapping of the waves against the side of the warship soothing. He closed his eyes, listening to the men grunting over their oars, talking about their escape and their hatred for Einar Thorsson, the bravery and skill of Rorik, their captain, their lord. They spoke of Gunleik and of his plan to surprise them on the beach and cut their warships free during the storm and how this Gunleik, surely a man who shouldn't be in the service of Einar, had trapped Rorik and forced him inside, into the inner yard where he was taken. They spoke of the battle, of how Rorik had fought like a *berserker,* how this same Gunleik had thrown his knife into Rorik's shoulder, but hadn't killed him. Rorik tried to smile for he knew that soon a scald would be recounting these feats, but it would become heroic, this failure of his.

He felt pain flow through him, knew that he must rest now else suffer more pain than he deserved later when he must have strength. He looked once again as the woman twisted onto her side, moaning softly, pressing against his leg. He leaned down and pulled the blanket more closely around her. He saw several of his men looking at her too. He said quietly, "She is my prisoner and my hostage. She is not to be raped or brutalized."

The men mumbled, but nodded slowly, one after the other. Rorik added, "She isn't really a soft woman. She's hard as a man in her thoughts, and she's proud. Leave her be and don't trust her."

Aslak said, "She leads men and they heed her. She has a woman's parts, but her actions aren't always that of a woman. She disagrees with men if she wishes to, even with her brother, and he allows it. I heard that he whipped her but just once I think. She leads the men in her brother's absence. Both the men and the women at Clontarf respect her and obey her. I didn't understand it at first, but heed what Lord Rorik says and take care, for she is dangerous, despite her small size, despite her delicate woman's looks. Why did she tend Lord Rorik so gently if not to keep him alive for her brother's tortures? Aye, and he is known to enjoy another's suffering. I wasn't whipped myself but I saw others whipped and he did it with great relish."

Rorik added, his voice just loud enough to be heard over the lapping waves against the side of the warship, "Attend Aslak's words. He's lived in that fortress for the past six months. Now, you have but three days before your rods can plow any field you wish. Leave the woman alone. We'll be home even sooner if you keep that thought in mind and hold to your oars."

Aslak laughed. Hafter, Rorik's childhood friend, a man closer to him than his own brothers, said, "Next time, Rorik. Next time you will succeed. At least we've all escaped nearly whole-hided. There will be another time." But as he spoke he was looking down at the unconscious woman, and there was hatred in his blue eyes. Then he rubbed his head where he'd been struck.

"Aye," he said. "There will be another time."

## Hawkfell Island
## Off the coast of East Anglia

NEARLY HOME AT last. Rorik looked hungrily toward Hawkfell Island, his home, the island his grandfather had captured, razing the monastery and killing all the monks who'd lived there thirty years before. His grandfather had also been in the band of warriors who had killed King Edmund and given East Anglia over to the Vikings. All of England was theirs now save for Wessex, which was still held by the Saxons, thanks to King Alfred, that wily old man who had journeyed to his Christian hell some ten years before.

Rorik shaded his eyes. The sun was bright overhead, the day perfect for a homecoming. The island glittered like the richest of emeralds beneath a golden sun blazing in its light blue sky. The island was rich with arable land, wildlife abounded, and the weather was temperate. It was his, granted to him upon his grandfather's death some seven years before. During that seven years two bands of marauders had tried to take the island from him. They'd both failed.

Hawkfell Island, his island, his home now for over two years. Before, he'd left men here and come three times a year. Now he left only to trade and to go araiding. And every time he returned he thought of the skald, Salorik, a master of the *kenning,* who, in a flight of lyrical fancy had called the island Hawkfell just after his grandfather had captured it. Hawkfell—such a melodious rendering for the hand that held the falcon.

Rorik's warship, *The Sea Raven,* took the lead into the narrow protected harbor. There was a single long wooden pier, its pilings built of sturdy oak. He watched men, women, children, two chickens, and one goat running and scrambling down the path from his farmstead atop the highest point on the island. Not all that high, really, just a gentle sweep upward, the flat land at the top covered with crops of barley, wheat, and rye. Thick copses of pine and fir and abundant low tangled shrubs formed nearly impenetrable protective boundaries around the fields.

The men who reached the quay first grabbed the lines thrown from the warriors on board and tied them securely. The chickens retreated and the goats just stood there looking for something to chew on. The women and children stood back, waiting. They were always waiting, Rorik thought, scanning their faces and those of the children, and sometimes when they returned it was with fewer warriors and he would see those faces turn from anticipation to despair.

Rorik's men jumped onto the pier, stretching and shouting to their comrades, hugged their wives and threw their shrieking children into the air. A familiar scene, Rorik thought again, one repeated each time they came home, and this time there were no tears, no laments. Two wounded men and their hard heads were healing. As was he.

Except there was no wife or child to greet him. He shook his head, damping the echoing and familiar pain, a pain so much a part of him he doubted a time would come when the pain would not be there, deep and constant. His shoulder ached and pulled. He saw others racing down the path from the farmstead to greet them, calling out, shrieking.

When the last man had jumped from *The Sea Raven,* Rorik said to the silent woman at his feet, "Come along. This is my home, the entire island belongs to me. There is no way to escape, as you can see. You will not try to. Now, keep your mouth shut and get onto the dock."

Mirana, who hadn't said a word since early that morning, managed to struggle to her feet and hold steady, despite the gentle rocking of the warship. She greatly admired the island, its location, and its strategic advantages—not that she would ever tell him. The island's natural harbor made it a possession of great worth. No storms would destroy the ships in this protective inlet. From the arm of land that curved outward into the sea, an enemy could be seen from a goodly distance and warning given in good time. She looked at him straightly, and said, "It isn't a very big island, barely a speck in the sea. I don't know why you're braying on so about it. It's just a chunk of land, a small chunk. I wouldn't want to live here. Why do you choose to live here instead of on the mainland just yon?"

He was tired, his shoulder throbbed, and he wanted to sleep until his muscles eased and he healed. And now she must question him and mock him, her sarcasm thick and double-edged.

"Hawkfell Island is big enough for me and my people. I willingly leave East Anglia to those who enjoy worrying about Saxon marauders poaching onto their lands and into their towns. Now, be quiet." He jumped onto the dock. He turned to look down at her. She was in pathetic condition. Her face was burned from the sun, her gown was filthy and wrinkled and damp from sea water that had splashed her for the past three days. Her hair was tangled and matted to her head. However, as he'd just seen, her tongue was mean as a demon's. "You look like a hag," he said, and offered her his hand. "If I wanted to sell you, I doubt I could find a man who would be willing to buy you."

She looked at that hand, strong, deeply bronzed by the sun, then looked away. There was black grime beneath his fingernails. It pleased her. She climbed onto the dock by herself. She immediately staggered for her legs wouldn't hold her. She'd been tied down to the plank by his feet for nearly the entire voyage. She would have sprawled on her face had he not grabbed her arm.

"You smell vile," he said, and dragged her after him along the dock. "I hadn't realized it aboard *The Sea Raven,* for the blessed sea breezes wafted your odor away."

"It wafted yours away too."

He turned back to look at her thoughtfully. "I thought at first that my men would try to ravish you, despite my warning to them. After all, you were somewhat comely with all that black hair and that white skin, unique perhaps, and a man enjoys trying something that is unusual. And those green eyes of yours, strange eyes, the color hints at mysteries and secrets. Aye, that's what I thought they'd see when they looked at you: a new sweet, a new animal to pet. I venture they wondered at the hair between your thighs, if it was as black as the hair on your head. But they kept their thoughts to themselves. There's been no danger of them wanting you for the past two days, has there? Why, they would have tossed you overboard had I allowed them to so do. You've given nothing. You did nothing save take up precious space. You smell like a gutted fish. You ate our food, drank our precious water, and reviled me until I wanted to strangle you."

"I only told you that Einar would find you and butcher you like the miserable bastard you are."

"You said it more times than I wanted to hear it."

That was true, she thought, but only during the first day, those first interminable hours when her anger had overcome her fear of him, her hatred had been stronger than her good sense, when exhaustion hadn't yet dulled her mind or her will. No, her strength hadn't yet been sapped, she hadn't yet slept like a dog at his feet for endless stretches of time, huddled and bound. Many times he'd even rested his foot on her neck, then on her back, for his own pleasure or to punish her, she didn't know. The two were probably one and the same. So many hours had passed that her brain refused to count them, to even recognize them as day shifted into night and back again. She was so tired, so stiff, she just wanted to sit down and never move again. But he just kept dragging her along, and she knew if she did fall, he would simply drag her along the ground.

"I also told you I would kill you," she said, drawing on a shred of strength she didn't know was still within her. Ah, that had been during those endless hours during the second day. For punishment, he'd kept water from her until her tongue was swelled in her mouth. He'd moved his foot from her back to her neck.

"Aye, my men thought that amusing."

"So you didn't tell them how I held my knife to your throat, and when you displeased me, I eased it through your tender skin?"

No, she saw, he hadn't told them that. A man's pride could only suffer so much. His hand went to his throat, to the healing ridge of flesh where her knife point had gone deep enough to draw his blood.

He realized what he was doing and dropped his hand. There was fury in his eyes, but he said quite calmly, "Can you walk without me supporting you now?"

"Of course."

He released her and she promptly collapsed.

He stood over her, watching her rub her legs through the filthy wool of her gown. He grunted, leaned down, and hefted her like a haunch of beef over his shoulder.

She jerked upward, and he said, "Lie still else I'll drag you by all that hair of yours."

She tried to lie still, she truly did. He walked up a narrow snaking path that was paved with quarried stones. Her stomach clenched and heaved at the constant jostling. She closed her eyes against the pain, only to hear bird cries, more cries and calls and shrieks than she'd ever heard at Clontarf. She opened her eyes. From upside down, she saw several birds scurrying about just off the trail—ah, so many. An oystercatcher, a half-dozen dunlin, and a pair of curlews. She liked birds, she always had, since she was a child. Birds, she thought, gritting her teeth against a wave of intense nausea. Only someone losing their mind would think of birds at a time like this. She saw a ringed plover nestled down in the thick loam beside the trail, admired it, and knew she must be nearly dead.

He continued to climb. She counted ten more steps up the deep-set quarried stones. By the eleventh, she was trying to rear up on his shoulder to relieve the pressure on her belly. He slapped her buttocks.

There was no hope for it. She yelled, "Let me down! I'm going to vomit!"

With no hesitation he dropped her on the sloping side of the path into a low scrub bush that scraped across her exposed arms. Mirana rolled over, feeling the pain from the harsh scrub needles, to come up onto her bruised and torn hands and knees. She retched and retched. There was no food in her belly to come up, thank the gods for that. She felt sicker than she'd ever felt in her life. She hugged her stomach and continued to retch, dry heaving that felt like her belly was being ripped apart. Her throat was dry, and hurt so badly she didn't want to breathe. At least he couldn't see her face for her hair hung like a filthy black curtain to the ground.

She felt him behind her then, saw the slant of his shadow over her left shoulder through the matted strands of hair.

"There's nothing in your belly," he said, and she wished she had her knife. She would have stuck it deep into his groin.

"What's wrong with her, Rorik?"

It was Hafter who had come up to stand nearby. Some six other warriors were behind him, all standing there, all staring down at her. She could hear women talking too, even a child saying loudly, "Who is she, Papa? Is she a new slave? What is wrong with her? Will she die?"

They were all looking at her and she wished both for their deaths and for her own.

Rorik said to Hafter, "I was carrying her over my shoulder. She's weak, being a woman, and couldn't walk by herself. Now this—puking her guts all over my island. Perhaps it's all an act to gain sympathy. I should have let the men throw her overboard." He sounded like a man put upon, a man upon whom the gods had visited the worst of punishments.

She looked up at him and said clearly, "I hope your man's parts rot off. I hope this wretched island sinks into the sea and you with it."

There was dead silence, then he threw back his head and laughed, a deep, rich laugh filled with malice and fury, a laugh that should have warned her.

"I hate you," she said, unwarned, then leaned over and retched again. "You're naught but a brutal animal. You chain me like a wretched dog for three days, use me to rest your filthy feet upon, then expect me to dance about when I'm finally allowed to walk."

He grasped her beneath her arms and half dragged, half carried her back to the wooden dock. He swung her off the ground and flung her far out into the water. The shock of the cold water drove her breath from her body and sent her under. Her mouth was open on a scream and water rushed down her throat. The water was cold, too cold for the warmth of the day, the mildness of the spring air. She flapped her arms with her little remaining strength, but it did no good. Her efforts did nothing. Her wool skirts dragged her down. It was then she decided she preferred to sink like a stone to the bottom. He would kill her anyway. This way was quicker, easier. She ceased struggling and fell cleanly downward.

The men were laughing. That was the last sound she heard as she went under the water—that gleeful laughter of theirs. Rorik was massaging his shoulder, looking at the rippling water where she'd gone under. Time passed, too much time. She didn't come up.

He cursed and jumped forward to the edge of the dock. Then her head cleared the water, bobbing up as if pushed from below. She was choking, thrashing the water with her arms, and he realized then that she couldn't swim, that or she was too far gone to keep herself afloat.

"You damnable witch!" he yelled at her. "I might have known you'd do this to me!" and jumped into the water beside her. He grabbed her, but she flailed at him, striking his face, his bandaged shoulder, choking and coughing up the water. Pain from her blow to the shoulder nearly sent the breath from him. He struck her jaw and she sagged unconscious against him.

He cursed again and towed her back to the pier. "Hafter, take her!"

Rorik cursed all the way to the farmstead, through the thick wooden gates, into the longhouse built by his grandfather. He cursed even as Kerzog, a huge mongrel of a hound, barked madly into his face then leapt up against his chest. He cursed even as he calmed Kerzog, cursed even as he took her from Hafter and carried her into his sleeping chamber. He started to lay her on his bed, then shook his head. He leaned her against him, and stripped off her sodden gown. He ripped the shift off her, laid her on her back on the box bed and untied the leather straps and pulled off her shoes. He drew a blanket over her and left the chamber. Immediately, he cursed again, turned back, and strode to the bed. He pulled the blanket down, jerked her over onto her belly, and splayed his hands across her narrow back. By the gods, her skin was nearly blue with cold. He straddled her and pumped the rest of the water from her body.

She sputtered and coughed and vomited up sea water, too much water. He was surprised she had survived. At least he had the presence of mind to pull her to the side of the bed so that the sea water didn't end up soaking the feather mattress. Kerzog sat there, staring at the vomiting, heaving woman, just staring, not barking, just looking thoughtful at this stranger.

"She's a witch," he said to his dog, and Kerzog looked at him for a very long time, his tongue lolling from his mouth. "I should have let her drown. Keep your distance from her," Rorik continued, "she just might bite you."

He slapped her hard between her shoulders one last time, then turned her onto her back once again. She stared up at him, her lips blue, her face whiter than her very white belly that he didn't want to look at, that he refused to look at.

"Why didn't you just let me drown?"

"You sound like a wet rag that's been trod upon by a dozen men."

"Why?"

"I should have," he said, then pulled the blanket up to her throat. He looked at the thick black hair, sopping and matted and filthy, and quickly fetched a drying cloth of soft white cotton. He spread it beneath her head then fanned her hair out like a halo around her head to dry.

"Are you through puking?"

She nodded, so tired, so beaten, she had no more words. She wished he'd let her drown. She wished she'd let herself drown, but even though she'd wanted an easy death, something in her had rebelled and she'd fought her way to the surface, only to realize that she had no more strength. He'd saved her life, damn him. If he'd just walked away, it would be over. She thought of the past three days, the endless humiliation of it, ignored after a while even by his men, kept bound unless she had to relieve herself or eat. Aye, she wished he'd let her drown. And now there was this massive ugly dog sitting there, staring at her. She wondered if the dog were as vicious and unpredictable as his master.

"Stay here and keep quiet. I'll bring you some food."

He left her. Mirana immediately sat up and swung her legs over the side of the bed. The dog didn't move. She eyed him, then moved some more. The dog still didn't move or growl, just sat there, looking at her. She whistled, then sang a verse from a child's song her mother used to sing to her, but he still just sat there on his raw-boned haunches, looking. The chamber was dim. She was cold, shivering, despite the warmth of the room, despite the warmth of the sun that shone so brightly upon the thatched roof above.

She wrapped the blanket around her and rose. She stumbled and sat down again. She drew a deep breath and stood again. Her legs were stronger now, but she was so weak, so very weak. Kerzog didn't move.

What should she do?

# 5

SHE WAS STANDING when he came into the room again, a wooden bowl of stew in his hand. He stared at her as she was bent forward like an old woman, wrapped in a blanket, her hair streaming down her back and over her shoulders, staring at him, her eyes dull, her face too pale. He saw a brief spark of anger, of defiance perhaps, in her eyes, but it was quickly gone. As for Kerzog, he was being watchful, but nothing more. It appeared he'd made no move to stop the woman from rising from the box bed.

He said to her, "I told you that my men really have no interest in you. You're skinny, not at all appetizing. A man would have to be starving for a woman before he would turn his eyes to you. Although the dousing in the sea relieved you of the worst of your smell, you still look like a wet scrap. You will not go into the main chamber. Get back into bed. I won't tell you again. Kerzog, watch her. Keep her here."

She didn't move. His dog, raised by him from a tiny pup, merely kept looking at the woman.

He frowned at his dog, then at her and took a step toward her. She still didn't move.

"Where were you going?"

"I must relieve myself," she said, and hated him for forcing her to say it aloud, though it shouldn't have mattered, not after the three days on his warship.

He cursed, plowing his fingers through his hair. "Come along." He set the bowl of stew on the end of the bed, told his dog to keep away from it, then turned and left the chamber. She trailed behind him, wrapped in the now-damp blanket, half of it dragging behind her on the beaten earth floor. Kerzog slowly followed.

She followed him from the longhouse, aware of the boisterous conversation that quieted when she appeared. He took her to a small shed and said, "This is the privy. Hurry. I will wait for you here."

When she emerged from the small shed a few minutes later he simply looked at her, just like his damned dog was still looking, then motioned for her to follow him again. This time he led her into a large stone and wood building. Inside there was an outer chamber with benches along the sides of the wall. It was the bathing hut, and she felt a spurt of hope. Surely he wouldn't bring her here just to watch him bathe. She followed him into the inner chamber, small and square, filled with heat and steam drawn from the pile of burning embers filling the fire pit in the center of the chamber. Wooden planks covered the floor and more wooden benches lined the walls. He stood her in the middle of the room, pulled the blanket off her, and said, "Stand still. If you move, I'll toss you in the sea again. I'll have my dog kill you. He's vicious. He protects me and my island that you have so freely scorned."

She stood there, shivering despite the billowing heat and the thick steam, trying to cover herself, and knowing that she failed and knowing too that he was looking at her, but that he didn't care, that she repulsed him. She should be grateful for that, she thought, watching him coming into the chamber again, a bucket in each hand. She knew what was coming and nearly yelled with the anticipation of it. He threw a bucket of hot water on her. He handed her a piece of soap carved into the shape of a small bird. A tern, if she wasn't mistaken. She was going mad, she knew it. A tern!

"Bathe, all over, and hurry."

She did. She didn't even notice that he'd left her alone. She'd never before in her life realized the luxury of a bath with soap. It was wonderful. He'd left another bucket on the wooden plank beside her. She rinsed her hair and soaped it again. Once clean, she had nothing to do but wait. She couldn't fetch her own water, not naked.

When he appeared, he looked at her, his expression grim. "Hold still." He poured the water slowly over her head as she rinsed herself. Then he backed up several feet. She looked at him even as he raised the bucket and threw ice-cold water on her.

She shuddered and heaved and yelled even though she'd known what was coming.

He laughed. She reacted just as he always did. Evidently Einar had a bathing hut on Clontarf like this one.

Once she was dry, he handed her the damp blanket again, and motioned her to follow him.

Conversation became muted once again. Mirana looked neither to the right nor to the left. She followed him into his sleeping chamber and sat down on the edge of the bed. He tossed an antler comb onto her lap. Kerzog hadn't come into the sleeping chamber this time.

"Eat first else you might collapse again. I don't wish to have to untangle that witches' nest on your head."

Obediently she took the bowl of stew from him, the stew now long cold. She took a bite, and gagged. It tasted like congealed grease and strangely sour. The bits of meat were stringy, the sauce filled with lumps as nasty as rye root. She was hungry but she wasn't starving. She forced down another bite, then set the bowl aside. Any more of it and she'd vomit again. Her stomach was knotting and unknotting in painful spasms.

Rorik looked at her, his frown building. "Finish it."

She looked up at him, holding the blanket tightly over her breasts. "It tastes like pig swill. There is so much grease on the top that it has hardened."

She thought he would burst with rage but she didn't care. If he struck her, perhaps he would kill her. At the moment, it didn't matter, nothing mattered.

He seemed to get control of himself. He lifted the bowl and took a bite. It was bad, he thought, very bad. Worse than it usually was, though that was usually bad enough of late. Even the women who prepared food well seemed to have forgotten over the past weeks. It was Entti, he thought, the women had given the task again to Entti. He sighed, but he didn't give in, he was still too furious with her. She was his prisoner, less than a slave, and yet she dared to speak her mind as if she were the mistress here. She dared to show her disgust for him and for his farmstead. She dared to scorn the food that only a halfwit would eat. She dared to allow Kerzog, the dog he'd raised from a pup, a very small pup, just watch her but make no threatening growls or moves. He said, "You will consume it as you would a feast. Every bite. If you don't, then you may go hungry, I care not. You can starve."

"I can't eat it," she said, and knew immediately that he would indeed not give her anything else to eat. "I won't eat it." For how long? Would he let her starve to death? "No one could eat it." She looked at him, at the closed expression, at the anger in his eyes. She didn't want to starve. She fancied it wouldn't be a very pleasant way to die. It would be far too slow even though she was already so hungry she'd believed she could eat anything. She'd been wrong.

Drowning would have been better. She would simply have to escape, that was all, and then when he caught her, as she was certain he would, for it was an island, after all, he would kill her. It would be over.

She smiled at him. "Give me the comb."

He tossed it at her, then left the chamber without another word.

Mirana knew it was late at night because the loud voices that had filled the silence for hour upon hour were now silent. Nearly everyone must be asleep. She'd slept most of the afternoon, but she'd awakened, hungry and alone, and laid there. Her stomach churned and clenched and growled. No one had come. She'd had no desire to rise and go into the huge outer room.

She wondered where he was. This was his sleeping chamber, she was sure of it. Where was he?

As if conjured up by her mind, he came into the room. There was a fresh bandage of soft white linen wrapped around his shoulder. He was clean and dressed in a fresh tunic belted at his waist. He was big and powerful, his hair thick and blond on his head, his eyes the light blue of a Viking whose blood wasn't tainted, as was hers. He was clean shaven. He was a magnificent animal, she supposed, but she didn't care. She wished she'd killed him. Her fingers itched for her knife.

He held a rush torch light in his right hand. He held it high and looked at her. "You're awake, are you?"

She said nothing.

"Good. Now I shan't have to rouse you and listen to your endless complaints. At least I had the foresight to have you bathe."

He was going to ravish her. She held perfectly still, preparing herself for his attack. She wouldn't give in to him easily. She would fight him until he was forced to strike her, perhaps kill her. She waited, her muscles tensed, ready. If only she had her knife, if only.

He doused the rush torch light. She heard him removing his clothing. He sat on the far side of the bed, so close to her really, and she pictured him taking off his boots.

Then he rose and she knew he was coming to the other side of the bed, to her. Her heart thudded hard and heavy. She tasted fear in her mouth. Fear and hatred of him and resolve that her rape wouldn't be easy for him, that she would hurt him badly if she could. She heard him brush against his trunk that sat at the foot of the bed. She was ready for him, she had to be.

He was standing next to her, bending down over her, saying nothing, but she heard his breathing. Suddenly, he grabbed the blanket and wrapped it tightly around her, trapping her arms. He lifted her and tossed her onto the floor beside the bed.

She landed on her side, stunned and winded.

He threw another blanket on top of her.

He said nothing more. She heard him ease down onto the bed, heard him draw in a deep breath, then he was silent.

Then he laughed, and it was a rich mocking laugh.

A knife, she thought, if only she had a knife.

"You thought I would rape you," he said, and laughed again. "Rape *you*? Even though you're clean and more sweet-smelling than otherwise, I doubt I could have forced myself to take you, you who are nothing more than an ill-tempered witch. I'd rather be forced to plow an old crone than to plow your belly. You're so fond of your brother, you who would do anything for Einar, a swine who deserves the cruelest of deaths. Do you lust after him, your own kin? Is that why you're still unwed? Perhaps he has already bedded you. You aren't young, after all. Does he hold you above his other whores?"

It was odd, she thought, as she rose silently to her feet. So very odd that it would happen now, that he would taunt her beyond what she could bear. She wrapped the blanket around her and walked to the entrance. She pulled the hide aside. A small sliver of light shone in. She wondered where Kerzog was and what he would do. Would he kill her, his fangs buried in her throat?

It was then that Rorik heard her. He said loud and clear, "Do not leave this chamber, damn you. Get back here or it will go badly for you."

She ignored him, something she knew had never happened to him in his life, and walked into the outer room, still filled with the dying warmth from the fire pit. She breathed in the light smell of smoke, thinning out now, until the morrow when the fire pit was lit again, the room filling once more with smoke turning the air a pale blue. There was snoring coming from all the benches along the walls. She saw Kerzog sleeping by the fire pit. He raised his head and looked at her. Then he lowered his head and went back to sleep. He was indeed a ferocious animal, she thought as she kept walking. Then she broke into a run, for he was behind her now.

She dashed to the doors, and heaved up the heavy wooden cross-beam. She couldn't manage it.

She heard him behind her and she jerked up with all her strength. The cross beam flew upward and fell to the side with a heavy thud. She shoved open the door and dashed outside.

She stumbled on the blanket, falling to her knees. She was up in a flash, running, ignoring the pebbles and shards of wood that dug into her bare feet. She heard him behind her, but he wasn't saying anything now. No, this chase was a silent one, one that would end with her death.

There were four guards at the huge gates of the palisade. They saw her coming, saw Lord Rorik behind her, naked.

They didn't move. They said nothing. It was as if she were alone with him.

Rorik caught her hair and stopped. She cried out with the burning pain and fell back against his chest.

He wrapped the thick hair around his wrist again and again, until her head was pressed tight against his shoulder.

"You wish to relieve yourself again?"

He sounded calm, not at all angry, but she wasn't fooled. He would kill her.

"Nay," she said, gritting her teeth against the pain as he again tightened her hair around his hand. "Nay, I wanted to escape you, to force you to catch me and kill me cleanly. But that isn't your way, is it? You would prefer to torture me, with your words and your threats and your deeds."

"Kill you," he said. "Aye, that's a thought, isn't it? You've caused me nothing but annoyance, forcing me yet again to hurt my shoulder running you down."

He said nothing else, merely jerked his hand lightly. She was close to him, pressed tightly against his side. She couldn't move away because he held her hair wrapped tightly around his hand. The blanket slipped and she jerked it up.

He laughed, nodding to the men standing silent by the palisade.

There were men awake in the longhouse. One called out, "My lord, what goes?"

"Seek your dreams again, Gurd. The woman wished to see the moonlight above Hawkfell Island. She believes this island to be beyond any land she has ever before seen. Aye, return to your sleep."

Once inside the sleeping chamber, he unwound her hair and shoved her down onto the bed. He lit a rush torch.

He opened his trunk and pulled out a length of chain from the bottom. She watched as he fastened one end of the chain to the post at the foot of his bed. He held up the other end and straightened. "Come here."

A chain, she thought, staring at it dumbly. She shook her head. He would chain her like an animal? He wouldn't kill her cleanly?

He strode to her, grabbed her right hand and wrapped the chain around it. The blanket fell to her waist.

He fastened the chain securely, then straightened again. He grabbed her left hand as she tried to pull up the blanket.

He said nothing, merely stared at her breasts. Slowly, knowing that she was watching, knowing well that she hated him looking at her, he reached out and cupped her right breast in his palm.

She froze for an instant with fear and humiliation. Then she jerked back. He grabbed the chain, laughing now, and pulled her forward. She hit at him with her free hand.

He pushed her down onto her back and came over her, straddling her. He again lowered his hand, all the while looking at her face, watching her staring at his hand. This time he ran his fingers lightly over her breasts, from one to the other, again and again. His expression was unreadable. Then he frowned and jerked his hand away, staring at it as if he were unclean, as if she'd befouled him.

He rose off her and jerked the chain, bringing her to her feet. He looked down at her, said nothing. He hooked his leg behind her knees and sent her sprawling onto the floor.

She watched him extinguish the rush torch. She heard him fall onto his bed. She heard him drawing deep steadying breaths.

She was awake when his deep breathing evened into sleep.

# 6

RORIK TENSED AS Old Alna probed at the pink flesh around the wound on his shoulder. She pressed more, made more noises he didn't understand, then rubbed a noxious-smelling paste over the healing wound. She looked hard at the paste and the wound, made more noises, patted him as she would a small boy, and said, " 'Tis good. You'll live, my lord. Whoever tended you after you were pricked did a fine job. Saved your lordly hide, I'd say."

Rorik grunted, easing now as she bandaged his shoulder again in soft clean white wool. When she'd tied the knot over the bandage, he rose, and smiled down at the bent old woman. "Thank you. It doesn't pain me so much now."

"Aye, it shouldn't. You heal well and that's because of your mother, aye, never a scratch on her that wasn't well in a day's time."

Rorik didn't know this, but he only nodded. He rose to leave the longhouse.

"The girl," Old Alna said. "What will you do with her? The men tell of how she kept you alive only for her brother to torture. Is she the one who tended you? Nay, that doesn't make sense since the men say she would kill you if she could, that she's not really a woman but only a woman's form and that she's vicious and cold and a black-hearted witch." Old Alna spit into the fire pit.

His men had said all that? It was doubtful, Rorik thought. Old Alna had an imagination to rival a scald's. She could plant an acorn and quickly raise a full-branched oak tree from it.

"She is Einar's half-sister and my hostage," he said, and turned away, saying more to himself than to the scrappy old woman, "Her intentions aren't always clear to me. She is my prisoner. Keep away from her. She isn't to be trusted around any of us."

A scraggly brow rose in question. "Will you keep her in your sleeping chamber?"

He allowed the impertinence, though he gave her a look that would halt most of his men in their tracks. She'd helped bring him into the world, she'd not left his mother's side when she'd been so very ill with the bloody flux, and he remembered then that it had nearly broken her, for she dearly loved his mother, as did he. Aye, it had been a bad time, but in large part due to Old Alna's constant vigil, his mother had survived. Rorik shook his head. He was Old Alna's favorite of all his three siblings and she'd journeyed here to Hawkfell nearly two years before when he'd left his small farmstead in the Vestfold, just west of the trading town of Kaupang. He suspected Old Alna and his mother had discussed it and that both women had decided she should come with him.

He had no intention of answering her. He looked over her left shoulder at Erna who was efficiently working the loom. Her withered right arm didn't hinder her work at all. He'd heard stories when he was much younger of how her mother had seen her baby and had wanted to leave her to die on the mountainside, but Erna's father had looked at her withered arm and said no, this was a girl to be proud of. She was wedded to Raki, one of his warriors with immense strength, his own two healthy arms the size of his chair posts. Their two boys were whole and strong as their father. Rorik heard her humming softly to herself as she worked. He turned back to Old Alna, "She was still asleep when I left her this morning."

"When she awakens she will be hungry. All she needs is good food to regain her strength." She cackled at that and gave him a sly look. "Not that Entti is such a good cook. Shall I take your prisoner some porridge?"

He thought of his orders to her to eat the inedible stew or go hungry. Damn her. He said aloud, "Why do you continue to make Entti cook if her results are so terrible? Why do you make us all suffer?"

Old Alna shrugged. " 'Twas her turn. What could I do? It is all done by vote. You gave me the responsibility, my lord Rorik, to oversee the homestead, for two years now. I am doing my best. Will you strip me of my duty?"

Rorik gave her a harassed look, knew the pathetic voice was a sham, but let it go. It always seemed to be Entti's turn of late, that or she'd given the other women lessons on how to prepare swill to cramp the belly. "I'll see if she's awake. Did Entti prepare the porridge?"

Old Alna cackled again. "Nay. Ottar's girl, Utta, was up before the dawn. Aye, a born cook that one is. A pity she's only eleven years old. She cooks only on rare occasion. Aye, a wondrous cook, that little one. No black lumps in the porridge this morning. She'll grow up soon enough, in three years or so, and then she'll take her turn with the other women, that or wed and leave Hawkfell."

Rorik was so hungry at that moment he gave thought to marrying the child himself. He stood by the fire pit and fed himself first, eating two bowls, savoring each spoonful of porridge, then dished up a bowl for the woman, dropped a dollop of butter on it, and walked to his sleeping chamber. He pulled back the hide covering the doorway. Light flooded in.

She was lying on her side on the floor, her legs drawn up, her hands folded beneath her cheek. He stood over her, saying nothing. She looked defenseless. She looked helpless, but he knew the truth. He'd felt her damned knife in his throat.

What was he going to do with her?

He nudged her buttocks with his foot.

She mumbled something in her sleep, then quieted again.

He nudged her again, saying, "Wake up. I have much to do and wish not to waste more of my time with you. You try me with your very presence."

She was awake in the next instant. She sat up slowly and brought her hands up to push her hair from her face. It was in the next moment she remembered that her right hand was chained.

He watched her face pale then saw the anger build in her eyes. He said again, "I have porridge for you. You will eat now. I have no more time to waste."

She was so hungry she wanted to snatch the bowl from him. The smell made her mouth water. She forced herself to nod slowly, very slowly. She could smell the porridge and the melting butter. She swallowed convulsively, eyeing that porridge. She looked at the large man standing over her, the man who'd smashed his fist in her jaw and taken her from Clontarf, the man who'd set his big foot on her neck and on her back during the long voyage back to this island, and said, "Is it better than the offal you offered me last night?"

Rorik dumped the porridge on the floor, turned on his heel, and left the sleeping chamber.

Mirana stared at the porridge, that beautiful porridge with its rich smell and the sweet melting butter, all of it now seeping slowly into the packed earth. She cried. She didn't make a sound, just cried, the tears falling over her cheeks, dripping onto the blanket. It was her own fault. Why had those words come from her mouth? She hadn't planned them, they'd just come out without her permission. Why hadn't she just kept silent? Just nodded and accepted the porridge from him? After she'd eaten it she could have told him it was offal. Why had she baited him? She lowered her head in her hands.

She didn't know how much time had passed, perhaps minutes, perhaps hours, but suddenly she heard a movement, thought it him returning, and quickly sniffed back the tears. To have him see her weak like this was more than she could bear. She sniffled and wiped her eyes. She couldn't bear to look up, to see him staring down at her, doubtless pleased at her failure to control herself, more than pleased that he'd beaten her down so easily.

A soft young voice said, "I brought you some bread. I made it myself. It's very good. Lord Rorik and the men have left. Would you like it?"

Mirana raised her head. On her knees directly in front of her was a young girl with hair so blond it was nearly white. She was slight and very pretty, wearing a pale blue wool gown with a darker blue tunic over it. Two simple brooches of pounded silver fastened the tunic at her shoulders. More importantly, in her hands she held a wooden plate and on that plate were four slices of flatbread. Smeared on the flatbread were butter and honey. The smells were beyond description. It was a gift from the gods.

"Thank you," Mirana said, her eyes never leaving the bread. "I'm very hungry."

"Old Alna said you would be. She said Lord Rorik came out of his chamber looking like a man ready to commit murder, his face all red, the cords standing out in his neck. She said she doubted you got any of the porridge, he looked just that mad. She is always saying that men have no patience, that their spirits are too easily irritated and their actions the result of too little thought. They can't always control themselves, she says."

"Old Alna sounds wise." Mirana said no more. She tried not to stuff the flatbread into her mouth, but it was difficult. She concentrated on taking one bite at a time and chewing thoroughly. She knew the girl was watching her intently. She also knew that she was silent because Mirana was so very hungry and she didn't want to disturb her eating.

She ate the fourth slice of flatbread and reached out her hand. There was nothing more on the plate.

"Old Alna also said that you shouldn't eat more right now or you would be sick and vomit it all up. She said if you could bear it, you should just rest for a while and then I'll bring you some more food. Is that all right?"

"Aye, that's wonderful," Mirana said. She sighed deeply, ignored her still hollow belly, and lay back.

"Lord Rorik is gone hunting with the men."

"There is game on the island?"

"Aye, but he's been careful to breed as much as he kills so that we'll never starve when there is a long storm and he and the men can't fish or row to the mainland to hunt. This morning he and my father and some other men have sailed to shore to hunt there. The coast is flat and there are salt marshes and bogs, but there are wild boars there that are quite tasty. Everyone was tired of fish, though I know a very good recipe for roasting herring with juniper berries."

Mirana wanted some roasted boar right this instant or some roasted herring, she didn't care which.

"Would you like to get into Lord Rorik's bed?"

Mirana thought of other body parts than her stomach and nodded. She slowly rose, her back stiff, her buttocks sore, her right arm numb. It was then that Utta saw the chain. Her eyes widened with surprise.

"Why did Lord Rorik do that to you?"

"Because he didn't want to kill me just yet."

Mirana lay on the soft feather mattress. Utta pulled a blanket over her, then straightened.

"If you would like to relieve yourself, I will bring you a pot. I don't know how to unfasten the chain so you can go to the privy."

It was humiliating, but the young girl treated it so matter-of-factly that Mirana felt boundless gratitude. She said, "I will repay you for your kindness, Utta. If someday I can, I will repay you."

Utta merely shrugged. "I thought you were a witch, that's what all the men were telling the women. But you're not. I hope you aren't too frightened. You must sleep now. Later Old Alna will tend to the cuts on your hands and knees."

"Thank you."

Utta turned in the doorway. "My mother was sick for a long time before she died. I learned to care for her. Do you know how to cook?"

"Aye, certainly. I was mistress of my brother's fortress until Lord Rorik brought me here as his hostage."

"Are you a very good cook?"

"Aye."

Utta was silent for a long moment. She fiddled with one of the brooches at her shoulder. She said finally, "Why does Lord Rorik treat you like this?"

But Mirana, her belly lulled, the feather mattress soft beneath her back, was fast asleep.

Rorik and his men returned late in the afternoon, covered with blood and smelly dried bog mud. He himself had brought down the wild boar they'd seen and hunted down, cornering it finally at the edge of a deep salt marsh. He'd been pleased with himself and his men. He was elated at the kill, he always was when his skill was sufficient. But, since that time, his thoughts had gone to her. He thought of her lying on the floor, chained to his bed, unable to relieve herself, no one to give her food. He hated worrying. He hated even caring if the damned witch lived or died. He shouldn't have left her there, on the dirt floor, chained. She had saved his life, for whatever reason.

He would treat her a bit better. He needed her alive. He would use her just as soon as he figured out how to do it. He would use her to bring Einar to him.

Hafter said over the flapping of the square sail, "A wild boar, full grown and enough meat for the next two days. 'Twas a fine spear throw, Rorik, though I feared for a moment he would gore you."

Ottar agreed and spat over the side of the warship. Rorik merely nodded.

"Did you hurt your shoulder anew?"

"Just enough to remind me of all my sins," Rorik said, and the men laughed, watching him unconsciously massage and work the shoulder.

They rowed into the inlet. The men on the dock secured the warship and kicked its bow clear so it wouldn't scrape against the wood. They hefted the boar onto their shoulders and started up the stone path to the palisade, singing and bragging of their prowess.

Hafter said to Rorik as they fell in line behind the other men, "I have prayed to every god in Valhalla that Entti hasn't prepared our meal tonight. My ribs are striking together."

Ottar laughed. "Aye. But the other women say that she must take her turn, that it isn't fair she just perform one task—no matter how well she performs it."

"She has remarkable talents," Hafter said, grinning, his blue eyes lighting up. "Surely it is enough to occupy her time."

Ottar just laughed. "Aye, 'tis enough that she part her legs for me, for you, Hafter, for Gurd, or for you, Sculla—"

"Nay, not for me," Sculla said. "I would crush her were I to take her." This, Rorik thought, was probably the truth. Sculla was so tall he had to bend over to enter the longhouse. Sculla and Amma were well suited, at least in their respective sizes. Ah, but Amma was a sharp-tongued woman, taking no orders from the men, even her husband.

"Entti much enjoys herself," Rorik said. "She is a woman of calling. You, Ottar, may cease your listing of men's names." He sighed. "It's not just Entti's cooking, though it is bad enough. The other women seem to have forgotten what ingredients go with what and the most simple of preparations. I don't understand it. I have asked why anyone would put onions in porridge, but Old Alna just shakes her head and grunts. If the women don't regain their skills, we will all be dead or lying about with cramping bellies. They suffer just as we do, which makes it even more a mystery."

Hafter shook his head. "Perhaps they will take a new vote and decide to remove Entti from the cooking pots. It's been nearly three weeks of her cooking—Old Alna swore to me Entti had cooked all the time whilst we were gone. She said the other women were trying to teach her, but it was not a skill she took to easily."

"Alna is a treacherous crone," Sculla said, hunching down so his head didn't strike against the low-lying oak branches just off the path. "She lies like a virgin born, the old crone. I've always admired her. So does Amma."

"Women are stubborn," Ottar said, "mayhap even dangerous, for their thinking isn't reasonable like ours. Even my little Utta gets a notion and I can't move her from it. Her mother was the same way. Sweet and gentle one moment, then her chin would go up, her eyes would turn black, and I knew I would be stupid to open my mouth to disagree with her. By Thor's hammer, we'll all starve before the women reverse their vote. Mayhap you should speak to Old Alna, Rorik."

"I did," Rorik said. "She spoke of how I had made her responsible for the homestead and how she was doing her best. She then gave me a look that clearly said I would be a brutal monster were I to complain more."

Aslak stared at them, laughed until he choked, spat on a rock in his path, and marveled aloud, "You are all blind. I have been here only a day and have seen that the women are preparing wretched meals apurpose. You surely don't believe they're eating the same food they prepare for us, do you?"

"That is foolish," Hafter said, swatting at a fly. "You're wrong, Aslak. They wouldn't dare."

"Ha!" Aslak said, louder this time, shaking his head at them. "Don't you see? The women are punishing all of you for taking Entti to your beds."

Sculla said, "None of the men who are wedded seek her bed, or if they do they are cautious about it, they don't boast of it to their wives. Aye, they creep about very carefully. Gurd is very sly about it."

"I wonder," Rorik said.

"You are all fools," Aslak said. "I know it is the truth. It's as obvious as the snout on that boar."

"Women," said Ottar, "are occasionally shrewd in their cunning. They shrink from nothing. I think Aslak might be in the right of it. We should—that is, *Lord Rorik* should simply order that Entti doesn't touch another piece of food. It is for the women to obey, especially to obey you, Rorik. You will simply tell them what to do and what not to do and who is not to do it. You will tell them they are to remember how to cook properly or you will punish them."

Rorik looked at him as if Ottar were mad.

Raki flexed his mighty fists. Rorik knew he could slay six of the enemy with ease and bellow with joy all the while. But with Erna and his two sons, he was a man of gentle parts. He'd been thoughtfully silent until now. He said, "The crops grow well. Not all of us are needed here for protection or for hunting or farming. We could sail up the Seine, and go araiding on all those rich little towns. Ah, aye, 'twould be good sport and our pockets would grow heavy with gold and silver. Or we could go to Hedeby to trade some of Gurd's swords for wine from the Rhineland. Aye, we could trade some soapstone bowls for leather and ornaments. There is no reason to stay here and starve. Even bedding Entti isn't worth that, though all of you say she passes the time most pleasantly. What say you, Rorik?"

Rorik sighed. "I will speak to the women again. Then we will see."

The men looked at each other without much hope.

OLD ALNA SAID to Asta, who was Gurd the blacksmith's wife, "Lord Rorik keeps the woman chained to his bed. He tells me to stay away from her. What think you?"

Asta, always laughing, wasn't laughing now. She shook her head. "It is all strange. Lord Rorik isn't brutal, particularly to women. Is she really so vicious, so cold and cruel? I know she is the sister of Lord Rorik's avowed enemy, but still, why would he treat her so meanly? She did nothing to harm him, at least I don't think she did. But the stories the men have told could curdle the goat's milk."

"Little Utta thinks she's very nice and she's been feeding her all day—her cooking, not Entti's—the same as we've been eating. Do we do the right thing, Asta? With the good food, the girl will regain her strength in no time at all."

"Aye, and when she does, Alna, what then? It makes no difference. Let her eat, let her belly sing with happiness. The child is an excellent cook, and the men wouldn't ever suspect her of duplicity, even Ottar, her father. Aye, let them suffer and let the prisoner grow fat. Do you know that two of the wedded men have taken Entti since their return not twenty-four hours ago? I suspect Gurd, but he is sly, and when he returns to me, he complains of loose bowels and belly pains. Ha! The wives are furious. I'm furious. No, Alna, let them eat Entti's cooking until they come to reason."

"It is a good plan, this one of Amma's," Old Alna said. "She is smart and determined to teach the men a lesson. She is always saying that Sculla is constant and that the others should be as well. She says that they can starve unless they come to reason.

"It takes a long time for a man to starve," Old Alna continued. "Mayhap starvation takes longer than it takes to bring him to reason."

Rorik strode into the sleeping chamber. He'd bathed all the wild boar's blood off him, all the rotted marsh mud, and donned a clean tunic. He stopped, surprise and fury combining to make him flush red. She was propped up against his feather pillow like a lady taking her ease. Her hair was combed and braided. Soft curls had come loose to feather around her face. She looked very different, aye, that lady or princess ensconced in her bed, waiting for her slaves to attend her. He frowned down at her. She looked up at him, saying nothing.

He saw the chain around her wrist. It made him feel better. She might look like a princess, but she was, indeed, his hostage, chained by him. Aye, he was the master, he was the one who held her future in his hands. He wouldn't allow her to forget it. "Get up," he said.

She rose slowly, to stand before him. "Give me your hand, your right hand." It was heavy with the chain but she thrust it toward him. He unfastened the chain from her wrist and let it drop to the ground.

She was wearing a gown of soft gray wool, a white linen tunic over it, belted. He frowned, sudden anger roiling in his belly. "Who has aided you?"

"If I tell you, will you chain them to the floor and beat them?"

"I haven't beat you," he said, watching her massage her wrist.

"Now you will because I have given you the idea."

"Who?"

She saw the pulse quicken in his throat. He was angry, and becoming angrier by the moment. He was the lord here and yet someone had aided her, his prisoner.

"Hafter helped me." Oh aye, Hafter, his man, let him chew on that one.

Rorik didn't chew long. "Ha! Hafter help you? Even if he would ever be so unwise, nay, so stupid, he wasn't this time. He was with me all day. Stop your damned lies. It was doubtless one of the women. Who?"

She turned from him and walked toward the doorway. He grabbed her arm and jerked her around to face him. She raised her other hand to strike him, and he grabbed her wrist. He saw then the scrapes and cuts and eased his hold on her hands. He saw the red marks still sharp and angry on her wrist from the rough links of the chain.

"Are you hungry?"

"Since you have starved me since you dragged me here, I am ravenous. I nearly gnawed at the chain. Will you offer me food or pig swill again?"

He frowned. "I don't know. Sit you down on the bed, and I will bring you what there is. If I don't deign to eat it, then you won't have to either."

He returned shortly carrying a wooden plate. On the plate was a pile of mashed peas with some sort of red berries crushed in, a reeking pile of cabbage boiled with small chunks of what seemed to be bark from a pine tree. In the center of the plate lay a large herring, headless, not boned, and burned blacker than a Christian's sins.

She looked at the plate. "Is there naught else? Is all the food like this?"

"Aye," he said, and looked grim.

Mirana didn't know what was going on here. Also, it threw her off balance to see another side of this man. He'd been only vicious to her, but now he looked ready to howl or weep at the sight of the inedible slop on the plate. Mirana thought of the wonderful bread, the delectable roasted herring she'd been fed earlier, the big plate of beans seasoned to perfection. But now this. She said nothing. It made no sense.

"I would rather starve," she said deliberately, and glowed at the thought of her full belly. "Take this miserable swill and grind it under your heel, or act an enraged child again and throw it onto the ground like you did this morning with the porridge."

Instead, Rorik dumped the plate onto her lap, stepped back, rubbed his hands together, and said with a good deal of mockery, "If it was Hafter who aided you—which of course seems very likely for I see him wearing gowns all the time—why then, he now owns one less gown." He gave her a long thoughtful look. "Though I must say that this particular shade of gray with the white tunic doesn't match his eyes. Why then, he will surely be displeased for this gown is ruined now. I will tell him what you have said and watch his face turn purple with fury."

He strode from the sleeping chamber. She stared after him. She realized a few moments later that he'd been so angry, he'd forgotten and left her unchained. She stood, wiping gobs of food from the skirt of her gown.

The gown had belonged to Utta's mother. Now it would need to be washed, vigorously, and hopefully be saved. She walked into the great hall, a folded blanket over her arm, and was again aware that conversation flagged. She could feel the men staring after her, distrust in their eyes, uncertainty, since she was free. She felt only curiosity from the women. Perhaps something more than just curiosity from them. Whatever they were thinking of her, she didn't feel the chill she felt from the men.

She looked neither to the right nor to the left. She walked to the front doors. They were pushed wide open. Not a word, not a shout, not a yell from Rorik. She wondered why he hadn't at least ordered her to stop.

She went to the bathing hut. There were buckets of water in the outer room. She stripped off the gown and the tunic and washed both garments. She wrapped herself in the blanket, spread the gown and tunic over the benches to dry, and left the hut. She turned toward the palisade wall, just to see what was there, how thick the walls were, what the gates were like, what . . .

She came face-to-face with Rorik. He held three good-sized silver bass by hooks on a line. Kerzog was standing at his side, his tongue lolling.

She stared at the fish.

He looked at her face, then down at the blanket wrapped around her. "What are you doing out here?"

"I had to wash the gown you ruined with the swill. What are you doing with the fish?"

He looked undecided, then shrugged. "Come with me."

She followed him, her blanket held firmly to her neck. He squatted down near the wall at the eastern corner of the palisade, and built a small fire from the pile of twigs and small branches stacked there. Kerzog fell onto his haunches close to the fire and watched his master, his big head cocked to one side, as if in question.

Rorik motioned for her to sit down. She watched him scale the bass with a small knife as sharp as the one she'd lightly speared into his throat. Then he lifted an iron pan he'd obviously brought from the longhouse, smeared the bass with thick sweet butter, and laid all three of them with near reverence into the pan. He set it over the fire, sat down cross-legged and stared at the pan, as if willing it to heat quickly and cook that fish.

She laughed, she couldn't help it.

"I'm starving," he said matter-of-factly. He continued looking at the fish, now beginning to bubble and spit, and said, "I'll give you one of them."

"It seems fair. I did feed you in your captivity."

"Aye, and you tried to gullet me."

"Had I wanted to kill you, I could have, easily. You were as helpless as that gutted bass."

"I am tired of your swaggering. Be quiet. Watch the fish. Do you think this one in the middle is nearly done?"

It was hissing in the thick butter, darkening nicely, looking quite delicious.

"No, it is still raw on the inside. Must you feed yourself every night?"

He grunted. A fat half-moon shone down overhead. The night was clear, the stars vivid in the black sky. The air was warm and still. The birds had quieted for the night. It was so quiet, the water lapping against the rocks sounded faintly in the distance. She saw him quite clearly, the planes and shadows of his face in the firelight. He was staring as hard as he could at the frying fish.

It was difficult to hate a man who looked as if he'd cry if something happened to that frying fish.

"Will you chain me again tonight?"

"Probably. I cannot trust you to keep your word—you are Einar's sister, after all, and he is a murderer, and much worse. I will chain you, aye." He stuck his knife into each of the fish and flipped them over.

She watched them sizzle and brown for several minutes, then said, "What did he do to you? I have never heard him say your name."

"The fish is cooked." He picked up a wooden plate, realized he had only one, then shrugged. He knifed each of the fish onto the plate, then set it between them. "You will use your fingers. I have only one knife. Take that fish nearest you. It's the smallest."

She simply nodded, but made no move as yet. She was blessedly full. She watched him slice the bass, carefully cut it, and spear it. He eased it into his mouth as one would present a gift to a god. He chewed, the expression on his face blissful. He said nothing, just ate, one bite after another, until all that was left on the plate was the smallest bass he'd said was hers and a half of another.

He looked at that half of bass. Then he looked at his dog and sighed. To her astonishment, he offered the remaining half to Kerzog. To her further astonishment, after Kerzog sniffed at it, he wuffed softly, and refused it, looking at Rorik as he rested his head on his front paws. Rorik frowned at him but said nothing.

She said, "There is something strange going on here. I was fed all day, the most delicious porridge and fresh bread with butter and honey, and then there was stewed beans in onions and eggs, all delicious. Yet you bring that horrid swill for dinner. You are starving. What is happening here?"

He continued to stare at that half fish and at the small one that was hers. He said, more to himself than to her, "So Aslak was right." He cursed. "By all the gods, my damned dog is full bellied! That's why he disdains the bass I offered him. It is only the men the women are torturing. Even Kerzog is blissfully full."

"Eat the rest of the bass. I am very full, perhaps even more so than your dog. As I said, the women fed me all day."

He did, saying nothing until he'd wiped his mouth on the back of his hand, wiped his knife on an oak leaf, and tossed the leaf into the embers of the small fire.

"Aslak said the women are punishing us because Entti beds the men. The women don't care if the men aren't married, but married men are seeking her out as well and that makes them very angry."

She stared at him. This was the man who'd tried to kill her brother, who had fought over a dozen men with naught but a sword and a knife? This was the man who'd borne the wound in his shoulder like the warrior he was, contemptuous of weakness and pain, until, finally, he'd escaped, taking her with him? He'd been cruel, treating her like an animal, abusing her endlessly, yet saving her from drowning, even though at that moment she'd wanted to drown, to end it. She was thankful now that he'd saved her. But all of it came down to this—he and his men were being punished by the women for their faithlessness.

He'd caught his own dinner and cooked it.

"I don't know why the women fed you," he said absently. "You're their enemy since you're also my enemy."

He sat back against the palisade wall and sighed in contentment, lacing his hands over his belly.

"Aye," he said, filling the silence, for Mirana said nothing, "aye, I must do it, there is none other. I will stop this women's rebellion. My men said I should put a halt to it and I will, though in all truth, I don't think they believe me able to succeed. But I will succeed. If a man wishes to bed a woman, it is his right to do so."

"Even if he is wed?"

He looked into the fire, his blue eyes gleaming brighter than the flames. "The man rules. It is he who protects the woman, he who provides shelter and food for her. It is his right to bed with a bear if he wishes to. It is I who am the lord here and all obey me. I will endure no more."

It was in that instant that Mirana decided to take a hand. His words, spoken with such arrogance, made her want to strike him. So, he believed a man could be unfaithful to his wife, did he? She wished now she'd known the reason for the inedible cooking before speaking to him, for she'd been too frank in her words to him, and now he planned to retaliate. She would do something, she had to.

She bided her time. He led her back to the longhouse, into the sleeping chamber, and again chained her wrist. Then he left her. Mirana waited. When she'd passed through the longhouse with Rorik, she'd looked directly at Old Alna, a look that conveyed a woman's meaning that was instantly recognized and accepted. She waited now in his chamber, knowing the old woman would come if she were able.

Both Old Alna and Amma came only minutes later.

Old Alna said as she lit the rush light set in the wall, and pulled the bearskin down over the opening to the sleeping chamber to give them privacy, "Lord Rorik and the men are all drinking and braying like goats over their prowess on the mainland hunt today. Aye, on and on how brave Rorik was to face down the boar with his wounded shoulder. He will gain too much affection for himself if it continues. I also overheard Gurd telling the men that Rorik would stop the women's rebellion and then he laughed and laughed, and poured mead down his throat in Rorik's honor. Don't you worry, Mirana, that Lord Rorik will come here to look in on you and thus surprise us. Nay, Lord Rorik won't think about you, he's too busy thinking about himself and how wonderful he is. We're safe. This is Amma. It was her idea to punish the men until they learned to keep their men's lusts at their own hearths."

"I'm glad you came," Mirana said. She looked at Amma, who nodded back to her. "I had wondered at the terrible food. Unfortunately I spoke of it to Lord Rorik. If only I'd known the reason for your actions, I wouldn't have said anything. I'm very sorry. Amma, 'twas an excellent idea. Tonight Lord Rorik said he would stop it, that he would give you orders that Entti would no longer cook, that you would no longer play these games with the men's bellies. It was Aslak who saw the truth immediately and he told the men, but Rorik didn't want to believe it."

"Rorik's soft when it comes to the women," Old Alna said and grinned at Mirana and Amma. "I wondered when one of the men would realize what we were doing and why. But Rorik is soft with women, as I said, all except with you. I don't understand that, he is different with you, but with us, he won't lift his voice or his hand."

Mirana shook her head. "He is ready to order and command and yell. Perhaps he is even ready to do violence. Rorik is starving. He caught his own fish and cooked them himself tonight. I have never before seen a man look at food the way he did at that frying fish. He will do what is necessary and if that is terrorizing the women with threats and punishments, that is what he will do. That is why I looked toward you, Alna, when he brought me back inside." Mirana drew a deep breath. "I want to help. I want to try to stop him if I can. I want you to gain what is right."

Amma said, "I have pushed the women into this. Nay, Alna, don't excuse me. I did think it was the best way to gain their attention. You see, Mirana, Sculla, my husband, doesn't sleep with Entti. He is faithful, but the others, they are rutting stoats. There is something else. I wouldn't have you fault Entti. None of the women do. She's a simple-minded girl, sweet and gentle. 'Tis not her fault that she was captured and brought here as a slave and made to sleep with the men. We don't blame her, even though she appears not to mind who plows her belly. It is those men who deserve punishment. 'Twas my idea to make them suffer with inedible food. What think you, Mirana?"

They'd recognized her as one of them, Mirana thought, relieved and pleased and strangely touched. They were including her, looking to her. "Aye, I do have an idea, but let me say first that yours is an excellent punishment. But now I think it is time to withdraw, just a bit, to make them guess, to make them uncertain and wonder about what we will do next. Men don't realize that women can select a course of action and devise excellent strategy, and that is what we will do."

Old Alna smiled at Amma, nodding. The prisoner, this girl whose brother was indeed Lord Rorik's enemy and theirs, was one of them. She was smart and she had recognized what they wanted and agreed with it. There was something about her, perhaps a confidence, a determination, but both of them trusted her. Amma motioned Old Alna to sit on one side of the bed and she sat close to Mirana. "What do you think we should do? What do you mean, we should withdraw?"

Mirana sat forward, her eyes bright with plans and excitement. "Tomorrow, make the food sublime. Put no pine needles or black bark into the porridge. Don't pour any smashed sour reeds or turnip roots and rotted oak leaves into the stew. Add no sour spices. Make all the food as sweet and delicious as if it were a gift to the gods themselves. All day tomorrow feed the men wondrous dishes, and give them fulsome smiles. Act like worshipful sheep."

"But they don't deserve it!" Amma said. She bounded to her feet and began pacing the small chamber. She was very tall and hardy and Mirana smiled as she watched her, this strong-willed woman who was a natural leader. "Sculla doesn't approve of the men's faithlessness, but he won't chide them. He says naught, damn him! He, the man I've been married to for twelve years, doesn't even realize that I talked the women into ruining all the men's food."

"I know," Mirana said, "but men are different from us. Listen, Amma, we need to keep them off balance. Rorik won't understand when everything suddenly changes on the morrow, none of the men will, and he won't know what to do. He'll have to think, but he won't have any idea what are the right thoughts."

"Ah, I see the way her ideas are stringing themselves," Old Alna said. She cackled. "I like it, Amma. 'Twill make the louts wonder if they're on their arses or on their heads! Aye, 'tis a good plan."

Amma said slowly, "And then the next day, we'll give them swill again?"

"First we will see what Rorik does. I doubt he will do anything. As Alna says, they won't know what to make of what has happened, all without a word or an order from Rorik. Perhaps he will conclude that you've heard that he plans to break the rebellion and have submitted without a whimper."

"Men reason that way," Old Alna said. "When a woman is a submissive little sheep, he thinks it's because she finally realizes he's a prince and a god and is ready to worship at his feet. Dolts, all of them, even my perfect Rorik sometimes." She gave Mirana a long thoughtful look. "You're a bright sweeting," she said suddenly. "Just like Rorik's mother, Tora. Strong-willed too, and stubborn as a flea on a goat's back."

"Aye," Amma said. "Tora is strong. Aye, and inventive. Her husband never knows which way to think when she weaves her web around him. I remember she always stands toe to toe to Harald, her husband. She shouts louder than he does, despite the level of his ire. He would never strike her or threaten her. Alna is right. You are fearless. You are like her."

Mirana wondered about that, but said, pleased, even as she shook her head, "Well, we won't shout as yet."

"Ah, no, obedient sheep we'll be," said Amma and she gave Mirana a fat smile.

"Say nothing to Sculla," Mirana told Amma. "Even though he is a faithful husband, he is still a man, and a man is more loyal to other men in many things than to his wife."

"I'll say not a word," Amma said, then she laughed. "I will prepare a barley soup that will make the men weep with pleasure."

"And what of Entti?" Mirana asked.

"Ah, that sweet little simpleton will do as she's told," Old Alna said. "She has cooked the swill, we've not lied about that. Asta hands her pine bark and she adds it to the stew. Amma gives her turnip root and she merrily grinds it into a paste to throw into a soup."

"Aye, with a sweet empty smile on her face. Now we'll let her watch," Amma said.

# 8

SHE LAY ON her side on the floor, wrapped in a single blanket. Her left wrist was chained tonight because he'd looked at the bruises on her right wrist, said nothing at all, and chained her left.

He hadn't fondled her again, had scarcely even looked at her once they'd returned to the longhouse. She thought about her meeting with Amma and Old Alna. She was doubtless a fool to involve herself with the women's problems, but the urge had been strong inside her and she'd done it. She hoped her plan would work. She hoped Rorik would wait to make his threats to the women, just a day, just to see if perhaps their fear of him would better their cooking. Aye, and when it did, how he would preen. How all the men would strut about, feeling so pleased with themselves. But not for very long. She wished she didn't like the women so very much, but she did. She felt kinship with them now.

She listened to Rorik's deep even breathing. She closed her own eyes and tried to copy his rhythm. It didn't work. She lay there wondering what would become of her, wondering what Einar was doing to find her, if he was doing anything. She might brag of her half-brother before Rorik, but to herself, she admitted the truth. No, she had no idea at all what Einar would do. He was a strange man; she'd never understood the way he thought, why he behaved as he did.

Suddenly, Rorik's breathing hitched, his chest heaved, and he groaned deep in his throat. He cried out, and then moaned, his voice deep and raw and filled with pain, "Nay! By Thor, nay! Inga, don't leave me! By all the gods, no!"

He heaved and jerked. She felt the box bed moving in his frenzy. She came up onto her knees. He was thrashing, moaning, in the throes of a nightmare.

"Rorik! Wake up!"

He cried out again and again, softly, cries of great pain, of helplessness and misery too deep to bear.

"Rorik!"

He jerked upright in the bed, gasping for breath. She could make out his outline, but not the expression on his face.

"You had a nightmare," she said calmly, leaning forward so she could see him better. The chain rattled as it struck against the wooden bed frame.

He looked over at her, kneeling up so she could see him, the chain dangling from her left wrist. The sound of that damnable chain clinking against the wooden bed. He shook his head. The nightmare . . . always there, the horror of it, the pain of it, always there in the back of his mind, freed at night to sneak in unchecked and hurt him and make him relive it again and again. He hated it and he couldn't seem to escape it.

He said nothing to her. He hated her for hearing him relive the monstrous memory, for sounding defenseless as a child, hated her too for waking him from it even though he knew he should be grateful to her because she'd kept the dream from continuing to its terrible end, an end that didn't always come because he hadn't been there to see it. He had arrived too late, too late to do anything, save witness the misery and breathe in the acrid stench of death, and he'd felt it deep within him even as he'd fallen on his knees and keened his own agony and cursed his impotence, cursing himself because he hadn't been there. He rose, realized he was naked save for the white bandage around his shoulder, and jerked a tunic over his head.

He drew a deep breath. His hands were shaking. He hated that too.

"Are you all right?"

"Aye," he said shortly. "Go back to sleep. Attend to your own dreams and leave mine to me."

He left the sleeping chamber without a backward glance.

Mirana eased back down and wrapped herself securely in the blanket. Who was Inga?

The next morning Old Alna came to release the chain. Rorik hadn't returned to the sleeping chamber for the rest of the night. It was well after dawn now. She handed Mirana the gown and tunic she'd washed the night before.

"It was an excellent plan," Old Alna said, "but it didn't work. I had hoped he would wait, but he didn't. Lord Rorik is speaking right now—before he or the men have had a chance to eat the wonderful porridge and flatbread. The gods have frowned on us." The old woman sighed. "Come along, we might as well hear what he has to say. Perhaps you will have another idea."

She led Mirana into the long hall, where at least three score people stood about or sat on the benches around the wall. But no one as yet had eaten, curse the fates. Rorik was speaking, his voice firm, but she heard the deep anger and wondered if the rest of them did. He was standing in their midst, his hands on his hips. He looked like the ruler he was; he looked determined. He also looked calm as a Christian priest and, at the same time, primed for violence. It was odd, but it was true.

". . . I have had enough of this, as have all the men. You women will cease this cruel game with our meals. No more. It is ended. If there is one more foul stew presented, one more pot of cabbage mixed with oak bark, one more dish of anything that isn't at the very least ordinary to eat, I will personally whip the woman or women who cooked it. Then each of my men will whip one of the women in turn. The only woman who won't be punished is Entti. She will be spared, for it is not her fault that she has no skills with food. It is not her fault that you have forced her to continue, if it is indeed all her own efforts, which I strongly doubt. All of you understand me, for I do not spout these words for my own hearing. There will be no more of this, or the whippings will take place. I am the master here and I have spoken."

He turned on his heel and left the hall.

Mirana wondered if there was an equal number of men to women. If there weren't, then some women might escape the whipping, or if there were more men, then some . . . her brain stopped. Once Rorik left the hall, there was a babble of protest from the women. They'd moved away from the men, and were huddled into groups, shrieking, moaning, clearly unnerved. Old Alna merely stood to one side and grinned, showing her three remaining teeth. It was a pitiful grin indeed.

Most of the men were laughing and cheering, some were even rubbing their hands together in anticipation. The blacksmith, Gurd, bellowed, "Asta, bring your buttocks here, my fine wife! Aye, come or I will whip you now, with our lord's good wishes, nay, his orders!

Aye, he is not a man to disobey. You heard him, he is the master here."

Asta shrieked, "I will see you rot in a salt marsh, you miserable unfaithful sod!"

Gurd, whose upper body was massive, the muscles bulging in his arms and chest, swaggered to his wife, grabbed her hand, and hauled her against him. He took her chin in his smoke-blackened hand, and said aloud, for all the men to hear, "I'll plow Entti's belly or any other woman's belly whenever I wish it and you'll not say me nay. Aye, you'll feel the flat of my hand on your plump buttocks if you gainsay me ever again. Nor will you whine or goad me with tears or plaints. Get thee to the chores and bleat not with those other sheep. Aye, and bring me porridge. It had better be tasty or you will feel my anger."

Mirana said nothing. She saw flashes of fear on some of the women's faces, on others', outrage, and utter defiance, and challenge. She saw the little girl Utta look at her father and frown. Amma looked defeated, but only for a moment. She was a determined woman, and very soon, her shoulders were squared and she was staring first at her husband, Sculla, then at the other women. Mirana knew there would be a meeting as soon as the men had left for the day to hunt. She wondered if the women would include her. She'd done them not a whit of good as of yet. She cursed quietly.

She left the longhouse. They would tell her if they wished her to be involved further. She hoped they would. She would enjoy teaching them the use of weapons. The prick of a knife was a more lasting memory than a pot of bark-filled stew. Aye, a man who knew that a woman could slice up his manhood with skill and no hesitation, that was a man who wouldn't be so eager to brag about his rights and his power. Ah, but she was naught but a prisoner. How could she have forgotten that, even briefly the previous evening? There was nothing she could do for herself, let alone the other women.

It was a bright warm morning, the smell of the sea strong on the gentle breeze that was blowing from the east. Gray plovers, redshanks, and curlews flew overhead, dipping low, then soaring toward the white clouds. She smiled at their antics, identifying each one, savoring each one's existence. There were so many of them, some she didn't recognize. She drew a deep breath and looked for Rorik. He was at the palisade gates, speaking to several men. Probably telling them to fetch out their whips, she thought. She wondered how they would like it to have a whip slash across their backs. Kerzog sat beside Rorik, looking up at him, his fur ruffling in the breeze.

Mirana combed her fingers through her hair, then tied it back at the nape of her neck with a string Old Alna had given her. She wanted to bathe; she wanted to relieve herself. But more than that, she wanted to know what Rorik planned, if he truly meant he would whip the women if the food continued badly prepared. And why had he acted so quickly, even before he'd eaten the morning porridge? It didn't seem right to her.

She walked to where Rorik was standing and stopped not two feet from him, her arms crossed over her breasts. Kerzog looked at her and wuffed softly. He didn't move from Rorik's side, but he began to wag his tail.

"Thanks be to Frey," one of the men said gratefully. "They'll obey you, my lord, aye, the women know you can only be pushed so far." He grinned, then added in a wistful voice, "I wish I could have been there to hear you, to watch their sly expressions turn fearful."

Rorik didn't say anything to that, but remarked instead, "Yet I look at Kerzog here and he's not suffered a bit. They fed the animals, themselves, and the children good food, and us, they gave swill."

That, Mirana thought, was because Kerzog and the children didn't bed with Entti.

The other man whistled. "Aye, the women played a deep game. I hope our food isn't filled now with crola berries, 'twill send our bowels galloping to the mainland. We'd be too weak to punish them. Think you they'll try to poison us in their anger?"

Rorik shook his head. "I will inform Old Alna that tonight we wish to have boar steaks."

Four widgeons flew over. Kerzog wuffed at them, then sprawled down, his head resting on his front paws.

One of the men noticed Mirana. He nodded to Rorik, who turned around very slowly.

He took one step toward her then stopped. "Who unchained you? What do you want?"

He sounded mildly annoyed, as if she were naught but a dog who'd chanced to come upon him at a time that wasn't convenient to him. No, he would have been delighted had it been Kerzog that came to him. No, he viewed her as less than his damned dog. Her chin went up and she said sharply, in a voice filled with unconscious arrogance, "Come here, Rorik. I would speak to you now."

He stiffened as straight as an oak tree. He was still furious at the women for their duplicity, still smarting from his feelings of outrage that they would dare do such a thing to him and to his men. "You dare? You will show me proper respect. You will say, woman, 'I wish to speak to you, my lord' or 'If it pleases you, my lord, I beg a moment of your time.' "

She just stared at him. It was true; she hadn't sounded at all conciliating, at all willing to compromise with him.

"It is my title. Say it. Change it, if you wish, to your own words, but you will show me respect and obeisance. Now, say my title."

She shook her head. "You aren't my lord. You aren't my master. You're the enemy, nothing more. Ah, I forget. You're also a vicious monster who threatens women who nurture you and care for you and feed you and—"

"Feed, ha! I counted my ribs this morning. I was starving last night, you saw it. No more of it, so I have told them and so it will be if they dare to disobey me again. Now, Mirana, say my title. Address me as your Lord Rorik. Be quick about it for I grow weary with the taming of you."

The moment he shut his mouth, Rorik realized he'd gotten himself in a situation that wouldn't win him a thing. He'd given her an order in front of his men. Had he given it any thought at all, he would have known that she'd stand stubborn as a mule before paying him any homage. Still, he couldn't let it stand. Not in front of his men. By Thor's hammer, he'd ordered her to say it. He could still hear the damnable arrogance in her voice, *ordering* him to come to her. It galled him to his toes. In addition, she'd sided with the women, calling *him* a vicious monster, when all he'd done was bring it to an end.

He said slowly, as if to a witless child, "I am your lord and your master and your enemy—all of those things. Right now, I am your lord. Say it."

She turned on her heel and walked away. She heard one of the men suck in his breath and say, "Lord Rorik won't let that pass. He can't."

"Aye, I pray he won't kill her."

Kerzog wuffed softly but didn't move.

She wasn't at all surprised when she felt his hand close over her upper arm and jerk her to a stop. He whirled her around to face him with such force that she would have fallen had he not held her upright.

He said low, "Listen to me, Mirana. You will obey every order I choose to give you, just as will every other damned woman on Hawkfell Island. I am the lord and master here. You will temper your voice and the words that come from your mouth. You will treat me as you would a god. You must, there is no choice. My men have excellent hearing and I am their leader. Do you understand me?"

She shook her head.

He took both her arms in his big hands and shook her hard, snapping her head back in her neck.

He leaned down, his breath warm on her cheek and said low, just for her ears, "Don't force me to whip you in front of them. Don't be unyielding about this. Don't wallow in your damned pride. It will gain you nothing but pain. Don't be stupid. Say it now, loudly, so they will hear you. Say 'my lord.' "

"I cannot," she whispered. "You know I cannot."

Rorik cursed. "How like a woman you are, when all is said and done. You have lost because you lack judgment, because you don't understand how to reason properly. You must learn to pick your battles. This one you couldn't win. It is already lost. Now, say it." As he spoke, he turned slightly to see that his three men were watching him avidly. He cursed again. He'd done it to himself and now she would suffer for it. He'd told her the truth. There was no choice for her or for him. But she'd made the decision not to obey him. It was her fault, after all. He waited. She said nothing.

"I will give you one more chance. Say it." He shook her again. Kerzog wuffed again, but still didn't move.

She looked at him helplessly, then shook her head.

He cursed very softly. She knew only she had heard him. He held her right wrist and took off his belt with his other hand. She stared at it. It was wide supple leather. It would hurt, for he was very strong. He grabbed both her wrists and held them high with his right hand, bringing her to her tiptoes. He wondered briefly at her passivity, but only briefly. In the next instant, she spun about, jerking her hands free, and sent her fist into his belly, her knee toward his groin. Her fist in his belly hurt but he was quick enough to have her knee land hard against his thigh. She was on him, her fingers going for his face. He cursed her, dropped the belt, and managed to grab her quickly enough. Still she fought him with amazing strength and agility. Well, why not? She, after all, had been eating like a stoat for the past day and a half. She was no longer weak, curse her and curse the women for seeing to her needs and not his. "You will only make it harder on yourself. Hold still, damn you."

He ended up binding her wrists together, then holding them high in his right hand. She struggled, but she couldn't break free of him. She cursed him now, vicious curses that impressed him with their range and intensity.

He turned her so that her back was to him, her face to the three men. He knew he wouldn't hurt her badly for he had no leverage, though his men wouldn't realize it. He picked up the belt and swung it, wrapping it around her back.

She jerked, but didn't make a sound, not even another curse. She didn't struggle anymore. She looked over her shoulder at him, and her eyes were deep and calm, as green as the moss grass in the salt marsh. "You are naught but an animal. I will kill you if I have the chance. I should have killed you at Clontarf when I had you caged. Aye, I just pricked your pretty throat to give you a taste of pain and the sticky feeling of your own blood, but I should have sunk my knife deep."

"You didn't, so it doesn't matter what you spout out now. I am your lord. Say it."

He gave her several moments, wishing to Thor, to Frey, to Odin All-Father, that her stupid pride would bend. But she remained silent. He saw her tense for the next blow, but she didn't try to escape him again. He swung the belt. It stung her back harder this time, he knew it, he felt her shudder, heard her sharp intake of breath.

"Say it."

She remained silent as a tomb. He stopped after the fourth swing of the belt. He'd given her only a small jolt of pain, nay, not really pain, just the warning of it. She'd given him more pain when she'd stuck her damned knife in his throat, and she had the gall to call it naught but a prick.

What he had forced on her was the knowledge of her helplessness against him. That humiliation wouldn't leave her for a very long time. He turned her about and looked silently at her pale face.

He released her, hooked his foot behind her leg, and sent her sprawling to the ground. Again, there was little or no pain, but another dose of humiliation, which for her was a more powerful lesson. Slowly, he fastened his belt around his waist. "Get up," he said. "Go bathe. Your smell offends me."

The men were nodding in approval. She got to her feet, felt the pulling in her back, but walked away, not speaking, not looking at him or the men. She heard

Kerzog wuff to Rorik, as if in agreement with what he'd done, she thought, anger flooding through her, momentarily blocking out the pain in her back.

She heard one of the men say with great satisfaction, "Aye, no more from her. Well done, my lord. She is only a woman and she is our enemy. She deserved a lesson. She will know better next time. Let her tell of her beating to the other women. If they were wondering whether to obey you, they won't wonder now. Aye, they'll now do as you bid them to do."

Rorik didn't say anything. He wondered what she had wanted to speak to him about.

To her surprise, Mirana heard another man say, "Nay, Askhold, she's a small girl and proud. Her pride does honor to her parentage. Despite her brother's dishonor, she has honesty. She's a true Viking woman. She shouldn't be abused, Rorik, she should be protected."

Mirana resolved to discover the man's name. Unfortunately she couldn't turn around to see him.

She heard Rorik curse.

What she was, she thought, wincing with each step from the stinging in her back, was stupid. He'd been right. Her pride had kept her silent. Her pride had seemed her only choice until he'd struck her back with his belt. All she'd had to do was bend, just a small yielding, but she hadn't. So simple really, just say *my lord* to him, nothing more, just a simple *my lord,* for it meant naught, she could even have said it with revulsion in her voice and he would have known she didn't mean it. But she had to be stubborn.

What had Einar done for the man to call him dishonorable?

ASTA RUBBED THE white medicinal cream into her back, made from the oily tender root. The belt hadn't broken the skin, had only sliced through the tunic and gown in two places, and the material could easily be mended. There were only welts on her back, Utta said, as she watched Asta rub the cream into Mirana's flesh.

Mirana would have choked before she'd have told anyone, but Utta had come into the sleeping chamber when she was naked, holding the gown in her hand, examining the damage.

But the girl had said only, "I will fetch the healing cream from Old Alna. It will take the stinging away." She paused in the doorway and added, "I will tell her I have a bee sting and it pains me."

Mirana had smiled at her, wondering at her wisdom, at her youth, remembering herself at twelve years old, a lanky, proud girl, ready for any mischief, ready to fight any boy. She'd not had a dollop of wisdom. She smiled at her now. "Thank you, Utta. Do you have thread and a needle so that I may mend this lovely gown?"

But Asta had come with Utta, Asta, the woman married to Gurd the blacksmith, the man who had insulted his wife before all the assembled company this morning. To Mirana's surprise, Asta was smiling at her, soon laughing as she told her of the old shoe the goat had chewed and chewed until the women had stirred it into a stew for the men. Before she'd left the chamber, she said, "Don't worry. Both Utta and I frequently suffer from bee stings. You try to rest now, Mirana. I thank you for what you tried to do, as do all the other women. We believe that Rorik spoke so quickly because he dreaded doing it and just wanted it over and done with. But you tried, and we do thank you."

Mirana just shook her head. "I did naught of anything. I'm not sure, though, if that is why Rorik made his speech so very early, even before he tasted the wonderful porridge. It doesn't make sense to me, but perhaps you are right."

Both Utta and Asta just sighed and left her alone. Asta said from the doorway, "I will tell you later what the women are thinking. Amma is very angry, but I know she must be calm for us to determine what is best to do now."

Mirana was sitting on the side of the bed, wearing the gown again, now mending the tunic, when Rorik walked in. He stopped and looked at her.

"Utta told me she'd rubbed cream into your back."

"Aye," Mirana said, her eyes on her mending.

"She said there were only red welts."

"That is what she said."

"She said I wasn't to tell anyone else. She said that would shame you."

Mirana said nothing. So he didn't know Asta had been here as well. She wondered why they hadn't told him. To protect her, she supposed, but didn't understand how it could. Then it struck her. They'd had Utta speak to him. Surely if there was guilt to be felt, he would be made to feel it from an eleven-year-old girl. She wanted to smile, but she didn't, for he said in the next moment, "I didn't hurt you. I was careful."

At that she did look up. She said mildly, "If I had my knife with me, I should show you how I can slice you nicely without much pain. Shall I thank you, Rorik? Is that what you want? You want me to kiss your hands for whipping me in front of your men? For proving to me that you are the stronger? For humiliating me? That final move of sprawling me to the ground was well done of you, Rorik, and I doubt not it was also important for your men to witness."

He wasn't about to admit to the truth of her words, and said firmly, " 'Twas your own fault. All you had to do was bend that damnable pride of yours just a bit and say the truth—for I am your lord, damn you. All you had to do was say it. I can even hear the words on your tongue now, all dripping with hatred and scorn and contempt. If you'd but said them I wouldn't have been forced to whip you. I wouldn't have been forced to do any of the other. Your fault, not mine."

She wondered if he truly believed that. Her fault? Of course, Einar whipped women or slapped them or hit them with his fists whenever he wished to. It never required much provocation. He also beat those men who were weaker than he was, and slaves of both sexes whenever the urge claimed him. He'd whipped her several times. He'd tied her to a pole because she'd fought him the last time he'd whipped her. She'd even hurt him, though he would never have admitted it. He'd swung the whip with great relish, slicing open her back with the strength of his blows. He'd said to her when he'd tired of wielding the whip, "Now, my girl, you won't ever try to protect someone from me again. I gave you a good lesson, don't you think? Aye, you should thank me for this valuable lesson, but I won't force you to. I know you won't, and I have no wish to kill you. My men wouldn't be pleased, though only the gods know why you have their loyalty."

Mirana clearly remembered the young man, a boy, really, who had displeased Einar. She couldn't remember what he'd done to anger Einar, if indeed she'd ever known. But it couldn't have been anything severe, nothing all that bad. She'd taken the boy's side and hidden him. That's what had provoked Einar's fury. He'd had her whipped and as she lay on her belly, gritting her teeth against the pain in her back, she was told the boy was dead. Einar had come in then and looked at her bare back, at the ugly welts, and said, "Aye, 'tis a pity." She never knew if he was speaking of the dead boy or of her back.

"What are you thinking? You are silent too long. I don't like it, for your thoughts are dangerous even though you are but a woman and ungoverned."

She shrugged. "Bad memories, nothing more."

"Is that all?"

"Very well. I was remembering that first day in the warship when you put your foot on my neck and I bit your ankle. You yowled, I hurt you so badly. I saw my teeth marks there for two days."

"Aye, you hurt me well enough," Rorik said, remembering mainly the shock of her act. She'd been screaming at him that he was naught but a vicious animal, that she should have plunged her knife through his neck. Aye, she'd still had her fury and her strength to sustain her that first day out of Clontarf. To punish her, he'd pressed her face to the plank and held her down with his foot on her neck. She'd turned red with rage. The bite had hurt. He said only, "I can't see that it would be a bad memory for you. That memory would make you laugh with pleasure. Thus, you are lying to me. Tell me the truth now, what were you thinking?"

"If you would know, I was also wondering if it really bothered you to whip me. I doubt it. Men are violent. They enjoy hurting those weaker than themselves. I was thinking of the times Einar whipped me. And now you did. Both of you said it was my fault."

He grabbed her arm and jerked her to her feet. The tunic slid to the ground. He shook her. "Don't compare me to your brother, ever again. You gave me no choice but to whip you and you know I stayed my strength. You know well enough that I could not allow my men to see me as bending to a woman's wishes, particularly after I've been played the ass by the women since our return to Hawkfell Island. I am their lord and their leader and I cannot be seen to be weak or irresolute. I had no choice. Damn you, admit it!"

He'd done it again, given her an order. She stared up at him, fury banking in her eyes, and this time, he just shook his head at himself.

"Finish your mending." He released her, leaned to pick up the tunic and threw it at her. He shoved her down onto the bed. She made no move to escape him.

Her hands were quiet in her lap. She stared up at him, and said, "Were you unfaithful to Inga?"

His face, deeply bronzed from the sun, paled at her words. His hands fisted at his sides. He raised his right arm, and she knew he wanted to strike her. She knew too that he would control himself. She didn't know how she knew it, but she did. She had no doubts at all. He did. He turned on his heel and strode away from her. She called out, "I think you must have been, for you threatened to beat the women just because they don't want their husbands to be unfaithful to them. What power do they have save ruining your meals? Were you my husband and you bedded another woman, I would kill you, not just give you belly pains from eating swill."

He jerked, then strode from the sleeping chamber, never looking back.

Rorik drank deeply of the mead. His belly was full and now his mind was fast dulling with the drink. He heard his men laughing, bragging of their victory over the women, and, indeed, it was truly a victory, for the meal had been the best any of them had eaten in a very long time. The boar steaks had been broiled over the pit fire, wrapped in oiled tartar leaves. The herring and bass, both baked to tenderness, turning to tender flakes in the mouth, had made them groan with pleasure.

Rorik finished the mead in his cup. He leaned back in his chair and closed his eyes. The woman was chained in his sleeping chamber. He'd refused to have food sent to her. Let her suffer as he and his men had, damn her. She'd already eaten enough—given to her by those damnable treacherous women—to hold her steady for a good week.

She'd dared to demand if he'd been unfaithful to Inga. He'd wanted to kill her, at least to strike her at the sound of Inga's name on her lips.

He heard someone approach, and slit open his right eye. It was Entti, and she was holding out a pitcher of mead. He allowed her to fill his cup again.

She was smiling at him, a very sweet smile that added warmth to the near vacant expression in her eyes. She was simple, this girl he'd captured on a raid the previous summer in the Rhineland, but kind. She harbored ill will toward no one. There was no malice in her. That she was a slave to a Viking seemed not to bother her at all. She seemed to enjoy the men who had bedded her here on Hawkfell Island. She'd not drawn away or screamed and pleaded. Even the women were kind to her despite the men's lust for her. Their revenge had been against the men, not against Entti. Rorik thanked her. Her smile widened, showing dimples, and he realized that she wanted him to bed her. She was really quite pretty, with her thick rich brown hair and her brown eyes, but those eyes were too childlike for him to appreciate, too blank in their intent, for him to consider bedding her. She was tall and slender, full-breasted, really quite lovely, but still, he couldn't bring himself to want her. It would be like taking advantage of a child even though she was a woman grown, all of eighteen, he was certain. Hafter had taken her first upon her capture. Rorik wondered if she'd been a virgin.

He said quietly, his voice low and gentle, "Nay, Entti, not tonight. I must attend our prisoner."

Another female would have shown displeasure, but not Entti. She said, looking down at his empty plate, "The food is delicious. I am so glad."

He laughed at that. "Aye, all of us are glad. Seek out your bed, Entti, you have labored enough. I am sorry. I had not realized the women had fed you the swill they'd given to us."

She lowered her eyes and her fingers began plucking at her gown sleeve. He realized that she didn't wish to sleep. She wanted a man. He saw Hafter looking at Entti with more interest than a man should show a woman who wasn't his wife, and said, "Hafter looks unhappy. I release you from your work. You may see to him."

She nodded happily, and left him.

Rorik rose, felt the chamber spin around him, shook his head as would a mongrel hound caught in the rain, and walked toward his sleeping chamber, Kerzog at his heels.

Ottar called out, "Lord Rorik, do you go to whip the prisoner again?"

Hafter laughed and called out, "Oh nay, Ottar, he'll plow her belly, that's his thought."

Sculla raised his head from his conversation with Old Alna and said, "Rorik is too sodden to plow a field, much less a woman."

Old Alna cackled.

Sculla's wife, Amma, said, "He isn't used to so much drink like the rest of you louts. His belly won't like him for this."

Rorik turned and said, "All of you, keep your tongues behind your teeth. You chatter because your bellies are content."

"Aye, that's the truth of it," Askhold said. "Beat the witch, Rorik."

Rorik didn't hear him. He was thinking about his belly and his dulled head. He prayed Amma was wrong in her prediction but knew that she wasn't. He didn't hold drink well.

The sleeping chamber was dark as the deepest pit. He brought in a rush torch and fastened it into its holder on the wall. He saw her on the floor, on her side, her legs drawn up to her chest. He couldn't see the chain, but he knew it was there, wrapped around her wrist.

She was awake. She hadn't moved, hadn't breathed, it seemed to him, but nonetheless, he knew she was awake. He didn't care.

He pulled off his clothes, doused the rush torch, and flung himself down onto his bed.

"You drunken lout. You disgust me."

He laughed, a drunken laugh that sounded demented. "I begin to believe you have missed me, Mirana."

"I would that you had rotted, you and all your vicious men."

"You have been left too much alone," he remarked to the darkness. "Even I am welcome after your overlong solitude. You obviously have grown bored with your own company. Aye, that's a woman's plaint, isn't it? She cannot bear to be alone."

He could hear her breathing, harsh and deep.

"Shall I tell you about the delicious meal we enjoyed? It was quite excellent, truth be told. The boar steaks were broiled; the fat sizzled on the sides. I decided to let your belly shrink a bit—you've eaten too well in your captivity. Now, it is your turn. Would you like to say something?"

"Unfasten the chain."

He came up onto his elbow, weaved a bit, looking in the darkness toward her. "I just might if you would say, 'Please, my lord Rorik, I would be your willing slave if you would free me.' Say it and I will consider releasing the chain."

Her breathing was deeper now and hoarse. He was glad she didn't have a knife.

"Say it, Mirana, else I will leave that chain on your wrist until you do."

He was drunk, he knew, and it was his only excuse. But he wouldn't bear more from her. She would obey him else he would make her life a misery.

"Please, my lord Rorik, I would be your willing slave if you would free me."

He stared toward her. He couldn't believe it, yet the words he'd demanded from her hung in the silence between them. She'd done as he'd asked. He didn't understand. His brain, filled with too much mead, suddenly rebelled. He couldn't make sense of her. He wanted to demand that she tell him what she was planning now, but his belly chose this moment to rebel as well. He groaned and leapt from his bed. He managed to run to the palisade walls before retching. His body shook and trembled. He leaned his forehead against the wooden planks and waited for his belly to calm. It had been thus all his life. He couldn't drink much of the delicious mead or even the fruity wine from the Rhineland without becoming violently ill. He would not drink more than a cup of anything for months at a time and then he would forget, and drink too much. And this was his punishment. It was the woman's fault. If she hadn't taunted him, if she hadn't then given in to him and dared to call him *lord,* he wouldn't have become so ill.

He shuddered and straightened. He was so thirsty his tongue felt swelled in his mouth. It was some time before he returned to the longhouse and to his sleeping chamber, his belly emptied of the vile mead as well as of the wonderful boar steaks, the vegetables, and the bread.

Mirana waited until he was stretched out on his bed. He'd run as if a Christian demon had been after him. She waited another minute, slapped down her pride, hating herself even as she said, "If you please, my lord Rorik—"

She heard a deep snore.

She fell onto her back. Her hand was numb, the flesh on her wrist rubbed raw. It hurt her so badly she would have begged him to release her, she would have called him Odin All-Father had he demanded it of her. She wanted to howl and cry at the same time. She did neither. She fell asleep with his snores sounding in her ears.

**Clontarf, Ireland**
**Danish Fortress**

EINAR CARESSED THE soft cheek, smiled as the warm open mouth turned to him, and leaned down to kiss it. His tongue smoothed over the lips, then slipped inside. He heard the gentle sigh, took it into his own mouth, and tasted the sweet honeyed almonds they'd shared an hour before.

He drew back, patted the smooth cheek, then lay on his back, his head cradled on his arms.

"You please me," he said.

"Aye, there's truth in that, my lord. But you are too tired to bring me much pleasure tonight."

Perhaps in a week, perhaps even as long as a month from now, Einar would slap that smooth cheek, or wield his whip on the flawless back, rage overflowing at such impertinence, but not now, not after only three days. The impertinence, the moments of insolence, aye, it was pleasing to him now. It whetted his passion and his interest.

He said slowly, "I have brought you to pleasure two times, more than you deserve. Cease your plaints. I am thinking of my sister, Mirana. I must have her back."

"I hear she is but your half-sister."

"Ah, is that jealousy that stings your agile tongue?"

"She is not golden as am I, so I have been told. Her hair is black as sin—"

"Aye, like mine. And her eyes are also like mine—as green as Erin's hills after a spring rain. Her flesh is as white as goat's milk, unlike yours, which is shaded with a rather ugly olive tinge."

"Aye, but the gold of my hair and that olive tinge is unique, quite out of the ordinary, so you said yourself when you bought me from that fat French merchant in Dublin. You have said that you could drown in my golden eyes, a gold like rich sweet mead, you said. You have endlessly admired my black lashes, so thick you've said more times than I can remember, more lush than any of your women's."

Einar merely smiled. He enjoyed the show of jealousy, the preening vanity, the edge of viciousness to gain his attention, but Mirana—ah, where had the Viking taken her? He must find her quickly or he would surely find himself in grave difficulties. He thought of King Sitric, but didn't worry overly about him. No, it was Hormuze who made his blood slow, made his stomach curdle and cramp. Hormuze was an old man, tottering in his years, but he was still a man to fear and Einar recognized it deep inside himself. The old man's black eyes held passion and determination, not the dimming and clouding of old age. He had no desire, ever, to face Hormuze and have to admit that he'd failed. Well, he wouldn't have to admit anything. He would find her in time.

Rorik Haraldsson was the bastard's name, at least that was the name he'd told Mirana. Einar had forgotten, truth be told, about that day well over two years ago, a long time, after all. He'd done much in two years, too much to remember Rorik Haraldsson, a man he'd never even seen, a man whose farmstead in the Vestfold he'd visited and reduced to ashes and death.

But the Viking had found him. And Gunleik, the damned old fool, had been tricked. The Viking should be dead; they could have and should have butchered him easily, but they hadn't. Mirana had even seen to his wound. He'd been pampered as a sultan in Miklagard. All that talk about keeping him for Einar's pleasure he discounted. On the other hand, Gunleik never lied to him. But still . . . He wished Mirana had been here so he could have beaten the truth out of her. Had she admired the Viking and that was the reason she'd allowed him to live? Nay, Gunleik and his men were cowards. The Viking had frightened them, made them believe he was beyond them, and thus to be respected and held in awe.

The Viking had kidnapped his sister—nay, his half-sister. He grinned, but sobered almost immediately. He had men out searching for any word of her, of this Viking Rorik Haraldsson. It could take a long time, a very long time, more time than he had. He thought of Hormuze again, and felt bile rise in his throat.

He felt long fingers stroke over his belly, downward, to tangle in the thick hair at his groin. When the fingers closed around him, he sucked in his breath, his fears momentarily forgotten. He knew what was coming and all his senses focused on the mouth that was now on his belly, wet and soft, nipping at his flesh, moving ever downward.

His pleasure, when it took him, arched his back off the bed and made him scream. He forgot Mirana in those long incredible moments. He thought only of that warm skilled mouth and knew that it would take perhaps even more than a month for him to be bored with his new slave.

"By all the gods," he managed to say after his heart calmed, "you are a beautiful animal."

"Aye, more beautiful than your black-haired half-sister with her flesh whiter than a virgin's teeth."

Einar didn't even consider a slap or a whipping. He merely smiled as he stroked his hand down a slender thigh.

It was nearly an hour later. Einar was sitting in his massive oak chair, his hands curved around its ornately carved chair posts. He accepted a plate of food from a slave.

As he chewed on the leg of mutton, tougher than it should be, he thought again of Mirana. She wouldn't have allowed any meal to be served unless it was perfect. He'd remarked too that the turnips mixed with sweet onions and peas weren't seasoned properly. He frowned. Nothing was quite as it should be without her here. Damn Mirana for not simply killing the Viking. He had to get her back, by all the gods, his own life depended on getting her back. He wanted to see her again, to hear her voice as she gave orders to the slaves, a calm voice, many times gentle, but also sharp if need be.

He looked up to see Gunleik chewing on his own mutton, his face down, silent as a stone. He'd aged ten years in the days she'd been gone, and rightfully so, since it was his fault that she was taken in the first place. Einar handed his wooden plate to a waiting slave, a girl not older than eleven, a sharp-featured child he didn't like. He called out, "Gunleik, I have decided you will find Mirana. You will take three men and you will leave on the morrow. Two of these men will be Emund and Ingolf—my men—and thus I will be certain they will tell me the truth of things when you return. Aye, you will leave and you will find her.

I have no need of you here. You have proved your worthlessness as the fortress commander."

Gunleik looked up, trying to prevent the look of joy that washed away the drawn pallor of his face, but Einar saw it. "Ah, so you would go after her, would you? You lost her and now you will find her. Kill the Viking, I care not, or bring him back to me. I wish to punish you again, but now, even though it pleases you, I don't wish to see your face until you've succeeded. Now, get out of my sight before I have you whipped anyway."

Gunleik obeyed quickly, though it was difficult for him still to walk upright, his stride steady. The long deep welts on his back still burned and pulled, making him lock his jaw to keep his pain to himself. He'd deserved the beating. Had he been Einar, he would have done the same thing. The only difference was, he wouldn't have enjoyed wielding the whip with such ferocious ecstasy.

"I do not like that old man, Einar. I am glad that you will send him away. He looks at me with contempt."

"I have not asked that you like him. I punished him and now he will leave and find my sister. He will go because I believe him to have the best brain of all my men. Aye, he will find her, if she still lives." His hand clenched into a fist. "I must have my sister back here or I will lose more than I can afford to lose, mayhap even my life."

"No one would dare!"

"You think not?"

"You are a warrior, above other men. You are strong and brave and cunning."

"Aye, that is true, but the forces against me would be overwhelming, forces even stronger than I, forces even more powerful than I could withstand. Nay, I must have my sister back and very soon."

"Your half-sister."

Einar calmed himself. He wouldn't die, for Gunleik would bring her back. As for the golden-haired quite beautiful little savage seated gracefully at his feet, he found he was still amused at the show of jealousy, at the little jabs of impertinence.

He sat back and closed his eyes. He'd done all he could. There was naught to consider now, and so he smiled, for the aftershocks of pleasure still pulled at him, making him calm and easy, despite the gnawing fear in his belly that grew with each passing hour.

"I do not like this meal either."

"Do you not?" Einar said easily, opening his eyes. "Well, then, why don't you prepare it?"

"I have many skills, my lord. Food is something to enjoy, not sweat over."

Einar laughed and ruffled his fingers through the golden hair, as silky as a babe's yet thick enough to wind about his hand many times. "Then pray that Gunleik finds Mirana. She is an excellent mistress to Clontarf. When she returns I daresay she won't like you at all. Mayhap she'll even punish you when I am not about to protect you. Aye, mayhap she'll take the whip to you or set you to working in the fields, ruining those soft little hands of yours."

"You'll not let her touch me. You think I'm beautiful. You won't let her hurt me."

"You think not? Well, perhaps you're right. We will see, won't we?"

He felt slender fingers lightly stroking his inner leg. He leaned back in his chair, closed his eyes again, and said nothing. But he thought, Were Mirana here I couldn't have allowed this. There was something about her that always stayed him, something in her eyes, the way she looked at him. But that would change now. When she returned, he would do as he pleased, for she would be gone again from Clontarf soon enough. He looked up now and caught several looks from his men, furtive looks that held surprise and a goodly measure of disgust. She'd never looked at him with disgust, no, it was something else, something deeper, more powerful. But she'd never said anything; he'd always reined himself in when she was about.

As for his men, they'd said nothing before, they'd kept their silence. Of course they wouldn't dare say anything. He felt his power over them and was pleased. The soft hand continued upward on his thigh.

### Hawkfell Island

Rorik was furious. He stared from Sculla to Askhold. Finally, when he had himself well under control, he said, teeth clenched, "Why did you not tell me what you intended? She is my prisoner, my burden, and yet you send her to the mainland to collect herbs with the women?"

"Rorik," Askhold said patiently, wondering at him, for surely this was absurd, this worry of his. "Old Alna said she should do some work. Chaining her in your sleeping chamber gains us nothing. Let her be useful. She is a slave—less than a slave. An enemy, a prisoner. Aye, let her work."

Rorik cursed. "Neither of you realize that she is skilled with a knife and doubtless other weapons as well?"

Sculla, bent over to protect his head from a thick fir branch, looked fit to burst with laughter, which he did, loud guffaws that made his lean belly shake. Rorik just looked at him, waiting for him to be silent. When his laughter died down, Rorik said, "Listen, both of you. You underestimate her. It is a mistake."

"She's a small girl," Sculla said. "She could do nothing against Hafter. He's a powerful warrior, nearly as skilled as I am."

"Every female is small compared to you," Askhold said, and slapped Sculla on his broad back.

Rorik said nothing. He wanted to believe what Sculla said was true, but Mirana was smart. And her hatred probably made her even more cunning. He didn't trust her. "How many women went to the salt marsh?"

"Asta, Old Alna, and Entti. Hafter rowed them over, cursing the entire time that it was his lot to do it, but he knew that he had to watch the prisoner. He knew you would be displeased had he allowed another to take his place."

Rorik shook his head, for a moment distracted. "I pray that Entti understands what it is she is to gather. I fear death at her hands, all a mistake, naturally."

"Now you will cease to worry," Askhold said. "The girl is an enemy. I dislike having my enemies lying about doing nothing, just as the women apparently do as well. You whipped her for insolence, and now she will work or she won't eat. Old Alna was right to make her work for her food."

But Rorik was gazing toward the mainland, bathed this afternoon in thick low-lying clouds. Mallards and oystercatchers suddenly burst from the gray clouds, as if flung from a slingshot. The clouds would soon become dense, impenetrable fog, he knew the signs. They'd been gone for three hours. He was worried, though he knew it wasn't at all likely she could do anything. Still, he couldn't help it. Something bothered him, something that wasn't right, that had nagged at him for the past two days. He realized in that moment what it was. It was the women and how they had treated Mirana, how they behaved when they came near her. It was as if she were one with them and they looked up to her, which was ridiculous, for he'd kept her chained and alone. But Sculla had said that Old Alna agreed with him, that she considered the woman an enemy. He was creating difficulties where none existed.

It was late afternoon. Rorik knew his men were eyeing him with some amusement, but he didn't care. Finally, he lowered his axe to the ground, wiped the sweat from his face with his discarded tunic, and said, " 'Tis time to go to the mainland. She has done something. I feel it."

None of the men argued with him, not even Askhold, who appeared to dislike her heartily, or Sculla, who simply believed that since she was small and female, she was thus of little consequence, since he could, naturally, crush her easily with one hand.

There were eight men, all of them rowing the second longboat. All of them were armed. There were always outlaws lurking about in East Anglia, just beyond the salt marshes. They always took care. There was only the sound of the water slapping against the sides of the warship and the raucous cries of the black-headed gulls overhead. They rowed into the estuary, strokes strong and steady. They were silent, concentrating on their task. From the thick clouds overhead, dunlin wheeled in tight flocks, disturbed by their presence.

There were more animals and birds here than on the island, the salt marshes on either side of the estuary pulsing with life and movement, and sudden shrieks of death as well. Rorik listened, trying to block out all the animal and bird sounds. He heard no sounds of people. They drew alongside the other warship, tied to a tree trunk alongside the trail they normally traveled to hunt. It was deserted.

The men were silent, but they still held no doubts that Hafter would crush the girl were she to try to escape or avoid the work, aye, and the women would help him, for she was a prisoner, an enemy.

Rorik doubted mightily. He led the men quietly through the salt marsh, knowing from long experience where to find the firmer ground. Suddenly there was the muted yell, a woman's yell.

They burst through a dense cover of tangled overgrowth into a small clearing. There was Old Alna, bound to a straggly fir tree, shrieking again around a wad of wool she'd managed to work to the side of her mouth. Beside her, bound to a large yew bush was Asta, her gag firmly in place.

There was no sign of Entti or Hafter.

The men rushed forward to untie the two women.

Rorik remained standing, his hands on his hips. He said to Old Alna, "This was your idea, was it not? You wanted her to work and look what has happened. Tell me quickly. Where is she? Where are Hafter and Entti?"

It was Asta, Gurd the blacksmith's wife, who said quickly, working her mouth to regain moisture and feeling, "Nay, my lord, do not blame Alna. She wanted the girl to have some exercise. She was growing weak chained to your bed. We saw no danger—"

"You are fools," Rorik said shortly. He watched Asta rub her arms, numb, he imagined, from being bound for so long. He waited, then said, "Tell me and be quick about it."

Asta shrugged. "Hafter took Entti with him to dally away the afternoon. He said he feared letting her collect roots and herbs; he said none of the men wanted their bellies to cramp or their bowels to convulse, but he was looking at her as would a hungry wolf at a boar steak. It was after they left that the girl Mirana managed to get a rock without Alna or me seeing her. She hit me on the head and knocked me down. Then she tied up Alna and then me."

Rorik felt no surprise at all. Why did none of the others see her as he did? He cursed low and long. "How long ago?" he asked finally.

"Three hours at least."

He cursed again, infuriated with himself and with Old Alna and with his damned arrogant men who couldn't imagine a woman besting them at anything.

He would find her, he didn't doubt that, but he did doubt he would find her alive. She was a woman and she was young and comely, and that thought froze his blood. If outlaws or Saxon raiders or other Vikings found her, they'd rape her in turn, abuse her endlessly, and probably kill her. He didn't want her dead. Damnation. He raised his voice and yelled, "Hafter! Come to me now!"

But there was no answer from Hafter. They found him ten minutes later barely conscious, a large lump just over his right ear, tied securely to a tree with long strips from a woman's tunic.

Entti was nowhere to be found. Nor was Mirana.

# 11

IT WAS DARK, the sliver of moon overhead giving little light through the thick fir and pine branches at their camp. Crickets sounded loud in the warm night. There was an occasional splash in the bog just feet from where they sat, for the most part silent. Rorik stared into the small fire, his hands stretched to the flames, feeling the blessed heat warm him.

His men continued silent. They'd eaten dried fish and apples and hard flatbread. Their bellies were filled, unlike the women who hadn't even eaten any of the food brought over for the noonday meal.

Rorik had sent two men back to Hawkfell Island to fetch supplies. He didn't know how long it would take to find a sign of her. He had no idea of the direction she'd taken. She and Entti. Why had she taken Entti? None of the men had any idea. Surely she didn't intend Entti to be a hostage, for the woman was a slave herself. Just because all the men lusted after Entti didn't mean they wouldn't hesitate to kill her if need be.

Mirana must have known she was courting nearly certain death if she managed to escape, yet she hadn't cared. She would obviously rather die than remain his prisoner. She cared that much for that cursed brother of hers. His mouth tasted sour at that thought.

He'd made her desperate; he'd made her consider death rather than remain chained to his bed. He spat and continued to stare into the flames.

The gods knew he hadn't abused her, not really. She had bitten his ankle when he'd rested his foot on her neck on their voyage to Hawkfell Island. But she could have fallen overboard if he hadn't held her still, that or jumped from the warship just to thwart him. His mind continued in this vein even though he knew he was lying—and to himself, which was the worst kind of lie there was.

He'd had to whip her but he hadn't hurt her and she knew it as well as did he.

He'd had no choice but to chain her in his sleeping chamber. She would have caused havoc had he allowed her to run loose. She would have run all right, all the way to the dock to steal a warship and try to row it by herself, anywhere. And now she was out there, somewhere, in the darkness, she and Entti, and she had no protection, no food.

Hafter said, looking into the fire, even as he continued to massage his head where Mirana had struck him, "I had Entti under me. She was smiling and kissing me, her legs already around my flanks. I was just ready to come into her body when the witch struck me hard on the head."

"You're a fool, Hafter," Rorik said, his voice emotionless. His rage, his fear that Mirana was already dead, all that he felt, he would keep to himself.

"I know," Hafter said and sighed deeply. "My head is killing me. I have a lump here that does naught save grow and grow."

"You deserve it," Gurd the blacksmith said, and chewed on a cord of dried fish. "She could have killed my Asta if she'd had the notion to do it. And then I would have had to kill you for allowing it."

"Aye," said Sculla. " 'Twas your responsibility and you failed because you wanted to stick your rod into Entti. Your lust has brought us all low. Now we must needs track two women, one of them a prisoner, the other one—well, I'd not believed her ruthless and cold as any witch that lives under the earth, but now perhaps I must change my thinking."

"She stole my sword and my knife," Hafter said. "She's not completely without protection."

Rorik cursed. Hafter hadn't told him that before. By all the gods, this added a new danger, both to the women and to Rorik and his men when they caught up to them. He rubbed his fingertips over his throat. He asked now, "But why in the name of Odin All-Father did she take Entti?" He didn't look at any one of his men, merely stared beyond their camp into the dark forest beyond.

"Aye," Askhold said, shaking his head. "It makes no sense to me either, Rorik."

"Who can understand the mind of a woman?" Gurd said. " 'Tis of no real importance. We must needs sleep now. We can begin to track them at dawn. The two of them trekking inland curdles my belly. They'll not make it far, that's certain." He paused a moment, then said, "I want Entti back. Now that you've broken the women's rebellion, Rorik, I can take her whenever it pleases me and Asta will say nothing about it or I will whip her, just as you said."

"I had not meant that exactly," Rorik said, and frowned at the blacksmith. He was remembering Mirana's words, words that had riled him, had made him shake with anger at her. She'd asked him if he'd been faithless, demanded to know if he approved married men bedding other women in front of their wives.

He didn't approve, but damnation, he couldn't dictate to his men, couldn't demand they not bed Entti. Mirana had been right, damn her. The women had few choices; they'd punished the men with inedible cooking and he'd threatened to whip them for it.

"Astá will obey me," Gurd said. "She is a good wife. She must obey me, her husband."

Aye, Rorik thought, that was the crux of the matter, but still, it didn't settle well with him.

Mirana laughed softly. All men were gullible. She'd proved it yet again. Even mighty Rorik, ah, she'd fooled him and his damned men.

She and Entti had cut the second warship adrift and settled down in the other one. Now they were quietly rowing toward the mouth of the estuary. It was just before dawn. She'd wanted to leave hours before but knew they couldn't possibly navigate in the sea and they couldn't take the chance that Rorik would send men back to Hawkfell Island again. They would see that the other warship was gone. Thus, Mirana and Entti had spent their night within twenty feet of Rorik and his men and they'd heard all their talk.

Gurd, Mirana had decided, needed more lessons in how to properly treat Asta, a woman of whom she was very fond, a woman filled with laughter and joy and kindness. She hoped the bonds hadn't hurt either Asta or Old Alna. She'd had to take them by surprise because she couldn't depend on them agreeing to help her escape. If she had asked them and they had agreed, then she would be endangering them, for she imagined if Rorik were to discover that the women had helped her escape, he wouldn't have shown much kindness to them. He might have had them whipped. He might have done even worse.

She and Entti had watched the other warship return to the island, both Asta and Old Alna aboard. She'd said a silent good-bye to them both. They'd watched it return with more men and provisions. And they'd waited.

"I doubt they'll come back this way," Mirana said now in a low voice, pitching it to the night sounds surrounding them. There was the soft slap of the water against the sides of the warship, the occasional sound of a frog or cricket, a slithering sound near the side of the longboat that made Mirana's flesh pucker and crawl. Once, something long and solid had bumped against the longboat and Mirana had had to stifle a yell.

"Nay," Entti said, satisfaction in her husky voice. "They believe we fled like empty-headed females through the salt marshes deep into East Anglia itself. They're fools to believe us such empty-headed fools. But they are naught but men, after all."

Mirana smiled at her new friend. Entti was no simpleton, she thought again as she turned to look at Entti's vague outline in the darkness. What a wondrous surprise that had been when she'd snuck up on Hafter and Entti had stared up at her, and smiled and nodded, bringing Hafter's head down to hers, holding him tightly against her chest, wrapping her legs around his flanks, so Mirana could slam the rock against his head.

"There is still grave danger," Mirana said. "It would be foolish of us to be overly confident. By all the gods, Entti, I don't know. Perhaps you were safer staying on Hawkfell Island. You were not abused. The women were kind to you, they protected you."

"Aye, they were," Entti said, "but the act was growing more and more difficult." She fell silent as she drew again on the oar, her motion steady and smooth. "You believe pleasuring one man after the other not to be abuse, Mirana? They had endless appetites, and a few were animals. They believed they were doing me such a favor, giving me such joy, the rutting stoats. Hafter was different, but still, the chance to escape, the chance to be free once again, it is worth all the danger to be rid of even him."

"And Rorik?"

"I never bedded Rorik. I tried to gain his attention, but he kept to himself. I had hoped that if I bedded him, he would keep the others away from me. But it never worked. I realized that he felt sorry for me, for my simpleness, for the innocence of my mind. I believe he thought to bed me would be like bedding a helpless child." She laughed softly. "I wasn't wise. I decided to play the lackwit shortly after the Vikings captured me. I decided I could bear the men bedding me, that I would be able to suffer it and keep my mind and soul free of them, but it became more and more difficult, as I told you. I would rather die now than return to Hawkfell Island. I would rather die than be a whore again."

"You survived and that is what is important. With luck, both of us will continue to survive. Thank you, Entti."

And that was that. Mirana sat opposite her on the narrow wooden plank, both women drawing on their oars together. It took a while to gain a rhythm, but they'd at last managed it. Each draw took them farther and farther away. Soon they would reach the mouth of the estuary and the North Sea. Two women rowing a warship. It would be difficult, near to impossible, but Mirana knew they would manage somehow.

Entti said, "I found it amusing when the women took their revenge, and I wanted desperately to help them, but how could I? I was naught but a blank-brained child. They were so furious when their husbands took me, but they never blamed me, particularly Asta. Even she showed me no dislike or blamed me for Gurd's infidelity. I disliked him more than any of the others. But then Amma's plan, and what they did to the men until Rorik made his threat! I heard Amma talking to some of the other women of your idea, but then Rorik made his threat immediately, giving it no time to work."

"Aye," Mirana said. "I wondered why he did it so soon. He didn't even eat any of the porridge that next morning, and it was very very good, Entti."

Entti chuckled. "I saw him go to his sleeping chamber when Amma and Old Alna were in there with you. He didn't enter, but just paused outside. I believe he overheard you and the women making your new plans. He knew he had to act quickly and so he did. He isn't a stupid man."

"There will be no more rebellions, Entti. All the women know he whipped me even though they don't know why he did it. It was enough to make them forgo any more thoughts of defiance. 'Tis a pity and yes, Rorik is many things, but he isn't stupid."

"Mayhap he was this time. We have escaped him. By the gods, Mirana, we listened to him and his men calling us naught but women, small and helpless and insignificant as insects. Aye, this time we've won." Entti looked heavenward for a moment, then said, "Why did Rorik whip you?"

"It was silly, really. I was too proud to bend, and that's the truth of it. Oddly enough, he was very careful not to hurt me." Mirana added, shaking her head, "Naturally, he blamed me for making him have to whip me."

"Men," Entti said, "they behave as if they actually

believe what they do is right. It is astounding that they can be so blind."

"Lucky for you that they are, my friend."

"Aye, if you would wish to regard my captivity in that light. I was lucky. I survived to escape."

They rowed in silence, for their breaths were beginning to hitch with the strain. It was nearly impossible for the two of them to keep the warship exactly on the right course. They had to make constant corrections, and it was exhausting.

Mirana said, "I know weapons and have a certain skill with a knife and a sword. If only there had been time, if only Rorik hadn't overheard our plan. All the women need is the proper training, for they have grit and heart. A man whose parts or whose throat is threatened by an agile hand wielding a knife isn't a man to go against his honor, to spite his wife."

"Mirana?"

"Aye?"

"You would have them gullet the men? Nay, don't answer. I like it very much. I can see Amma sitting atop Sculla, a knife pricking his throat. Except, of course, Sculla is a faithful hound. He loves her, nay, he worships that woman. Raki is the same. Poor Erna has but one good arm, yet it makes no difference to him or to their sons. She is a good woman."

"If we both still live on the morrow, tell me that again."

"We will be alive," Entti said, and for a while, at least, Mirana was content to believe her.

It was sheer happenstance. Askhold had forgotten a skin water bag and had returned to the warship to fetch it before they set out to journey inland at dawn the following morning.

Both warships were gone.

"Gone?" Rorik repeated, staring blankly at Askhold.

"Aye, both of them."

"No accident," Hafter said.

Gurd said, "She did it. The woman is cunning and treacherous as a snake. Rorik is right. She has a brain. She thinks like a man. She did it. I will strangle her skinny white neck when we catch her."

Rorik nodded, feeling rage flow over him, but mingled with that rage was respect. She was good, very good.

"But she still has to worry about Entti," Hafter said. "That will slow her. By Thor's hammer, if she harms Entti, I'll strangle the witch myself. My poor Entti, so helpless against such as her. She probably doesn't understand what is happening. Ah, the woman has much to answer for, Rorik."

"But I wonder if she could make Entti row?" Rorik said to no one in particular. "It is impossible for one man to row a warship."

"And she is still naught but a small female, despite all her ploys," said Gurd. "And she must control Entti as well. Entti is simple, Hafter, but she must realize sooner or later that the woman isn't her friend. Perhaps she will slow the woman. 'Twill not take us long to get her back."

"We must find the other warship," Rorik said, and they set off just as streaks of dawn were penetrating the thick foliage in the salt marsh.

They found the warship run against a log near the shore nearly a mile distant. They were sweating and filthy from walking in the bog. They rowed to the mouth of the estuary very quickly, scenting their victory. When they reached the sea, there was nothing in sight.

Rorik hadn't really imagined that she would be here,

perhaps run aground, but nonetheless he felt a shaft of fear and disappointment.

"Where did she go?" Hafter said.

"Back to Ireland," Rorik said. "Back to her damned bastard of a brother."

When the storm struck four hours later, Mirana and Entti were close to shore, staying just behind the breaking waves. Rain poured down, waves splashed over the sides of the warship, soaking them, the water resting in the bottom of the boat to lap over their feet. It was misery.

"We must get ashore and find shelter," Entti said finally, so tired, she thought her arms would surely break off. With the force of the rain and the wind, they were making little headway. The effort wasn't worth any distance they were gaining.

"Aye," Mirana said. "There isn't much of a choice now. The tide is tugging harder at us. I have no wish to be pulled out to sea."

"I have no wish to have the boat fill with water and sink. Mirana, they won't find us. They were going inland to search. Don't worry about Rorik. This time we have outsmarted him, we outsmarted all of the men."

"He's clever," Mirana said, looking behind her, but seeing nothing through the impenetrable gray sheets of rain. "He's very clever and smart and shrewd."

They managed to run the warship ashore, but it took all their combined strength to pull it far enough onto the beach so it wouldn't be whipped by the storm and the waves back out to sea.

They stood there, breathing hard, their heads down, their arms dangling uselessly at their sides. The rain pounded down, but still they didn't move.

"It's far enough in," Mirana said at last, her chest still heaving. "If no one comes across it, it will be safe."

Entti only nodded. It really made no difference. Neither of them had any more strength to pull it further. It would remain where it was.

"Let's get under the trees. Those thick oaks will provide some shelter at least."

They huddled together as the storm raged overhead. The thick oak leaves did provide protection, but they were both soaked to the skin and there was naught they could do about it.

"We cannot become ill," Mirana said as she and Entti pressed as close together as possible. "We cannot."

The rain slowed to a drizzle in the early afternoon. The leaves overhead dripped on them, but it wasn't bad.

"I'm very hungry, Mirana," Entti said.

"I too. We will have to eat berries and roots. I know what things are safe to eat, so you don't have to worry that I will poison us."

Entti gave a rich laugh. "Aye, you believed my fiction as well as everyone else. I cook very well, for I was the daughter of a jeweler who loves his food as much as his silver. It's possible I know more than you since I am a bit older than you. Let us get on with our hunting."

They found strawberries and blueberries, not terribly ripe, but ripe enough. They also dug up some cadmus roots. Without its tough skin, the cadmus was mushy pulp that tasted like bland porridge.

In the middle of the afternoon, the rain stopped, and the sun came out. It grew warm and soon their gowns were dry.

"I would like to sleep for a full day," Entti said, on a

sigh, stretching. She felt her arms, stiff and sore. "How long will it take us to reach this fortress of yours?"

"With just the two of us rowing? I don't know."

"Then we'd best get to it."

They were just on the point of pushing the longboat back into the water, when there was a bloodcurdling yell. Two men were running down the beach toward them. They were wearing leggings and woolen trousers, and leather tunics. They were local Danes, and they'd seen two women and were doubtlessly overwhelmed with their unexpected find.

"Can you use a weapon as well as you cook?" Mirana asked.

"Nay, but I imagine that my fear will sharpen my skills. Give me the sword. I will have a better chance with something bigger."

"But let us try to fool them first," Mirana said. "Aye, let us be simple helpless females."

She slipped the knife back into the pocket of her gown. Entti held the sword in the folds of her gown. Both women waited, not moving.

The two men stopped some ten feet from them. They were young, well formed, and there were huge smiles on their faces.

They called out a greeting.

Mirana, looking as frightened as a young virgin, backed up a step, her face pale, her left hand fluttering helplessly in front of her.

"We mean no harm," the taller of the young men called out. "We've come to help you. We will take you with us."

"And the boat," said the other man, short and muscular as a bull. "Aye, we'll take the boat."

They walked toward the women, swaggering now, still smiling, their teeth gleaming white in the sunlight, as happy as two men could be having two lone women and a warship thrust into their waiting hands.

"Hold yourself ready," Mirana said, still shrinking back in fright, her face creditably pale.

"BY ALL THE blessed gods, what do you two women here? You are alone?"

The older man's eyes darted behind them, suddenly suspicious. There was a magnificent warship dragged out of the water onto the beach, but no men to have pulled it to safety from the storm, no men to have rowed it, no men in sight, that was.

Mirana, who thought them heedless fools, nonetheless trembled as violently as a leaf tossed about in the wind, and shook her head. "We're alone," she whispered. "We have been so afraid."

An unseen enemy was forgotten at her soft words. The man grinned and walked to Mirana. No, it was more like a swagger, she thought, the ass. She made no move when he clasped her chin in his callused palm and lifted her face. He brought his face close to hers and she could see the pock marks on his skin. She doubted he was as old as those ugly marks made him look. He said in a tender voice, "Aye, little bird, you're safe now. I'll take you. I am called Odom and my younger brother yon is Erm. You're quite beautiful. I have never before seen such hair—ah, the color, it's as black as a raven's belly. Is she your sister?"

Entti wore the same frightened look as Mirana. She stuttered and trembled, and nodded as Mirana said yes. She and Mirana looked nothing alike, for Entti's hair was a rich deep brown, her eyes an even darker brown—certainly not the green of Mirana's—and she was tall for a woman, as tall as the man who was in front of her, certainly much taller than Mirana. But the men didn't seem to notice all these differences, at least Mirana prayed they wouldn't until it was too late. The man Odom, who was holding her, was built like a bull. He was clutching her to him now as if she were a treasure he feared losing. She gave him no resistance. She was limp and submissive.

"Ah, Erm, look at the warship. It is well built. Our family will put it to fine use. But we, brother, we have found two beautiful women to ease us. I cannot believe our good fortune."

"Aye," Erm said and released Entti. "This day the gods have smiled on us." He actually rubbed his hands together as he strode toward the warship, saying over his shoulder, "Stay together, little birds. My brother and I will take care of you. You have no more reason to be afraid."

When Odom the bull moved off to join his brother, Entti said in a low voice to Mirana, "I'll lay you a fine wager just how they'll take care of us. What say you, Mirana?"

"Let us wait until they are completely lulled, completely without suspicion. Then we will act."

Mirana gleaned from their talk that the brothers had wives and children and a farmstead just inland. The beach upon which they'd landed was just beyond the Thames estuary. The brothers were there to hunt, aye, just to hunt and perhaps to fish if there were no pheasant or wild pigs about. She saw them look at each other then, their expression sly. They were very pleased with themselves, that was obvious to see. They slapped each other on the back. Two new slaves, both young and lovely too. It was a treasure they'd found and all because of this trip down to the beach to fish. Aye, they were happy men.

When they returned, Erm suddenly grabbed Entti, pulling her to him, and clutched wildly at her breasts. Obviously he'd looked his fill at his new warship and now he wanted the woman. She was soft and firm and he was eager, more than eager. He was ready to ravish her to his heart's content. She was nearly as tall as he was, but he was the stronger. He was a man and he was her new master.

He said into her face, his words meant for his brother, "Let's sate ourselves with them now. I have no wish to argue with my wife. And our other men will want them. There will be trouble, but I am willing to fight for them."

"Aye," said Odom as he smiled down at Mirana. "Please me and I'll see you're not abused. I'll protect you from all the others. Aye, I'll give you a new gown. This one you're wearing is very ugly and old."

Entti heard Odom the bull's words and very nearly laughed aloud.

Mirana's fingers itched and tingled, tightening about the knife. She was ready. She prayed that Entti wouldn't panic.

It happened quickly. Odom grabbed Mirana about her waist and flung her to the sand. He straddled her with his knees on each side of her waist, content for the moment just to stare down at his gift from the gods. He reached out his hand and began to fondle her breasts. She made no move, merely lay there, waiting, waiting. His breath came more quickly and she knew it wouldn't be long now. It wasn't. When he ripped up her gown and he fell atop her, he impaled himself on the knife she was clutching between her breasts. He reared up and stared down at her, blood bubbling from his shoulder, dripping down the knife handle onto her gown. He cried out, jerked back, and grabbed his shoulder. His fingers fluttered about the knife handle, but she could see he was afraid to pull it free of his flesh. Let him rot with it in him, she thought. She said nothing, merely waited. He could still kill her, despite the knife in his shoulder. She waited, silent and still.

Odom threw back his head and yelled, his voice filled with both pain and astonishment at what she had done to him, "Erm! Help me!"

Erm whirled about at his brother's strangled cry. His hand was on Entti's thigh, all his thoughts, all his concentration, on the soft flesh, on his lust, on how the woman wasn't fighting him, how she was accepting him. He yelled back in surprise, then leapt off Entti and ran to his brother. At that instant, Entti jumped after him, and jabbed the sword in his side. He yelled louder than her father ever had when he'd been bested by another jeweler.

"She is but one woman, Rorik," Askhold said again, as if to reassure himself rather than Rorik or the others. "Entti is her prisoner. The woman has some hold over her, threatening her in some way, or promising her a better life with her brother. That, or Entti is just too simple to realize what is happening to her. If Mirana acted like her mistress, she might have just obeyed her blindly."

Hafter frowned. "This has already been discussed, Askhold. I've already rejected that. Entti's not that simple. The woman is hurting her, she has managed to gain some hold on her. I don't understand it, but it must be so."

"Not that it matters now," Askhold said. "Two women alone—they had no chance. The storm was brief but very deadly. My arms feel as though they've been pulled from their sockets. There are only two of them to handle the warship. They had no chance, Rorik. They must be dead. Mayhap we'll never find them."

Rorik stared at Askhold. He said only, "Nay. Mirana is smart. I have told all of you this again and again. Believe me now. She has managed, I know it. Despite Entti's slowness, her simplicity, Mirana will survive. She would keep the warship close to shore. When the storm became too strong, she would beach it and wait for the weather to clear. Keep a sharp lookout, Gurd. We must have gained on them considerably."

It was Hafter who saw the warship.

It was Rorik who saw the two men attack the women. He felt a curdling of fear in his belly, then he smiled, not at all surprised, when the man on Mirana reared back and fell onto his side, Hafter's knife sticking from his shoulder. But he admitted to astonishment when he saw Entti leap to her feet, run after the other man, and ram Hafter's sword into his side. She nearly missed, but she was strong, and the glancing blow carried enough force to knock the man down and make him yowl with pain.

"Let us go in quietly," he said. "I do not wish to startle them."

"Startle them, ha!" Gurd said, and spat over the side of the boat. "That damned woman, she's playing the man. We should kill her."

It was Entti who saw them. The wounded men at their feet were forgotten.

Mirana cursed, pulled her knife from the moaning Odom's shoulder, and ran, Entti behind her, Hafter's bloody sword dragging in the sand.

"Why is Entti running away?" Hafter said. "She is Mirana's prisoner no more. Surely she must realize that. She should be running to me. I know she saw me and recognized me. She can't be that witless. She knows I will take care of her, save her from the witch."

Rorik said nothing more until they'd pulled their warship onto the beach to rest beside the other one.

The women had long since disappeared into the trees by the time the men jumped from the warship onto the dark sand. The wounded men were also gone, both of them leaving trails of blood in the sand. The sun disappeared behind thick gray clouds. More rain threatened.

"Come," Rorik said, and ran to where they had disappeared. When they reached the treeline, he stopped, and said, "Askhold, come here. We must track them now."

"We will hear them," Gurd said. "Rorik, you believe this woman to be beyond a woman, and that is madness. She is naught but a female when all is said and done. Aye, the two of them will make more noise than ten boars thrashing through this heavy undergrowth. They have no skill in—"

Rorik just shook his head, silencing Gurd.

"It is difficult," Askhold said at last. "There are different footsteps here and they are merged together. It is the two men who were with the women, but I cannot be certain whose feet belong to the women, there is too much confusion, too much overlapping. See the spots of blood? It's from one or both of the men, but again, there is too much confusion to know which blood spots belong where."

"So," Rorik said, "she saw their steps and is trying to copy them to lead us astray."

"Aye," Gurd said, and spat in a mess of leaves, "now you'll be saying that she cut herself to mix her blood with theirs to confuse us all the more."

"I wouldn't be surprised at anything she would do," Rorik said. "I will tell all of you again, but you, Gurd, you will really listen to my words. Mirana is smart; she knows guile, she sleeps with cunning close to her breast."

"Aye," Askhold said, his eyes gleaming. "You were right, Rorik. She has a man's brain. Hold your thoughts to yourself, Gurd, they are useless to you and to us."

Gurd looked both furious and uncertain, an unusual combination in the blacksmith, who had always known the way of things even when he was in the wrong. Then he just shook his head, and held his tongue.

Rorik said nothing more. He walked back to the beach and sat down two feet beyond the water line. He stared over the water, at the roiling heavy waves, churning and crashing onto the dirty sand.

His men looked at each other, but said nothing.

Rorik sat there quietly for some minutes. Then he rose, stretched, and said in surely an overloud voice, "Hafter, you will stay with me." He divided the other men into two groups and told them what to do, again, his voice loud and carrying. They looked at him oddly, but nodded.

"And where will we go?" Hafter said, watching the other men disappear into the trees.

Rorik didn't look at him as he said quietly, "We will go into the maple woods just yon. Then we will double back and go over there, just beyond the point, and hide behind those black rocks."

Hafter started to laugh, then he frowned, and slowly, his eyes never leaving Rorik's face, he, like the other men, nodded. "So that is why you nearly yelled in our ears."

"Aye," Rorik said, and grinned. "Now, let's make a good show of it."

The two men slung water bags over their shoulders, arranged their weapons, strapped small packets of food to their waists, then strode toward the woods in the opposite direction of the other two groups. They looked purposeful; they looked determined. They looked ready to search until they collapsed from exhaustion.

"Patience," Mirana said, lightly tugging back on Entti's sleeve.

"But they've been gone a very long time."

"Not long at all," Mirana said. "Rorik is smart as a snake. Doubt it not. I don't trust him."

"He's a man and thus he believes women are weak and silly and without subtlety. He and Hafter are at least a mile from here now. You saw how he gave the other men orders, you saw how they walked—so sure of themselves—the direction they took. Let us go, Mirana. What if those men we wounded return with others? They will kill us, do not doubt it."

Entti was right, but still Mirana didn't like it. The sun was shining again, the bulging gray rain clouds dispersing, and she knew they could gain distance from Rorik in the warship, even with just the two of them rowing, but still, she didn't trust him. She didn't know why she felt so strongly, but she did. Why would Rorik leave no one to guard the warships? Aye, that was it, that was why she knew, simply *knew* that something wasn't as it appeared to be. And why had he spoken so loudly? Still, Entti was right. If the men they'd wounded returned with others, they would be in grave trouble.

Entti said, "We will steal the food from their warship and then cut it adrift. We will escape them for good this time. They know we are holding close to shore. Did you not tell me there were several large islands just off the coast? We could hide amongst the inlets. That would confuse them if somehow they managed to regain their warship, if somehow they managed to keep after us."

Mirana sighed, for Entti was speaking to her with a bit of sarcasm, as one would to a stubborn child. She smiled at the irony of it. "You're right and your plan is a good one. Perhaps it is time. Perhaps I am wrong about Rorik this time, ah, but it vexes me, Entti."

"You worry overmuch. I feel so itchy to move, I think I'll scream if I have to hide here a moment longer. There are sand fleas here, Mirana."

She and Mirana rose and stretched, then walked slowly forward, peering through the dense foliage onto the beach. There was no one to be seen, not in any direction. It was silent. Odom and Erm were probably back at their farmsteads, getting more men together. She'd been surprised that they could move so quickly with their wounds, but they were running from the beach the moment they'd seen Rorik and his men leap over the side of their longboat into the surf. Entti was right. They had to leave and they had to do it quickly. It made no difference that Rorik had left both warships unguarded.

"All right," she said. "Quickly, Entti!" They bolted from the cover of the trees and ran as fast as they could toward the longboats.

"Hurry, Entti, fetch whatever there is from Rorik's warship, but move quickly!"

She herself was pushing with all her strength at the bow of Rorik's warship, grunting as it eased very slowly on the wet sand toward the water. She felt fear pounding through her, and strength she didn't know she had. She pushed harder, then harder still. A huge wave burst onto the sand and the warship finally slid forward toward the water.

Entti shouted that she'd found water skins, food bags and weapons. She was crowing, rubbing her hands together, smiling as Mirana had never seen her smile before. "Aye, perhaps I'll leave Hafter his sword. It has that fool's blood on it. Aye, here's a clean one I'll take!"

"Hurry, Entti!"

"Mirana, they're leagues from here. You give Rorik too much credit. He isn't a god, he's just a man, like all the other men. Stop your fretting."

"No, Entti, you're quite wrong."

At the sound of Rorik's voice, Mirana felt herself grow very still. She felt suddenly very cold. She'd known, by all the gods, she'd known how smart he was, how treacherous.

She slowly turned to face him. Hafter stood at his right, his eyes on Entti.

"I knew," Mirana said, her voice dull, "I knew we wouldn't trick you."

"Ah, I knew as well that you wouldn't dash off into the woods, not knowing where to go. You're not a fool. And there are those men you and Entti wounded. It was well done of you, but again, I knew you wouldn't leave because those men and their families just might be waiting for you. You did well, but you couldn't escape me, Mirana. You will never escape me."

Slowly, Mirana drew the knife. There were still flecks of Odom's blood drying on it. "We're leaving, Rorik.

Entti! Come here and bring the food and water."

Hafter looked at Mirana as if she were a fool. He grinned toward Entti and called out, "You don't have to obey her any longer, sweeting. Be a good girl and come to me. I will take care of you. I won't let her hurt you anymore. If she has promised you rewards to help her reach her brother, she is lying. Come, sweeting."

Suddenly Entti looked perplexed, like a child who couldn't understand why her parents were arguing. She looked from Mirana back to Hafter. He stretched out his hand to her. "Come, Entti, I'll see that she doesn't hurt you ever again. You can believe me, trust me."

"All right," Entti whispered. Only Mirana saw the glimmer of Hafter's sword she'd slipped alongside her body, hidden in the folds of her gown. Hadn't Hafter heard her speaking? Was he so caught in his belief of her as a sweet halfwit that he couldn't grasp anything else?

Hafter was smiling at Entti and nodding, his expression gentle and reassuring, the look one would give to a slow child. But his stance was smug and confident. As for Rorik, he never looked away from Mirana's face. She saw him begin to frown and wondered if he were beginning to doubt Entti.

She held herself perfectly still, as if deep in thought, waiting tense and anxious.

Suddenly, Rorik heard a choking yell. He whipped about to see Hafter falling slowly to his knees in the sand. He was clutching his head and he stared up at Entti, who stood over him, the sword handle extended.

"Don't move, Hafter," she said, this voice very different from the voice he knew. It was the voice he'd heard just before he and Rorik had come out to catch them, but then he'd thought he was mistaken, he'd thought . . . He wanted to vomit, from the blow and from his own stupidity.

Rorik yelled, "By Thor's hammer, what is the meaning of this!" He took a step toward Hafter, then stopped in his tracks. He shook his head. "Never," he said, looking from Entti to Mirana, "never again will I underestimate a woman. You are no simple female, are you, Entti? No sweet-faced child to warm a man's bed and smile at his jests. You aren't Mirana's hostage and you never were. By all the gods, I was a fool to disbelieve what my good sense was screaming at me. I was a fool to disregard the very words I heard you speaking to Mirana, no witless child's words they were."

"Go away, Lord Rorik," Mirana said, her voice cold as the night wind. "Go away. Hafter will be all right. Evidently Entti has some liking for him and thus didn't kill him. Go away. I have no wish to hurt you and now it is the two of us against you. We will win, Rorik. Entti knows weapons as well as I do. Aye, she is vicious with that sword and she won't hesitate to stick it through your belly. Do not forget the feel of my knife in your throat. I will do it again, only this time, your blood will spurt out onto the sand. Go away."

She didn't believe what she'd said for a single instant, but there was no hesitation, no uncertainty in her voice.

Rorik looked undecided. Had he believed her? She had sounded vicious, very sure of herself. Was it possible he was frightened of her? She had never seen this expression before and was instantly wary. No, she wouldn't fall into his trap again. She would sooner trust Odom the bull. She took a step back from him, keeping the knife pointed out in front of her, aimed at his chest.

He sighed, then said, his hands splayed in front of him, "You plan to push both warships into the sea. What will I do? I have no wish to be stranded here. Those warships are valuable. They cost me much silver."

"I am sorry, but you would follow us, and I cannot take the chance."

"What if I swear to let you go," he said very quietly, his eyes never leaving her face.

She stared at him, not knowing what was in his mind, but this man who sounded as if he were pleading, as if he were trying to bargain with her, she didn't recognize. The Rorik she knew never bargained. He commanded, he ordered. He never gave an inch, never faltered or acted the supplicant. Something wasn't right and she felt her belly knot and twist. She took another step away from him.

She shouted over her shoulder, "Entti, come here. Leave Hafter. You've downed him. Don't worry about him now, he will survive the pain to his head."

Entti, after one final look at Hafter, turned away to do Mirana's bidding. Suddenly Hafter jerked upward and tackled her, slamming her facedown onto the sand, coming down hard on her back. He twisted the sword from her hand and flung it beyond her reach. She struggled wildly with him but it did no good. He was large and he was heavy and he simply lay flat on her, forcing her face into the wet sand.

As Mirana cried out, turning to run to help Entti, Rorik was on her, grabbing and twisting her wrist until he felt the bones twisting, ready to break beneath his strength. Still, she didn't release the knife, if anything her fingers tightened around the ivory handle. He hardened his grip. He stared down at her face, saw her eyes nearly black with pain and determination.

"You cannot win now, Mirana, for I am the stronger. Surely you will realize that. I can tighten my hold and break every bone in your hand. Drop the knife, damn you. Drop it now."

# 13

SHE COULD ONLY shake her head, biting her tongue to keep from screaming. He suddenly jerked her arm upward, changing his grip, two fingers pressing on the inside of her wrist. Her fingers went instantly numb and the knife dropped to the wet sand, making not a sound.

She kicked him, but he was fast, and her knee struck his thigh, which was pain enough. A soft keening noise was coming from deep in her throat. There was a sheen of blankness in her eyes, the vivid green dull and glazed. She fought him mindlessly now, and he knew he had to put a stop to it. Rorik knew she was out of control.

He struck her jaw hard and clean. She sighed softly and sagged against him.

He yelled over his shoulder, "Have you gotten Entti conquered, Hafter?"

"Aye, but she has broken my head, and all because I wanted to care for her. I just wanted to save her from Mirana's folly. I will never understand a woman, Rorik."

"At least she didn't stick the other end of the sword through your flesh. Be grateful for that."

"Aye, I am. She must know I've a hard head. Ah, her perfidy still shocks me." Rorik thought Hafter would burst into tears. "All I wanted to do was care for her."

Entti tried again to rear up, to break away from him, but Hafter was strong and big. He pressed her back, even as she screamed at him over her shoulder, "Care for me! You stupid bastard, you're naught but a selfish cruel animal! You bray like a mindless lout. You believe yourself so kind, so tender with a simpleminded slave. Aye, and why not? I never said you nay! If I had, you would have clouted me and raped me or just killed me! I should have killed you, more fool I. Aye, dead you would look as fetching as you believe yourself to be."

"I do not believe you," Hafter said slowly, still unwilling to accept this woman who was so different from the one he'd taken to his bed. She'd been such a simple woman and he'd given her so many smiles, all of them gentle, all of them filled with kindness, and he'd patted her as she'd passed him in genuine liking so many times, on her shoulder, on her bottom, aye, he'd even taken her hand and gently squeezed it. But the truth of it was that she was a shrew and a termagant, just like the other one whom Rorik was holding unconscious against him.

"Hafter," Rorik called, "come now and get off her and tie her securely. Think before you act whenever you deal with either of them. After you tie Entti tightly, call the other men. They are but twenty yards inland."

"You told them to remain close by," Hafter said slowly. He shook his head, saying low, "I am a great fool. I have seen nothing clearly, understood nothing."

"Stop condemning yourself," Rorik said. "All of us believed Entti to be different. I told the others to remain close by because I didn't want them to get lost or come across any family or friends of the men brought low by these two docile females."

He swung Mirana up into his arms. She didn't weigh much, this woman who had too much fight in her, this damned woman who wouldn't give up, even when she knew she couldn't win, even when she knew he could kill her.

He didn't want to kill her. He felt profound relief that he'd found her unharmed. If there was any abuse to be done, he wanted to be the one to do it.

"You killed her, you bastard!"

Rorik merely smiled at this new Entti with her narrowed, vicious eyes and a voice to pierce a man's eardrums, and said, "Nay, her jaw is as hard as her head. I didn't break it. I simply don't wish to have to fight her more for a while. Hafter, tie those ropes more securely or she might do you in again. Get it into your brain that she isn't simple, she isn't willing or soft or meek."

Rorik looked down at the woman in his arms. Her head lolled back, her white throat was bare. She looked defenseless. She looked very female, very soft, but by all the gods, he should know her better by now. The only thing soft about her was her white flesh. He needed her if he was ever going to gain revenge on her damned half-brother. But how to keep her from killing everyone on his island? He didn't want to have to be on his guard all the time. But how to avoid keeping her tied to his bed? He hated doing it, hated seeing the raw flesh of her wrists when he changed from one wrist to the other. But he knew as well that the women would find a way to unchain her just as soon as he was gone from the farmstead, damn them for their loyalty to her, his enemy.

He considered several alternatives as they rowed back toward Hawkfell Island, Mirana on the planking, hands and ankles bound, his left foot resting on her neck.

It was but moments later when she said, her voice vicious and low, "Get your foot off my neck."

He heard her easily over the slapping of the waves against the side of the longboat, over the smooth motion of the oars dipping into the water and rhythmically drawing hard, over the talk of the men, over the whipping wind and the cawing of gulls overhead, for her voice was mean and hard and furious, and it pleased him very much and, too, he'd been waiting for her to speak, even looking forward to it. He'd won and he knew that she knew it. Aye, it made him feel quite good. He left his foot on her neck. This time, he placed his foot so she couldn't manage to bite him again.

He leaned down and said quietly, right into her ear, "If I do, do you swear not to try to jump overboard again? That or try to push me over the side?"

"I wasn't trying to jump. Do you think me witless? I don't want to die—"

"Ah, so you were trying to shove me out of the warship. I should have known. I wouldn't have bound you if you hadn't tried violence again. But you forced me to tie you up. You forced me to fling you at my feet. Well, at my foot, really, since my other foot is on your neck. You do look uncomfortable. Actually, you're looking very miserable. There's water in the bottom now. Soon it will come over the planking and splash in your face. That will be true misery, won't it? Saltwater in your mouth? Well, do you swear to lie still if I remove my foot, if I untie you? No more violence?"

She nodded. He saw she didn't want to, but his foot must be quite heavy on her neck and her wrists and ankles must be growing numb. Also, there was the water in the bottom of the warship and he knew that probably decided her, for soon it would reach her face. Aye, he'd won.

He lifted his foot. For a moment she didn't move. He wondered if she was able to move. Just before he would have helped her, she shook herself and sat up. She stared at him, holding her bound hands toward him. He untied her hands and ankles. She rubbed the back of her neck, then her wrists, then massaged her ankles. "I will pay you back for that," she said, not looking at him.

Rorik merely smiled, not at all disappointed. He looked over at Entti. Hafter had tied a rope about her waist and the other end was about his waist. Perhaps that's what he should do with Mirana. She looked calm now. No, defeated was the word. Her shoulders were slumped and she merely sat there, staring at nothing in particular, her eyes dull and indifferent, methodically rubbing her wrists. Rorik discovered that didn't please him. She was utterly withdrawn. He frowned.

It was raining hard when they returned to Hawkfell Island. All were soaked to the skin by the time they reached the dock. Mirana said nothing as she trudged beside Entti back up the trail to the longhouse. It continued to rain, heavy thick rain, hard and cold, a rain that the high winds gusted about, making it impossible to go out of the longhouse. Everyone was inside, even the pets and two goats. Smoke filled the longhouse, turning the air blue, making it difficult to breathe. Ah, but the food was delicious, the mead sweet and warm. The women were quiet, the children played and chattered and argued. Kerzog barked madly when one of the children threw a leather ball, then raced after it. The huge mongrel never tired of the game, spinning the ball over and over with his nose. There was the long constant sound of the loom and spinning wheel. One of the goats was chewing on a rope. All was normal.

Entti sat beside Mirana, both of them altering gowns Old Alna had given them. The men gave them both wide berth. The women did as well, but not because they were angry but because they were wary of the men if they came too close. Still, Erna had brought them food balanced on her left arm, the withered stub of her right arm up to steady the platter if it slipped.

"Raki told me what happened," she said very quietly. "I am proud of both of you. You tried." And then she was gone, saying nothing more, leaving Mirana and Entti to stare at each other.

Mirana supposed that Rorik and the men had made it clear the women were to keep away from them. Mirana caught Amma's eye once and saw her wink. She then looked at Entti and smiled widely. So the women knew now that all Entti had done had been naught but an act. Soon, surely, once the rains had stopped and the men were out of the longhouse, the women would come to her again. She wanted to make amends to Asta and Old Alna for tying them up. They hadn't seemed angry with either her or Entti, more accepting than anything else, for Mirana had been bound to try to escape, hadn't she? As for Entti, Mirana thought the women believed her very smart.

"I should have killed him," Entti said now as she looked over at Hafter, who was drinking a wooden cup of mead, laughing at something Askhold was saying. She speared her needle viciously into the wool.

"Even if you had," Mirana said, not looking up, "we couldn't have disarmed Rorik. He's too smart and he's very strong."

"He isn't all that smart," Entti said. "Certainly no smarter than Hafter, who is a witless fool. 'Tis just you who believe Rorik to be close to perfect, and that only because he continues to prevail over you. But it's true, if I had killed Hafter then your Rorik probably would have killed me. He would have had no other choice."

At that, Mirana looked up. "Surely you don't believe that I see Rorik as smart only because he beats me? The sun beat too brightly on your head, Entti."

"It rained constantly, Mirana."

"No matter. Now, what do you mean he would have no other choice? He doesn't need choice. He doesn't need any sort of excuse. He would kill you because he would enjoy it, he would savor his revenge for the killing of his friend. Most men are like that. They bring misery because it pleases them to do so."

Entti shook her head. "Nay, Rorik isn't like that. Before you came, I heard talk about what had happened in the Vestfold. Everyone always spoke freely in front of me because they believed me simple."

Mirana sat forward, her eyes on Entti's face. "Please tell me," she said. "Rorik has said naught about it."

Entti stabbed the needle into the material and laid it on her lap. "Your half-brother came to Rorik's farmstead when Rorik and many of his men were trading in Birka. They killed everyone they could find, including slaves, old men and women and children, the reason being, so I heard, that your half-brother had been told that Rorik was hiding much silver. But I don't know if this was true. It didn't matter. Some, like Old Alna, were hiding in the forest beyond the barley fields, and thus were alive, when Rorik returned home only hours after the slaughter, to tell him what had happened. They murdered Rorik's small twin son and daughter and raped and killed his wife.

"Shortly after that, Rorik moved here to Hawkfell Island, all his people with him, those who had survived the slaughter, that is. Even some of his father's people came as well. They rebuilt the longhouse, planted the crops, and strengthened the island's defenses. Then Rorik began his search. It took him nearly two years to find Einar. He heard of him quite by chance through a traveling scald, who sang of his heroic deeds at King Sitric's side against the treacherous Irish chieftains."

"I don't believe that," Mirana said slowly. "It is beyond vicious. If Einar had heard about hidden silver, then he would have known who Rorik Haraldsson was, but he didn't know his name, not until Rorik told me at Clontarf and I told Gunleik. And since Rorik wasn't there, why would Einar kill everyone so cruelly? Nay, it makes no sense, surely Einar wouldn't—" Her voice dropped away. She felt his presence before she raised her head to look at him. Rorik was standing directly in front of her and he was pale as death, his hands fisted at his sides.

"It is all true," he said, and she hated the roiling pain she heard in his voice even though she guessed he was trying to sound calm and emotionless. Ah, but the pain and his fury sounded through, at least to her ears. "I would impale your half-brother through his miserable guts on a dull-tipped stake and let him squeal like a pig. I would let him die slowly, and I would feel joy at his every scream."

She was shaken. She just stared up at him. He hadn't lied. Not for a moment did she believe that he lied. Perhaps Old Alna had exaggerated. No, she didn't believe that either. She closed her eyes against the knowledge. She'd seen Einar in his rages, though he was careful to hide most of them, both from her, and from his most powerful men and allies. He laughed even as he wielded a whip. The louder a victim screamed, the more he delighted in it. He was ungoverned; he lost control. He was frightening. She allowed herself to remember all of it now, to see him now with clear eyes.

She stared up at Rorik. She felt the tension in him. Then, finally, when the silence grew too painful for her, she said, "What would you have me do? He is still my half-brother."

Rorik dropped to his haunches beside her. "I would have told you had Entti not done it now. When my foot was on your neck and I was goading you, mocking you with my sarcasm, I knew I couldn't allow this to continue, this unending tug of strength between us. Aye, it was my decision to tell you, for I could determine no other way to gain some loyalty from you, to keep you with me of your own wish perhaps, to keep me from having to chain you to my bed. I cannot allow you to escape and return to him, to tell him of Hawkfell Island. He holds powerful sway with King Sitric in Dublin. Do you understand? I must find a way to get to him, some way to use you to help me get to him."

He simply stopped talking and looked at her, studying her now pale face, her every expression. Finally, he said, "Do you believe me, Mirana?"

"Aye," she said with no hesitation. "I believe you, but I don't believe this tale of hidden silver. Einar is many things but he isn't stupid. But, why then did he attack your family and your farmstead? Vikings don't raid and plunder and kill other Vikings, at least it is not the common practice. And he went to the Vestfold, and he would know it would enrage Harald Fairhair, the king. He couldn't be certain that he wouldn't be recognized. He even killed your slaves instead of capturing them. It makes no sense. Einar isn't wasteful. He wants more slaves, as would anyone with power and holdings. Why did he do it?"

"I don't know. Perhaps it amused him, all the pain and death gave him a sick pleasure. From what I know of him, he would find enjoyment in causing all that suffering and death. Is the tale about the silver true? I don't know that either. But I do know that Einar is a vile man. I don't understand such a man or such a mind."

Rorik paused a moment, looking at a rush torch light just beyond Mirana. His voice was low and deep and hoarse as he said, "He raped my wife, making a big show of it, having all his men and all my people who weren't yet dead stand in a wide circle and watch him do it. She fought him, mayhap even hurt him a bit, and so he had his men hold her arms and legs away from her body and watch her and him whilst he raped her. He laughed as she screamed. Then he gave her to all his men. And he laughed whilst they raped her. Then he killed her. Old Alna was one of those who saw him rape her and beat her, then stick his knife through her heart.

"Then he had my twins brought before him. They were babes, not yet two years old. He spitted them both on his sword."

She felt bile rise in her throat and quickly swallowed. Entti looked from Rorik to Mirana. "How could a man be so very evil? Mirana, did you ever see such viciousness, such cruelty, in your brother?"

Slowly, very slowly, Mirana nodded. "I refused to recognize it as such. I looked away. I pretended all was well. Einar is like his father, Thorsson, a man who nearly beat his wife to death—our mother—before a slave killed him to protect her. Einar killed the slave, of course, to give a show of revenging his father's murder. He wanted what was his father's. He didn't care if his mother lived or died. When she married some months later, my father took her away from Clontarf. She must have known even then that Einar had grown crookedly. I went to live with Einar when I was eleven years old, upon the death of both my parents. An Irish chieftain looted our holdings and killed them." She spoke calmly, with acceptance. Life was many times violent. There was nothing to be done about it. The pain of her parents' death had dulled over the years. She could sometimes remember her mother's scent, a soft fragrant rose smell, and the sound of her voice when she was humming.

Rorik frowned at her, saying, "I'm sorry. It was a bitter thing for a child to see. Did Einar treat you well enough? He didn't abuse you, did he?"

"Nay. At first he simply ignored me, but when I showed interest in weapons and in the war games he and his men played, he allowed Gunleik to train me. I think it pleased his conceit to have a sister who could both fight and kill and cook and sew. I think Gunleik wanted me to learn all I could so I could protect myself. He is honorable. He knew all about Einar, but still, he looked away. I know from Gunleik what happened to Einar's father and what Einar felt about it."

"Gunleik," Rorik said. "He is the man who sent that knife into my shoulder."

"Aye. He could have killed you but he is not like that. I regret that he was left at Clontarf to brave Einar's fury when he discovered you'd taken me."

Rorik said nothing, but Mirana saw him rubbing his shoulder, doubtless an unconscious gesture. She wondered if the wound was completely healed.

"I wonder why this Gunleik told you so much."

"He cares for me." She added, "I believe he told me so that I would have some understanding when and if Einar turned on me." Mirana paused, then looked up into his face. "I fear that Einar has probably killed him because he allowed you to escape and to take me."

"If he has killed him, he is a fool. Gunleik is an excellent warrior. That is more wasteful than I can comprehend."

She sighed then, deeply. "I have not looked at Einar straightly. I know now that he would kill Gunleik for letting you escape. It wouldn't matter to him, no it wouldn't. He was only seventeen when he became master of Clontarf. He has become very strong over the years. Those who have known him since he was born would say that he has gained his mature years, for he is thirty-five years old, but he looks much younger, not much older than you, Rorik. He is very handsome. Gunleik has only forty years, yet he looks old enough to be Einar's father."

Rorik looked away from her. There was rage in his eyes, clouding them. She knew that he must be picturing this handsome half-brother of hers raping and killing his wife.

"What will you do?" she asked finally. There was fear in her voice, but she couldn't help it. She despised herself for letting him hear it.

"I will decide soon what I will do." He paused a moment, looking beyond Mirana to the weapons fastened to the wall of the longhouse. His grandfather's sword hung there, still gleaming, its silver bright, for Gurd's father had fashioned it and Gurd cared for it. He looked away, thinking now about Kron, a man who'd just come home today, the man who had been his eyes and ears for six months in the king's garrison in Dublin. What he'd told Rorik made him realize he had to act, at least he had to do something about Mirana, and quickly. He'd been very surprised to learn the nature of King Sitric's dealings with Einar, surprised and disgusted. Aye, he had to act soon. Should he tell her? He nearly shook his head, but kept himself still. No, now wasn't the time.

He said, staring again at his grandfather's beautifully wrought sword, not looking at her, "I have told you the truth. I can do no more. Can I trust you now? Will you remain here with me?"

Mirana rose from the chair and stood beside him, lightly touching her fingertips to his forearm. It forced him to look at her. She said very matter-of-factly, "You kidnapped me. You treated me like you'd treat a frenzied dog. You showed me no mercy. You forced me to remain chained in your sleeping chamber. You whipped me. You set your foot upon my neck."

He was silent. It was all true, except perhaps for his lack of mercy. He would have to ask her to be specific about that.

"However," she continued after a moment, her voice clear and low, "had I been you, I would have done the same."

This was unexpected. And to hear such words from a woman's mouth was beyond Rorik's experience. It sounded odd, but somehow, it sounded true and he realized it and accepted it as well, and knew he was pleased with his acceptance. He felt the strength of her in those words, felt the honesty of her. Fidelity from her would mean something very rare, something valuable, something, he realized, he wanted very much.

He said again, "Will you remain here? Can I trust you?"

# 14

IT WAS MIRANA'S turn to look away. She looked at Entti, who was still seated on the bench, mending the hem of the gown, seemingly paying no heed to them now. She was even humming to herself. It didn't matter. Mirana drew a deep breath, and said, looking at Rorik's left ear, "If I say that you can trust me, if I promise I won't try to escape you—"

"You mean try to escape me again."

"Aye, again. Well, what will you do? Will I still be your slave? Your prisoner, your hostage?" Even as she spoke, he was shaking his head, but she couldn't prevent the questions, for they welled up in her. "Will I remain an outsider, to be despised and hated by all your men? Will you chain me to your bed? In the warship, will you set your foot on my neck? If I refuse to call you lord will you whip me and fling me to the ground?"

"Nay," he said, and nothing more.

She waited, but he remained quiet.

"I do not understand you," she said at last. "You say you won't hurt me again, but what will you do?"

"I would have you wed with me."

The words, completely unplanned, lay heavy between them. Rorik sucked in his breath, but no more words came out. By the gods, he'd said it, asked her to be his wife—surely he'd known he would have to take another wife again before he was too old to beget sons and daughters. Nay, but with her that wasn't all there was to it. He wanted a family again—the warmth, the giving, the joy and the pain. He wanted all of it. It had been so damned long, too long. He hadn't realized until the words had come out of his mouth how very much alone he'd been, how inward he'd grown, how empty he felt. But to take to wife this woman who'd come to him in such a way? This woman he'd stolen? This woman whose half-brother was his sworn enemy?

Well, he'd said it, and he knew himself well enough to realize that somewhere deep inside him, perhaps very deep, buried under layer upon layer of cold logic, he must, for some important reason, want her for his wife. He wanted her for himself. It was a mystery. He waited. He refused to think about the Danish king in Dublin, that jowly vein-handed old King Sitric, and what he wanted and what he was prepared to pay Einar to gain.

Mirana didn't move either. She knew he would say no more. To wed with him . . . He'd shown no caring for her, not really. He'd not even shown lust for her, for when he'd caressed her breasts, it had been his man's punishment, not for any pleasure either of them would get out of it, not to appease his man's appetites. She didn't understand him, but she knew that he was a man she could trust. Looked at from that attitude, it was really quite simple. There was nothing for her back at Clontarf, save Einar, and the thought of being with him again curdled her belly.

Rorik Haraldsson was a man to trust, a man to depend on. She also admitted to herself that he was a handsome animal, lean and strong and powerful. He wasn't stupid, and he was brave. And he was smarter than other men, despite what Entti had said. He didn't ever count the cost to himself. He was a man she could admire. His bad habits, his likes and dislikes, weren't yet all that clear to her. If she married him she would learn them soon enough, as he would hers.

Still, to wed a man she'd only known as her enemy. Was there nothing left to her in Ireland? Was her home irrevocably gone from her? She felt tears building, felt the knot in her throat. She willed the tears away and swallowed the knot.

Rorik understood her confusion, her wariness. He also saw the sheen of tears in her eyes, but he didn't touch her, didn't try to comfort her. She was a woman who despised weakness in herself. He wouldn't shame her by calling attention to what she would see as a fault in herself. She didn't know him, not really, and Hawkfell Island wasn't her home. She was a stranger here, and in her mind, how then could she belong?

He wanted to keep quiet, he didn't want her fear to bring her to acceptance of him, or her seeming lack of choices, but he realized suddenly that he wanted her very much to agree to wed him, he wanted to take no chances. He supposed that he didn't mind not being certain why she agreed, only that she would agree.

Thus, he said, "My man, Kron, just returned from Dublin. He was my eyes and ears at the court there. I knew that the king had dealings with your half-brother, but I didn't understand the nature of them. I wanted very much to know."

Rorik drew a deep breath. "Kron told me that King Sitric has negotiated with Einar to buy you, to make you his wife. If you return to Clontarf, you will be given over to the king and Einar will gain even more silver and slaves and power, and you will be abused by an old man." She would still be a queen, but Rorik knew that such a thing would not sway her. Strange, but he knew it to be true.

She stared up at him, surprised and horrified, yet it wasn't so unlike Einar to betray her or anyone else for that matter. But to sell his own half-sister to King Sitric, to that paunchy old man she'd met only once some six months before? He'd smelled of sickness and of age, and any pity she might have had for him vanished when he'd looked at her as would a hungry man at a honey-sweetened almond. He was old enough to be her grandfather; he was old enough to have been dead for many years. She'd borne his fulsome flattery, his old man's touches on her cheek and on her arm, though she'd hated it. She'd remained polite to him, she'd remained respectful, she'd kept her eyes down whenever possible so he couldn't see the distaste she felt for him.

There had been the other old man with him, his advisor, Hormuze, an old man with a long gray beard and brilliant dark eyes that seemed to regard the world with deep cynicism, and a belly as paunchy as that of the old king, who never left his side. Did he have a part in this? By the gods, she would never have dreamed that the king could want her for his wife. Why her? She was not a princess of significant holdings, not a daughter of a great household to woo and hopefully gain in an alliance. It made no sense to her.

"I would protect you," Rorik said, once again speaking when he wanted to keep his mouth shut, but the words just kept rolling out of him. "You would be my wife and safe from both Einar's plotting and the king's lust." He was pleading his case—though he sounded only calm and reasonable—like a lovesick swain, which was ridiculous, but still he didn't like seeing himself in the role of supplicant to a damned woman. He shut his mouth. He'd said enough, more than enough.

She looked up at Rorik, recognized the tension in him, and wondered at it. She also recognized a basic truth deep inside herself. What Einar had done hadn't really pushed her toward wedding with Rorik. No, she'd already decided.

Rorik was indeed a handsome man. She'd seen him naked and found him interesting, more than interesting, truth be told, fascinating. His body was intriguing, so very different from hers, all bronzed and lightly furred with golden hair, his body lean, his strength exciting as it was deadly, aye, those differences were dazzling, they made her eager to know more, to learn things she'd never really considered significant before. He was dangerous and that made her want to test those boundaries as well, for she imagined that it was all tied up in his warrior's essence. He was dangerous and he was vital and she wanted to learn about him, all of him. She smiled at him and watched his eyes widen just a bit. Surely he couldn't know what she'd been thinking.

"I have never before seen you smile," he said as he continued to stare at her. "It makes you look different, softer perhaps. I would also hear you laugh."

"Mayhap you will smile for me soon. Mayhap even laugh for me as well."

He gave her a wary look.

She said now, the smile gone from her face, "You, Lord Rorik, I have tested mightily. The gods know I have pushed you and tormented you and made you want to strangle me. Despite all this, if you wish it, I will wed you, my lord, and I will be constant as the North Star. I will never allow another to harm you as long as I have breath in my body."

Rorik smiled and Mirana found it the most beautiful smile she'd ever seen in her life.

Suddenly, Entti laughed, slapping her hands on her knees, laughing until her eyes teared.

Both Rorik and Mirana stared at her. She laughed louder. The gown slid off her lap to the ground. "Ah," she said, gasping for breath, "it is too much. The two of you are like proud yet noble warriors, uncertain that you aren't still enemies, circling each other. You call for marriage and you strut out all your warrior attributes, admire each attribute in the other, then prattle on about your honor. There is no talk of affection, of caring, only all these manly virtues each of you seek in the other. By all the gods, it is a wondrous amusement, this courting dance you two have performed." She began laughing again, now hugging her sides.

Hafter heard her, frowned, and roared to his feet, striding toward them. "Has she insulted you, Rorik? Shall I punish her? Where is the rope? I shall tie her to me again and drag her about. But it's that woman's fault—she taught Entti bad things, made her smart and loud, then made her hate us and we don't deserve it, she—"

Entti looked up at him through her laughter-teared eyes. "Ah, another big warrior, intent on his own prowess, his lordly rights. Go away, Hafter, you annoy me. Your tongue flays itself with its own stupidity. But first, wish your lord Rorik and Mirana happiness. She will be the lady of Hawkfell Island and your mistress."

Hafter stared at Entti, then looked blankly at Rorik. "You would wed this girl who would have killed you more times than I can count? She who would slit your throat even when you bed her, Rorik? By the gods, she will bite your tongue when you try to kiss her!

She will send her knee into your manhood and bring you low. Aye, she'll unman you and laugh and enjoy herself whilst she does it. Entti was simple but now she isn't. You, Rorik, you were of full wit and thoughtful brain, but now you're quite mad. It is all her fault—this woman with her sin-black hair and her green eyes that hold secrets—she has this mystery about her that makes men and women behave differently, makes them do things they shouldn't do.

"I must fetch your father from Malverne. He will make you see reason. If you lust for her, tie her down to protect yourself, and plow her belly until you tire of her. But do not wed her, Rorik, she will surely do you in."

Entti rose swiftly and leapt at Hafter. She sent her fist into his belly, shouting in his face, "You fool! You are less full-witted than the stoats rutting in the garden! Kerzog has more wit than have you! Have you no heart, no feelings? Did you not listen to Lord Rorik?"

Hafter was again distracted by this new Entti. "Shut your mouth, woman! You are the stupid one. Nay, not stupid, you aren't that, are you? The woman saw to that. You are simply unaware of the woman's hatred for Rorik, for all of us—except she seems to like you and the other women overmuch—which I still don't understand."

"Hafter," Rorik said quietly. "That is enough. I do not need your defense. Enough."

"Nay, it is all passing strange, and you, Rorik, you will awaken on the morrow and wonder what demons possessed you and then you will—"

"Hafter, it is done."

Hafter stared at his friend, a man who was closer to him than his own brothers, a man he'd known all his life. "Rorik, you do not jest?"

Rorik shook his head. He smiled. "Nay, jests are far from my mind. Mirana has accepted me. We will wed on the morrow. We will have a feast and all will be well. You must trust me. If she is willing to, why then, for you, it should be nothing more difficult than breathing. Trust me. I know what I'm doing."

"But her half-brother slaughtered Inga and your children and many of our people!"

"Aye, but she didn't. Why should she shoulder any of the blame? She accepts what Einar is now. She gives her loyalty to me."

But Hafter couldn't accept it. Loyalty from a woman? It sounded preposterous. The woman had been nothing but a thorn, nay, more a bramble or an entire forest of thorns and brambles. He said, "Kron told all of us about the king and how he wants to have the woman as his wife. She could be a queen, Rorik! Why would she want to wed with a simple man like you when she could be a queen and have everything a woman could ever want?

"It makes no sense. So what if King Sitric is old and repellent and will give her no pleasure in her bed? He is still the king and he has power and wealth. You must think about her motives, Rorik. I do not trust her any more than I trust this new Entti the woman created.

"You are being noble, Rorik. You do this only to protect her, don't you? It is nonsense. She needs no protection. Send her back, use her as a lure to get Einar, or is that what is really in your mind? Tell me true, for I must know."

"Hafter, were you to plead my case for me to Mirana, I should have her trying to kill me rather than accepting to wed me. You will be quiet. I have told you the truth. I want this woman. She will be my wife and the mistress of Hawkfell Island. She will be loyal to me, to you, to all of us. I trust her, as you must also. She isn't deceitful, she is honest. She doesn't want to be a queen."

"Ha! You aren't stupid, Rorik, at least you weren't before we had the misfortune to voyage to Clontarf. You captured her and everything has changed. It is beyond too much to understand." He closed his mouth then, only to open it once more, saw Entti frowning at him, and closed it again. He looked at Mirana, who'd said not a word. He really looked at her now, and he saw a young woman who was passing pretty, quite lovely really, small and fine-boned, her flesh as white as newly fallen Vestfold snow, her hair thick and black as a midnight revel. Her eyes were a green color that looked like dark moss, beautiful eyes that were soft and mysterious, aye, there were secrets in those eyes of hers, with the thick black lashes that added to their mystery, and he wondered how he would feel if she looked back at him with warmth and caring in those eyes, and with desire. And she was brave and smart. Ah, but still . . . it wasn't right. It wasn't smart. But there was naught he could do about it. He prayed that Rorik knew well what he was doing. He himself didn't really believe Rorik was doing this to protect her or to somehow use her to capture Einar. Rorik wasn't that kind of man. On the other hand, Hafter had been wrong about a number of things of late. He'd humiliated himself in his wrongness and his head still hurt from it. Only the gods knew what was in the woman's mind and in Lord Rorik's mind.

He looked at Entti, still frowning at him, tense, ready to attack him again, and scratched his head where she'd struck him. Yet another one whose mind was now hidden from him. He didn't like this new Entti. He turned away, shaking his head. He heard Entti say behind him, "That's right, you lout, turn away, go hide, don't face the truth that's staring you in your goat's face!"

He said nothing, though the irritation at her words was great. He walked away, silent and thoughtful.

But it was Hafter, only minutes later, who yelled for silence and gave all their people the news. He sounded enthusiastic. He looked over at Entti and she smiled at him, making him feel like a trained pet who had performed just as she'd wished.

As for the women, they surrounded Mirana, hugging her and kissing her loudly, telling her that finally Lord Rorik had shown good sense. "Aye," Old Alna said, trying to look wise, "finally he's wedded a woman like his mother, wise and kind. Aye, and strong. 'Tis a strong woman Lord Rorik must have for he is a warrior, a Viking, and at the bottom of things, he is a man, and thus rough and untidy, sometimes unmeasured in his talk and actions."

"A good thing I say," Amma said. "You didn't really bind Alna or Asta very tightly, so you don't need to feel guilt about it. They understood. All were proud of you and your cunning."

"Now Gurd will keep to me at night," Asta said, laughing and hugging Mirana. "I am very fond of the new Entti and know now that you won't allow any more married men to abuse their wives with their infidelities."

"I will do my best," Mirana said, smiling at all of them, these women who'd taken care of her and fed her and treated her as one of them, without question. Mirana felt very lucky. She saw Utta standing at the edge of their circle, and quickly drew her in. "I thank you, little one. I am nearly as good a cook as you are." And Utta hugged her close. "Aye, Utta, you and I will deal very well together, never doubt it or my affection for you. Would you be my sister or my daughter?"

All the women laughed at that.

And there was Erna, drawing back, as she always did, but she was smiling, moving slowly closer, her face softly pretty. "Utta must be a sister, I think," she said, looking from little Utta to Mirana, "for none would ever think you her mother."

That night Mirana slept in Rorik's bed. He slept in the outer hall, wrapped in a wool blanket. She happened to see the chain lying next to the bed on the floor. She just looked at it. She didn't touch it.

She smiled. What she was doing was right, she felt it deep inside her.

# 15

THE FOLLOWING DAY dawned warm and sunny. More birds than Mirana had ever seen in her life seemed to have visited the island for their wedding, flying overhead, swooping downward, spinning through the clouds, their keening cries filling the air. It was magical.

It was a perfect day to be married.

Mirana stood opposite Rorik, beneath a sweet-smelling apple tree, her hand held in his across the space between them. His men flanked him, with Hafter at his right hand. The women, led by Old Alna, stood behind her, Entti at her right hand.

The women had done wonders. They'd sent Mirana off to bed the previous night, and immediately made their plans.

Mirana was now wearing a gown of the softest wool, dyed a rich saffron. Her tunic was a pale cream, fastened at her shoulder with two beautifully pounded silver brooches, a gift from Rorik. She wore soft leather slippers on her feet, a gift from Erna, who'd said softly, "I haven't two good hands, but I do have two good feet and they are just your size."

The slippers fit her perfectly. Mirana's hair was loosely plaited, as one would a belt of soft leather, and wound up onto the top of her head with pale saffron-colored linen ribbons threaded through the thick coils.

She felt calm. Her decision was a good one. Even if Rorik were marrying her to forward his revenge against Einar, she didn't care. She still believed him honorable. She held to that thought, now looking at Rorik, who said slowly, his voice deep and sure, "I will take you to wife, Mirana, daughter of Audun. I give you all that is mine and promise you my honor and loyalty and fidelity until I die. Before all our gods and all our people, this I vow."

Some of the men cheered, several slapping him on the back, but most were silent, their eyes on the ground, uncertain and wary. When there was again full silence, all eyes went to Mirana.

"My Lord Rorik," she said, looking up at him, and now she smiled, for he was looking very serious, overly serious, and it charmed her. She'd thought about what she would say to him and to his people, words that were critical to all of them. Her fingers tightened about his. "I come to you with naught save myself and what I am. I will be faithful to you and to your people for as long as I live. I swear to place your welfare above mine own, to honor you as my husband and as the lord of Hawkfell Island, and hold your interests first in my mind. I will never betray you. This I vow before our gods and before all who are here with us."

Now the women cheered, much more loudly than the men, full-bodied cheers that rang out over the island, sending the birds winging upward, shrieking wildly. Kerzog barked madly, danced about the two of them and licked Mirana's feet. She felt pats on her shoulders and back. "Well done," Entti said in her ear.

"Thank you, Mirana," Rorik said. He looked at his men. Then he raised her hand and slipped a small golden band on her middle finger. It was tight. She wondered to whom it had belonged. To his first wife? She made a fist, thrusting her arm high toward the cobalt-blue sky, symbolizing her acceptance and commitment to her marriage with Rorik.

The cheering began again, but not as loud as it could be. The women were shouting their heads off, making up for the men's wariness, Mirana knew, and felt a stab of anger for Rorik because his men were holding back, still uncertain of his decision, looking at her and knowing that she was of their enemy's blood. Rorik took her fist in his hand, gently opened her fingers, and laced his own fingers through hers. He grinned like a happy boy. The men eased, Mirana saw it and felt it. They began to cheer. When Rorik pulled her against him, lifting her high off the ground, his arms wrapped around her, and kissed her long and deep, the men began to laugh and jest. The women giggled and nudged each other. Chickens clucked wildly some feet away. The dozen or so children present looked uncertain, staring from their parents to Mirana and Rorik, then they were laughing and hooting and stomping their feet as loudly as the men and women.

Mirana felt such relief she would have shouted herself, but then what she felt was Rorik's mouth, warm and soft and firm. He wasn't particularly insistent, nay, he wasn't trying to savage her. He was more like an explorer, feeling the texture of her mouth, letting her learn him, taking his time, moving ever so slowly. Mirana, who had never before been kissed, hung there in his arms, relaxed as she could be with her blood crashing through her body, her hands on his shoulders, not understanding what all this was about, this strange concoction of feelings that were rioting in her belly. He said against her lips, "Kiss me, Mirana. It's only right that you do so. You are now my wife, before the gods and before our people, who are finally yelling their throats raw."

"I don't know what to do," she said, her breath warm against his mouth.

"Open your mouth and I will show you."

She did. His tongue slid between her lips. She gasped, wriggled unconsciously, much to the uproarious delight of all their people.

"He already makes her wild. Rorik won't contain his seed until the night falls!"

This was from Aslak, the only one of Rorik's men who truly approved his master's choice, for he'd lived at Clontarf for nearly six months and seen Mirana as she was. He quite liked her, save for her skill with weapons. That, as it should be for any reasonable man, was a bit frightening, for females were unpredictable at the best of times.

"She wriggled like a happy little stoat, she did. Did you see her bottom?"

"Rorik will make her scream with pleasure and all of us will be awake to hear it."

"No longer will he be a sullen bear in the mornings, envying us the moans wrung out of us by our wives. Not with her beside him, ready and eager to make him smile."

Their jests and laughter finally pierced Rorik's brain. Reluctantly, he eased Mirana down the front of his body until she was standing once again on the ground. He started to release her, realized dimly that she wasn't standing on her own, and leaned down to say in her ear, "Mirana, sweeting, we must wait. Come now, and we will let them jest with us and give us impertinent advice. They will drink themselves silly and soon we will be free of their attentions."

She was breathing hard. It was very strange, this difficulty she was having drawing air in and out of her body. And her heart was pounding as if she'd run farther than her body wished to. Her skin felt hot, particularly where his fingers were touching her bare flesh. All of this from a man who was more a stranger than not, and yet she'd just enjoyed having him kiss her, enjoyed having him hold her, enjoyed the strength in his arms and his body pressed hard against hers, and knowing he wouldn't drop her. Ah, more than enjoyment, more than the growing insanity, she'd wanted something that was still a mystery, a deep incredible mystery, a mystery she knew was there, waiting for her, to be granted to her by him.

"Rorik?"

"Aye?"

"I don't understand. Give me another moment, please. I feel quite odd."

He looked like a man who was immensely pleased with himself. His blue eyes were gleaming brighter than the sky. He stood tall and straight, the lord of his domain, and said loudly, "I will give you whatever you wish."

Hafter, who had heard their words, hooted with laughter. He turned to Entti, who was looking at him as though he were naught more than a slug to be ground under her foot. "Hear you that, girl? Rorik is so besotted with her that he offers her anything she wants."

"Well, you needn't worry, conceited oaf, you are quite safe, for never will she want you."

Hafter narrowed his eyes, riled instantly at the mocking in her voice—her very intelligent voice. "I hope she won't want me, for I plan to be very busy with you in my bed. I will keep you to myself for a while. Hear you!"

he shouted, turning to the men. "This wench is mine. You will have to wait!"

Entti spat at him. Right in the eye.

Hafter, normally a man of good sense and fine humor, yowled. This girl, this slave, this vicious witch he'd always treated well and kindly, even patted absently, had spat on him. He grabbed her arms and jerked her up against him and shook her hard until her head snapped back. "Damn you, Entti, I've held you in my arms and given you more pleasure than you deserve!"

"Pleasure, ha! You're naught but an animal, a filthy selfish beast who cares only for himself. You pass me around as you would a platter of boar steaks! Take yourself to the Christian's hell, wretched bastard."

He paused. He frowned down at her. "Do you really think I am selfish?"

"All men are alike, all of you selfish goats."

"I'm not. Surely I gave you pleasure. Surely you must agree with me. And you said I was filthy. No Viking is filthy. I bathe each day in the bathing hut. Yet you must say that I am filthy. What mean you?"

"Let me go, Hafter. You speak a man's nonsense."

"Not until you answer me. You are a slave. You will show me obeisance and respect. You will answer me, you will—"

He had no warning, no clue, though he should have been more careful, for she was no longer the innocent child who'd smiled at him so simply, so sweetly. There was no smile now. She brought up her knee and kicked him in the groin. She caught him squarely. He yowled again and dropped her.

Entti heard his raw moans, saw him drop to his knees and hug himself. She started to run. She saw the men staring at her. Then she stopped, frowned down at his bent head. "I'm sorry," she said, and came down to her haunches in front of him, and placed her hands on his shoulders. "I'm sorry, Hafter, it wasn't well done of me. You are what you are, after all, and I shouldn't have punished you so severely for it."

He moaned, his head still down. Rorik grimaced, for he and every other man could imagine the relentless waves of nausea that were holding Hafter bent down like a frail old man.

Finally, Hafter said, panting, "No, it wasn't well done of you. Ah, I wish you weren't so smart now."

"I'm sorry. I had to protect myself. I will no longer allow you or any man to bed me. I cannot do it. It was difficult for me before, but now, I will not be a whore. If you will promise to restrain yourself and what emerges from your mouth, I promise never to do that again. I am sorry."

"Do you truly not wish to bed me again? Did you truly never wish to bed me? Did you truly never enjoy me?"

"Everyone is listening to you. Be quiet. I shouldn't have blamed you for believing that I would now willingly bed with any of you louts. But it is so. There will be no more of it. Now, stand up, you've mewled quite long enough. You're a man, stand up."

Hafter stood, with difficulty, but he stood. "I never thought of you as a whore, Entti."

"Ha! What then, Hafter? Your beloved mother? A virgin come to Hawkfell Island to be admired and worshiped? Forget not, all you ever had to do was snap your fingers and tell me to part my legs and I did. I will do so no longer. Never again. So, Hafter, if you didn't think of me as a whore, then what?"

He just looked at her. "You were Entti, that's all. You were sweet and gentle and gave me all I wished to have. You never yelled at me in anger."

Entti snorted and turned away from him. "You're a fool," she said. "Keep your distance!"

Mirana and Rorik could only stare, as did all their other people.

"This is passing strange," Rorik said, then clasped Mirana's fingers with his. "Why doesn't Hafter clout her? Why does he just look at her so pathetically? By the gods, he would kill a man if he struck him, much less tried to destroy his manhood."

"He has a care for his hide, though he did sound as though he were dying," Mirana said.

"He was, or at least he prayed that he would. The pain is beyond normal suffering. It is worse than belly cramps, worse than a knife wound in the shoulder. I wonder what he will do to her once he recovers himself sufficiently. Unlike Hafter, when you tried to unman me, I was fast and saved myself from dire pain. Poor Hafter didn't have a chance. Entti still surprises me."

"She cooks very well."

"That doesn't surprise me at all. All you damned women—"

She giggled. It was an odd sound, an unexpected sound. He stared down at her. Slowly, he smiled, showing his even white teeth. Then he leaned down and lightly kissed her mouth.

"Let us go to the food tables and leave Hafter and Entti to sort themselves out."

It was late. The beautiful day had become somber, with dark storm clouds thickening overhead. The wind was whipping up the crops and making the more narrow fir trees bend and sway. The birds had quieted as had the animals and the children. Even Kerzog was still, lying with his big head on his front paws, asleep, for he'd eaten every scrap of food thrown to him, and still begged for more.

The rain began. It was quickly dark. Rorik was smiling like an idiot, Mirana walking at his side, toward his sleeping chamber.

He fastened a rush torch light to the holder in the wall, then turned to face his wife. Her face was flushed for she'd drunk a bit of his small store of wine from the rich vineyards south of the Seine herself. She looked beautiful. She pleased his eyes and his senses. At the moment, he didn't care why he'd married her. If something was done it was done and nothing could change it, a philosophy his sire had dinned in his ears since he was a boy.

It was indeed done, and now he would have her, surely an excellent consequence of this marriage.

"I have only one other gown," Mirana said, fingering the fine cream wool of her overtunic. "This beautiful tunic and gown I will pack in your trunk. I was careful not to stain it."

"Aye, you were," he said. "Let me remove the brooches for you. It is one of Asta's gowns, from many years ago. She told me she'd been saving it, for what she didn't know, just that she was far too stout to wear it now."

"The women have all been more than kind to me."

"Aye. I didn't understand it. Perhaps someday one of you will explain it to me. But it is good now that you are my wife and their mistress."

As he unfastened the brooches, Mirana said, "I have no weapons."

"No, you don't. But I do."

"I always had my own knife, since I came to Clontarf. Gunleik gave it to me."

"Ah, the one you used to prick my throat?"

She nodded.

"If you don't wish to use it to torment me or to flay the flesh from me, then what is your reason for having it?"

He laid the brooches on top of his chest, and stepped back to watch her as she eased the tunic down over her hips, stepped out of it, and carefully folded it. He watched her lay it gently in his chest, placing the brooches on top of it.

She straightened then and turned to say very seriously, "It was just a part of what I wore every day, like my gown or my shoes."

"You're a woman."

"Aye," she said, standing very close to him now, her gown very much still in place. "This is very strange, Rorik. Are you certain about the king? Would Einar truly have dishonored me by selling me to him?"

"That is what Kron said." He waited, wishing she would tell him that her fear of that hadn't pushed her into marriage with him. She said nothing. Well, he'd given her an excellent reason for accepting him, and if it had been her reason, why then, it was his own fault, his own doing. She slipped off her shoes and toed them across the floor until they were lying against the trunk.

She looked up at him then. "Many girls are sold in marriage, their consent unimportant. Perhaps Einar thinks he honors me. The man is, after all, a king. Perhaps—"

"Don't weave a false thread, Mirana. Einar had no more notion of honoring you than would a bear."

"You're right. If he believed it would honor me, why then, he would have told me, bragged of his negotiations to me, of his brilliance. He kept silent."

"Enough of your half-brother. There are other things I wish you to consider this night."

She started to pull off her gown, then stopped. She looked at him straightly. "When you brought me here you stripped down my gown and looked at me. You played with me, but there was no enjoyment, either for you or for me. It was awful. Will you do that again?"

He gave her a fascinated look. He was remembering her breasts, their softness, their weight. "Aye, but it will be different this time. There will be play between us, but it will give you much pleasure."

She was silent for a long moment, standing motionless. Then she waved her hand about her, toward the bed, toward the clothing trunk that stood at the foot of the box bed. "You have been married before. You had a wife and babes. You know what all this is about. You slept with a woman every night and awoke with her every morning. You must have known her habits and everything else about her. You understand things that I don't yet even comprehend. It makes me nervous, Rorik. It makes me feel as helpless as a warrior who has no weapons."

He saw Inga in that moment, her hair a rich golden blond, shining as brightly as ripe barley in the bright sunlight. She was frowning at him, her pale blue eyes narrowed fiercely, angry at something he'd done or something he'd said. He couldn't remember. Odd that he would remember a frown and not a smile, but the gods and men knew that life was filled with both. Should he tell Mirana that? They would fight, but they would hopefully find pleasure and joy in each other as well. No, she would discover it for herself. She'd already known rage at him. If he gave her joy with him now, it would balance the scales. And he wanted those scales balanced. He wanted them well tilted.

"What did you say? Oh, you speak of intimacy between a man and a woman. You worry about my experience and your inexperience. It will not matter in a little while, for we will begin that intimacy right now, Mirana. Come here and I will help you off with that gown. It is lovely and you are lovely wearing it. I do not remember Asta ever being so slender, but I suppose she was when she was a girl."

Mirana didn't want to be naked in front of him but she didn't see there was a choice. Too, since he'd already had a wife, he knew what was to be done and when it was to be done. She would have to trust him. Once the gown was neatly folded in his trunk, once she stood there wearing only a soft cotton shift, he smiled down at her. "Sit on the bed and I'll free your hair from the ribbons and braids."

She did as she was bid. His fingers were gentle, and when he splayed his fingers to comb them through the braids, smoothing her hair into loose ripples down her back, she smiled up at him.

"That feels better. My head feels lighter."

"Now your shift."

"I would prefer it if you would take off your clothes first, Rorik."

He grinned at her, stepped back, and stripped off his clothes very very quickly. He stood there naked, letting her look her fill at him. "You've already seen me," he said, when she remained quiet and staring for a very long time. He began to fidget. Did she find him repellent? He drew himself up straighter. He was a man and his body was very different from hers. He was large and hairy and his rod, swelled now and jutting toward her, might frighten a maid.

"But it is different now," she said, still staring at his belly and his groin.

"I suppose it is," he agreed, and kept his arms at his sides, but it was difficult to remain still with her just looking and looking at him, unmoving. His member swelled more, he couldn't help that, and seeing her looking at him so intently, so very absorbed in what she was seeing, made him only bigger. "Your shift, Mirana," he said at last.

"Could you please douse the rush light?"

He shook his head. "Nay. A husband has rights. One of them is to see his wife, to see all of her, in every fine detail, to study her and her endowments, so that he will have no questions, no doubts, about his acquisition."

"Just as you're letting me see if my acquisition pleases me?"

"If you will, though the comparison isn't much to my liking."

"Nor to mine."

"Then neither of us will be acquisitive this night," he said, and walked to the bed. "We will be a man and a woman coming together for the first time. There is magic in that, Mirana, and in the future if we are fortunate."

"I think it is good fortune that brought you to me," she said, and held out her arms to her husband.

For an instant, he thought of the misery that had been responsible for bringing him to Clontarf. But that was over now and he wouldn't let the past touch them.

He smiled at her, at his wife.

RORIK KNEW WHAT he should do. She was right, he was a man who'd had his share of women, enjoying them as he trusted they'd enjoyed him as well, and much more than that, he'd had a wife, and she'd been a virgin when they'd first come together, so he should be completely confident in himself. He should know when he should do what and how he should do it and for how long. Aye, this night was the beginning of their life together. He'd spoken smoothly to her; he'd spoken with sincerity, and gently. He was scared to death.

He wasn't ready for it, not for any of it. With all her strength, Mirana was still helpless against him. She knew naught of what was to come. Thus, he thought, he would simply try to enjoy himself and her and hope that she would come to him willingly. He didn't want to hurt her.

He pulled the shift over her head, then took a step back to look at her. He'd seen her naked in the bathing hut, and he'd looked his fill at her then. He'd fondled her breasts, to torment her, to punish her, but not for pleasure, she'd been right about that. But this, by all the gods, this was different. This was his wife and there was no anger in him now, and none, he prayed, in her toward him.

But she was hesitant, she had misgivings about him and his body and what would happen, and he saw it. He would go slowly. That was the only thing he could make his mind comprehend at this moment.

His eyes fell from her face to her breasts to her belly. He was, he realized, staring at her as intensely as she had stared at him. He was the one who knew what would happen so it wasn't well done of him to scare her now by looking at her like a hungry wolf.

"You are very nice," he said, forcing his eyes back to her face. "You are pleasing to me."

"Thank you," she managed. "You are too, Rorik. You're very different from me."

That made him laugh. He crossed the few feet between them and pulled her into his arms, pressing his hands against her buttocks to bring her firmly against him. "Ah," he whispered, feeling all of her, and knowing deep inside that it was good, beyond good, and that it was right. His hands came up her back, and he felt the suppleness of her, the narrowness of her waist, as he stroked the soft flesh, feeling the lithe muscles. He hugged her, kissing her ear. Then he took her face between his hands, drawing her up, and he kissed her, very gently, light nipping kisses.

"You feel very strange to me, Rorik," she said, her breath warm in his mouth and very sweet from the wine she'd drunk. "I like your mouth especially."

He laughed. "A woman who knows her own mind. That pleases me too. Now, kiss me. That's right, open your mouth and give me your tongue."

Mirana was glad she didn't hesitate, for the feelings that stormed through her when his tongue touched hers made every uncertain thought flee her mind. She gave herself to him in that moment, gave him herself and her trust, and Rorik felt her acceptance. It amazed him and astounded him and made him want to fall to his knees and thank Thor and Odin All-Father and especially Frey, who would surely bless their union with many children.

He kissed her, holding her head in his hands, feeling her soft hair, stroking through the deep ripples, and growing harder by the instant.

He pressed against her, never releasing her, until she fell back onto the box bed. He came over her, his knees gently opening her thighs. He came down between her legs, felt her breasts soft against his chest, felt his member pressing hot and hard against her woman's flesh.

He dimly realized that she was lying very still beneath him. He was going too rapidly for her. She was a woman, slower to peak in her desires than a man, and more than that, she was a virgin, untried in the ways of men and women. He forced himself to draw up onto his elbows. He looked down at her breasts, soft and white as her belly, and closed his eyes against the intense pleasure as he pushed himself against her. He felt the warmth of her, the smoothness of her flesh, the lingering softness of her thighs and her belly.

He watched her as she closed her eyes. Very slowly, she pressed upward.

Rorik groaned, fell on her and kissed her until both of them were panting for breath. It shouldn't be possible, but it was. He wanted her so badly, he knew he'd spill his seed if he didn't have her, now, at this very instant. "Mirana, I must have you now. Will you accept me?"

She stared up at him, knowing what he would do, but still just looking at him, at his beautiful eyes that were glazed with his need, at the flush on his cheeks. She stroked her hands down his back to his buttocks.

Very slowly, she opened her thighs wider.

"Aye, Rorik," she said, nothing more, and he went wild with her acceptance of him, rearing back, pressing her thighs wider apart, and then he was staring at her woman's flesh, his fingers there, parting her, and he was breathing so hard he thought his heart would burst within his chest, but he didn't care, he only wanted to come inside her and stay there until he . . .

"Mirana," he moaned, and slowly came into her. "By all the gods, it is too much." Coming into her was more than he'd thought it could possibly be, though what he'd thought, if anything reasonable, he didn't remember. Her warmth, the smallness of her, made gaining entrance difficult and this tightness chaffed his flesh, making him mad with lust, but he held himself in control, going very slowly, now watching her face, seeing her begin to feel the pain he couldn't prevent, seeing her want to pull away from him even though she didn't move, and he tried to draw back just a bit, but she lifted her hips, now biting her lower lip in her pain, but he came in more deeply and he couldn't have pulled out of her had the longhouse been afire. *Slowly,* he repeated to himself over and over, he must go slowly. He mustn't savage her. He finally felt her maidenhead, and he shoved against it, going out of his mind now, lust pounding through him, shoving at him, making him want to thrust deep into her, so deep he would be at her womb and he would feel all of her and *know* her, actually be a part of her for a few precious moments. By the gods, it was impossible not to thrust with all his strength now, to breach that barrier that kept her from him, that kept him from his ultimate knowledge of her. And so he did, throwing his head back, thrusting deep, hearing her cry above the pounding of his heart, above the mad swirling of his blood throughout his body, hard and driving and hot, and he was deep inside her, pressing frantically against her womb, and he knew he couldn't wait, simply couldn't hold back for another moment, another instant.

She felt him tensing over her and opened her eyes. He was arched back, all his weight on his hands, the muscles bulging and knotting in his arms, and the cords in his throat strong and working wildly, and he was moaning, deep raw moans, and then he was tearing into her and crying out as if he were dying. She felt the wet of his seed then, felt him stiffen with the power of his release.

He almost fell on top of her, but managed at the last moment to keep some of his weight from her. He was breathing heavily, his body sweating and limp against her.

*A man's pleasure,* she thought, but didn't begrudge him his short eternity of madness. The pain had lessened, it was nearly nothing now. Only a weak fool would bemoan the discomfort. He wasn't so full inside her now and there was his wetness to ease her. She felt herself begin to relax beneath him, though his weight flattened her into the feather mattress. She lightly touched her palms to his back and his shoulders. She threaded her fingers through his thick hair, and tugged.

He raised his head and looked down at her, his eyes beautiful and quite vague.

"I want you to kiss me," she said.

He smiled and did. For a very long time. Until she realized that he wasn't inside her any longer, that he seemed oblivious of what he was doing.

She gently shoved at him. He gave her another vague look and rolled onto his side. His arm fell over her belly, his fingertips lightly stroking her pelvic bone. In the next moment, he was deeply asleep. Mirana moved his arm to his side, then came up on her elbow to stare down at him, this time enjoying her freedom to study him, without him watching her, without him knowing she was looking her fill at him. His member was flaccid, wet from himself and from her, and now nestled in the thick golden hair at his groin. She saw blood on herself and on him and knew it was from the rending of her maidenhead. She felt no fear. She continued to stare at him. Strange that he could change and grow so very much in such a short time.

Lightly, she splayed her palm on his belly. The feeling of the crisp golden hair, the dampness of his flesh, the unconscious clenching of his muscles beneath her fingers, it all delighted her. Very lightly, her fingers touched him, gently encircled him, but when he suddenly moaned, deep in his throat, his hips coming up, she released him. He quieted again.

She leaned down and lightly kissed his mouth. She was quite pleased that she'd married him. This part of it hadn't been so very bad, aye, the kissing she had much enjoyed and, too, his strength. She admired strength. But to have his strength bring her pleasure was beyond what she'd ever imagined. The rest of it was interesting, and she accepted it. She also knew there wouldn't be the rending pain the next time they came together. He had gained much pleasure, of that she had no doubt.

She was glad she had pleased him. She was glad she had pleased him so much he'd fallen off her and dropped into a deep sleep. She'd brought a mighty warrior low with his lust, and she was a female of no experience.

She felt somewhat proud of herself. She'd never before imagined this sort of power a woman could wield over a man. She wondered if it would always be so. She thought of Einar's two mistresses, silly sheep, both of them. She doubted that he thought of them beyond the pleasure they gave him. She doubted they had ever held any power over him.

Mirana looked down at her husband again. She wished he would wake up. She wanted to kiss him again.

When she woke again, Mirana was sprawled on her back, her legs spread, and he was between them, staring down at himself and at her, as he pushed inside her. The sleeping chamber was dim with early morning light. She stared up at him, not understanding for a moment, then she realized that he was scarcely awake himself, his eyes closed, his body full on her now, his sex hard inside her, moving in and out, until before she even had a chance of bringing his head down so she could kiss him, he was arching, his head thrown back, and his seed was deep inside her once again. Nothing more than that and it was done. So little warning, no kisses at all, just him over her, deep inside her, and it was done.

She frowned, tightening her hands on his shoulders.

He awoke completely from one instant to the next. He stared down at himself, now pulling out of her body, feeling the profound lethargy that followed release. Then he looked at his wife, saw her frowning in confusion, and shook his head at himself, trying to clear away the sleep from his mind, the pleasant dreams that had brought him to take her again, trying to understand the pleasure that had been so intense he'd lost himself completely in it and failed her of course, falling asleep like a dolt. And now he'd done it again, not even fully awake, he'd come into her. He'd never done that in his life.

He'd taken her again without giving her anything in return. It wasn't well done of him.

Rorik swung over to the side of the bed. He stood and stretched. He saw the wet of his seed on his member and her virgin's blood. He said, "I hurt you last night and I'm sorry for it. Did I hurt you again now?"

He had, but not that much. "I was asleep," she said. "You woke me but then you were through with me. It seems to be a very fast thing, Rorik. Is it always so speedily accomplished?"

"Nay. I'm sorry for it. It was strange. A man normally knows what he is doing, enjoys looking forward to doing it, for it involves all of him, not just his sex. Nay, a good man, one with control and experience, can pleasure his wife for hours, not just the minutes I gave to myself. Come, let's go to the bathing hut. I'll bathe you and you can steam away the soreness."

Even as she lay on her back on the warm oak bench, sweating in the steam-filled hut, she knew he wanted her yet again, for his sex was jutting outward, and he seemed in pain, the flesh of his cheekbones drawn tight, but he was controlling himself. He'd even moved to the other side of the chamber, and lay there on his belly, not looking at her.

When he caught her by surprise, dumping a bucket of cold water on her, she bounded up, shrieking, then laughing, for it felt wonderful. She returned the favor, and he yelled just as loudly as she had, shaking himself like a mongrel.

Asta had prepared porridge for breakfast. Entti had made fresh bread. Utta had churned butter. Erna was spinning, using only her one whole arm, her motions smooth and graceful. Kerzog had slept atop Raki the entire night, snoring in his face, and Erna had just laughed and bade her husband not to complain, for he was the only warrior strong enough to bear Kerzog's weight.

All this was told to Mirana by Old Alna the moment she and Rorik stepped out of the bathing hut. All the men were still within, waiting, it seemed, for Lord Rorik to show himself. Thus, when Rorik and Mirana came into the longhouse from their bath, there was a moment of silence, then knowing looks and some laughter, and more of the seemingly endless advice.

Rorik looked momentarily annoyed, then he shrugged and smiled. He wrapped a long tress of her damp hair around his fingers. "So very black," he said. "Rich and deep as the night." He raised the tress to his mouth, stroking it over his lips. He inhaled the scent. "Sweet," he said. "I dislike the braids. Leave your hair long and free."

She smiled up at him. "Very well."

"Ah, she becomes easier than a babe in arms," Gurd said, chewing on a piece of warm bread. "But be careful of her, Rorik, do not forget that she is capable of killing a man after she bestows a smile upon him."

"Rorik always tames his women," Sculla said, looking down at them from his nearly seven-foot height. "This one would be no different."

"You men," Amma said, standing on her tiptoes to cuff her husband's head. "I prefer—all the women do—to think it's Lord Rorik who is tamed."

"Nay," said Aslak, " 'tis Lord Rorik who understands where the power lies here, and he will teach his wife obedience even as he gives her smiles."

"All of you will hold your tongues," Rorik said. "She

is at ease at the moment, but if you needle her pride, she will stick a knife in my gullet. Show her respect else I'll be the one to suffer for it."

There was more good-natured laughter. Rorik joined his men. Old Alna filled a wooden bowl with porridge, poured honey over it, and took it to the master. She cackled when she gave him the bowl. "Aye, a fine time you had last night! The little mistress made you into a limp fish, didn't she?"

"How would you know? I saw you snoring in the corner yesterday, your mouth on its hinges so wide flies were buzzing about your remaining teeth. You didn't even awaken when Kerzog barked in your face."

But Old Alna just laughed and laughed, then spat on the packed earth.

Mirana stood there by the fire pit, the heat pouring off the burning embers making her sweat, uncertain what to do. She was the mistress here, but all had been taken care of. She looked for Entti, finding her at last by Asta, who was standing next to Erna, winding the warp on the upright loom. Entti stood on her other side, loading a shuttle with thread from a distaff. Rorik was with his men. Even Kerzog was at his place at Rorik's feet, his big head resting on his paws. Should she join him? Aye, she thought. She was his wife and mistress of Hawkfell. She belonged here. She belonged next to her husband.

He was seated in his ornately carved chair, his bowl settled on his thigh. She sat next to him on the wide bench that lined the wall of the longhouse, and listened to him speaking with Kron, the man who'd come from King Sitric's court in Dublin, the man who'd told him of Einar's treachery, the man who had probably, with his news, been responsible for Rorik wedding her. She accepted that. She wasn't silly or a lovestruck maiden. She respected Rorik, even found his body—ungoverned though it be—quite to her liking, and it was enough.

Kron shut his mouth when he saw her.

# 17

RORIK FROWNED AT him. "Come, Kron, I wish the details. Tell me."

Kron merely nodded toward Mirana.

"I wish to hear them as well," she said, her chin going up. "Since it is my brother's treachery, it is my right."

"He is your half-brother," Rorik said. "Do not taint yourself overly with his blood. Tell us both, Kron."

Kron still looked uncertain. "With her gone, and once the king learns of it, he will kill Einar, or rather his advisor, Hormuze, will have Einar killed. From all I saw, it is Hormuze who decides who is to do what and when, the king included. His influence is very strong, this foreigner with his strange name and his long gray beard and his mystic's eyes."

"No!" Rorik's anger was clear and bright. He slammed his fist against his thigh. "No, he cannot. Einar is mine. By all the gods, I will have him. I must have him."

Kron sat forward, his voice pitched low. "Nonetheless, what I have said is true. My lord, I do not believe that Hormuze or the king will accept any excuses from Einar. Sitric grows old and he is greedy, and he is desperate for sons. He is desperate for the renewed youth Hormuze promises him. Hormuze is more a mystic than an advisor, and he's convinced the king that he will have renewed youth. He has convinced the king that he must have the woman—this woman, Mirana, daughter of Audun—by the first day of the fall, so that her youth and her purity will cleanse him, make him healthy again, restore his vigor. He prophesied that September was the month to wed her. The woman had to be her—Mirana, daughter of Audun—no other virgin would do. He promised the king she would bear him sons, proud and strong and brave. The king believes him, doubt it not, and thus, when you were at Clontarf hoping to find Einar, Einar was in Dublin, at the king's behest, making his contracts and his agreements.

"I chanced to overhear this old man, Hormuze, talking to one of his private guard. He said that he would pay a visit at the end of the summer to Einar and take her then. He doesn't trust Einar either, though he gave no reasons for his distrust. He said he knew she would be safe until the fall. He said he knew Einar could have no overweening desire for her, after all.

"And then he laughed and laughed, an old man's bloated laugh. I assume he laughed because she is of Einar's blood, but still, I don't understand it, not really. There is naught more, my lord."

Rorik ate his porridge in thoughtful silence. Finally, he said, "You have done well, Kron. You will visit your family now?"

Kron's wife and three babes all lived just beyond the salt marshes on a large farm owned by Kron's parents.

"Aye, my lord, if it pleases you. When you act against Einar, you will have me fetched?"

"I will."

Rorik turned to Mirana once Kron had left them. "The porridge is good."

"Aye."

"It is odd," he said after a moment, staring off toward his men, who were eating their porridge or playing with the children or polishing their swords. "The king or this foreign advisor of his, Hormuze, will doubtless kill Einar, if they can, thus saving me from the risk of trying again. Ah, Mirana, I cannot allow it. You understand, do you not? It is I who must wipe his life's blood on my hands. I must be the one to speed him to his coward's death, and spill his blood in the earth. All those he butchered demand that I avenge them."

She understood him very well. She nodded. She ate her last bite of porridge. "Do you yet have a plan?"

He shook his head.

"It doesn't matter yet. You heard Kron say that the king and Hormuze wouldn't move till the end of summer. Perhaps the old king will die before then. He is very old, Rorik. I met both the king and Hormuze earlier this year. They were both old. Very old. I disliked the king."

Suddenly he grinned at her. "I've heard he's wicked enough to outlive us all. In wickedness he is old, but not overly so in his years. A man overaged with guile and battles and treachery. But enough of him for the moment. Perhaps you and I could spend a little time learning about each other, about what it is like to have me for your husband. What say you?"

Her voice was firm and strong, her eyes on his mouth. "I would like that, Rorik."

"Mirana," he said, his voice low, warning. "Look not at me like that. It is early morning and there is much to be done. I must see to the fields and to hunting. Also when you and Entti stole one of my warships, you damaged it. I must see to its repairs."

"I know, but it is not badly damaged, merely the one plank came loose when we pulled the boat ashore. Ah, look, there is Hafter going to Entti. I wonder what she will do to him."

"Or he to her."

"Do you believe Hafter is agile enough in his brain to outsmart her?"

"You females," Rorik said, and stood. "None of you is to be trusted." He grunted, then leaned down and kissed her mouth, and strode out of the longhouse, shouting for his men as he went.

Mirana stood still as a statue, staring down the winding path to the sea. Rorik stood on the end of the long wooden dock with a dozen of his men and a dozen more men she'd never seen before, laughing and talking, a line of bass held in his right hand, and in his left hand, he held a girl's hand, a long graceful hand, and the girl was beautiful with her white-blond hair to her waist, thick and curling, nearly silver beneath the brilliant sun, and her slender body that was fully endowed, her breasts so full they strained against the soft linen tunic she wore.

She was laughing as she looked up at him. Behind her were an older man and woman, and one younger man. They all resembled each other, but then again, Mirana thought, they were Vikings and they were all blond and blue-eyed, tall and strong. Only she was the different one—like her Irish mother, short with hair as black as a lump of coal.

"Ah," said Old Alna, at Mirana's shoulder. "They've come. I wondered if they would visit this summer. That's Rorik's mother, Tora, and father, Harald, and his younger brother, Merrik. Aye, he has only your years, Mirana, but a great warrior he will be. His passions run strong, stronger than Lord Rorik's, for he yet has to learn to control them. The girl is Sira—look how beautiful she's become. Even more beautiful than before. Ah, a little princess, that one, proud and knows her own worth."

"Who is she?"

"Rorik's cousin, daughter of Dorn, brother of Rorik's father. Her mother died birthing her, her father was killed on a raid to Kiev. Lord Rorik's parents took her in. She must be all of eighteen summers now. That is your age, is it not? Ah, what a pretty she is."

"She seems very fond of Rorik."

Old Alna gave her a sideways look, then gave her now familiar scrappy shrug followed by an arcing spit that landed at the base of a yew bush. She patted Mirana's arm as she said, "She thought to wed with Rorik after Inga died. She was there, wanting Rorik, quite willing to wed with him, aye, I think she even sought out his bed, but his grief held him apart, his grief and his rage and guilt, and he refused to have her. You must never doubt him, Mirana, for now he has you."

"Aye," Mirana said, "now he has me." She turned away and walked down the path to greet her new relatives. She was aware of Old Alna's rheumy eyes following her.

She saw Rorik suddenly pick the girl up in his arms, hug her tightly and whirl her about. The line of bass fell to the ground, to be picked up by his brother, who was laughing and shaking his head.

She watched Rorik kiss the girl on her laughing mouth. She kept walking down the path, feeling very much like an outsider. There was a smile on her mouth. It didn't reach her eyes.

* * *

Mirana slowly walked inside the low timbered barn that stood just behind the longhouse. There was sufficient hay for the six cows, the two oxen, the two horses and three goats. Ploughshares were stacked neatly against one wall. There were iron blades for the ploughs and axes to chop wood and clear the fields. She'd escaped here, she knew it, freely admitted it to herself. She stood there in the middle of the dimly lit barn, simply staring at the hay spilling over the top of the wooden troughs. It was early summer, warm sunlit days, with enough rain to make the crops grow fully.

"You are wed to Rorik."

Mirana looked up to see Sira, so beautiful in her fairness, her face framed in a fall of silver hair, that it hurt to look at her. She was alone. She must have followed me here, Mirana thought. "Aye," Mirana said, "we were wed only yesterday."

"I know. I had wished to make our yearly visit earlier this time, for I am old enough to be wed, but Rorik's mother fell ill and thus . . ." She shrugged, but her eyes weren't at all accepting. They were deep and hot with rage. She looked Mirana up and down, and the rage was momentarily banked. "You look like a foreign slave. I have never cared for dark-haired women. I have always believed they look coarse, overly used."

Mirana walked back outside, Sira on her heels. She looked beyond her toward a splendid flock of goldeneyes, ducks who dove into the sea with more skill than any other bird. "I am pleased that Rorik's family is here. They seem kind."

Suddenly, without warning, Sira grabbed Mirana's wrist and jerked her toward her, twisting viciously. She was stronger than she looked. Mirana was but inches from her face, and so surprised by the girl's actions that she didn't move.

"Listen to me, slut, you have somehow tricked Rorik into wedding with you. You are coarse and common and you parted your legs for him and now you carry his child and that is why he felt he had to marry you. But he will see what you are, he will realize that his parents—aye, his entire family—hate what you are, whose blood it is that flows through you, and he will send you away, very soon now. His parents were kind to you, for they were pleased that at last Rorik seems content with life, and they want him to be content, to find some peace, but at the same time they will never forget their grief for Inga and his babes, and nor will Rorik, not really, not in the depths of him. They won't allow him to either, not until the man who butchered them is dead.

"Even though they wanted me for their new daughter, they were willing to accept you until they realized who you were—the black-haired witch who is blooded with our enemy, aye, they know now who you are, they ask themselves if you knew about your brother's deeds, if you approved of them. They will see to it that you are returned to your brother."

She leaned closer, and her breath was hot and sweet on Mirana's face. "Or perhaps Rorik will kill you. Perhaps I will kill you. But you will be gone, witch, soon you will be gone. Then Rorik will be mine as he should have been."

Sira flung Mirana away from her, turned on her heel and walked back to the longhouse. She didn't look back.

Mirana stood there rubbing her wrist. She realized quickly enough that Sira had spoken the truth, for when she returned to the longhouse, knowing it was her responsibility to see that a feast was properly prepared for her new family, she saw it on their faces when she came inside. There was coldness now where there had been warmth and acceptance before. There was now contempt and hatred where there had been smiles and kind words and welcome.

Rorik's brother, Merrik, filled with passion, Old Alna had told her, looked on the edge of violence as he gazed at her. He stopped his talk with Gurd and stared at her, his look malignant. His hand went to the knife belted to his waist. Harald and Tora, Rorik's parents, stopped speaking to Rorik when they saw her, and there was stillness on his mother's face, utter frozen stillness. Harald's face, so much like Rorik's, lean and strong and expressive, was now empty of any feeling that she could see. He lowered his blue eyes—eyes the same vivid bright blue as Rorik's—as if he couldn't bear to look upon her.

She waited for Rorik to do something, anything, to stop this madness, this injustice, but he remained still and silent as his parents.

Entti came to her, and smiled. "I have seen to the preparations of the boar steaks and the hare and line of bass. We also will have a lot of beer and a bit of wine from the Rhine. There are vegetables aplenty—stewed onions and mushrooms, cabbage, and turnips that Utta—that sweet child and now your little sister—seasoned with cloudberries and a strange liquid she squeezes from the roots of this bush whose name I don't know. She just smiled and wouldn't tell me, said it was one of her mother's secrets. Ah, and there is flatbread, hot and ready for thick goat cheese—"

It was too much. Mirana laid her hand on Entti's arm. "Thank you, Entti. You are kind, but it won't help."

Entti cursed softly, saying, "It was Gurd who told them. He is angry with you, afraid that you will keep him from taking me. He rants on about how he is a man and you are naught but a woman and I am naught but a slave."

Mirana said nothing. She was watching Rorik, who had turned away from her and was speaking low to his parents. His younger brother had joined them. Sira stood nearby, a wooden cup of mead in her hand. She was smiling as she stared into the cup.

Old Alna came to Mirana then and said, "We will begin to feed everyone shortly. Lord Rorik will give his chair to his father. And then—"

"Do what is normally done," Mirana said. "I will sit by my husband," she added. If he had changed his mind, then she would know it now.

She went to their sleeping chamber and changed into the gown and tunic she'd worn the previous day at her wedding. It was the only gown she had that was fine enough for a feast. She belted it at her waist. She combed her hair with the antler comb Rorik had given her. She fastened the beautiful brooches Rorik had given her to the tunic. She pinched her cheeks and changed into soft leather slippers. She drew a deep breath and walked out into the big hall again.

The air was filled with the tangy smell of the sea bass, wrapped and baking in oiled maple leaves. The boar steaks spat and sizzled atop the grating of the fire pit. The goat cheese, freshly made, smelled tart.

The men were drinking steadily, the women as well, though not as quickly for it was their job to serve the food, and they had to keep their wits about them to carry the heavy platters. Rorik sat beside his father. Sira sat on his other side and next to her, his mother, Tora. She wondered what was in his mother's mind. Her stillness made Mirana uneasy. Old Alna had told Mirana that she was much like Tora. She didn't see any likeness, not a bit. The remaining places at the table held his brother and all Harald's men. There were no other women save Sira and his mother, Tora. All Rorik's people sat together, away from Harald's. She assumed this was simply the way of things. Rorik had granted his father and all his men the best places in the longhouse. Mirana smiled at the slaves and the wives who were serving with them. She picked up a tray of mutton and leeks and walked to the table. She took it to Rorik and held it out to him.

"My lord," she said.

He looked at her then, though she knew he didn't want to. In that moment she saw such pain in his eyes that she nearly gasped aloud. Instead, she said calmly, "Would you like some mutton? Entti prepared it."

"Aye," he said, no emotion in his voice, his eyes blank of feeling. "It looks excellent."

She served him, saying nothing, then turned to his father. "My lord Harald," she said, and offered him the platter.

Harald didn't look at her. Indeed, he turned away from her completely and spoke to Merrik, his voice overloud. "You will go trading to Kiev soon now, boy. Press me not just at this time. Soon you will go, I promise you."

Sira said loudly, "I wish some. Don't just stand there gawking at me. Serve me."

Mirana looked at the girl, then looked down at her wrist. There were purple bruises where Sira had gripped her so tightly, then twisted.

"Why do you just stand there? Do you not understand me? Are you witless? Serve me now."

"I have learned from my husband," Mirana said loud enough so that all would hear her, "that rudeness can be dealt with simply and practically, with no undue anger or insult."

She dumped the platter of mutton and leeks on Sira's head, turned on her heel, and walked out of the longhouse, paying no heed to the shrieks and wails of fury and outrage behind her. She thought she heard Amma laugh, but she couldn't be certain. She did hear Kerzog bark loudly, and could easily imagine the huge mongrel trying to lick the mutton from Sira's face.

That image made her smile.

IT WAS COLD and becoming colder still, the sky black with turbulent clouds, roiling and bursting against each other, harbinger of a violent storm to come. The wind was whipping the waves against the rocks below her, sending plumes of spray thirty feet upward only to crash downward again hard and fast, the sound of mad thunder. She felt the cold mist on her cheeks and stepped back from the cliff edge. She shivered and rubbed her arms but didn't even think of returning to the longhouse and the pandemonium she'd left behind her.

She grinned suddenly, the picture of Sira shrieking like a witch, as leeks and mutton thick with gravy slithered off her head and face and onto her gown, ah, it was a vision that would probably stay with her until she died. Without a doubt, Mirana had made an enemy.

But Sira was already an enemy.

What would Rorik do?

She felt a shaft of pain slice through her belly. Her marriage of one day—surely a hopeful beginning—had collapsed into a pile of cold ashes.

She saw his pain again in her mind's eye, unguarded in that instant, such pain she couldn't comprehend.

What would he do now? Would he send her away? Kill her?

"The little princess is still shrieking like a goat, with Rorik's mother trying to calm her. There is laughter, but it is muffled behind hands. Kerzog holds no respect for her plight. He is trying to lick the gravy from her neck and face."

Mirana turned to smile at Entti. "Kerzog is an excellent dog. You shouldn't have come out here, Entti, though I'm glad you're here. You know, I am the stranger here, not any of them. I am the outsider. No one owes me loyalty; no one owes me anything."

"Don't be a fool, Mirana. You are the mistress of Hawkfell Island. Rorik owes you loyalty as do all the people here. He swore his loyalty to you before all the people. Were it only Sira, the women would not hesitate to openly show you their loyalty and affection. It is Rorik's mother who holds them back. They respect her and don't wish to hurt her. They don't understand her hatred for you; they say she refused to let the pain fall away from her. She nurtured the pain, both she and Harald. Still, it doesn't matter. You are the mistress here, none other, and soon his mother and father and that wretched Sira will be gone."

"My being mistress here—I believe that is now in question."

"Did Rorik really dump food on you?"

"Aye, I taunted him and he retaliated. Not on my head, but just on my lap. 'Tis better than striking someone, and I wanted to hit her, Entti, I wanted to hit her very much. But the leeks slogging down her face—it was a nice sight."

Entti grinned. "Aye, it was."

Mirana looked out to sea for a moment, then looked again at Entti, saying low, "Is Lord Rorik angry?"

Entti wrapped her cloak more closely around her. It was, actually, naught more than a ragged piece of wool, and Mirana frowned at it. Entti would have a real cloak on the morrow. She started to say something about that then closed her mouth. She had no idea if she would even be the mistress of Hawkfell Island on the morrow.

"I don't know what he is. There is something going on here I don't understand, Mirana. Oh, I know that Gurd told them all about you being Einar's sister, but this hatred for you—it makes no sense to me. They don't wish to give you a chance. And Lord Rorik—"

"They have reminded him of his pain and the horror of what happened. They have reminded him of his guilt. They have made me a part of it. I wonder now what he will do."

Entti sucked in her breath. "You are being too understanding. Truly, you don't believe he will send you away? By the gods, you are his wife!"

Mirana shrugged. "He is close to his family. He listens to them. He may kill me. Or Merrik, his brother, might or even Sira. She is capable of it, doubt it not. She is a girl of strong passions. She wanted Rorik and I believe she still hopes to have him. Thus, I must be made to leave or die. There are doubtless many who would gladly volunteer for such a task, including any one of the men who came with them."

Entti said then, her fingers on Mirana's sleeve, "Let's take one of the boats and leave tonight. Let's leave now. We could make it this time, I know we could."

Mirana smiled at that. "A storm is coming, Entti. Remember our last adventure with a storm?"

Entti moved away from her, closer to the edge of the cliff. She stared down at the roiling water. It looked black, even the froth of the waves. It looked terrifying.

She looked beyond, to the south, where the longboats were tied securely to the wooden dock. Even in the protected inlet, the waves were tossing them about like leaves. Still, it made no difference, not now, at least not to Entti. She said, "I can't stay, Mirana, you know that. If I do, I will have to protect myself from the men, for I will play the dull-witted whore no more. I have no wish to kill one of them."

"No one will touch you. I will not allow it."

"As you told me, you are in a rather uncertain position right now yourself. I have been left alone because of you. But now neither of us can be certain that you will remain untouched and alive."

"You're right, of course. I'm being stupid, believing that Rorik will realize what is happening, that he will speak to his family, convince them that I am no threat to them, that I am not guilty of my brother's crimes."

"He is your half-brother."

"Aye," Mirana said slowly. "He is my half-brother. But in their eyes, his blood is my blood and thus I am tainted with his wickedness. I am as evil as Einar is."

"This is madness. How can Rorik be so blind?"

"Rorik isn't blind, girl. Speak not of your master in such a way. Lord Rorik is a man who has suffered grievous pain, pain you cannot begin to imagine."

Both women whirled about to see Hafter standing there, still and silent in the black night, a thick wool cloak about him, the wind whipping his dark golden hair about his head. He looked big and strong, his shoulders stiff with anger. Mirana took a step closer to Entti. She wished she had her knife.

"Aye, I know," Mirana said, "but I was not a part of it."

Hafter shrugged. "His family believe differently. You left them raging, Mirana." Then he laughed suddenly. "I always believed Sira to be more beautiful than any goddess. With leeks dripping off her forehead, she looked quite human. Aye, a good dose of humility you gave her. She will hate you forever now."

"Mirana could have stuck her knife in the girl's gullet, Hafter. A leek or two atop her head is nothing."

"Women see things differently. Sira is after your blood, Mirana. She was calling for your death when I left the longhouse."

Mirana didn't want to ask him but she did. "What of Rorik? Do you know what he will do?"

He shook his head. "He remains within, with his family. They are very angry." He turned to Entti and he smiled, holding out his hand to her. "Now, I am here to fetch you. You will warm me tonight and I will take you until I am sated on your soft flesh."

Before Entti could speak, Mirana lightly touched her forearm to hold her silent, and said, "Nay, Hafter. No man will touch Entti again unless she wishes it. This is her wish and I honor it."

"I will give her pleasure this time, I swear it. I have a man's needs and she must fill them. She will enjoy herself as she does. She must do as I wish."

Entti straightened as stiff as one of the palisade posts. "Take yourself back to the longhouse and stick your head in your mead, Hafter. I will have naught to do with you. Did you not believe me yesterday? Do you wish me to unman you again with my knee?"

"You said you were sorry. You said you wouldn't do that again."

"Aye, I said I wouldn't hurt you again if you kept your distance from me. I don't want you. Go away."

"Which of the men do you want?"

Mirana was fascinated at the sudden very jealous tone of his voice. She saw that Entti was about to laugh, and said quickly, "Entti doesn't wish any man right now, Hafter. Surely you understand. She has been sorely unhappy. You are a man of sense and kindness, are you not?"

"Aye. Mayhap. Not in this instance. I want her, Mirana. Don't interfere, it is not your right."

"If you force her, Hafter, she will kill you or hurt you badly and then she will have to die and all because she was protecting her honor. Do you wish her to die because of your lust?"

Hafter had no real thoughts, only a burning need to bed Entti. He didn't want another woman, only her. He stared at Mirana, the woman who was the wife of Lord Rorik, a woman who could possibly be dead soon by the hand of one of Rorik's family. He said slowly, turning now to face Entti, "I don't want you dead."

"What do you want then, you boorish lout?"

"Speak not so meanly to me, Entti. I am a man and you are naught but a slave. It is I who am in the right. You will do as I bid you."

Entti shook her head at him, so frustrated with his stubbornness she wanted to hit him. "You are more obtuse than the goat who must eat cow dung! I will not be your whore, Hafter. Understand me, for I grow tired of repeating it. I will not be your whore or any man's whore. No more."

He looked perplexed. "But no other man will have you. I've seen to that. I have told them that you are mine and they are to keep their distance. I am protecting you."

Entti said to Mirana, "It is of no use to speak to him. All men are dull-witted goats when lust possesses them.

He is no different from that man Erm who wanted to rape me." She turned then and walked away, pulling the ragged square of wool more closely around her shoulders.

Hafter said, "Entti is wearing a rag. It isn't right. I don't like it."

"Aye, you are right," Mirana said. "I will see to it that both of us have better clothes to wear."

"She's leaving me and I am not done with her. Entti! Come back to me! I will give you a new cloak. Just come back here, now."

He gave Mirana a distracted frown, then turned to run after Entti. Mirana didn't think he would catch her.

It was so very cold and yet it was a summer night and she had pulled hay over her to keep warm, but it wasn't enough. It was still dark, so she didn't believe she'd slept all that long. The wind was howling outside the barn and she wished she could stuff her ears to keep out the loud dinning of rain, the cracks of thunder that made her jump. She remembered the storms at Clontarf, vicious and unrestrained, tearing the sod from the roofs of the huts, making the cattle bawl in fear.

It was so very cold.

She burrowed deeper into the pile of hay. A cow shuffled nearby, but made no sound. The oxen stood with their heads down, sleeping, she supposed, oblivious of the storm. The goats were trying to eat the leather straps that held them tethered in their stalls.

What would happen on the morrow?

It was Old Alna who found her, curled into a tight ball, only her head showing from the pile of hay.

"Aye, mistress, 'tis time for you to rise, for the sun is climbing in the sky and there is much to be done. The storm is done and it will be a hot day, both outside and inside. Aye, his family is like a pack of wolves, unheeding of naught but their hatred, a festering thing it is, deep and burning, and they've not let it go. They've not healed since your half-brother killed Ingá and the babes. They've gotten but more bitter. It is not a good thing. And they believe what Sira told them—you seduced Rorik, claimed you were with child, and he was honorable."

Mirana sat up and began picking off straws of hay. Her hair was stiff with it. So this had added fuel to their hatred. They believed the tale Sira had spun for them. She should tell them how long she'd known Rorik. Why had Rorik not told them that she'd come to him a virgin? She said without looking up, "There is no reason for me to return, Alna." She looked toward the goats for a moment, then added, her voice so wistful that Old Alna frowned, "Unless Lord Rorik sent you to find me?"

The old woman spat as she shook her head. She scratched her shoulder. "Nay, the master has said naught of anything. He is different. Last night he was different, this morning he awoke with the same blind pain in his eyes. They came and poisoned him and he is different. Lord Rorik spent the night next to his brother and some of his father's warriors. They spoke long into the night to him. They drank too much mead, and Lord Rorik doesn't hold mead or wine or ale well. It makes his bowels churn and his head ache fiercely. He pukes up his guts. You'd best come into the longhouse now. You are still mistress. It is your responsibility to oversee the slaves and the chores and the comfort of his family."

"Have you seen Entti or Hafter?"

Old Alna cackled. "Aye, Entti struck him down with an iron pan last night. Hit him solid, she did, and he just spun away like a drunken duck, sitting down finally, holding his poor head in his hands. She slept next to me, complaining this morning that I snored. Ha! An old woman doesn't snore. I didn't snore. I was awake most of the night, listening to Hafter moan. Then that Gurd tried to take her." Old Alna cackled again. "I told him to go back to Asta, where he belonged. I told him that Entti was having her monthly flow. That got him away from her."

Mirana stood up and picked more straw from her tunic. She badly needed to bathe. Her beautiful wedding gown and overtunic were soiled and wrinkled. She had nothing else to wear. Old Alna frowned at her, but said only, "Hafter is still sleeping. That Entti, now she's afraid that she really hurt him and he won't ever awaken."

"Hafter is as stubborn as Rorik. He'll awaken all right and then it will all begin again."

Old Alna regarded her in rheumy silence, saying finally, not unkindly, "Come, little lamb, 'tis time to return to the longhouse. I don't know what will happen, but you have no choice. Come now. All the women await your instructions. They dance on the fire coals, you know, but 'tis not their fault. They all have great liking for Tora. They don't know what to do."

Mirana followed her into the longhouse. The people were stirring, the men moaning from the surfeit of mead, the women punching at them, some laughing, for the men had been lusty from drink and thus lusty with the women. "Aye," Old Alna said, "some of the women—the younger ones—are humming and singing and are ready to begin the day. They chirp like happy hens.

The men have nothing more than they deserve."

Mirana only nodded. She began the morning tasks, setting the various women to work, careful to avoid looking toward Rorik, who was awake now and speaking to his brother. What else was there to say to him? Or Merrik to him? Were they deciding who was to kill her? Would they draw lots? She was stirring the porridge that was steaming nicely in the heavy iron pot suspended over the fire pit when she felt him near her. He'd said nothing; she hadn't heard him approach; she just felt him there, right behind her. She stilled, waiting.

"I will go to the bathing hut now. There is straw in your hair and on your clothes. Your gown is soiled."

"I know," she said.

"My parents still sleep in my chamber. I will fetch you what you need."

She turned slowly then, looking up at him. He'd said *my* chamber, not our chamber. "There is nothing there for you to fetch. I have no other clothes."

He looked as if he would say something, then closed his mouth. "The porridge smells good. It is a relief that the food is again fit for men to eat."

She only nodded.

"Hafter is groaning, only his pain is from an iron pan and not from indulging in too much mead. You will cease your interference. If he wishes to have Entti, he will have her. She is a slave. Before she slept with any man who would bed her, and all wanted her. It is no different now. Indeed, Hafter would have her to himself until he tires of her. I have given her to him. Cease your plaints. You can no longer protect her. It is I who will determine who and what she will be, not you."

"She won't be a whore again, Rorik."

"She will be what I order her to be. Nay, now she will be what Hafter wishes. She belongs to him. Do you understand?"

"Do not order her to be a whore. She cannot do it. It is different now. Don't let Hafter shame her."

"You will not interfere. Gurd is right in this instance. You are the cause of this. You will leave her alone and cease your meddling."

He left her, saying nothing more. She instructed a slave to fetch him towels and leave them in the outer chamber of the bathing hut.

# 19

SHE WENT ABOUT her work, every once in a while plucking off another straw from her hair or from her clothing. When Entti began mixing dough for the flatbread—so many loaves needed that it was mixed in a deep wooden trough—Mirana saw that she too was still dressed as she had been the night before.

She went to her and said only, her voice low, "We will leave when it is possible. You were right last night, there is nothing for either of us here now."

Entti only nodded. Mirana knew she understood, for she'd seen Rorik speaking to her. She knew that she now belonged to Hafter, that no choice remained to her.

"Perhaps tonight when all of the men are drinking again. The storm has blown itself out."

"Aye," Entti said. She looked at her straightly now. "You must take care, Mirana. I am afraid one of them might try to kill you before tonight."

"I will get my knife from Rorik's trunk when his parents leave his sleeping chamber. I will steal one for you, Entti. Also, if you can, set food and water aside for us to take with us. It will be a long journey."

Entti nodded, wondering where they would go. Certainly not back to Clontarf, for Mirana knew what awaited her there. She didn't ask. Mirana would decide where they would go, and this time they would succeed.

But an hour later, Rorik came to Mirana and said, "Here is a gown that belongs to Asta. It is now yours. Asta says she and Erna will make new gowns for both you and Entti. Come now to the bathing hut. It is very hot in here and your face is red."

She didn't want to go with him. She was afraid that when she was naked and vulnerable, when they were alone, he would kill her. Her heart pounded as she walked beside him. But she'd managed to retrieve her knife after his parents had left the sleeping chamber. It was something; she prayed she would be strong enough to use it.

His father and mother had ignored her completely when they'd emerged from Rorik's sleeping chamber, and she'd set a slave to serving them. There had been no sign as yet of Sira. Rorik's brother had left the longhouse not to return as yet.

"You have already bathed," she said, stepping outside into the bright morning sunlight.

"Aye," he said, not looking at her.

"There is no need for you to accompany me."

"There is."

He would kill her. His family had convinced him that she was as evil as Einar, as untrustworthy, as foul. She didn't want to die, not by his hand, not now. Nor did she want to leave Hawkfell Island.

But there was no choice for her. She wondered if he would choke her or stick a knife into her heart. She knew, too, that she would protect herself, and that brought her more pain than she wished to consider.

When they were in the outer room of the bathing hut, he told two of his father's men who were there, naked and still wet from their bath, to get out.

Once alone, he said, "I will help you." She stood quietly while he unfastened the brooches that held her tunic to her shoulders. She stood quietly when he unfastened her belt and held out his hand for her knife. He said nothing about the knife though he must know that she'd gotten it from his trunk. She looked at his hand, then at her knife. In that moment, she knew she couldn't strike him with that knife. She simply couldn't do it. She handed him the knife. If he killed her, then so be it.

She stood quietly when he lifted her gown over her head. Only when she was naked, did she move. She cried out, seeing him look at her, no emotion in his clear blue eyes, no hint of how he meant to kill her. She ran into the inner chamber and pressed herself against the far wall. Steam rose and she couldn't see him clearly.

"Mirana!"

She dropped to her knees, pressing herself even more firmly against the wall, her hair cascading down to cover her face.

"Come here and I will bathe you."

Bathe her? She frowned. So he wanted her to be clean whilst he killed her? Or was it a ruse?

She rose, pushing back her hair, knowing that if he were lulled, she could slip by him and into the outer chamber. Her knife was there, lying on the bench with her clothing. She would grab both and run. Surely there was someplace to hide on the island.

But he wasn't lulled. He took her arm as if he weren't aware of her fear, and stood her in front of him. He dumped a bucket of hot water over her, then began to wash her. She was so stiff, so afraid, that she didn't at first realize that he was also now naked.

When she did, she nearly doubled over with fear. He would rape her, then kill her.

"Nay," she said, but he was washing her face and she got soapy water in her mouth.

"Nay what?"

"Don't rape me first."

Rorik rubbed his soapy hands over her breasts, then downward to her belly and lower to her soft woman's flesh. His fingers were light and teasing and when he eased his middle finger, thick with soap, upward and high inside her, she jerked back from him, crying out.

"I will rape you if you force me to," he said, his finger tingling from the feel of her, the heat of her body. He wanted her now. "Come here."

He felt violent; unreasoned rage flowed through him; he could feel the savage heat of his blood. He also felt more uncertainty than he'd ever felt in his life. He felt as though he were dying, not of wounds valiantly gained, but from deep inside him where there was naught but emptiness and pain and regret and guilt. He hadn't been there to save Inga or his babes. He hadn't succeeded in killing Einar. Nay, he'd wedded Einar's sister, a foul creature who'd worked her wiles on him. He had watched her withdraw from him, watched her blank her expression, watched her pull completely apart from him. She'd remained hidden the previous night, leaving him to deal with the uproar she'd caused. It was then he smelled her fear. She deserved the fear.

"Come here," he said again, and his body was pulsing with lust, his heart was pounding in his chest, and he was near to panting with need. He was on the edge of violence. He wanted her now, and he would have her.

She didn't move, just stood there, trying to cover herself, shaking her head.

He grabbed her hand and dragged her to the bench against the wall. She was still covered with soap and very slippery. She jerked away from him, but he caught her and slammed her against the wall beside the bench. He pulled her hard against him, forcing her legs to straddle his thighs. He thrust two fingers up into her and felt her flinch with pain. But she didn't make a sound. He was swelled hard, painfully full, and he didn't wait. The violence in him erupted. He lifted her, then violently forced her down onto him, impaling her, pushing into her, his hands digging into her hips, until he was touching her womb, and it was easy, this powerful entry of his, and he didn't hurt her, for she was slick with soap. Then he clasped her to his chest. He worked her, but it wasn't long, just a few strokes of his sex deep inside her, for his lust was part of his violence and he couldn't contain either. He yelled his release, feeling his own pain and fury, the grinding helplessness of it, all pouring out of him.

He lifted her off him. He dropped his hands from her hips as if he couldn't bear to touch her more. He staggered away from her, sat on the bench and leaned back against the wall, closing his eyes. His breath was harsh, deep and raw. He felt the drain in his body, the easing in his mind. But still his heart pounded so fiercely he wondered if he would die. No woman had brought him to such violence before. He hated himself for it, and her, hated her for who she was and what she'd brought him to. There was no fairness in what he had done, but he didn't care. He was, in these few moments, beyond guilt and thought, emptied of violence and savagery.

Mirana, free of him, stumbled, nearly falling, as she turned to run. She stopped suddenly. She felt his seed on her legs, could still feel the pounding of him so deep inside her. She grabbed more soap and scrubbed him out of her body, scrubbed herself until her flesh was raw. Then she took buckets of hot water and rinsed herself thoroughly. She looked up then to see him staring at her. There was no smile on his mouth, no expression in his eyes, languid now, even dazed. Then he slowly straightened. He would kill her now. He raised his arm, thick with muscle, deadly with strength. She cried out and raced out of the inner chamber.

Rorik didn't move for a very long time.

The afternoon was warm, the sun bright overhead, the storm but a memory now. Mirana sat outside the longhouse, in the shade of the overhead beams. She looked to see Tora, Rorik's mother, walking toward her. She was a tall woman, hair so blond it shone nearly white beneath the bright afternoon sun. She was deep-bosomed, her face once lovely, but now there were bitter lines scarring the flesh about her eyes and mouth. She looked hard and unforgiving.

Tora's shoulders were squared, her step firm, her lips thin in their meager line. Mirana drew herself up, knowing that she was to be attacked, but knowing too there was nothing she could do about it. She set down the gown she was stitching. It was a pale blue wool and she thought the material beautiful, a present from Old Alna, who'd been hoarding it for herself for more years than she could count.

Mirana stared at Tora, wishing she could make her believe she wished her or her family no harm, wishing she could convince her that she was innocent of her brother's crimes. She opened her mouth, but Tora forestalled her. The woman stood in front of her, blocking out the sun.

"I have come to warn you," she said, nothing more, just those few stark words.

Mirana merely nodded.

"Sira will kill you, very soon now. I cannot stop her."

"You warn me so that I will leave?"

"Aye. Leave. Now. If you die, my son will feel but more guilt. He is innocent of any evil. He is a good man and I don't want him hurt more or beguiled by a woman with no honor."

Mirana looked away from Tora, out over the water, which was a glittering blue-green under the bright sun, and calm, for there was little wind today. For an instant she smiled, for there were pinwheels spinning and diving over the water. "Do you now believe that I didn't trick Rorik into wedding with me?"

"Of that crime, you are innocent. Rorik said that you came to him a virgin, and that on the night of your wedding. No, you are not a slut, more's the pity. Sira still refuses to believe it. Leave, Mirana, else she will kill you. Or you will kill her because you must save yourself. To kill her would destroy Rorik. He has known her all her life, has known that she loves him and wanted to wed him, but he wed you and thus he hurt her badly. It would force him to seek but more vengeance were you to kill her. Stop it, Mirana. Leave now."

"Very well."

The woman looked stunned. "You agree?" she said, uncertainty and surprise in her voice.

"I want no more pain for Rorik. He doesn't deserve it."

"No he doesn't."

Then there was a shadow behind Mirana and she turned, afraid it was Sira, a knife raised, but it was

Merrik, Rorik's brother. He was broad-shouldered and tall, and would become as large as Rorik when he gained his full man years. He was hard, no warmth in his eyes, no giving in his mouth.

"Don't accept her lies, Mother," he said, so much rage in his voice that Mirana knew in that moment that his family would never change, that there would never be any hope for her, for Rorik.

"She will leave, Merrik. She has agreed to."

Merrik looked around quickly, then said, "I'm pleased that Rorik isn't here. I don't know what he would do if he heard she was willing to go. But I don't trust her, Mother. She probably lies. She will go to Rorik and plead and cast her woman's spells over him and make him forget what he owes to Inga, to his dead babes, to us."

"What does he owe to them, Merrik?" Mirana said, her voice low, steady.

"He owes them vengeance!"

"I agree. But why do you think I am deserving of punishment as well?"

"You will be quiet, you damned slut! You have torn my brother apart with your lies and your promises and your false understanding."

Mirana sighed. There was no hope for it. "That isn't true, Merrik, none of it. However, as I told your mother, I will leave. I don't want Rorik to be hurt any more than you have hurt him by bringing him back such pain."

"My two small grandchildren were impaled on your brother's sword! Such beautiful babes, so happy and full of life, and your brother butchered them!"

"I know," Mirana said. "But heed me. I am Rorik's wife. When I leave I will still be his wife. He needs children, Tora. He needs happiness. He needs a union free of guilt and pain, one blessed by the gods. What will you do for him then? Give him more reasons to hate? More reasons to keep remembering that awful time? More guilt until he manages to kill my half-brother? When will it stop, Tora?"

"Your death would be a start," Sira said, coming to stand beside Tora. "I don't want you to go, Mirana. I want you to die. By my hand, by Rorik's, I care not."

"Be quiet, Sira," Tora said, shaking off the girl's hand. "Your vengeance is mixed with jealousy; it isn't pure or noble. You speak with a mouth full of envy."

Merrik said slowly, his eyes on his cousin, whose features were twisted with hatred, "I had considered wedding with you for I believed your beauty great. But now you have no more beauty for me, for you have no more kindness of spirit. I don't wish to have you now, Sira." He turned then and walked away from them, his mother staring openmouthed after him.

"I didn't realize he wanted you," she said to Sira. "Now it doesn't matter, for you have lost him."

"I care not," Sira said, her eyes still on Mirana. "I will have Rorik once she is gone."

"I don't think so," Mirana said. "Alna told me that Rorik wouldn't have you after his wife was killed. Why would he have you now?"

Sira's breath came out in an ugly gasp. She jumped at Mirana, her hand hard and flat striking her cheek, throwing her from her stool and onto her back on the ground. She was on top of her, straddling her, slapping her, sending her fist into her breasts, her belly.

Mirana heard Tora yelling. She felt Sira's blows, then the rising of tears in her eyes. She had to stop this. Quickly, in a move Gunleik had taught her years before, she brought her knees up, striking Sira hard against her back, and at the same moment, she sent her fist into the girl's throat. Sira gave a strangled cry, grabbed her throat and fell off Mirana onto her side, gurgling and clutching her throat, for she couldn't breathe.

Mirana rolled to the other side and came up to her knees, panting as she stared at Sira, knowing that within a few moments, she would be all right again, and wondering if she would attack her again. She slowly drew her knife from its sheath at her belt.

When Sira regained her breath, when the pain in her back receded, when she looked at Mirana, she stilled at the sight of the knife.

"You filthy slut."

"Come here, Sira," Mirana said, her voice low and dangerous, beckoning her with her hand. "Aye, come here, and this time I won't be so very gentle. I will stick this knife into your cheek—aye, I'll mark you so you won't believe yourself such a goddess among women any longer. I will make you as ugly on the outside as you are on the inside. Aye, come here, Sira." Mirana tossed the knife from her right hand to her left, and back again. She knew she was taunting her, but she didn't care. She didn't want to be a victim, not anymore.

"So, you will knife my cousin?"

It was Rorik, fetched by his mother, and she was panting beside him from exertion.

"Aye, if she forces me to."

"Give me the knife, Mirana. I should never have allowed you to keep it. You stole it from my trunk and like a fool I allowed you to keep it with you. You are too ungoverned in your passions, too unpredictable, mayhap too vicious."

Mirana stared up at him. Without a word, she gave him the knife, sticking it toward him, its handle first. He took it, staring at her, surprise in his eyes. In the next moment, Sira jumped at her, sending her fist into her jaw.

Rorik wondered if the world had always been mad or if the gods had plunged him into a nightmare that would never end. He tossed the knife to the ground, grabbed Sira beneath her arms and dragged her off Mirana. She was panting with rage, and he shook her.

"Stop it! Enough!"

She cried out and twisted in his arms, wrapping her own around his back, pressing herself against him. "Oh Rorik, she is vicious, evil. I was but protecting myself. She hurt me. I couldn't let her believe me a coward. Save me, Rorik!"

He pressed her hard against him. He looked at Mirana and saw that her face was pale, without expression. He watched her slowly rise, feel her jaw with her fingers, then work it open and closed a few times. He saw her pick up her knife, sheath it again at her waist, turn without a word, and walk away. He started to call after her, demand that she give him back the knife, but he said nothing. He remembered thinking on their wedding night that he should return her knife to her, remembered being surprised that she—a woman—would consider a knife as part of her clothing, but he'd forgotten it in his need for her. He watched her walk away from him, walk away from the madness that was within him and surrounded him and seemed to infect the very earth he stood on. Her shoulders were as square as a quarried stone.

Aye, he thought, the world was surely mad, at least his world was, so mad in its madness that sense was nonsense and nothing had meaning anymore, nothing at all. This mad world was also without hope. He held Sira whilst she sobbed, aware of her body against his, aware that he felt no desire, no burgeoning lust, nothing but immense pain that wouldn't go away.

"TONIGHT," ENTTI SAID quietly to Mirana as she passed her, a platter of boar steaks on her arms.

Mirana merely nodded. "When all are asleep. But what of Hafter?"

Entti shrugged but Mirana wasn't fooled. There was both worry and another emotion in her eyes Mirana couldn't identify, but it puzzled her. Entti said, shrugging yet again, her eyes on a boar steak that was close to the edge of the platter, "I will deal with the lout if he forces me to." She turned, and began serving with the other women.

And what of Rorik? Mirana thought. She looked across the longhouse to see him sitting between his brother and his father, only this time they were all silent. He wasn't eating, merely sitting there, drinking the sweet red wine from the Rhineland his father had brought him as a gift. She wanted to tell him not to drink too much of it, for it would make him ill. Ah, but she could imagine how he would look at her if she even approached him, much less expressed concern for him. She felt sorry for him, but there was naught she could do. He'd avoided her since the scene several hours before. As for Sira, she was seated next to Rorik's father, head down, picking at her food, her beautiful hair clean and glimmering again in the rush torch light.

Mirana filled her own plate and joined the women. Asta said, "The gown becomes you more than it ever did me, Mirana. I think it's because of that black hair of yours and your skin that's whiter than the goat's milk I'm drinking."

"You just wait until she finishes the blue wool I gave her," said Old Alna. "Your gown is poor and miserable when compared to that blue wool. Aye, it's the color my eyes used to be when I was young. Then I was more beautiful than the lot of you."

Erna said, giggling through the fingers of her one good hand, "There is no one to tell us if she speaks the truth, for any who would know are all dead now."

"The wool probably has holes in it you've hoarded it for so long," Asta said and laughed, poking the old woman lightly on her scrawny arm. "Aye, I believe you had it when you were young and had all your teeth and a man about to warm you, but Alna, none of us can remember, it was so many decades ago, just as Erna said. How can you remember?"

"You'll talk and talk, won't you, Asta! Well, look you to Gurd, a mangy one, that man."

"Aye, but he's strong and hard in my bed, Alna."

"You'll grow old and lose your teeth, you'll see."

Asta laughed and laughed.

So very normal, Mirana thought. It was as though this part of the longhouse was in a world completely apart from Rorik's. These women didn't hate her. It seemed too that they'd made a choice. They'd chosen her over Tora. She looked over at Amma, the leader of the women's revolt, a woman she'd trust with her life. Her husband, Sculla, so tall Mirana felt like a child standing next to him, wasn't always a reasonable man, though he hadn't even slept with Entti. She wondered if there was still acrimony between them.

Utta said shyly, "Your recipe for the sauce is delicious, Mirana. Would you let me watch you make it next time?"

Mirana smiled and nodded. She looked over at Entti, silent as a stone, and she knew she was forcing herself to eat because she knew she would need her strength. Her rich brown hair hid her face, a long thick curtain falling forward to touch her forearm. Hafter was also staring at Entti, like a hungry goat, Entti had told her earlier, her voice sour and frustrated.

Mirana forced herself to eat as well. She knew that Entti had stolen food and water and hidden it down near one of the smaller longboats. Mirana still had to steal another knife, but she knew it would be no problem. Once the men were asleep, many of them sodden with drink, she would easily be able to slip a knife out of a sheath. Rorik had let her keep her knife to her, saying nothing, and for that she was grateful. She wondered why he'd let her. Didn't he fear that she would slip it between Sira's ribs still?

She ate and sipped sparingly at the rich mead. She listened to the women talk of smoking herring, arguing over which wood smoke was the most flavorful—oak or fir. She watched Rorik's parents and his brother, Merrik, and Sira, the violence in them silenced now, but for how much longer? It was like an armed camp, and she was the enemy, just out of reach, but not for long. Every once in a while, Sira raised her head and looked straight at Mirana. Tora was silent, withdrawn. Mirana ached for the older woman. Her position in all this was damnable.

Mirana oversaw the cleaning of the plates and pans and pots. There was always a seemingly endless supply. Finally, she dismissed the slaves and sent the other women off to their beds. She sought out Entti and the two of them took blankets to the far corner of the longhouse, not far from the front doors.

Mirana lay there, her heart pounding, wondering what would happen. In her experience the gods didn't suddenly smile upon a mortal's plans and allow them to act and succeed. The gods weren't like that. When she looked up to see Rorik standing over her, she wasn't surprised. He was either here to rape her or to kill her. She had rather hoped that his mother would keep him away from her. Tora believed she would leave, trusted her to leave.

Had Merrik said anything to Rorik about her promise? Had he told his brother that he didn't believe her, that he knew she was lying?

"What do you want, Rorik?"

"You. Come with me. We will sleep in the barn."

Entti stiffened beside her but remained quiet, pretending sleep.

He continued, "As for her, Hafter will come for her shortly. He won't bear with her woman's deceit any longer."

He reached out his hand to her. Mirana looked at that hand, strong, browned from the summer sun, a large hand, a man's hand that could soothe as easily as it could kill.

"I want to stay here, Rorik. I wish to sleep."

"I care not what you want. Come."

Mirana came up onto her knees. Her knife was at her waist. She would do what she had to do.

He took her hand and pulled her upright. He held her close, staring down at her. His eyes darkened, then cleared. "Come," he said again, and pulled her after him from the longhouse.

They were nearly to the barn. The moon was bright overhead. Mirana knew they must leave this night. There would be no better chance, but Rorik . . . what to do with her husband, a man she no longer knew, a man whose every action frightened her?

He pulled her into the barn and closed the door. The animals were silent. He said nothing, merely pulled her down atop a pile of straw. He didn't bother undressing her. He merely pulled up her gown to her waist and shoved up her shift. He sat back on his heels and stared at her.

"You are beautiful," he said, frowning. He laid his palm on her belly, then let his fingers widen outward to touch her pelvic bones. He massaged her for a long time, his gaze intent, saying nothing more, then his fingers went lower, found her and she sucked in her breath at the feel of him against her flesh. She'd not imagined anything like this. It was near pain, it was so intense, and she wanted more of it, until . . . until something happened. What that was, she didn't know, but she wanted it. She felt hot and damp-fleshed and it was disconcerting, this reaction of her body to his fingers. It was wonderful.

"I don't know what to do," he said suddenly, his voice filled with anger. Without another word, he pulled open his trousers and fell over her. He was pressing at her, opening her, and she began to struggle against him, all the intense feelings swamped in fear.

In that moment a cramp seized her belly and she cried out, trying to lurch up.

He came up onto his elbows. "Stop fighting me." She was breathing hard, truly frightened now, but not of him. "What is wrong?"

"My belly," she managed, shoving at him. He rolled off her and watched as another cramp doubled her over. She rolled to her side, her arms locked about herself, crying out softly.

He frowned. "What is wrong?"

"I don't know. It hurts, Rorik." The cramps came more quickly now, more viciously. Suddenly, she gagged, and came up onto her knees. She vomited her dinner, vomited until there was naught left in her belly and still she shuddered and gagged and heaved.

He held her shoulders, keeping her hair away from her sweating face. He felt the bone-deep shudders in her, the wrenching of her belly that spread throughout her body, making her weak.

Still she heaved until she was so weak she fell back against his chest.

" 'Twas something you ate," he said. "There must be others who are ill. Lie still. I will fetch you some water to clean out your mouth. Don't move, Mirana."

When Rorik returned, he held her against him and slowly fed her water from a wooden cup. She spat it out, then swallowed some. Her belly cramped immediately and she moaned.

"Asta is sick," he said. "No one else."

Mirana said nothing. She just wanted to die. She closed her eyes, her head lolling against his chest.

"I'm carrying you back to my sleeping chamber. My parents will sleep in the outer hall."

But then it would be more difficult for her to escape, she thought, but it wasn't a strong thought, merely a vague thought that went softly through her mind and was soon gone. A cramp twisted inside her and she knew then she would die. She couldn't bear this sort of pain, no one could bear it. It was beyond anything she could have imagined.

She was ill throughout the night. She was aware that Rorik's mother was there, and she put a cup to her lips and told her to drink, that it was an herb—the root of the brawly bush—that would help settle her belly, that it would calm her. She wondered if it were also poison that would make her sleep forever, but she didn't care. She drank it. It tasted sour, of old milk, but it did settle her belly, and she slept until the belly cramps woke her again.

Old Alna was beside her this time, wiping her face with a cool damp cloth, and it felt wonderful. She spoke of the cheese making that would soon begin in earnest, of the growing crops that were flourishing with the rain that had fallen so heavily during the past days, of Sculla, so tall that he would walk amongst the rows of barley waving his arms, and surely this scared the birds and animals away. Mirana listened and wondered why she should care. Surely she would die soon.

She awoke once and believed she was floating above herself, feeling light and insubstantial, as unfettered as a cloud or a western breeze. She felt a strange emptiness and sought to fill herself with something that would give her meaning again, that would give her substance. Then she was within her body again and she wanted to die at the twisting, roiling cramps.

And Rorik, he was always there, either lying beside her on the box bed or speaking softly to whoever was in the chamber with them. He would hold her, lightly rubbing her back, massaging her belly, holding her when she retched and shuddered and fell against him in exhaustion, the spasms temporarily ended. But they always came back and she knew she was growing too weak to fight the pain in her mind. Her body would give up because her mind would have no more will to combat the pain.

Near dawn she fell into a deep sleep, her head lolling in near unconsciousness against Rorik's chest. She slept until midday and awoke with no more cramping, no more pain. She lay there, waiting, distrusting, too afraid to move, but she was as she had been. Just so very weak. Her ribs hurt as did the muscles in her stomach. She had no more strength, no more will. She felt like an old woman, surely older than Alna. She wanted only to sleep.

She opened her eyes at a sound from the doorway. There was Rorik, standing there, looking at her. He said, "I have a bowl of broth for you, made by Utta. She said that her mother loved the broth and it was the only thing she could eat without vomiting before she died."

Mirana shoved herself up in the bed. It took all her strength. How, she wondered suddenly, now firmly back into her body and into the present with all its vast complications, would she and Entti escape now?

Rorik set the large wooden tray on her lap. Steam from the broth curled upward. It smelled delicious. "Do you want me to feed you?"

"Nay," she said, and took the spoon from him. She managed one bite, then dropped it. Her hand was trembling and her forehead was damp with sweat. Rorik took the spoon and pressed her back against the pillows. She wondered at this new gentleness in him but said nothing. There'd been none in him the previous night before she'd become so ill.

"Open your mouth."

She did. She ate the entire bowl of beef broth. It was the best broth she'd ever tasted in her life. Her stomach felt bloated and very content.

"Why didn't you let me die?"

"You weren't ready to die. You're young and strong. Speak no more about dying, Mirana."

"Was anyone else ill besides Asta and me?"

He shook his head. He looked away.

"How is Asta?"

He was silent for a very long time. She felt panic well up. "Asta! How is she?"

"She did not survive the night. She is dead."

"No!"

"We will bury her this afternoon."

But Mirana was beyond understanding him now. She was shaking her head back and forth, crying, jagged, ugly sounds from deep in her throat. "No," she said over and over, not wanting to believe it, not willing to accept it. Asta, dead, and just yesterday she had been laughing and teasing Old Alna about the blue gown, bragging about Gurd being hard in her bed, and Mirana had thought he didn't deserve any kind words from Asta. Just last night she had stayed close to Mirana, showing Rorik's family that she felt loyalty to Mirana, that she wouldn't scorn her. Her laughter was so bright, her smile so natural.

Now she was dead. Just like that. Mirana couldn't allow it to be true. It was too much. She turned away from him onto her side, clutching her arms around her, becoming a ball, rocking back and forth. "No . . . no . . . she gave me her gown, Rorik. She said it was very nice on me with my black hair. She said my skin was whiter than her goat's milk. She always treated me well, even when you first brought me here, and last night, she smiled at me and stayed near me to show your family I wasn't a vile person like Einar. Not dead . . . not Asta. Please no, tell me it is a mistake."

Rorik rose. He stood there staring down at her. He felt his own pain at their loss. Asta, so much a part of his life. Gurd was blank and silent. The women were preparing Asta for burial, quickly, quickly, for the dead mustn't be allowed to remain overlong around the living, for their ghosts would return as powerful monsters and destroy them.

At least Mirana had survived. But why were only the two women struck down?

Old Alna and Tora had tried to discover which dish the two of them had eaten that others hadn't. It made no sense.

It scared him to death.

Mirana stood beside Rorik as all the people clustered about the cliff overlooking the small inlet. They had buried Asta quickly, carrying her away from the longhouse feet first so her spirit couldn't find its way back. They buried her in a deep moss-lined grave, quickly covering her body with the rich black earth, quickly retreating once it was done.

Away from her now, safe from the threat of her ghost, they showed their grief openly, the women crying softly, the men standing behind the women, stiff and straight, their eyes fastened on the distant horizon.

Aslak stood over Gurd the blacksmith, his hand on his shoulder. Gurd seemed beyond all of them, unwilling to believe his wife was dead. He'd said nothing. Now he fell to his knees, not crying, no, never crying, showing nothing but a blank face to all as he prayed to the gods to lead his Asta over the mortal's bridge to Heaven.

Mirana felt Rorik's hand firmly under her elbow. She was weaving on her feet, so weak that every moment was a challenge to keep standing upright. But she'd had to come. She owed it to Asta, to honor her, to grieve for her.

Before the last prayers to the gods for Asta's safe journey, Rorik led her back to the longhouse.

# 21

RORIK SAID NOTHING as he carried her back into the sleeping chamber. He eased her gently back into the bed, pulling the wool blanket to her chin. He sat down beside her.

"You were going to escape me again," he said without preamble. "Entti with you."

"No."

"Don't lie to me. Merrik told me, and my mother did as well. Sira claimed you promised to leave, but she said no one could believe a slut and a liar like you."

"No."

He sighed, turning away from her, clasping his hands between his knees. She looked at his profile, its pure clean lines, the strong jaw, the curling golden hair that lay long on his neck. He was a magnificent man, young and powerful with strength, forceful, bursting with life and good health, but it wouldn't always be so. He would age and his strength would lessen, but he would remain what he was, a man to admire and respect, perhaps a man to trust. Something deep and mysterious swelled deep within her, something she didn't understand, but something she knew was there and knew she wanted to be there. It was Rorik, her husband. But she also knew there was no hope for them, not ever. And he was hurting. He was being gnawed apart from within and without. But he was still her husband, at least for today, perhaps even for tomorrow. But after that? She shook her head, silent and still.

"I would that you not lie to me."

And because he was Rorik and her husband, she said clearly, "Very well. It matters little now that you know. Aye, I promised them I would leave. I don't wish to die, Rorik. It is best. I won't return to my brother—"

"Your half-brother."

She smiled at his vehemence. "My half-brother. No, I will go somewhere else."

He looked at her now, his expression austere, his blue eyes as cold as the winter sea. He said, his voice remote, "You will go nowhere. I don't want you to go. You are my wife and you belong to me. You will remain my wife until I wish it otherwise. You will do as I tell you."

"And if I tell you I no longer wish you to be my husband?"

"It would matter not. It isn't true in any case. I wouldn't accept any words from you to sever our ties so do not waste your meager strength saying them."

She didn't begin to understand him. "Listen to me, Rorik, you hate me, you must. At the very least you don't want me here to remind you of what my brother did to your wife and your children and your people. My presence only brings you pain and the memory of your guilt because you weren't there to save them. Understand, Einar wouldn't have attacked your farmstead had you and your men been there. He is no fool and he is smart. He is not a coward, at least I never before thought so. Why he did what he did I don't know. But what he did remains and cannot be changed. Your family has made you see that I am not the wife you should have. They believe this strongly. They won't allow me to remain, Rorik."

He rose from the bed and began pacing the length of the small chamber.

She said again, "I do not blame them for their hatred of me. I do believe they should leave go of the past and allow the wounds to heal, for their unending bitterness shows on their faces and can be heard in their voices. It is deep within them. It makes them miserable. I don't wish them to destroy you with the past. It isn't fair of them to do so."

He turned then, back to her, and said, his voice harsh and low, "I won't lie to you. I listened to them. I was beginning to agree with them. They are my family. They love me. They loved Inga and the babes."

"I know," she said.

"Then you were so ill. I truly do not know what I would have done. Not kill you, Mirana, never that, though I can't expect you to believe me now. Nay, I realized that I had been a fool, that you had helped me to ease the past away, to put it where it belonged—in the past—where it would forever remain, not forgotten, nay, never forgotten, but distanced, the pain of it softened and mercifully blurred now. But then they came and it was as if the wound were slashed open again, raw inside me, and the past was the present, here with me now, full-blown and as filled with horror as it is in my nightdreams.

"My parents and brothers have kept it alive amongst themselves, and nurtured it and allowed it to feed on itself, and they wanted me to bow at the altar of their grief and hatred as well, aye, you're right about that.

And you were here, as wicked as the Christians' devil, ready for their fury and their hate. Your presence, who you are, helped their hatred grow and burst free once again. They now had a target, not just vague images that flowed through the mind. Your half-brother is still a man without a face to them, but now, through you, they could grasp their pain and see to its depths.

"There was Sira. She'd come to wed me, with my parents' blessing. I am not a fool. I knew it, and knew also that I would never have wed her. She is like a sister to me. How could I wed a sister? I watched her here, watching you. I watched her change, grow twisted and jealous when she looked at you, when she realized that you were my wife and who you were.

"I have never wanted her, Mirana, never given her any sign that I wanted to wed her. Her feelings are deep and violent. I see that now. I have decided that I will give her to Hafter to wed, if my parents agree. He has many times told me he believes her beautiful beyond all women, that he would want her were it possible. He can have her. Then he can take her from Hawkfell Island to the mainland. He has land there and family, near to Edingthorpe. He won't be here to rape Entti and Sira won't be here to torment you."

He fell silent now. Mirana had never felt so uncertain in her life; never had she felt more reluctant to accept words that would sway her. She was too afraid to be swayed. There was too much here, far too much. Always before in her life, everything had seemed so very clear to her, which path to take neatly marked. She'd believed that there'd been no grayness, no shimmering lies or half-truths to make her question herself or those around her. Ah, but she'd learned that her life had been filled with naught but lies, but she'd ignored them, turned away from them, refused to see them. She'd accepted her life at Clontarf with Einar as what life must be since her parents were dead. She hadn't recognized him for what he was, hadn't recognized what she was to him—naught but a pawn to be used to gain him more power, naught but a plaything for his amusement. Her mouth felt very dry. She swallowed. Rorik said nothing more, just waited, patiently. Finally, she said, "You are an honorable man, Rorik Haraldsson. Even so, I was very afraid. I thought you would kill me yesterday in the bathing hut."

"I know. I am sorry for it. My mind—I was maddened. I realized I could be as crazed as a *berserker,* but I wouldn't have killed you, Mirana, never would I have killed you.

"I had forgotten the passion of my brother, Merrik. His loyalty runs as deep as do his hatreds. He is a formidable enemy and a friend to value and hold close. I fear my parents kept his hatred festering, and because of his youth, it was easily done." He stopped then and paced the small chamber. He waited silently, patiently, as he had before.

She sifted through his words, afraid to find other meanings in them, meanings that would bring clearness, even hope. There was naught but a bitter truth, a truth that would always remain a truth no matter what she wanted or thought or wanted to believe. She had to face up to it, make him face up to it as well. By Thor, it hurt to say it, but she did, her voice low and clear, "I am relieved that you have no wish to kill me. But Rorik, your honor shouldn't dictate the woman you should have as your wife. Or your pity. Or guilt. And I know you felt both guilt and pity for me once you learned what Einar had planned to do with me. And that is why you wed me. To protect me, to save me from that wretched old king.

"You have taken care of me whilst I was ill and I thank you for it. You went beyond what one would expect of you. But it is your family to whom you owe your loyalty, not me. I am a stranger here, an outsider, and they are right, Rorik, I am of Einar's blood. You could never be certain that I was free of all taint. You could never trust me as you do Merrik or your parents."

He walked to the bed and stared down at her. Her hair was lank and dull. His mother had fashioned it in a loose braid that fell over her shoulder. She had said naught as she'd treated Mirana as matter-of-factly as she would have one of her own. She was strong, his mother was, sometimes too strong, too forceful, but in this instance he didn't understand her. He looked at Mirana, at the tendrils of black hair curled about her pale face. Her green eyes, so mysterious usually, were as dull as her hair and that bothered him though he knew now that she would regain her strength and her health.

He said again, his voice as cold as the Oslofjord, "You won't leave. You won't decide what it is I must want or not want. You will cease telling me what I must feel, both toward you and toward my family. You will not leave, Mirana. You will obey me now and always."

She said nothing, merely looked at him, then away, to her fingers that were fretting with the wool blanket.

He'd spoken honestly to her, yet he hadn't, for there was too much here, too much that was beyond him as yet, and beyond her as well. She would do as he told her. For a while, at least.

"You don't trust me," he said, and that surprised her, for surely she trusted him more than he did her. "Nay, don't shake your head. I don't know you well, but trust

I understand. I understand the feel of it in another, the smell of it, the expression of it in another's eyes.

"You will rest until you have your strength back. You will not leave. I will hear no more about it from you. I am protecting Entti, so you will not throw her up to me again. You will not have her as an excuse to escape. Her honor is now safe, as is Hafter's manhood."

He left her then. The rest of the afternoon passed very slowly. Far too slowly.

She slept and ate for the next two days. Rorik spent less time with her, as if knowing she needed to be with her own thoughts. But she wanted him to come into the sleeping chamber. Just to see him, to watch his mouth as he spoke, to feel his hands on her when he lifted her on the pillow. At night, he was close, his breathing deep and even, beside her throughout the night. But during the day he stayed away now.

His mother, Tora, was a different matter.

The following morning, it was Tora who brought her porridge, topped with rich honey.

"Will your belly like this?"

Mirana was salivating. The smell of the porridge and the honey filled the small chamber. She was pushing herself up on the bed, her eyes on that bowl. "Oh, aye," she said, then saw the look on Tora's face. She stilled, now uncertain. Tora said, her voice impatient and cold, "There was no one else to bring you food. If you want it, take it."

"Thank you."

Still the woman didn't leave. She sat on the end of the box bed, silent, watching Mirana eat the porridge. Mirana took the last bite, sighed deeply, and leaned back against the pillow, closing her eyes. "It was delicious."

"The child, Utta, made it for you. She said you liked the way she seasoned the porridge."

Mirana nodded. She said nothing, merely waited. Would Tora ask her to leave again?

"Sira has decided she will take Hafter. He is a good man. He will treat her well. He also looks a bit like Rorik and I suspect that is another reason she will have him."

"I see," Mirana said.

"They will wed soon. Sira will leave with him to the mainland."

Mirana was silent.

"I thought you should know."

"Thank you."

"Rorik will bathe with you on the morrow. I told him I would see to it, but he insists. He says only he knows how hot you like the bathing water and how cold you like the rinsing water."

She couldn't hold back the words. "But I thought you wanted Sira to wed Rorik."

"Rorik said he had no wish to wed her. That he would never wed her. It is done."

Tora left then, no more words between them.

The next day Rorik did indeed take her to the bathing hut. She was still very weak. Indeed his gentleness made her feel even more helpless, something she hated. He washed every bit of her, his large hands slick with soap, gliding over her back, her buttocks. He even had her balance herself with her hands on his shoulders whilst he washed her feet. He was matter-of-fact, saying nothing even as he held her against him with one hand, his other hand going between her thighs to bathe her there. She wished by the end of it that he would yell at her so she could yell back at him. Instead, he merely rinsed her off, doused her with a bucket of icy water, then wrapped her up warmly and carried her back to the sleeping chamber.

He combed her hair then left her.

He returned within five minutes, striding like a warrior into battle, frowning ferociously. Anger burned bright in his eyes. His jaw was working. Muscles corded in his throat. He looked ready to kill. Mirana brightened.

"It must be your doing," he said.

"And just what is my doing?" Ah, her voice rose, vibrating in the still room. It felt good. His kindness was irritating. She was bored with her own company and tired of his continued goodwill. Now, this was something to bite into. No longer was she a helpless child.

"Hafter just told me he didn't want to wed Sira."

"But why?" she asked, just staring at him, her joy at his ire momentarily forgotten.

"He just said he didn't wish it, nothing more."

"Surely this is strange, Rorik."

He had the look of a man forced to swallow bitter dregs, a man who didn't like it one bit. He yelled at her, full strength, "Damn you, Mirana, you know what he wants! He wants Entti, curse both your heads! I'm not blind or stupid. Hafter is as clear as the stream that flows shallow on the island. Aye, you've planned and plotted this. You're a meddlesome wench and won't leave things alone. Aye, and Entti is in this as well. It's all a woman's plot. That's why she's refused him and beaten him and kicked him. I won't have it, Mirana."

She grinned up at him, a taunting grin, full of mockery. She felt marvelous. She felt strength flow through her. She watched him rise to the bait. He actually shook his fist at her.

"You listen to me, woman. You will tell Entti that she's to take him into her. She's to let him sate himself on her body. Then he will be free of her and her damned wiles. Then he'll whistle and straighten his trousers and leave her without a backward look. Then everything will go as I have planned. He will wed Sira and we will all be free of her, and I do want to be free of her, do you understand me? I want that damned violent woman out of here!"

She continued to grin and keep quiet. She drummed her fingers on the blanket, waiting, ever grinning.

There was a strange chomping sound. She believed it was Rorik grinding his teeth.

"Mirana, I won't have it!"

She chose her words with fond disregard for peace. "Ah, I was just remembering how you told me that you would protect Entti's honor, how you would keep her safe so that I would not have to worry about her. Your vow did not last long, Rorik. Like other men, you make promises and scatter them to any willing female ears, then you break them just as easily, when it suits you."

"This is different and I know you see the differentness of it. You are merely being stubborn; you are merely enjoying yourself at my cost. You are enraging me, I see it clearly now. But I will tell you, Mirana, and you will not argue with me more, this is naught but a problem to be solved and the solution is simple and straightforward and Entti will do as she's told."

Mirana listened to him with growing joy. She was filled with such energy, nearly bursting with it, and she wanted to run and dance. She threw off the woolen blanket and swung her legs over the side of the box bed.

"Wait! What are you doing? Get back into bed, I won't have you ill again."

"Rorik," she said, grinning shamelessly up at him, "you want me to speak to Entti. I will speak to her now, oh aye, I certainly will. This differentness, I am certain she too will understand it well. She is sometimes slow in her thinking, but I will explain it to her carefully and at full length, giving her all your reasons and your man's logic."

"I will get her and bring her here." He said nothing more, merely leaned over, grabbed her legs and swung them back into bed. He covered her with the blanket. Then his hands stilled. He looked at her silently for several moments. "You look as healthy as a stoat," he said slowly. "There is color in your cheeks, your eyes are sparkling. I don't understand this, Mirana."

"I am pleased to see you, Rorik. There's nothing more to it than that."

"Why?"

She cocked her head to the side.

"Why are you happy to see me? That rings not of any truth I know. I think you're lying."

"You please me," she said simply. "I like to hear your voice, whether it's dark with threat or filled with laughter. I like to see you smile or frown or just stare at nothing. I like to see you stomp about when you're irritated. That I like particularly. You have been too considerate—not at first, mind you, just of late—and it has grown wearisome. But even that I can bear, if it be only rarely. I just like to see you. Just you."

That took him off guard. He frowned and straightened. He stared down at her from his great height. He would never understand her, never. "You would have preferred that I yelled at you when you were retching up your guts?"

"Oh no, but this tenderness of yours, Rorik, is rather like a father or a brother would treat me. Or a mother. You are a man, a strong man, and as I said, to see you furious, to see your face turn red with anger, why, that does please me. It brightens my spirits."

"You say nothing that makes sense to me."

"Perhaps not," she said, and smiled at him.

"I will fetch Entti to you now. You will speak sense to her, and not this morass of words that vex me even more. You will see that she obeys me."

"Very well," she said, crossed her hands over her stomach and smiled at his departing back, rigid with outrage and distrust of her motives. Ah, but she'd been tired of his endless kindness, the low-voiced gentleness that made her grit her teeth, for she'd known he was thinking other thoughts deep down, far more important thoughts for him, for her, for both of them together, yet he'd held them in, showing her only restraint and moderation, and the gods knew how irritated she'd become. But now he was angry and his brow had flared upward, and his jaw had worked in his anger, and it had pleased her enormously.

It was odd how life could be so very bleak one moment and make one want to burst with laughter the next. Odd, but it was so.

# 22

WHEN ENTTI STRODE into the sleeping chamber a few minutes later, she looked like a Valkyrie, her eyes mean with temper and outrage, nearly snarling, looking nonetheless like one of Odin's prized maidens in her tattered gown, the tunic held up with knots over each shoulder. Mirana knew that her feet were bare.

"Lord Rorik," she said slowly, as if that were sufficient.

Mirana remained silent.

Entti drew a deep breath. "He orders me, Mirana—*orders me*—to let Hafter take me until the lout is bored with me. Were he not your husband, I would have unmanned him."

"I am pleased you didn't. Doubtless Rorik is even more pleased."

Entti stopped cold, staring at Mirana. "You believe this is all a jest. You are laughing at me."

"Nay," Mirana said, sitting up now. "Sit down. We must decide what to do. Rorik is convinced he's being noble and wise, providing a beneficent solution for all involved. He doesn't know that—"

"Know what?"

"Entti, you are making my neck ache. Sit down. Aye, that's better. Stop waving your arms at me and listen.

Rorik wants Hafter to marry Sira, but he's refused. It is your fault—yours and mine—that Hafter refuses. He wants you, and in Rorik's mind, it is only lust, nothing more, and it is you who are responsible for this uncontrollable lust, and I, of course, because I am your friend."

"Of course it's nothing more! By the gods, Hafter is like all men—a randy goat who thinks of naught save that rod between his legs and shoveling it in a woman. I will not do it, Mirana, I won't. Using me to cure his lust so he will want to wed that venom-tongued Sira! Ha, Mirana!"

"No, you won't. And it's not lust. I have come to realize that Hafter wants you, Entti, but not just to assuage his man's unending needs."

Entti stared at her. She shook her head, sending a thick coil of rich brown hair to fall free over her shoulder. She said finally, bewildered, "You're mad, Mirana. Quite mad."

Mirana shook her head. "Nay, he loves you. Perhaps he doesn't yet realize it, but he did refuse to wed Sira. He must know something, or sense it, whatever it is a man does understand when he wants a woman forever, as his mate. As for you, my friend, you have been so busy fighting him and cursing him and escaping him, I don't think you know what you feel either."

"You're mad. I despise Hafter. He is—"

"I know, I know. He's an animal, a goat, he believes himself a stud, a stallion, a—"

"I don't mean to bore you, Mirana," Entti said, all stiff and cold. She rose and began to wring her hands. Mirana stared at those wringing hands and smiled.

"Listen, Entti. Why don't you tell Hafter that if he pleads with you, if he shows sincerity and suitable adoration in his speech and in his voice, you will consider accepting him for a husband."

"No."

"Make it clear to him that you won't let him take you until after you're wed."

"No." Entti flung off the bed and began pacing. "I don't believe what you are saying. We will escape, Mirana. You are nearly well. We will escape, perhaps tomorrow night. We will be free of all of them."

Mirana felt a deep misery. She shook her head.

"You believe yourself safe now that you've been so ill? I hear things, Mirana, since I am a slave and of no account. Everyone speaks freely in front of me, all save Hafter, who just stares and broods and looks sour. I heard Merrik and all the other men talking, and his mother and father as well. None of them want you here. Perhaps they don't want you dead, for surely that is too extreme a measure even for these cutthroats, but they want you gone. I think they fear you, fear that your half-brother will come for you, and thus it will begin again.

"As for Sira, that viper, the bitch would stick a knife in your ribs if she but has a chance. We must escape, Mirana, we must."

"Do you want to, truly, Entti? Do you truly wish never to see Hafter again?"

"What choice do I have?" Her voice was low and dull and filled with despair. "I have no wish to remain and be made into a whore again. Aye, a few of the other men are looking more closely at me now since they realize that you can no longer protect me. Particularly Gurd. They will force me, Mirana, 'tis but a matter of time."

Entti looked up to see Rorik standing in the doorway. He smiled suddenly, for he had heard her speak.

"Hafter is waiting for you, Entti. Go to him now."

She shook her head, not moving.

"I gave you to him. You need have no fear of the other men. They won't touch you. Hafter is now your master. Go to him now and do what it is he wishes you to do."

"May you go to the Christians' hell, Lord Rorik, and roast for all eternity."

He paled. Anger wiped away the fear of her curse. He drew himself up. He had no intention of striking her. He had never struck a woman and he wouldn't begin now. "You aren't a whore, Entti. However, you are naught but a slave. You will do as I bid you."

"She wasn't a slave until you raided her town and stole her."

"You will be quiet, Mirana," he said. "As for you, Entti, it matters not that you weren't a slave before. If your father or your husband or the other men couldn't save what was theirs, they deserved to lose everything, including you. That is simply the way of things."

Entti said nothing more. She drew a deep breath, and walked past Rorik, head high.

Rorik rubbed his hands together and smiled. "Good. That is done, finally. Surely Hafter will tire of her by tomorrow, for he is sorely tried, and will plow her belly until the sunrise. Then he will see reason. Then he will agree to wed Sira and remove her from here."

Mirana swung her legs over the side of the box bed and rose to stand nose to shoulder with him. "I won't have it, do you hear me? I won't have my friend abused just because you want Sira away from here." She was wearing only her shift, a white linen garment that came only to her mid-thighs, but she didn't seem to realize this. She walked from the sleeping chamber, her black hair in wild tangles down her back, her feet bare, her legs long and equally bare.

He stared at her, his brain at first refusing to work. Then he roared her name and ran after her.

He caught sight of her when she had reached the outer hall. She was in the midst of a knot of women and thus beyond his reach.

Erna was stroking Mirana's hair with her one good hand, pulling it free of tangles.

Old Alna was clucking through her few teeth—it sounded like hissing—and was patting her bare arm.

Utta was standing back, merely staring at her, worship in her young eyes.

And Amma, that damned woman who had brought the other women to revolt, that woman who should have been a man, so solid was she and so filled with guile and cunning, why she held her hand over Mirana's forehead, seeing if there was fever. Entti was nowhere to be seen. The other women just stood there, besotted looks on their faces. It galled him. Why did they give her their loyalty so quickly? Why had their loyalty escaped from him and flown to her?

Rorik gave it up for the moment. He went to Hafter, who was slouched on a bench against the far wall, a wooden mug of mead in his hand. He was staring at the floor between his feet. He did not have the look of a Viking warrior. He looked like a man beset, a man who had lost something dear and was at a loss as to how to retrieve it.

Rorik said, "Did you speak to Entti?"

"Aye," Hafter said, looking away from his feet up to Rorik. "She said she would kill me or herself if I tried to bed her. She said it mattered not to her. She walked out of the longhouse then, saying nothing more, as if daring me to force her." He paused a moment, drank deeply of the mead, and said, "She is strong, Rorik. She fights like a woman and her knee is as quick and as deadly, just like a man's weapon. I could take her, but it would be difficult if she didn't want me to. I would have to hurt her and I don't want to."

"Why not? She's but a slave. She belongs to you. You can do anything you wish to do with her."

Hafter shook his head. "She might be a slave now, but she wasn't before. And what she is now is more like she was before than what she's supposed to be now."

Rorik wondered why a mortal's plans must always go awry as he tried to sort through Hafter's words. There was sense there, but he was too tired, too frustrated, to delve deep enough to find it. His plan was noble. It would solve every problem. Except for Entti's, but she was a slave. What she was before no longer mattered. He bellowed down at Hafter's bent head, "You are a warrior! Tie her down, damn her!"

Hafter's eyes lit up. "I hadn't thought of that. Would you help me? She is very determined."

Rorik looked disgusted. He slammed his fist against Hafter's shoulder, sending his friend sprawling onto the earth floor. "Go tie her up yourself!" he yelled, then turned back to see his wife grinning at him.

Hafter shook himself as he rose. He drank down the rest of his mead, slammed the mug on the bench, and strode from the longhouse. Mirana felt a shaft of fear. She turned, only to feel Amma's hand on her arm.

"Nay, Mirana, leave him be. Entti can see to herself. She has surprised us all. I vow this is the meat for a scald's verses, at least those verses that make you laugh. I wonder what my husband Sculla thinks of all this."

"Ha," said Old Alna, "Sculla is out doubtless hitting his head against a low-lying oak branch, that, or polishing one of his weapons. 'Tis all the man thinks of—his weapons."

"He thinks about me when he is angered," Amma said, and smiled. "I have the skill to make him angry quite often now. Nay, he spends little time on his axes and knives when I am close to him, goading him to anger and to pleasure."

"Ah," said Erna, tears filling her eyes. "How I wish Asta were here. Can't you just hear how she would tease Hafter? How she would laugh and hit him on the arm? And tease him until his eyes crossed?"

"Aye, I can hear her," Mirana said, and wondered if Gurd had gone off by himself to grieve for his dead wife. She didn't like him, but she felt a small portion of his grief.

"At least you survived the bad food," Old Alna said, "though what it was I don't know. I've thought and thought, but I cannot imagine how only you and Asta were struck. Ah, it is too much for an old woman to bear. Aye, we'll miss Asta, a fine treasure that one was. I remember when she was born, came out of her mother's womb squalling louder than a Viking's battle cry. And then she gurgled, I swear to you, all were astonished."

"Aye," said Amma. "And I'll wager she made her mother laugh but moments after that. I remember when she first met Gurd. She said he had the strongest arms of any man in the world. She said she wondered about his temper, but then she just laughed and said that no man could resist a good jest and she would bring him many jests."

Utta said, "Mirana, you are very pale. Should you not be in bed?"

Mirana agreed and returned to the sleeping chamber. She lay there, wondering what Entti and Hafter were doing.

Hafter had found Entti at the dock, untying the mooring lines to one of the smaller longboats. He yelled at her, running full tilt toward her. She turned, then began to tug more frantically at the knots.

He caught her and twisted her about to face him. "What are you doing? Do you think yourself a man? Nay, a dozen men to row this damned boat? You are a fool, my girl. Now, I will follow Lord Rorik's advice."

"And what is that, pray?"

"That I tie your arms and legs and open you to me, and do whatever I want to with you."

She howled and sent her fist low in his belly. Hafter felt the bolt of pain, but this time it was high enough so that he didn't drop like a stone at her feet. He drew back his fist and hit her jaw, not too hard, for he didn't want to hurt her. She crumbled against him. He liked the feel of her limp and soft against him. It was different from the loudmouthed woman, all fists and meanness, that she'd become.

When Entti awoke, she was in the barn and her wrists were tied above her head to a stake, her legs spread, ankles tied as well.

She stared up at Hafter, who was seated beside her, his legs crossed. He looked like a man who hadn't a care in the world. He looked like a man who had gained what he wanted. He was whistling and chewing on a piece of straw.

He saw she was awake and gently felt her jaw. "You are all right. Your jaw won't even be bruised. Well, perhaps just a bit, but that you deserve. I controlled my great strength with you since you are but a woman."

"Untie me."

He shook his head and smiled. "I am not a fool."

She pulled at the bonds but they didn't loosen. She looked at him with murder in her eyes.

"I'll untie you," he said, enjoying that look, and unfastened the knots of her tunic. "Now I'll do more than untie you." Then he calmly pulled her clothes off. It didn't take him long for she didn't wear many clothes, not even a shift. She didn't have anything save rags, and it angered him immensely. He would see that she was well garbed, just as soon as he convinced her to trust him, to cease playing her woman's jests on him.

"There," he said, sat back again and looked at her as he would a platter of boar steaks. "I have missed seeing you. You please me."

Entti stared up at this golden man who had helped sack and destroy her town, his skills and enthusiasm well suited for such an endeavor. He was staring down at her, not at her breasts or her belly, but into her face. He was silent, just looking down at her. Then he began to frown.

Finally, he said, "What is wrong with you?"

She said nothing, merely turned her face away.

"Entti!"

He grabbed her face between his palms and jerked her back. "Don't you look away from me, damn you!"

She closed her eyes.

"All right, if this how you wish things to be between us I care not."

She heard him rise, heard the rustle of his clothing. She felt his body come down over hers, felt him hard against her, felt the hair of his chest rubbing against her skin, felt his hot breath on her cheek.

He moaned and moved over her. He kissed her ear, her jaw where he had struck her, her nose. "You're crying," he said suddenly, rearing back. "No, don't do that, Entti. You never cry. You are too mean to cry."

"There is nothing else to do," she whispered.

He cursed, then cursed again.

# 23

"I HAVE BROUGHT you some mutton broth and some warm bread with butter and honey."

"Thank you, Utta," Mirana said, took the wooden plate and laid it on her lap.

"Lord Rorik said you shouldn't yet have the mutton itself or the mushrooms or the cabbage. He said it was still too much for your belly. He said the broth was only for you and the rest of us weren't to touch it. He even told the men to keep away from the broth, but they were laughing and all were trying to tip some into their bowls, trying to annoy him."

"And they succeeded?"

"They annoyed him, aye," Utta said. "My father said Rorik has become too protective and that you, of all men or women, have little need of protection. I thought Lord Rorik would hit my father, but at the last moment he held back."

Mirana smiled.

"I think he held back because I was there, right beside my father."

"Aye, you're right." She tasted the broth, but it wasn't to her liking—it tasted of a strange condiment she didn't recognize—and she ate only a few bites. A pity Rorik couldn't have tended to his own business and left her to decide about what food she should and shouldn't eat.

"Who prepared the broth?"

"We were all working about the fire pit. All had a say in its preparation but Amma said we must add some brawly root."

"Ah," said Mirana, and ate all the bread, gently shoving the broth to the side of the tray.

When Rorik came into the chamber a few minutes later, she was full and sleepy.

He looked harassed.

"What has happened now?" she said, patting the bed beside her.

He eased down, not really heeding what he was doing, and said, "Hafter wishes to marry Entti. I don't understand any of this, Mirana. He says he tied her up just as I told him to, then she cried and he couldn't bear it, he said, and now he will marry her. He has freed her. He didn't force her, he said he wouldn't take her until they were man and wife. He has told her that if she wishes to unman him again, she must now consider closely, for he will be her husband and the man to give her babes. To unman him, he said he told her, would hurt her as much as it would him now. They will wed tomorrow."

She stared at his strong throat, and kept her smile hidden. "What do you think about this now, Rorik?"

He shrugged. "He will have his way. I told him not to leave now to live on the mainland. I told him he must stay, that you would be very unhappy were he to take Entti away."

"And you wouldn't miss Hafter, I suppose."

"Oh aye, I would surely miss the great idiot. I don't understand him, but I would miss him sorely."

"You have very nice legs, Rorik."

He whipped around to stare at her. "Are you all right?"

"Aye, I was just looking at your legs. I like the golden hair. They're strong legs. They could walk for a very long time and not tire. Very beautiful. I want to touch you."

He laughed then, softly at first, then he laughed louder, deep and full and free.

And then she said, "And your belly. It is covered with gold fur, all soft and thick, just like a goat's belly, and you are hard and lean, and mayhap your belly is more beautiful than your legs."

He stopped laughing and stared at her. There was something deep and brilliant in his eyes, something that drew her and made her want when she'd never wanted before, and she was smiling at him, reaching out her hand to him. She wanted to touch him, and she wanted him to touch her and kiss her, and aye, perhaps even the other, perhaps she even wanted that now, for there was a warmth in her, deep and curling and so very intense that she wondered how one could feel like that and not burst with the need of it. He was taut, leaning toward her now. His beautiful eyes were alight with her, with the thought of her with him, and she recognized it. Then she said, "Aye, Rorik, and your mouth, mayhap that is the most beautiful part of you, but it will take me many years to decide. You have a bewitching mouth." And he was smiling again, that beautiful mouth of his turned up at the corners, his lips slightly parted, then laughing and shaking his head at her. She wanted to bring more laughter like that into his life, she thought, then her stomach cramped viciously, and she scrambled from the bed and vomited up the little broth she'd drunk and the bread.

"By the gods, no!"

Mirana moaned, clutched her belly, and fell onto her side on the pounded earth.

She was ill for only two hours, for she'd eaten little of the broth, but she was white and pale and sweating profusely, lying on her side, her legs drawn up, waiting, dreading the next cramp. There was no laughter in her now, no joy, just the fear of more of the awful pain.

Finally, she slept. Rorik stood over her, shaking his head. He'd been a fool. He covered her with a woolen blanket, smoothed the damp hair off her forehead.

Hafter stood in the doorway. "Will she live?"

"Aye. I fear it is Sira."

"I believe so too, but I am sorry for it. I have known her since she was a child, as have you. But I do not understand her now."

"I am not certain that I do either. She must have poisoned Mirana. Poor Asta died because she liked the taste of the food and thus she ate most of Mirana's. But why would Sira do it again? It is you who turned away from her. Mirana was not involved."

There was a shout, then a scream.

Both men ran from the sleeping chamber into the main hall. Sira had wrapped Entti's long hair about her fist and had dragged her down to her knees, pulling her toward the fire pit. She had a knife in her right hand.

"By Thor, this is madness!" Rorik slammed through the men and women and children who were crowding close, uncertain what to do. Kerzog was barking wildly, his strong teeth tugging at Sira's skirt. Sira reached down and struck the dog with the handle of the knife. Kerzog fell sideways, whimpering for a moment, but then he was up again, his teeth sunk into Sira's gown, pulling, slowing her.

"Nay, Rorik, I will stop it. Entti is my woman."

Hafter grabbed Sira's forearm and shook it. Then he bent back her wrist, but still Sira was screaming at Entti, twisting and jerking on her hair, "You damnable whore! You slut—you are her friend and between you there is no man for me, no man that I want. I'll kill you and then I'll kill that other miserable bitch!"

Hafter calmly drew back his fist and cuffed her solidly in the side of her head. The knife fell to the earthen floor, Sira fell forward onto her knees, then fell to her side. Entti went down with her, her hair still wrapped about Sira's hand.

Hafter said to Entti, "Lie still and be quiet, or you'll just hurt yourself more."

He carefully unwrapped her hair from around Sira's hand, then massaged her scalp. He helped her to her feet and stepped aside, keeping her in the crook of his arm.

Tora leaned down and looked at her niece. "Harald," she called to her husband. "Take her out of here. Let her sleep outside the longhouse. Let her think about her lack of control. Let her think about her punishment, for surely there will be retribution to match her crime."

"I believe," Harald said, "that I will keep one of the men with her." When Harald lifted Sira and slung her over his shoulder, carrying her away, Tora said, "I am sorry. Entti, you seem a reasonable girl. I would be pleased were you to forgive her." She shook her head. "It is difficult. First Rorik and then you, Hafter . . . it is her disappointment. Harald and I have raised her gently, for her parents had died suddenly, and left her alone, and we wanted her to feel happy with us. We had no daughter, and thus we tried to make her into ours, but we gave her no boundaries. Mayhap we have given her too much, not reined in her temper, not tried to dampen her vanity. I suppose she came to believe that anything she desired would be hers. It is my fault, not hers."

Entti thought that was nonsense, but she held her peace. She was still rubbing her scalp. Her eyes were stinging from the pain of it. Sira had caught her off guard and she felt like a fool for letting the woman get the better of her. She looked up to see the pain on Tora's face. She sighed and said, "I forgive her," and thought she would surely kill the damned bitch the moment she got the chance. First Mirana and now her. Why was Tora commiserating with Rorik and Hafter as if they had been Sira's victims? It was she and Mirana who had suffered, not the damned men.

She knew Sira had tried to poison Mirana. All knew it had to be she. What would Rorik do? After all, Asta had died and so much laughter and jesting had passed with her. After all, Rorik was lord of Hawkfell Island. He had to do something.

He did. The following morning, Rorik ordered Sira stripped to her waist, tied to a pole, and whipped, first by Harald, since she was his responsibility, then by Rorik and finally by Hafter. Entti wanted very much to wield the whip herself, but only men were allowed to do it. Mirana, still pale and weak, stayed in her bed, Utta with her.

"You will be safe now," Rorik said when he came into the sleeping chamber after it was done. "Sira will not soon forget the pain of her punishment. It should slow her anger in the future, make her pause before she loses her control."

No, Mirana thought, it might slow her outwardly, but her anger and hatred would fester. She said, "You are certain she tried to poison me, Rorik?"

He stared at her. "Who else would it be? Forget not that she tried to kill you before you were poisoned, and then Entti last night. Aye, she had to be the one to put the poison in your food. She has learned a lesson. She will obey my father and mother now. She will do as she's told and keep silent."

"I spoke to the women. None were certain, but Utta told me that Sira didn't come near the broth."

"Utta is a child. She cannot be certain. Don't forget that Asta died. I told Gurd that he could whip Sira as well, for she has no silver to pay him *Danegeld* for Asta's life and he refused to accept payment from my father. He also refused to whip Sira. He said that I would provide the punishment. He said he didn't want to look at her. He didn't stay to watch. He grieves for Asta. It pained me to see his sorrow."

He paced the room several times, frowning ferociously. "Sira continued to swear she hadn't poisoned you, either time. Even as I brought the whip down on her back, she screamed that she hadn't done it. Had I not seen her attack on you and then on Entti last night, I might have believed her."

"I am sorry for all of it, Rorik," Mirana said. She'd brought him such misery, she thought, suddenly exhausted, too exhausted to think more, to reason out what she should do. She had never been so weak in her life. Even rising from the bed to relieve herself made her legs tremble and sweat break out on her forehead. She closed her eyes. She was asleep within minutes, a deep sleep without dreams.

Rorik sat on the bed beside her. He just looked at her for a very long time. He remembered what she'd said before she'd fallen ill again the previous night. She'd made him laugh and she'd much enjoyed doing it. She enjoyed his laughter as much as she enjoyed his rages. She'd also made him hard as a stone. And what she'd said to him—did she really believe him beautiful? His legs and his belly? Did she really want to touch him?

Life, he thought, still staring down at his wife, perhaps life could be just curious enough to bring trust and love to an unlikely man and woman. He prayed that it was so.

He also thought she would appreciate kindness and gentleness from him again, if just for a day or two.

The next day Hafter and Entti were wed. Gurd had sent all of Asta's clothes to Entti.

Sira lay on her stomach in the longhouse, her back coated with the white cream that leached out much of the pain from the lashes.

Rorik eased Mirana onto a blanket in the shade, her back against the longhouse wall. He brought her food and joined her, giving her a goblet of Rhenish wine. Kerzog lay at her feet, his head on her ankles. The dog's belly was stretched taut with all the food he'd eaten. He snored.

Rorik frowned down at his dog. "The brute wanted to stay with Entti, but Hafter told him to wait his turn for her affection. Thus he comes here and you feed him until he falls into a glutton's swoon. Damned hound."

"He is fond of Entti," Mirana said and patted the dog's neck.

"You are too pale. Drink this and smile at me and tell me that you believe my arms are beautiful, mayhap even more beautiful than my legs and my belly."

She smiled, but it didn't reach her eyes, for she was staring at the food, and he saw her fear.

He picked up a piece of mutton and took a bite. He chewed it slowly, then nodded. He closed his eyes a moment and waited. Then he opened his eyes, smiled, and held the mutton toward her. Kerzog raised his head, sniffed, looked at the mutton, then barked. Rorik gave him a piece, just shaking his head as he did so. The dog, as was his wont, grabbed the mutton from Rorik's fingers, coming within a whisper of his flesh. He snarled and worried the mutton as Rorik made a show of trying to hold it from him.

"Did he ever bite your fingers?"

"When he was a pup, aye. But not now, 'tis a game with him."

"That dog," she said, staring at Kerzog, "was never a pup."

She ate then, but not enough.

"Kerzog is getting fat," Rorik said as the dog finished Mirana's mutton and gave him a look that clearly said he deserved the mutton and much more. Rorik punched him lightly on his shoulder. Kerzog belched and slept again, but not before he'd looked about to find Entti. Seeing her laughing with Hafter, kissing him, feeding him bits of food, the dog let his head fall back onto Mirana's ankles.

Rorik gave her more wine. When she was smiling and laughing at nothing that was funny, just laughing because the wine had loosened her thoughts and her tongue, he fed her honeyed almonds. He didn't leave her until she, like Kerzog, was asleep. He hoped her head wouldn't feel like bursting when she awoke from all the wine. He'd stopped drinking the wine in good time.

All the men had begun to build Hafter and Entti a small house of one chamber on the north side of the barley fields where all his married warriors and their wives slept during the summer months. All his people ate together in the longhouse, and lived there during the coldest months, but the married men liked their privacy with their wives when it was warm enough. There was at least a roof over the beams so the two of them would sleep there this night. The jesting was in fun and there was no mention that many of the men had already plowed her belly when she'd been a slave and seemingly a half-witted woman who hadn't cared who did anything at all to her.

Entti sought out Mirana before she went with Hafter to their small hut.

"She sleeps, Entti," Rorik said. "She is nearly well again, thank the gods and her dislike of the broth." He leaned over and kissed Entti's cheek. "You are a good woman. I am the lord of Hawkfell Island. You are free now, Entti, forever. You are now one of us. You are now a Viking woman and a Viking warrior's wife."

"Hafter is crowing like a rooster, Rorik. I have not heard him laugh much before. It is a nice sound. He will never regret this marriage, I vow it to you."

That night Sira disappeared.

# 24

THERE WAS ENDLESS talk and argument and questions. It was a full day now and no one had found Sira. None of the boats were missing. She was dead, there was no doubt about that, for she couldn't have swum to the mainland because she couldn't swim, nor could she have flown there like one of the myriad birds, but the men were near to violence because they couldn't discover what had happened to her. And that troubled everyone the most. What if she hadn't wanted to be found?

Tora said little, just held her grief to herself. The women held their voices low and simply didn't speak of Sira. Finally, Mirana was able to leave the longhouse late that evening to find a few moments to herself.

It happened so quickly that Mirana had no chance to struggle or to yell or to even recognize who her attacker was. One moment she was staring out over the moon-drenched sea, alone, letting the warmth of the night enfold her. The next, a hand slammed down on her mouth, her hands were jerked behind her back, and bound quickly. She bit the hand, then opened her mouth. She heard a man's oath, then felt the pain on her left temple, then nothing save a deep pulling blackness. But the voice had seemed somehow familiar and she tried to hold to it even as she slumped unconscious.

When she awoke, she was aware instantly that she was in a longboat. She lay very still, becoming used to the rocking, the rhythm of the oars dipping into the water, rising, dipping again, smoothly, quickly. Her head hurt, but she became used to that too. Her fear eased. She heard four men speaking, and she knew all of them. Each of them excited, pleased, but one of them was furious.

It was Gunleik, and he shouted suddenly, "By Odin All-Father, you struck her, Ivar! She is still unconscious. You were to rescue her, nothing more, and bring her to me so that I could speak to her, to reassure her. But nay, you were a brute and rough with her."

"There was no time, Gunleik," Ivar said, and Mirana could picture him biting his lip, stiffening because the man he worshiped was angry with him. "You set me to watch the longhouse and when I saw Mirana, I knew I had to take her then, else risk our lives and perhaps hers as well. Forget not that the other woman told us that all want her gone, that Rorik Haraldsson hates her and wishes her dead, that someone has already tried to poison her. She was alone. I took my chance. I had to hit her else she would have screamed. When she awakens, you will speak to her, she will agree that I did only what was necessary."

"You struck her," Gunleik said again. He cursed, and Mirana saw him thrust his fingers through his coarse gray hair.

"Aye, but if I hadn't, she might have struck me. She is a good fighter, Gunleik, forget it not."

"I'm all right, Gunleik."

"Mirana?" He bent down and began to rub her arms, her hands, lightly touch his callused fingertips to her cheeks. "Thank the gods, you're awake. Listen, we've saved you. You're here with us now. You're not to be afraid. Aye, I have you again, little one. All is well now." He lifted her onto the bench beside him. The boat rocked to the side and one of the men cursed. It was Emund, and she wished it were any other save him. He was one of Einar's minions, a mean-spirited bully she had never liked. He abused slaves and women.

"Gunleik," she said. "You must listen to me. What Ivar said is true, but not really. What did he mean—'the other woman'?"

"The girl with the silver hair so wondrous that even I have stared at it. Her name is—"

"I know who she is." Mirana turned to stare at Sira as she spoke. She was sitting beside Ingolf, another of her half-brother's favorites. He was as ill-favored with his squinting eyes and his too-heavy black eyebrows as Sira was beautiful, her hair gleaming silver beneath the bright moonlight. She smiled at Mirana and gave her a small salute. It wasn't a nice smile. Sira merely looked at her, but there was malice in her eyes, and pleasure.

"All are worried for you," Mirana said. "All have been searching for you. Many believed you dead, by your own hand. Guilt and remorse, it is said. But Tora is distraught by your disappearance."

"I am sorry for that because Tora has always loved me and always tried to make me happy. But in the end, she lost to you, Mirana, and I knew she would lose to you, as would I. But that is over now. It is a new life for both of us. Are you not pleased? I am quite alive and so are you. Were it not for Tora and Harald, I would have no remorse, merely a sense of dissatisfaction that I failed so badly. But now you are here, Mirana, saved just as I was from certain death by these brave warriors. Aye, we are the luckiest of women."

Ivar said to Mirana, his young voice eager to placate, eager to reassure Gunleik that he'd done the right thing, "Sira was out walking about, just as you were tonight, Mirana. Ingolf took her last night and she told us all about you and the way you've been treated here." His young voice rose in his anger at what had happened to her, for he and Mirana had been playmates since she'd come to Clontarf years before. "We will come back to this place, Mirana, and we will avenge you."

"Aye," Ingolf said. "This Rorik, this little lordling of Hawkfell Island, is naught but a fool, a pretentious, impudent oaf, and we will kill him and fire his little island and take all his women. Gunleik should have killed him before. You, mistress, should have let him die from his wound. Your kind heart stayed your hand. The next time it will be my turn."

Mirana closed her eyes for a moment. She had to speak to Gunleik, but not in front of Ingolf or Emund. Her head throbbed where Ivar had struck her. Sira merely sat there looking beautiful and fragile and utterly self-assured.

"You look thin, Mirana, and very pale," Ivar said.

"Aye," she said, so distracted she scarce knew what she was saying. " 'Twas because I was ill. But I am well now, worry not about me."

"It is because they poisoned you," Ingolf said. "Sira told us all about it. She told us how you were abused and mistreated by all of them,. Einar will be pleased to have you back. It has not taken us too long to find you."

"Einar," she said, knowing from the first instant she'd regained consciousness that it was her half-brother who had sent Gunleik to find her, but not wanting to face it.

Emund laughed, reached forward and lightly trailed his fingers over her arm. "Einar will be most relieved to see you, mistress. We have all missed you."

"Leave her be," Gunleik said sharply. "See to your oars, Emund. We must move quickly now."

"I must speak to you, Gunleik," Mirana said, her voice pitched as low as she could manage it. Still, she knew that Ingolf had heard her, for his features sharpened and he leaned forward over his oars.

"Certainly, little one," Gunleik said, and patted her hand. "I am glad to see you. I have been very worried for you. 'Twas by the veriest chance we learned about Rorik Haraldsson's island and its location."

"Aye," said Emund easily. "We were in London, a nasty place with smells vile enough to make a man puke, but Rorik is known there, as is his family. We pretended to be his friends, and soon enough there was mention of his Hawkfell Island. He keeps the island's location secret, but we had silver and it wasn't long before we found someone to tell us. Aye, 'twas easy after that. We hid to the east of the harbor, in a small protected cove. We rowed from the mainland when the night was blacker than a witch's eyes. None saw us. This Rorik believes himself a warrior. He is naught but a fool, aye, and I'll slit his throat for him."

"Doesn't the man even have enough wits to post sentries?" Ingolf said, then laughed.

"Aye," Mirana said, nothing more. "But all have been searching for her."

Emund said, "They could have found us, even during their search, but they didn't. Aye, 'tis an island filled with fools and led by a stupid man."

"We were well hidden," Ivar said.

Mirana said nothing. She felt sick to her stomach and her head throbbed. She couldn't speak to Gunleik until they beached the longboat and camped for the night. She felt a knot of cold deep in her belly, and said, "When do we go ashore for the night, Gunleik?"

"We don't," he said. "We must continue without stopping, Mirana. Einar said to return as soon as we could else he would suffer for it, and thus we would as well. I know it will be hard for you, but there is really no choice."

Mirana knew it was true that Einar would kill Gunleik and anyone for that matter who didn't do what he wanted them to, anyone who failed. She drew a deep breath. There was nothing for it but to try. "Listen to me, all of you. Einar has made a contract with King Sitric. He will force me to wed that old man in exchange for more power, more slaves, and more silver. I will be given over to him the moment Einar has me again. I do not want this. I would ask that you return me to Hawkfell Island. I would ask that you tell Einar that I am dead, that, or you couldn't find me." She realized this wouldn't work, and quickly added, "Nay, do not even return to Einar. Come back with me to Hawkfell Island and become one with Rorik's men. They were well treated and there is raiding and trading, enough to make a man rich."

Gunleik was frowning. "But Einar said nothing of this, Mirana. You to wed with King Sitric? It doesn't seem likely to me, for you aren't of a royal house nor do you bring great wealth. How did you learn of it?"

"Rorik had a spy in the king's court in Dublin. He returned to Hawkfell Island and told him of it."

"Aye," Emund said, as he spat over the side of the boat. "Aye, this Rorik had many spies. Aslak was his spy at Clontarf. He is responsible for freeing Rorik and for him taking you. I would kill the fool if I could. I would go back to the little lordling's island—

to kill Aslak. But I don't believe you about this other man, Mirana. At the king's garrison? Not very likely, I say."

She shook her head numbly. "It is true, Gunleik. The man's name is Kron and he was at the garrison for some six months. He discovered everything. I don't want to go back. I don't want to be forced to wed that old man. By all the gods, he is old enough to be my grandfather! I know I am not of a royal house. I know it makes no sense, but Kron said that the king was told by his advisor, Hormuze, that he was to have me, Audun's only daughter, a virgin, and I would bring him back to his virility and to his youth, and give him warrior sons."

Mirana looked at each man in turn. They were staring at her as if she'd gained three heads. She said very calmly, her heart spurting fast with fear, "It matters not now anyway, for I am no longer a virgin. I am already wed, to Rorik Haraldsson. I am his wife and the mistress of Hawkfell Island."

There, it was said. Her words lay stark in the night. The men were silent, frozen, staring harder at her now, clearly disbelieving. Then Sira laughed, a delicious woman's laugh, filled with amusement and disdain.

"It's true, damn you, Sira, and you well know it!"

"Ah, Mirana, you lie to yourself just as you lie to these valiant men who have risked their lives to save you." She smiled in pity, continuing to Gunleik, "I know that you are fond of her, but Rorik didn't want her, though she tried hard enough to gain his attention. He didn't wed her. He left her virginity intact. She was naught but a hostage to him, despite all her tricks, nothing more than an enemy to his family who would have killed her, despite him wanting to keep her to bargain with Einar. Nay, I was the one who was supposed to wed him. His parents came to Hawkfell, bringing me with them for the wedding. You saved her, Gunleik, for surely they would have killed her."

"Don't believe her, please," Mirana said. "She lies. She was the one who tried to kill me. She wanted Rorik, but he was already wed to me."

Ingolf snorted, his heavy brows a single black line across his brow. "It sounds like naught more than a tangled weave of a woman's lies. You will be quiet, mistress. Your whining has no effect on any of us. Your lies are childish. Not a virgin! You, the manly little bitch who would let no man near you, who would kill a man before you let him caress you? Aye, I wanted you, but you would only stare at me, contempt for me writ plain on your face. You're a cold one, mistress, and I doubt not that you will die a virgin. Or, if your wedding to King Sitric is true, why then, you will have no choice but to part your legs for him and then you'll be a vessel for the old king's rod. You, no longer a virgin? It would take more than a single man to rob you of your maidenhead. And that is a lie easily disproved. If Gunleik doesn't wish to do it, why I'll stick my finger inside you and find your maiden's shield.

"Nay, there is no reason for this other slave to lie. You lie because you don't want to be wedded to an old man, your fine white flesh crawls at the thought, doesn't it? But mistress, he is a king, think you on that and on the advantages it will bring you. You will have slaves and jewelry and more gowns than you would wish for. Einar will gain from the bargain as will the rest of us as well. Lie down and sleep and keep your lies behind your teeth. Leave us in peace."

"Gunleik," Mirana said, grabbing his arm. "Please, I am telling the truth. Don't take me back to Einar. This whole idea of the king wanting only me—it makes no sense. Why would he demand to have only me when there are princesses of more value to him?

"Please listen, all of you. If you do take me back, then the king will discover that he's been deceived, and all of us will die, me, Einar, perhaps even all of you. Don't look away from me, Ivar. I'm not a virgin. I'm a wife. I'm the mistress of Hawkfell Island. By all the gods, if I weren't Rorik's wife, why then would I be out freely walking about for Ivar to find me? Why would I lie to you, men I've known half my life?"

Gunleik looked at her for a very long time. She saw uncertainty in his eyes. She felt sick. He said finally, sounding very weary, "I will think on what you have said, Mirana. Einar never said anything about the king wanting you though, and that is a fact."

"That's because he's a snake and cruel and a miserable bully. It pleases him to make people jump and crawl according to his wishes."

Emund struck her clean across her cheek. Then he smiled at her. "Ingolf told you to be quiet. Now you will obey."

Gunleik flung himself on Emund, his hands around his throat, squeezing, until Ingolf struck Gunleik and he slumped to the bottom of the boat. Ivar grabbed for the knife at his belt. "Oh nay, boy, you keep your sticker sheathed. I didn't hurt your hero, Gunleik, even though the old fool would have sent us all into the sea with his violent attack on Emund. Mirana deserved the slap. She deserves more, but she is Einar's half-sister, and thus I had to show restraint. But to speak of her half-brother like that deserves much more than a mere slap and Emund would agree. Einar would whip her back raw. Now, row, boy. We have many leagues to cover before we rest."

Mirana huddled next to Gunleik, her palm on his heart. Thank the gods it was strong and steady. She fell asleep finally, so exhausted she could no longer keep her eyes open. As she slipped away, she heard Sira singing softly, her voice lilting, a siren's song in the still night. She heard Ingolf speaking quietly to Sira. His voice wasn't that of a man to his newly captured slave. No, his was a lover's voice.

Why had Sira lied? What did she hope to gain?

Rorik felt the grinding fear miraculously vanish when his brother Merrik said, "We can't find her. She isn't on the island. It's as simple as that. Neither is Sira. Both of them are gone. I'm sorry, Rorik."

He was sorry? By all the gods, why? Rorik wanted to believe it, but he was afraid to. He'd seen her in his mind's eye, dead, killed by an animal or mayhap even by one of his family. And so, he was still silent, simply staring at his brother who said again, "I'm sorry, Rorik. I know you wanted the woman, but she is gone. She is dead."

Rorik had been so weary he'd wanted to fall down and curl against Kerzog, but now, with this wondrous news, he was once again filled with energy, he wanted to shout and to plan and to gain hope because now he knew, now he was certain.

Harald laid his hand on his son's shoulder and looked into blue eyes that held the same summer blue of the skies. "There were no boats missing, Rorik. She was very unhappy, son. Mayhap she jumped from the cliff. Mayhap Sira attacked her and both of them fell. Aye, that was probably the way of it. Both of them dead, washing out to sea."

Rorik smiled, straightened to his full height, and breathed in the fresh warm summer air. "Oh no,

Father, not that. It's very simple, really. Her half-brother, Einar, discovered she was here and he took her. He probably took Sira as well. It is too late to leave tonight. We will prepare and leave on the morrow."

He rubbed his hands together, leaving his father and brother standing there, staring after him. But he knew, he knew it deep within himself that he would find her. He just prayed it would be in time. As he released his mind to sleep, he realized that he would have given his own life were she not found because she would have been dead and lost to him forever. But now the gods had given him hope, and a new chance. He would find her. He reached over to put his hand on Kerzog's neck, but the dog wasn't there. He was probably with Entti, the damned disloyal hound, but still he smiled. She was alive, and as long as she was alive, he would know it and there would be hope.

Rorik's last thought was that he had to find her before Einar or the king discovered she wasn't a virgin, that, or worse, that they discovered she was his wife.

# 25

MIRANA STARED AT her brother. He was drunk, his clothes disheveled, his young, too handsome face set in mean lines. He saw Gunleik first and yelled, "Well, old man? Did you find her? Where is she? If you didn't bring her back to me, I'll flay the flesh off your back."

"She is here," Gunleik said. He took Mirana's hand and gently pulled her forward.

Einar simply stared at her for a long time, finally saying, "She looks like a filthy slut."

Gunleik frowned at his master. "We have been voyaging hard for nearly four days. We are all exhausted, dirty, and tired. She is alive and well, Einar. She is here. We have brought your sister back to you."

Einar sat forward in his high-backed chair, his fingers curved over the beautifully carved chair posts. "Well, dear sister, you are with me again. It has been a long time. Clontarf has missed its fine mistress. I trust you have missed me equally. Come here and let me embrace you."

Mirana was so tired, her mind so fouled with fear and exhaustion, that she merely stood there, unable to walk to him, unable to say anything, nor did she want to.

"Come here, Mirana," he said, his voice low and so soft her skin crawled. She hadn't feared him before, even when he'd struck her for her sharp tongue, her occasional disobedience, but now she did. Now she saw clearly that to show him any fear at all would be a grave mistake. He wanted to see fear, she realized suddenly, and wondered why she'd never realized that before. He reveled in it. It was an aphrodisiac to him, a spur to his passions. It made him feel powerful, strong. It made him feel more a man. Odd how she realized that so easily now, how she saw him so clearly. It had been the distance from him, she saw now, and Rorik, a man clean of mind and of spirit, a man untouched by any blackness. Aye, she could fear Einar all she wished to, but she had to hide it deep inside her. She realized now the path she must trod with him, and she prayed she could do it.

She smiled, a smile so brimming with falseness he surely would see it, but he didn't seem to. "I give you greetings, Einar. Forgive me for looking like a slut, but Gunleik is correct. It has been a hard journey." She made her voice mocking, difficult that, because she was shaking with fear. "Even you, my handsome brother, would look less like a god were you to live in a boat for four days. There was even a storm but we survived it with Gunleik at the helm."

Einar eased. She recognized the signs. She realized he was staring beyond her, and slowly, she turned. It was Sira he was staring at.

"This one," Einar said, pointing to Sira, "who is she? How did you come by her? By the gods, look at that magnificent hair!"

"We captured her," Ingolf said, stepping forward, pulling Sira with him. Immediately, Emund took her other arm, like two dogs fighting over a prized bone.

"There is much to learn here," Einar said, stroking his long fingers over his jaw. "Mirana, take the woman to the bathing hut with you. Both of you will come to me again for the evening meal."

Mirana didn't want to go anywhere with Sira, but she knew there was no choice. She turned to Sira, unwillingly, and Sira said low, "I hadn't expected this. Einar trusts you. How odd, and you a woman, and you obviously despise him, rather you are not obvious, at least to him."

"I hope that I am not obvious about anything, Sira. Aye, certainly Einar trusts me. Why would he not? I am mistress here. He is my half-brother. Come, we will bathe. I, for one, am in sore need of it."

"I too," Sira said.

Suddenly it seemed that all the women surrounded Mirana, laughing, touching her, hugging her despite her filth. They were all talking at once.

Finally, Mirana held up her hand. "I am glad to see all of you. Now, I am so tired I fear I will fall at your feet and surely that would not be considerate. Sira and I will bathe now." She turned to Tanna, a woman who was prized at Clontarf for her beautiful weaving. "Please have clothes fetched. My gowns should fit Sira well enough."

"By the gods," Sira said as she walked beside Mirana to the bathing hut, "it was just the same with Rorik's people. The women worshiped you and there was no reason that I could see. And here they treat you like a queen. Just wait until they hear the truth, that their little queen will soon be gone from them." She laughed, then said, "Your brother is very handsome. That is a surprise. In truth, I had expected a black-haired witch like you, but he isn't. He's got pure black hair, but it isn't coarse like yours, it's flowing and soft and looks made of silk. And his eyes are such a lustrous green, not muddy like yours. He is not as large as Rorik, but his body appears fine enough. There is no fat in his belly. And he is very young, not much older than Rorik. Aye, he is a man who draws me, he is a man who knows what he wants. Perhaps I will have him. Perhaps I will become mistress in your place."

Mirana was too tired to tell Sira the truth. Why warn her in any case? Let her learn for herself the kind of man Einar was. She would learn soon enough that Einar had charmed the years away from his face and body, mayhap through magic, mayhap through potions, mayhap because evil preferred to reside inward and not leave its mark for all to see. She merely stripped off her filthy clothes and began to bathe.

It was dark outside when Mirana entered the large central hall of Clontarf. She was dressed in her favorite dark green linen gown with its lighter green overtunic, fastened at her shoulders with two finely beaten silver brooches. Her hair was clean and brushed smoothly to nearly her waist.

"By the gods, you look incredibly beautiful. When I first saw you, I feared that your beauty—unlike mine—was forever gone."

It was Einar and he was smiling at her, his hand held out. "Come, little sister, and sit with me. The women have prepared your favorite dishes—look, 'tis roasted hare and mushrooms. And your wild apples, Mirana, all covered with nuts and cloudberries. Come here, aye, that's right."

She sat beside him, giving him a mocking smile. "As you will, brother." She knew she would have to speak to him, she would have to find the right words to convince him not to sell her to the king. She would wait to judge his mood. She would have to wait for him to speak of it first.

Sira entered then, and she was more beautiful than a princess of myth. She wore one of Mirana's gowns. It was too short for her, but the pale pink wool made her blond hair turn silver in the rush light. She looked slowly about the room, as would a queen surveying her holdings, saw Ingolf rise, then quickly turned to where Einar sat, now staring at her.

Sira walked to him, smiling now, shyly as a Christian nun, and said, "I am pleased with your hospitality, my lord Einar. May I sit here beside you?"

He raised a brow. "You are now a slave," he said. "You are a relative to Rorik Haraldsson. Ingolf captured you on this Hawkfell Island, both he and Emund told me of it."

"Aye, it is true enough that your men did capture me, but do I look like a slave to you, my lord?"

Mirana watched her with some detachment, as Einar weighed Sira, assessed her endowments. What would he do? She looked over at his two mistresses to see their reactions, but their heads were bent over their plates.

Einar did nothing for the moment, merely shrugged. "You will eat. I will decide other matters soon. Sit down, Sira."

The slaves served her. Einar cuffed one small girl for no reason that Mirana could tell. She bit down on her tongue. She wouldn't argue with him, not yet. Time passed. She ate and listened.

There was loud and boisterous talk and jesting. Men were always men and always the same, she thought, staring about the smoke-hazed large hall. The women drank as well, but they sat apart from the men, speaking quietly, occasionally giggling. The children were asleep long before.

Gunleik sat in the center of his men, but he was silent, eating slowly and methodically. Mirana had to speak to him alone. After Ingolf had struck him down, he had taken command of the longboat. It was only when they hit the storm that Ingolf realized he must recognize Gunleik's authority, for he didn't want to die. Gunleik looked better now, though his head still hurt him severely. She had to speak to him alone. Mayhap she could see him later when all were asleep.

Even after the long meal Einar wasn't drunk, but most of the men were. Ingolf came to his lord and said, his voice slurred with too much mead, "I have come for the woman, my lord. I captured her. I want her. I would have her now."

Einar spared a glance toward his minion. He steepled his fingers in front of him.

"I want her," Ingolf said again, his jaw thrust forward, and this time he sounded more belligerent in his drunkenness.

"Mayhap I want her too," Einar said slowly. "Surely she would not prefer your ugly face to mine, Ingolf. What say you to that? Would you still insist in the face of your lord's spoken desires?"

Ingolf began to laugh. Mirana saw that the mead he'd drunk had not only given him more confidence than was wise but that it also loosened his tongue. He said, "I've seen you with your new slave, my lord. Aye, a pretty one this time, so very pretty." He laughed louder when Einar merely looked at him, a brow raised in question. Ingolf belched. "Nay, it isn't Sira you want," he said again, and Mirana knew that his drunkenness had made him forget who and what his master was. He looked over at a beautiful young girl, sitting quietly and alone, pointing a shaking finger at her, and laughed and laughed.

It was the last sound he made. Einar rose in a single fluid movement, quickly unsheathed his knife and slipped it into Ingolf's heart. Just one swift movement inward then a slight twist upward. Ingolf stared at him, then sighed softly, and sank to the floor.

No one said a word. The air in the vast room seemed to have been sucked out. There was no sound, even the dogs were quiet. It was a terrifying silence, a disbelieving silence.

Mirana had despised Ingolf, had come to fear him on the four-day journey back to Clontarf, but to see him struck down as if he were naught more than a rabid animal, of no account at all, made her gag. If nothing else, he was loyal to Einar. He'd drunk too much mead, spoken too much, and now he was dead. Simply dead. He'd said something about a new slave, nothing more. He'd laughed. Why had Einar killed him? Just because Ingolf had laughed at him? Just because he knew Einar had another new mistress? She looked at her half-brother's serene expression, aye, serene save for his green eyes that gleamed with a ferocious light. She was frightened, very frightened. She leaned back in her chair and closed her eyes.

Einar said, "Get him out of here. We don't wish his spirit to remain with us. He was foul in thought and his spirit would be no different."

She didn't watch the men remove Ingolf's body. She looked at Sira. To her astonishment, there was a smile on her mouth. She was staring at Einar and she was smiling. She leaned slightly forward so that her radiant hair fell over her breast.

The men went back to their drinking. The women couldn't seek out their beds until the men stopped their drinking, which it didn't seem they would do for a good many hours yet.

It was some time later when Einar called out, "All of you, my brave men, the best warriors in all Ireland, listen to me. Some of you know my wondrous news, others don't. I said nothing until my dear sister was returned to me. Now all of you will learn of it. Our King Sitric wishes to wed her. Aye, our family will be allied with the royal family. Her sons will rule Ireland. It will be done soon now, the first day of fall. We will all benefit from this alliance, doubt it not. We will all add riches to our coffers."

It was done. She wasn't surprised. She looked at Gunleik. He looked pale and ill. He would help her, he had to. She realized suddenly—with a clarity and certainty that left no room for doubt in her mind—that if she told Einar she didn't want to marry that old man, that she was already married, that she wasn't a virgin, he would stick his knife into her heart.

He'd killed Ingolf with no hesitation, and the man had really done naught to anger him. But if she told Einar the truth, she couldn't begin to imagine the depths of his rage, or his disappointment. He would surely kill her for ruining his grand plans. She didn't doubt him capable of it for a moment.

She held her tongue. She couldn't plead or beg, although she imagined he would be amused by it.

There was much toasting and cheering. She noticed the women looking at her. They weren't cheering.

Sira was smiling and drinking the sweet mead Mirana had made the previous summer.

Einar continued speaking to his men, his closer friends, those men who hadn't drawn back when he'd so swiftly and easily killed Ingolf. Those same men were now drawn close, listening avidly to his plans of greater wealth and power and how they would all profit. For the most part, they were simple men, strong men, fighters all of them, but wealth and power and slaves beckoned to the most honorable of them.

Finally, Einar turned to her. He clasped her hand tightly in his and drew it up to his mouth. He kissed her fingers. She didn't move, didn't draw back, remained still as a statue.

"I trust this will please you," he said, looking at her directly.

"Nay," she said. "It doesn't."

The flash of rage was in his eyes, then gone so quickly she wondered if it had ever been there at all, but she knew that it had. She had to go carefully. She'd tested the waters and escaped, this time at least.

Einar said slowly, "You will be a queen. You will have everything you wish. You will have endless jewels and slaves. You will breed two or three sons, then he will leave his age-spotted hands off you. Mayhap even his rod is age-spotted. Does that happen to old men? I wonder.

"Even though we haven't the same father, I still honor Audun. Through my efforts, you, his daughter, will be a queen. I do suggest that you quickly produce a male child, else the old king just might have your lovely throat slit and another virgin fetched to his bed."

The truth prodded at her, but she was too afraid and too wise in her half-brother's ways to speak the words.

"As will you," she said and shrugged as if she didn't have a care. "He is an old man. Mayhap he will die soon." She paused and tried to make her eyes glitter as his did. "Mayhap I will assist him to his just rewards."

Einar laughed. He released her hand. He drank deeply. "Aye, I like the sound of that, but you will have to take care, Mirana. It is strange, but you have changed," he added, frowning a bit. "There is a difference in you. I will learn it quickly enough, for I know you well, don't I?" Still he frowned, then he shook it off, for the mead was thick in his blood and in his brain. "Tell me what Rorik Haraldsson did to you. Did he mistreat you badly? Don't lie, Mirana. Emund and Ingolf already told me all of it, including your paltry falsehoods to them about being wed to this Rorik. They said Sira told them how vilely you were treated, both by his hands and at the hands of his family. Sira told them how he hated you so much he even whipped you. Did it hurt, Mirana? How did he whip you?"

She wanted to vomit. "You have said many things, Einar. What do you wish to know first?"

He frowned at her, and leaned closer. "Tell me about the whipping."

She said calmly enough, "One doesn't like to be whipped. You whipped me, remember?"

"Aye," he said, and there was remembered pleasure in his voice. "You deserved it. Tell me, did he hurt you?"

"It hurt."

"Did he strip off your clothes?"

"I don't remember."

"Of course you do. Did he strip you naked and have one of his men hold you whilst he wielded the whip?"

She could only shake her head, knowing she was showing weakness in front of him and that it wasn't wise. But he was drunk, surely he would leave her alone tonight. "I don't wish to speak of it more, Einar. I am very tired, surely you can believe that. May I seek my bed now?"

He brooded, obviously displeased with her answers to him. "You keep things from me, Mirana. I don't like it. Your tongue is as sharp as always, but at the same time you are different. Mayhap it is your weariness that allows these evasions, this mockery I've heard in your soft voice. I suppose it has been hard for you, this captivity and your long voyage back to Clontarf. But I wish to know more of this whipping he gave you before I let you seek out your bed. Be certain that I will avenge you; that is why I wish to know." He leaned closer to her, his eyes on her mouth. "Tell me and I will make this Rorik's death longer and more painful than any before."

Very well, she thought. "He hurt me badly, Einar. He stripped me naked and threw me to the ground. He had one of his men hold my hair away from my back. He tied my wrists to a stake. He beat me until I was unconscious."

His breathing was coming fast now. By the gods, she'd given him too much, she'd made a mistake. She'd gone too far. Her tale hadn't excited fierce protectiveness in him toward her. No, she'd excited him surely, but her words had brought him pleasure, a dark ugly pleasure. His nostrils flared and his eyes gleamed with a light that terrified her. "Did he touch you afterward?"

She shook her head as she rose quickly. She said loudly, "I am glad to be home. You are all my friends and you wish me well, my dear brother most of all. Tonight, I sleep safely." Then she quickly turned on her heel and left the hall, praying that Einar wouldn't come after her and perhaps whip her to see if he could best what she'd told him Rorik had done. No, he wouldn't do that, now he could not afford to, for there was the king who wanted her. Nay, he would whip another, an innocent, just because she'd taunted him and excited him with a lie.

What if Emund told Einar what she'd said of him? He wouldn't kill her for there was too much at stake. But what would he do? She wondered now as she had many times before what was in his mind.

He was staring after her. Sira was looking at him. There was no smile on her lips now.

MIRANA KNEW SOMEONE was there even before she was fully awake. Gunleik, she thought, and felt a surge of hope. She opened her eyes but it wasn't Gunleik who stood there.

It was a beautiful young girl with golden hair—not the silver blondness of Sira—no, golden as the wheat in August, and brilliant golden eyes. She was dressed in pure white linen with a tunic of the finest white wool over it. Mirana frowned a bit for those thick, beautifully designed silver bracelets at her wrists and on her upper arms surely belonged to Einar. She realized then that it was the same girl Ingolf had taunted Einar about just before Einar had killed him.

"You're awake, witch," the girl said, her voice vicious and low.

"Who are you?"

"I am your brother's mistress. Those other two women no longer hold him except on rare occasion, the bleating sheep. I have been here since you've been gone. I am more beloved by Einar than any before me and that includes you as well. He found me in Dublin and brought me here, nay, begged me to come here. I am the one he loves. You are here only until he can contact that old bastard, King Sitric, to come and fetch you. Then you will be gone and I will be glad. All the people will realize that I am here to take your place, and then they will have to respect me and obey me as they now do you."

"What is your name?"

The girl straightened now and simply stared down at her. She appeared fine-boned, yet tall, lithe, and sleek. "Einar told me you were beautiful. He said your flesh was as white as goat's milk, that your eyes were the same color as his, but it isn't true. The green of your eyes is impure, dulled with other colors, not the pure vibrant green of his. Nay, you are nothing with your ugly black hair. Einar remembered you in his image and endowed you with his own beauty. I know why. It was because you have such value to him. He wants you to be comely so the king won't be angered. Aye, he was afraid you would be lost to him forever. I had believed that Einar feared nothing, but I was wrong. He fears that old king and that advisor of his, Hormuze.

"I listened to you speak to him last night. You spoke sharply to him; you were cold when you wished to be; you taunted him, surely you lied to him about that whipping the Viking gave you. You did not treat him with respect, with the honor he deserves, yet he didn't strike you. Mayhap he wanted to but he didn't want you marked for the king. Aye, that is it. You'd best pray the king will fetch you quickly, else Einar will grow weary of your bitch's deceit and insolence. He will strike you and I will enjoy watching him do it. Else he will stick his knife in your breast, just as he did to that bastard, Ingolf, and I will enjoy watching him to do that as well."

"Has he struck you?"

There was a frown that marred the beautifully

smooth forehead. The girl couldn't be more than sixteen years old, Mirana thought, so very young to have pride in being a man's whore. She felt no compassion, just sharp dislike.

"Once he did. I was sharp-tongued like you. I realized quickly enough that he enjoys that, but not all that much of it. It is simply difficult to judge when he is wearied of mockery and audacity. His moods change quickly, but that only makes me love him more. He did not strike me hard."

Mirana shook her head, sending her hair into a thick sweep about her shoulders. She laughed a little. "You have learned a lot about him in a very short time. Perhaps you will last longer than those before you, though I doubt it. That or you will become like the other women, submissive and silent and afraid."

"What do you mean 'those before you'? Surely you can't compare me to those two."

Mirana simply shrugged and smiled up at the girl. "You heard what I said. Do you believe my brother a virgin, mayhap? You don't believe he took women before the two he now beds only occasionally? At least that is what you say." She laughed more, then shoved herself upright in her box bed. The girl stepped back a step, and that pleased Mirana. Perhaps the girl believed her to be like her brother, perhaps she feared her a bit as well. She gave her another smile, a vicious smile, and it had some effect as well, for the girl took another step away from her.

"Einar also told me you might dislike me and might try to whip me. I know he won't allow it, so I warn you, keep away from me."

Mirana pulled her hair over her right shoulder and began to comb her fingers through it. She appeared bored, but she was thinking furiously. So the girl expected cruelty from her, and she feared it. She said easily, "I will warn you, for what reason, I don't know. Perhaps because I find you pathetic. Or perhaps because you are so very young. When Einar is bored with his women, he isn't necessarily kind to them. In the past he has occasionally dismissed them in rather violent ways. You see his other two women—you call them silly sheep. That is because they are afraid to say anything in his hearing for fear he will be displeased. And then he will hurt them. He enjoys hurting those he beds."

To her surprise, the girl smiled, her whole body radiating confidence, and said, "Ah, but I am different, very different from his other women. I knew you were a fool and now I've proved it to myself. I am not pathetic, 'tis you who are. Now I will prove it to you, and your blindness, ugly witch."

Then the girl giggled. She stood by Mirana's bed, straight and tall and giggling. Without another word, she stripped off her tunic. Then slowly, she turned her back to Mirana. The gown followed, then the soft linen shift and leather slippers. Mirana saw a tall girl with a straight back and long legs lightly furred with golden hair. Her buttocks were small, too small, and there was something strange here, something . . .

The giggles turned to laughter as she turned to face her again. "Behold, Mirana."

A boy stood in front of her. A beautiful boy with golden hair that brushed his shoulder blades. His flesh was smooth and tinged with an olive tint. There was little hair on him, only at his groin and on his legs, lightly sprinkled. His rod was soft against him. He was slender as a girl and as supple. But there was strength there as well, Mirana could see it. And a very strong will. And a vanity that went too deep, a vanity born of too few years.

"I told you I was different. Am I not beautiful?" The boy did a turn, raising his arms, preening. "What I do to Einar gives him great pleasure, more pleasure than those two stupid women ever give him. He will sell both of them, he told me he was going to. Also he will sell them because I have asked him to sell them. Their stupid faces and their witless sighs annoy me. Their breasts hang on them like cows' udders, ugly and bloated. Nay, he won't ever dismiss me. Mayhap he'll hit me, but only because of his uncertain tempers. He would never mark me, at least not overly much, or send me away."

Mirana could only stare at the boy. Memories flooded into her mind and she knew now that there had been other boys before this one, but she hadn't realized, hadn't guessed, that her brother had used them as he would use a woman. Did Gunleik know? Did his warriors know? How could they? But of course they did. Ingolf had known and laughed about it and Einar killed him for it. She closed her eyes a moment against the knowledge. But there had been women as well, many women, some kind to her, others frightened, yet others certain their beauty and endowments would hold his attention. None ever had for very long, male or female. She remembered the boy she'd tried to protect. Einar had whipped her for her interference and the boy had died. Was he one of Einar's lovers as well?

"Look at me, damn you! I am more beautiful than you could hope to be. Look at me! Aye, none of you white-fleshed bitches can approach my beauty. As for that slut, Sira, mayhap Einar will plow her belly once or twice, but it is to me he will return, always to me.

It is only her hair that charms him, nothing else about her."

"What is your name?"

The lad smiled. "You may call me Lella. Einar is pleased to dress me in a woman's name and in a woman's clothes. It amuses him. It tweaks his men's noses, for they too are forced to call me Lella. They despise me, but it matters not. Once Einar even had me flirt with old Svein Forkbeard. I thought the old sot would faint when I touched his shriveled rod. Aye, the men must smile or look the other way, for I am the lord's favorite and they must mind their tongues.

"But you, Mirana, I had believed you would be different. Aye, I had feared you, for there is something dark in Einar, something that confuses me, and I thought it was you there, in the shadows of him, lurking and hidden from sight, holding him from me. But now that I see you, I can laugh and be certain of myself again. You are nothing save a possession to be used to gain him more power, more wealth. You are no part of his darkness, no specter to obscure what he is to me. He merely praises you to make me jealous. He speaks of you with affection because he knows it will but make me love him more. And soon you will be gone.

"I had to see you alone, see your face close to mine. Now that I have looked my fill of you, I will return to Einar's bed and I will know that I have nothing to fear from you."

The boy Lella laughed again, dressed quickly, and walked to the doorway of Mirana's small sleeping chamber. He turned to face her, but she forestalled him, saying in a lazy, taunting voice, "You think not, boy? Now that I am returned, you will learn the meaning of true fear. Forget not, Einar is my brother. Think you we are so different from each other? You don't yet know the meaning of fear, little man."

He paled, she saw it clearly, but then he laughed, an uncertain laugh, turned on his heel and was gone, no more words spoken. She heard him singing in a voice high and pure as a woman's.

Mirana lay back, her heart pounding in loud, slow thuds. She'd come home to a nightmare. No, not home. Hawkfell Island was home. Mirana shook her head. She would probably never see Hawkfell Island again. Or Rorik. There was no home for her, not now.

She lay back, closing her eyes. The boy Lella was there again in front of her, laughing, then looking fearful. She'd perhaps won that small exchange, but it was she who feared him, deep down, she feared him for he'd shown her just how little she'd really known her half-brother. She laughed then, softly, because she realized the boy was nothing. It was Einar to be feared, no one else.

She wondered again, as she had so many times before, if Rorik believed her dead.

Rorik and Kron stood alone in the shadows of the king's fortress in Dublin. Hafter, Aslak, and Raki were hidden some thirty yards away.

Kron said quietly, "Yon is the private entrance to the king's chambers. As I told you, Rorik, there are three guards, *berserkers* all of them, very dangerous."

"Aye, we must kill them and it must be done quickly and quietly. Are there others we must worry about?"

"Early each evening a woman is brought to the king. If she fails to stir his rod, then she is sent away and Aylla is brought to him, always Aylla. She is the woman who sleeps with him, cradles him like a babe, his wrinkled old face against her breasts. She is the one who feeds him a nightly potion, prepared by Hormuze."

Rorik made a sound of disgust.

"Aye, 'tis true," Kron said. "I discovered all this from one of the women's slaves. She said that whilst the king sleeps, this Aylla recites an incantation over and over again, one to renew the king's vigor, to push away the demons that age him and shrivel his rod."

"Who gives her this incantation?"

"Ah, Hormuze again, the king's own advisor and physician. He's an old man like the king, but he's wily, smart, and dangerous. He is not one of us. His name is strange. I have heard it said he comes from a land even farther to the south than Miklagard, a land of deserts and vast burial monuments that go back hundreds upon hundreds of years. He speaks a strange tongue, this from a servant I bribed who said she heard him speaking to his daughter in this alien language. I heard it said that he controls the king, though I cannot testify that it is true. Few see the king, but enough to swear that he lives and gives the impression that he makes the decisions and gives the orders. He says to those familiar to him that Hormuze is his physician and advisor, and thus he is willing to trust him in matters of his health and in matters that need advice. Then he laughs his old man's laugh and says that in matters of the marauding Irish chieftains, it is he who commands and who rules. However, as I told you before, Rorik, I heard it said that both Hormuze and the king will come to fetch Mirana from Einar."

Rorik nodded, saying, "And what do the king's people and his warriors believe about Hormuze?"

"They believe what the king says, that he is his physician and advisor, and yet they are wary of him. They fear him, for his hold on the king is a strong one. Hormuze has told them that once the king has wed Mirana, daughter of Audun, on the first day of September, he will be reborn, he will be vigorous and young again, and he will give his people heirs to rule them forever. On that day he will appear to them and all will see that he has spoken the truth. On that day, he claims, the Irish chieftains and all their forces will be as insects underfoot. The people cling to this. They even now begin to dream of a vigorous man emerging from his bridal chamber, renewed and somehow young again and ready to lead them to undreamed-of glory."

"What kind of blank-brained fools are these?" Rorik said, and spat into the bushes. "Why did he choose Mirana of all women? She is of no great house, her birth isn't royal. Why her?"

Kron shook his head. "I don't know. No one does, save Hormuze and the king."

Kron had already told Rorik most of this, but there were more details he'd thought to add this time. Rorik smiled. He had an idea. He said to Kron, "Tell me, is there someone close to this Hormuze? A wife? A son or daughter?"

"Aye, there is a daughter. She is but ten years old if I remember aright."

"And he is an old man himself?"

"Aye, he appears beyond old, an ancient relic."

"Odd that he could sire such a young child. Is he attached to her?"

"Aye, my lord. Hormuze worships the girl. She is a sweet child I have heard it said even though he treats her like a princess. There is no wife. I believe she died well before Hormuze came to the court."

Rorik rubbed his hands together. "Excellent," he said. "That is excellent. We haven't much time, but we have enough."

* * *

Hormuze was a careful man, very careful. He trusted no one and he never would. Slowly, meticulously, he pasted down the gray beard that covered his face and hung down past his neck. He patted the woven mat of gray hair over his own thick black hair. With the skill of long practice, he lined his face, taking care not to use too much walnut oil. He did not believe people to be stupid as the king did. But he believed people saw what it was they expected to see.

They believed Hormuze an old man. Thus he was an old man. When he finished he rose from his rosewood chair and fastened the three layers of soft feather padding, belting it about his lean belly. He dressed himself, then looked at himself again closely, as was his wont, in the polished brass mirror. He was pleased. He looked as he was expected to look. The long straggly beard covered the strong cords of his neck. The door opened and Eze stood there, her head cocked to one side, staring at him.

"You are a true graybeard, Papa," she said, then came to him and lightly kissed his wrinkled cheek.

"Quietly, Eze," Hormuze said, as he stroked her soft black hair. "Ah, you are so beautiful, my little one. Just like your poor mother. It won't be long now. You are keeping your own council?"

"Aye, Papa," the child said, and kissed him once again. "Be careful, Papa."

"Aye, always."

Outside the small window, Kron drew back, stunned by what he'd seen. Lord Rorik had been right, but only in a part of it. By all the gods, this was strange, this young man who made himself old. Ah, and the little girl. Kron shook his head. And they'd spoken the strange language between them. Kron quickly pulled the guard's body from sight. He stole the man's boots and his beautiful pounded silver armlet. A robbery, all would believe it a robbery.

# 27

THE NIGHT WAS black. Bloated clouds roiled through the heavens. The air was heavy and thick with rain, the wind becoming colder by the moment.

Mirana waited patiently. She knew Gunleik would come. Still, it seemed an eternity since he'd nodded to her, just after the evening meal. Where was he?

Suddenly, from behind her, he said, his voice soft as a summer's breeze, "What do you out here, Mirana? You ate very little, yet the women prepared all the dishes you like. I do not wish your charms to waste away. Come inside and let me feed you roasted fowl from my own plate."

He sounded so very loving and tender. It scared her to near speechlessness. But when she turned to face Einar, there was a sweet smile on her face. She touched her fingertips to his arm, feeling his flesh ripple beneath her touch, feeling the strength of him. "I thank you, brother, but I fear my stomach is displeased. It was doubtless something I ate earlier. I will be well again on the morrow."

But he was frowning. "Sira told of how Rorik's family had poisoned you, how you nearly died that first time, how another woman did die. I don't like this, Mirana. Are you certain your ailment is a mild one?"

She nodded. "Aye, I am certain."

"You are here at last. By all the gods, I was worried. Endlessly, I worried for you. Gunleik became an old man. I beat him for his failure. Then I sent him after you. He is wily and cunning, smarter than any of my other warriors. I knew he would find you if you still lived."

"Ah, that is why you didn't beat him to death?"

"Aye," he said, "that and he is still useful to me." He pointed toward a lone gull who sat perched on a piling near the end of the wooden dock. "Lella loves birds, just as you do. She feeds that one daily. She calls him Gorm. I scold her, sometimes discipline her for her benefit, but she is young and filled with excitement over foolish things."

Mirana laughed softly. "You mean the young lad who dresses like a girl?"

He stiffened and she felt a tremor run through him. "How do you know, Mirana?"

"Your Lella wanted to meet me. She came to my chamber last night and took off her clothes to show me she was different from the others, that you would never tire of her, that you loved her because of her differentness, because she could give you pleasure a woman couldn't give. Your Lella is a lovely boy, Einar. How odd that I did not know this about you. Odd that everyone else did know yet no one told me." Her voice was matter-of-fact, utterly without judgment, without revulsion or disgust. It was difficult, but she managed it, and she saw that he eased slowly, but he did ease.

"I will beat the boy," he said mildly. "He shouldn't have done that. I didn't think I had to tell him to keep away from you. He acted on his own. Aye, I will beat him for that. As I said, he is young and needs firm discipline. I would have told you in my own time, that or I would have tired of him and it would have made no difference, for I would have sold him and he would have been gone."

She shrugged. "It matters not what pleasures you seek or where you seek them. Surely a man should do as he chooses. And you are a leader of men, Einar." She watched him preen with her words. She had to learn well to dole them out—the flattery, then the spurs. It was finding the balance that would be difficult.

"Did Rorik do as he pleased with you?"

She felt her blood gathering, pounding through her. "What do you mean, Einar?"

"I was thinking about what Sira has told me, what Gunleik and the others have told me as well. You claim you were married to Rorik Haraldsson, that you are no longer a virgin, and thus you cannot wed the king. You will now tell me you lied. And you will tell me why you lied. I wish to hear the words from you, Mirana."

She looked at him, her eyes clear. She realized that she didn't want to die. She didn't want Einar to stick a knife in her heart and twist it upward with a flick of his wrist when she sent him into a rage with the truth. She saw herself clearly in that instant falling to the ground, a knife deep in her heart. No, she thought, no.

So she said, her voice firm and steady, "Aye, I lied. I didn't want to marry an old man, Einar, be he king or pauper. I have no care for jewels or slaves, you know that. I would say anything to prevent marrying that old man, even claiming to be wed to our enemy, Rorik Haraldsson. Aye, I would claim to be married to Gunleik were it to save me from marrying him. I beg you, don't force me to do this."

"There are things you don't understand," he said, and looked up into the heavens. A star appeared through a brief clearing in the clouds. "It is the North Star. There are men on the sea who are cheering at this moment, doubt it not."

She prayed one of those men was Rorik.

"What things?"

"I cannot tell you as yet. Just trust me, Mirana. What I do benefits not only me but you as well. Trust me."

She let her voice grow smooth and mocking, for pleading would never gain anyone anything with Einar. "And if I tell you I don't trust you, brother? What would you do to me then? Beat me? Kill me?"

"Nay, for the time is too short when the king and his advisor, an old ancient named Hormuze, will arrive at Clontarf to fetch you. What I will do, though, is examine you myself. I cannot take the chance of the king finding you unchaste after he has married you. I want my own finger to feel your maidenhead, Mirana. You will come with me now. If you wish it, I will even give you pleasure as well. You've never known a woman's pleasure. Come." He held his hand out to her.

She stared at it as if it were a snake to bite her.

She continued to stare at his hand as she said, "I told you the truth, Einar. I lied about a marriage to Rorik Haraldsson. Nor did Rorik touch me. I was his hostage, a valuable hostage to be used against you. He did not ravish me. He had no interest in me in that way."

She realized then that this was but a pretense. Einar wanted to touch her, perhaps for his corrupt pleasure, perhaps to humiliate her, she wasn't certain, nor did she care. She'd been a fool not to see it immediately. Now she saw the darkness in him so clearly, shining as black as the night in his eyes, beautiful green eyes full to brimming with a strange intensity, and knew in that instant that he'd placed her in the center of his dark soul, that the boy Lella was quite wrong.

She felt the perversity in him reaching out to her, remembered many times now when she'd seen the depravity, the darkness of him overflow onto others, causing pain and humiliation and even death. And now she was his focus. She remembered believing that Rorik would kill her. Now she wondered if her half-brother would as she said calmly, "No, Einar."

He smiled at her. He lifted her hand in both of his and stroked her palm with his thumbs. She was deadly cold yet her palm was sweating.

"I am your brother, Mirana, and until you wed the king, I am your master. You will always do as I bid you."

Again, she said, "No. It isn't right. It isn't normal or natural. You are my brother, I remind you of it and remind you of its significance and obligations. You will not touch me in such a way."

"It is because I am your brother that I do not wish to humiliate you by having another man do it."

"Then it will be a woman if you disbelieve me. If you truly think I am lying to you now, we will ask Hannah to do it."

"You lied before. You claimed he was your husband. A husband plows his wife. The women love you and would do anything you asked of them. I could not believe what Hannah would tell me. You lie and you don't lie. I no longer see what is right, what is the truth. Which is which, Mirana?"

She drew herself up. She looked skyward and said, "If you do this to me I will not wed your king."

He slapped her, hard, his open palm smacking loud against her cheek. Her head jerked back. She would have fallen had he not held on to her arm. He pulled her upright, jerking her against him. He held her there, whispering against her temple, "Do not go against me again. Now, come, for I wish to see you and feel you. I have waited a long time for this. I will not be denied. No longer."

She drew back and spat at him in the face.

She said softly, "Kill me now, Einar. I don't care. Or mark me, then you will fail, for the king won't have me then, will he? He is an old man but I do not believe he is blind. Ah, and then he would kill you, wouldn't he, because you would have failed in your agreement with him. Aye, kill me, Einar, then follow me into death."

He was shaking with rage and incredulity. He said, "You spat on me," and he looked at her as if she were something he couldn't comprehend, something alien and not of his experience. Slowly he wiped his face. He looked at her, her face pale in the night, so very pale, so very beautiful, and how he wanted her in those moments. He saw her fear of him, tasted that fear. It drove him mad. He reached for her, but she flung herself away from him. She ran across the inner courtyard and up the wooden ladder to the fortress ramparts.

"Mirana!"

She paid him no heed. He raced after her, his blood hot, his anger burning even hotter. He reached the wooden walkway, only to stop, for she was not ten feet from him and she looked suddenly calm, suddenly accepting, and he was terrified, for she'd been right. If she died so would he.

"You will swear upon the head of our dead mother that you will not touch me. If you do not swear, I will jump. I will be dead and you will lose everything. I have heard it said that the king has little patience for failure, beginning with your worthless life. He is much like you. Swear now to me, Einar, or I will be dead and you will lose."

He took a step toward her.

The king was tired, so very tired, for the day had been long. He'd had little appetite for the evening meal. He wanted to be young again, a vigorous man in his prime. Hormuze had promised him this again and again. But he felt so weary, his body flaccid and weak. He was afraid he would die. He wanted to go now to fetch Mirana, daughter of Audun, but Hormuze had cautioned against it, always against it, as he did now.

"Nay, sire, we must wait. It isn't yet time. I have consulted the stars and their paths and formations, and done my calculations. Soon now we will fetch her, but not sooner than is right, for then you would not have what you want. Nay, we must wait, then you will be as I promised. Ah, sire, the sons you will fashion in this woman's body."

The king listened to Hormuze speak of the sons he would sire, these sons who would rule until the world ceased to be and then beyond, perhaps, for his progeny would challenge the gods in their perfection. He listened to Hormuze until a slave was brought to him. Then he turned from his advisor to watch her.

She was young, not more than fifteen, and she was supple and talented in her dance. Soon she was naked and soon she was crouched before him, leaning up to stroke his bony knees, gently caressing his thighs, upward, to finally touch him, and this time, this once, he felt himself swell.

He yelled for Hormuze to leave him. His advisor smiled and left the chamber. The girl continued to caress him, to make him swell and swell until he fell forward on top of her and was able to enter her body. When his release came, he swooned with the pleasure of it.

When he awoke, Aylla was holding him against her, stroking his head, singing her soft incantations. He nestled against her soft breasts, nuzzling close. He was happy and proud that he was still a man.

"I pleasured her," he whispered against her soft flesh.

"Aye, she spoke of your sweetness, sire, of how you made her scream with pleasure."

"Aye," he said, and kissed Aylla's breast.

"Soon, sire, very soon now, you will have your wife in your bed and you will pleasure her and she will give you such fine sons and you will be changed. You will be vigorous and ready to fight again, to crush your enemies, all those petty chieftains who nibble at our people's lands and steal their goods."

Then he slept, her sweet insistent voice sounding the chant in his ear, and he believed the words she said, believed them to his very soul, and was glad.

Mirana leapt up to grasp the two sharp-pointed wooden poles that lined the ramparts. She would probably kill herself simply trying to get over them to jump. She didn't care. She wouldn't allow Einar to touch her. It was too much, simply too much, and she knew if he did, she would be irrevocably damaged in her spirit. No, she preferred death.

Suddenly, she heard Gunleik shout from below, "My lord Einar! You must come now, the boy Lella has attacked the new slave, Sira! Come, the men are hesitant to interfere. None want to meet Ingolf's fate."

Einar stared at her. She saw the frustration in his eyes, saw the truth of her threat as well. "I do not believe you would jump," he said slowly, but she knew in that moment that he didn't believe his words. She'd convinced him. He continued, "But you will be safe from me now, I swear it. I won't touch you." He turned on his heel and climbed back down the wooden ladder, not looking back at her.

Mirana stood there for a very long time, watching him stride back to the longhouse. She rather hoped that Sira would slit the boy's vicious throat. But then what of Sira? That made Mirana laugh. She nearly fell to the ground when Gunleik said quietly, "It is true, the two are fighting. Now we have a few moments before Einar remembers you and asks for you. I am sorry, Mirana, for not believing you. What shall we do?"

"I won't marry that old man, king or not."

"Aye, I know. We will escape then. This Rorik is your husband?"

"Aye, he is." She turned away from Gunleik. "I pray he will come, but I cannot be sure of it. I know that his family will want to come for Sira. It is all uncertain, Gunleik."

"You are no virgin."

"Oh no."

"Then you cannot wed with the king. Your virginity, I am told, is why he wishes to have you, that and who you are, or so Einar has claimed."

"But I am nobody, Gunleik! Why me?"

He shrugged. "None know, even Einar. He pretends it is your beauty and your purity, but there is no belief when he says it. Once he even tried to convince me it was because he was your half-brother that the king wanted you."

"Since it is a fact, I suppose there is no reason why we must understand it as well. There is really little hope, is there?"

"I will think of something," Gunleik said. He glanced down at the whistle from one of his men. "It is Ivar. We must go." He paused a moment, then added, his voice low, "Do not give up, Mirana."

SIRA WAS STRADDLING Lella, her breasts smothering him as she stretched forward to jerk and twist his wrists above his head. He was throwing himself upward, arching madly, striking her back with his knees. She slapped him hard, but before he realized he was free, she'd grasped his wrists again, then dipped down and bit his cheek.

He shrieked. She bit him again, on his other cheek. The boy stopped struggling. He was whimpering.

"Ah, at last you will be quiet, you wretched little fool. Don't dare try to hit me again else I'll rip your pullet's throat out."

Sira looked up to silence. There was Mirana staring at her, Gunleik at her side. Einar was there also, and he was smiling, stroking his long fingers over his chin, watching, saying nothing, merely watching. For how long?

"There is blood on your lips," Einar said to Sira.

"I know, and it is a foul taste, for it comes from this little savage."

"Is that what you are, Lella?" Einar said, coming down to his haunches to stare at the boy whose eyes were overflowing with tears. "Are you in truth a little savage?"

The boy looked up at his master, his lover, and his tears streaked down his face, running in crooked rivulets over the bloody bites on his cheeks. "She marked me," he whispered. "She has ruined my beauty."

"Get off Lella," Einar said to Sira. He offered her his hand and pulled her to her feet. "Now, tell me what brought this to pass."

Lella started to open his mouth, but Einar shook his head, and turned to Sira. "Tell me."

"This smug little bitch told me she would kill me if I tried to seduce you to my bed. I told her, my lord, that I wasn't a whore like she was, that I am a virgin, that I am a cousin to Harald Fairhair, the king of Norway. I told her I wouldn't willingly seek your bed until you married me."

There was utter silence following Sira's words. Every eye was on Einar, waiting for his reaction. Would he whip the new slave right now, his eyes darkening to near black when she screamed from the bite of the oil-soaked leather strips? Or would he shove his knife into her breast and watch as she bled to death?

Einar looked at Sira, at her hair—ah, that beautiful hair, thick and long and almost silver—now disheveled and spilling wildly down her back and over her shoulders. He looked at the passion in her pale blue eyes, at her full mouth, open now for she was panting from her exertions, and her heavy breasts, pushing against her gown that Lella had ripped. He saw the line between her breasts. There would be bruises soon on her white throat, for Lella had gotten a few good hits before Sira had beaten him. He knew Lella was strong; it pleased him that this new slave was stronger, that she hadn't hesitated to retaliate, and viciously. By the gods, she'd bitten Lella on his cheek twice, and he was bleeding, and there was blood on her mouth, and she had as yet made no move to wipe it away. He didn't disbelieve her for an instant—oh aye, she was a virgin and she was kin to the king of Norway. How odd that she would also be kin to Rorik Haraldsson, a stupid man whose honor would one day most likely kill him.

Lella had scrambled away and now stood on Einar's other side, waiting for his master to turn to him, waiting for his master to strike the new slave. But he wanted to be the one to kill her, perhaps beat her until she was pleading with him to stop, but he wouldn't, oh no, he surely wouldn't. There wasn't much blood on his cheeks, but the bitch had actually bitten him. He knew a bolt of fear that seared deep in his belly, for Einar was still holding himself silent, that intense look again on his face. Lella feared that look, for it went beyond what should be in Einar's mind, it went deeper, into that puzzling blackness. He saw Mirana standing back, Gunleik at her side. She was paler than her white flesh; he saw the revulsion clear in her eyes. He hated her more in that moment than he feared and hated Sira. He plucked at Einar's tunic.

"My lord," he said, his voice soft, so very soft, just the timbre he used when he was bringing Einar to his release, encouraging him with all the words that old Dublin merchant had taught him. Einar didn't say anything nor did he turn to Lella to reassure him, to kiss him perhaps, as he'd done many times in front of his people, warriors as well. He hadn't kissed him since Mirana had returned, but he would, he had to, and he had to do it now. He had to prove that he loved his Lella still, Mirana watching, that bitch Sira watching.

"My lord," he said again.

Einar turned to him and gently caressed his chin with his fingers. "Take off your clothes, Lella."

He jerked back as if Einar had struck him.

"You heard me. Remove your clothes this instant or I will beat you witless."

Lella quickly pulled off the tunic, the gown, the soft shift beneath. He stood naked, head down, his rich golden hair thankfully hiding his face. He was humiliated and defeated. He couldn't bear all their eyes on him, all their sneers.

Sira stared at the boy. Then she looked at Einar, her head cocked to the side, and then she laughed, a deep rich laugh that rang out, filling the longhouse. She gasped on her laughter, then stopped when Einar took her arms and shook her.

"Ah, my lord, this bit of offal thinks you want him?" She laughed again, the blood smearing on her mouth, and Einar said nothing now, merely waited.

"He does believe that," Einar said finally.

"He is wrong. I am the one who will hold you, my lord." She smiled at Einar, then rose on her toes and kissed him full on his mouth, and he tasted the sweet coppery taste of Lella's blood. He didn't move.

Lella shrieked and threw himself on Sira's back. His hands were around her throat and he was squeezing with all his strength. Einar calmly turned and nodded to one of his men, a huge man with grizzled red hair, Malle by name, a man who hated the little pederast. He grabbed Lella by his neck and lifted him off Sira. Malle held him in the air, dangling, his face turning red then washing to blue as his air was cut off, then he grinned, shook Lella once more, and said, "What do you want done with the little beggar, my lord?"

"Take him to the storage hut. Anyone who wants to use him may use him, my women included. Do not beat him. I will see to him later. Ah, give him a blanket, I do not wish him to become cold."

Sira was rubbing her throat. She looked at Einar now, and said, her voice and manner remote as a queen's, "I would have killed him."

"Aye, I believe you." He touched her face, the smooth cheek, the soft hair at her temple.

"What of me, my lord?" she asked now.

Einar was staring at her breasts, then at her belly. "I haven't made up my mind," he said, "but I will. There is much to consider here," and he walked from the longhouse.

Mirana knew she had to escape, tonight. She didn't care about the risk. She didn't want to die, but she knew well enough that if Einar found her again she would yell out the truth to him and he would kill her, that or humiliate her first, and he would do it more brutally than he had Lella. Ah, but perhaps death was preferable to the madness that festered here.

Hormuze was furious—with himself. He'd believed that once the king had managed to spend his passion with the young girl he, Hormuze, had found in the slave market and had personally trained, that the king would be content to wait now until the exact day and the exact month Hormuze knew from all his studies was the first fall month, and the first day of the fall month. Not before, not after.

But now Sitric wanted to fetch Mirana immediately. He didn't want to wait to be transformed again into a young man, vigorous and potent, a man who would once more be able to take a woman as many times a night as he had three decades before. He wanted it now, despite the risks, despite the dangers Hormuze had cautioned him about.

Hormuze wanted to stick his dagger in the old man's ribs. He tried to reason with him, even threatened that his youth would probably slip away like a fragment of a dream were he not to wait until the time exactly foretold by all the signs, but such lyrical reason was beyond the old man's mind. No, Sitric wanted it now, he would risk all the dangers, the failure that could result by not listening to Hormuze.

He drew a deep breath and ceased his pacing. Very well. It was not far from the first day of the first fall month. It lacked but another cycle of the moon. It couldn't really matter, could it? But no matter how he rationalized it, Hormuze knew deep down that his studies and his conclusions drawn from stellar signs hadn't lied to him.

He was taking a big risk to fetch Mirana sooner, that moon cycle was critical, and deep down, he knew it.

But he also knew he had no choice. He couldn't afford to lose the king's trust, or he would lose everything. If he refused, Sitric would simply go fetch Mirana himself. No, he had to accept the risks. He would overcome the obstacles fate would doubtless place in his path. He always had.

He had heard rumors that Einar had lost his half-sister, that some Viking marauder had stolen her away, but then the rumors ceased and so he discounted them. The king's court was always rife with rumors. Still, it worried him. Einar wasn't a man of any honor to speak of. He trusted him only because Einar knew what riches lay in store for him if he delivered up his sister to Sitric. And she had to be a virgin; she had to be pure. She had to be clean of mind and spirit to be worthy.

Thus it was that the king, fifty of his warriors, and Hormuze left at first light the following morning for Clontarf, the Danish fortress held by Einar, son of Thorsson.

* * *

"They've left, Rorik."

Kron was out of breath. Rorik waited a moment, then said, "Aye, I know it. Did you learn why?"

Kron nodded, then calmed his breathing. "I spoke to Aylla, the woman who owes her loyalty to Hormuze, the woman who nightly holds the king and chants her incantations to him. She said the king wanted Mirana now. He refused to wait longer. He wants his youth and his vigor returned to him now. Hormuze is displeased, but he had no choice but to obey the king's wishes."

Rorik turned away from Kron and looked down at the glowing embers of their fire. They were close to Dublin, camped in a pine thicket whose branches overhung the shallow tidal river, Liffey. It rained all the time, or so it seemed to Rorik. The air was many times so thick and heavy that it was difficult to breathe; the land was too green, too lush for Rorik's tastes. It choked a man. The pine trees were crowded close by thick-branched strawberry trees and yew bushes and strange bloodred flowers that grew wild in the hedgerows.

He looked toward their two flat-bottomed longboats that had easily navigated the shallow muddy river and were now hidden beneath layers of pine branches not many yards away.

Rorik turned back when the embers suddenly sparked, striking each other loudly, and exploding small volcanoes of fire upward. He drew a deep breath and rose. He kicked sand onto the embers. Then he turned to his men who were waiting silently.

"We get the daughter now."

It was easy, too easy, and Rorik worried about that. Hormuze's daughter, Eze, was alone with her servant, an old woman with failing eyes. Kron lightly tapped the old woman against her head, caught her when she crumbled, and laid her gently onto a floor mat.

The girl just stared at the big men who filled her room, all of them staring at her.

Rorik knelt beside her. He took her hand and held it gently. "I won't hurt you, Eze. My name is Rorik. I will take you to see your father. He wants to take something that belongs to me and I must have you to trade. I intend you no harm. I know your father loves you. He won't endanger you. All I want is what is mine. Do you understand?"

Eze nodded. Her papa was above all men and he would see that she was all right. She looked at this man, younger than her father, stronger perhaps, larger. But he didn't frighten her.

"I understand you," she said.

"You are a brave girl," Rorik said and rose to his feet. "We must be away." He stared down at the girl as she watched Hafter fetch her cloak from the trunk at the foot of her bed. She looked thoughtful, studious, a serious child. Then suddenly she smiled and something froze within him. He stared at her hard, then came down on his knees in front of her again. He turned her face to his. "Bring the light closer, Raki." When it shone directly on the child's face, Rorik felt his heart slow and his breath shorten. "By all the gods," he said slowly, wanting to disbelieve but unable to. "This is a mystery beyond any I had ever expected."

He took the cloak from Hafter and wrapped it around her. They were away from Hormuze's spartan chambers within minutes. They were in the longboat and rowing down the Liffey by late afternoon.

"My lord."

Einar turned at the sound of Gunleik's deep voice.

"Aye, what is it you want? I must think. There are many problems to deal with."

"I know, but one of them is going to arrive here at Clontarf shortly." Gunleik drew a deep breath. "The king and Hormuze will be here within the hour. They bring many warriors with them."

Einar cursed.

"Our runner just brought word. There isn't much time." Gunleik wanted to tell him then that Mirana was already wedded, that she was not a virgin, but he knew it was too late now. He'd failed Mirana.

"I will prepare my sister."

"My lord, perhaps Mirana can be spared, perhaps—" He broke off at the look on Einar's face.

"Don't say it, old man. She will wed the king. Aye, Sitric will give her all a woman could want. She will have to suffer his meager fumbling, but not often for he is old and frail. She will take him or I will kill her. Do you understand me?"

Gunleik nodded.

"I would have to kill her if she refused, for I too would die for failure to deliver her to Sitric, and believe me, I will never die alone."

Einar found Sira in Mirana's bedchamber. She was looking through the gold-banded trunk at the end of the box bed. She didn't look the least bit guilty or worried when he suddenly appeared.

She smiled at him. "I have need of ornaments, Einar, to enhance my beauty."

"Take what you wish," he said, and left her. "Have you seen my sister?"

"Your half-sister, my lord. Nay, I saw her earlier with the women, but then she was gone. I know not where."

He grunted and left her without another word.

Sira stared after him. He was behaving differently. It made her uneasy.

She'd heard that one of the men, an old man with crooked ways and a brutal manner about him, had visited Lella in the storage shed. She wished she'd heard the little pederast scream. She looked into the trunk until she found arm bracelets that pleased her and earrings and a necklace. Aye, she would look much more beautiful than that bitch, Mirana. What would she say when Sira appeared in her jewelry? Would she whine to Einar because she had taken her jewelry? Would Mirana plead that he dismiss her? For a moment, Sira hoped she would. She'd felt her power growing over Einar, and she knew now there was a good chance she would win. She would have him. He was dark and his darkness fascinated her. Aye, she would have him and learn to control him as she would a dog.

Perhaps, when the king came, Sitric would want her, Sira, instead, if she hadn't wedded Einar before he came. She was still humming, feeling quite confidant, when she heard that the king was nearing, that he had come to wed Mirana.

So soon, she thought, then rose. Very well then, she would take Einar. She fingered the beautifully pounded silver bracelet that encircled her right upper arm. Aye, Einar would suit her well enough. He would give her whatever she wanted.

She smiled when she thought of the king's fury upon discovering that his new bride wasn't a virgin. She hoped he would kill Mirana slowly, perhaps strangle the last living breath from her, or perhaps give her to his men and let them ravish her until she was dead. But what of Einar? Would he be in danger too? She smiled again, for she was beautiful, far more beautiful than that black-haired bitch, and more importantly, she was a virgin. Ah, life was suddenly rife with possibilities.

She decided to take the boy Lella some food. The pathetic scrap just might beg her for it. She wanted to see if she'd scarred the little beggar's cheeks. She wanted to see what the brutal warrior had done to him.

She wondered, as she carefully stepped over cow dung in the outer yard of the fortress, where Rorik was. Surely he would come after her, his family would demand it. She wanted to see him. She wanted Einar to capture him. She wanted to wield a whip and flay the flesh from his back. She trembled a moment at the thought of his treachery, at his rejection of her, at the pain as he'd whipped her.

Mirana stood just inside the longhouse entrance, looking toward Ivar, who wouldn't meet her eyes. She frowned, wondering what was happening or what had already happened. Then Einar was there beside her and he was smiling down at her and taking her hand to hold between both of his.

"King Sitric comes," he said. "He will be here very soon. I will assist you to change into clothes to dazzle an old man's eyes and bring his rod to renewed life. Trust me, Mirana, this is for the best."

She opened her mouth, but he forestalled her. She heard the fear in his voice. "By all the gods, I pray you are a virgin, that it was all a reckless lie you told—this wedding you claimed between you and that Viking, Rorik Haraldsson. But you have never lied to me, have you?

"I should have tied you down and seen to your maidenhead last night, but I was distracted by Sira and

Lella." He paused a moment, looking toward a knot of his warriors who were preparing themselves for the king's arrival. "Listen to me, Mirana, and listen well, for I give you excellent counsel. I accept now that you told me the truth, that you always have in matters of weightiness. I accept that you are wed, but you must forget the Viking. You will never see him again. Save yourself, pretend to great pain when the king enters you tonight. Suffer loudly and whimper of the agony he inflicts upon you so the king will not doubt your purity. Aye, then he will ply you with favors and jewels in his gratitude. You will see. You must trust me in this."

He stopped then, and ran his hands down her arms. "Come, I will help you to gown yourself appropriately. Sira was in your chamber, taking your jewelry. I will have her show herself to you, and if there is anything that would become you, I will have her give it to you."

Mirana nodded. She realized that as long as she was alive, there was hope. She didn't want to die. She'd been a fool to ever consider it. She had no intention of dying willingly even though it might mean her loss of honor. Death was too final to accept because of beliefs that men had fashioned and preached and held so dear, particularly when it came to women. She would survive until . . . She would survive.

"Come," Einar said. "We have little time."

"I'm coming," Mirana said. She didn't look back.

# 29

HE WAS FRAIL, the flesh hanging from his arms and his jowls, but his eyes flamed with excitement, rheumy eyes, heavily lidded, filled with too many years of living, of too much power and abuse of power, now nearly black in the dim light of the longhouse.

He was smiling down at her. Now he was reaching out his hand to take hers. The backs of his hands were spotted with age and the flesh was slack. There were small knots of hairs over his knuckles.

"Mirana, daughter of Audun," he said, squeezing her hand, feeling the coldness but believing it from her young girl's excitement over the honor he was conferring on her. "I will wed you and you will be my queen and the mother of my sons. All hear what I say. From this day forward, she is Queen Mirana and all owe her obeisance." Ah, but it was an old man's voice even though it rang out to every corner of the longhouse, staying strong and certain, not dissipating in the thick smoke that had gathered.

She looked away from him into the black eyes of his advisor, the old man, Hormuze, another whose eyes betrayed that he was something else, something more and mysterious. She feared him. But he was smiling at her, and unlike the king, his teeth were white and straight and healthy. As if sensing questions in her, he quickly lowered his head, resting his hands on his paunch.

"Say that you will have me, Mirana."

The king's voice was low, but the command was there, the same timbre as was in Einar's voice. No one would disobey him, no one. Including her. Especially her.

For the second time in her life, Mirana said, her voice calm and steady, "I accept you, sire, and pray that you will know happiness with me. I will be your queen and the mother of your sons. I, Mirana, daughter of Audun, swear it before all our gods and all our people."

He leaned down and kissed her mouth. His lips were cold and dry. His breath was hot and smelled of his frailty, musty and strangely dry. She made no move, merely stood there, pliant, silent. It seemed to please him, this utter submissiveness of hers.

He whispered against her left temple, "You are shy and that pleases me. You are a virgin, you know nothing of men and what they demand. I will show you, Mirana, and then you will please me, and all will know that you have succeeded, for your belly will swell with my son. Hormuze has promised it. Ah, and when you awaken on the morrow, it will not be this old man's body beside you, but a young man, strong and hale. I will be as I used to be and you will be greatly pleased for it is you who will have renewed me."

She heard his words but she didn't understand. He believed by tomorrow he would again be a young man? Surely this was madness. Such a thing wasn't possible, not in this world, not with these gods overseeing the affairs of men.

"Aye," he said, his voice still low and soft, "this is why you are my bride, Mirana. Only you. It is you who will restore my youth and my strength. Only you. Hormuze has promised and he is never wrong. He is a mystic, a priest of an alien religion, and he comes from a faraway land where such things are understood, where such things are common occurrences. He has promised and you will believe him as I do."

She looked at Hormuze then. She'd never seen a man more contained, so held within himself. She knew he'd overheard the king's words. Was he frightened of his mad promise? Surely he couldn't possibly believe it. None of it made any sense. Surely upon the morrow, the king would be as he was now, and he would see that nothing had changed. Would he not then kill Hormuze?

Einar said loudly to all those assembled in the longhouse, "We will have wine and ale and mead now. The women have prepared a feast, sire, and we will eat now until you wish to take my sister away."

The king smiled at Einar. "You have done well. You are now my brother and you will gain by it, as I have promised you. Once I have regained my vigor, you and I will crush the Irish chieftains who still threaten our lands and our trade.

"But now, I have no wish to befoul my body with drink. I will take your sister—and my wife—away. Hormuze has constructed a boat from his homeland, a royal conveyance that sails upon the Nile. There is a sumptuous chamber on this barge that is furnished with silks and pillows and precious carpets. It is covered as if a fine chamber from the chill of the night and from any rain. It is there I will take my bride now."

The king was holding her hand as if he feared that to release it would cause his death. The bones hurt from the strength of his grip. Einar came to her then, leaned down, and kissed her cheek. He said quietly against her left temple, "You will survive, Mirana. Pretend to a virgin's pain and all will be well. Do not forget or we will both know death."

Hormuze said nothing, merely nodded to the king, stepping back and walking away, an old man who was bowed with weariness, his feet shuffling, his shoulders stooped.

"There will be a feast served us on board the barge," Sitric said to her as he led her from the longhouse. "Then I will dismiss the servants and you will be able to come to me as I bid you to."

She nodded. If he believed her shy, so be it. She felt so deep a pain, a helplessness so profound, she didn't know if she even wanted to survive it. But she would, she had to.

She wanted Rorik. She wanted her husband. She had to hold to that else she would go mad, perhaps reach the depth of madness that possessed this old man. She would not allow the thought to intrude that Rorik didn't want her, that he had rejoiced when she had disappeared. No, he had come after her. She clung to that belief even as she thought of ways to escape this old man with his too hot breath and his age-spotted hands.

"Ah, Hormuze, you are here. I am glad. Is she not beautiful, this new queen of mine?"

"Aye, sire, she is beyond beautiful. She holds a spiritual beauty, nearly a rebirth of a beauty, so incandescent that it overflows the soul."

"What you say is poetic, my friend, but not to the point. She is my wife now. It is done just as you said it must be done. It matters not that I wanted her sooner. Once I've taken her maidenhead, once I've spilled my seed in her, I will be young again, and on the morrow, and all will see me as I was once, as I am now, and as I will be in the future. You have planned this, have you not, Hormuze? All my men will be awaiting my appearance in the morning? They are eager and ready for my transformation?"

"Aye, sire, they are ready. Excitement runs high. All are praying for this. Despite my warnings to you of the misalignment and confusion of the relevant signs and the position of the stars and their houses, I know all will go well. You are a great king; the gods will heed you and not spin things awry."

"I pray that you speak true," Sitric said. His eyes narrowed. "Truth, my friend, the ultimate value to a man and to a king. Without it, there would be chaos. Without it, you would be dead. Do you understand me, Hormuze?"

"Aye, sire, I understand you very well."

Mirana said nothing. She stared from one old man to the other. Hormuze was a priest of some sort, mayhap more likely a wizard, and he'd promised the king his youth. It was amazing. It was also more real to her now than it had been before, for now she was a part of it, an integral part. She felt a spurt of cold, felt the hair on her neck bristle at the strangeness of this. It wasn't customary or expected, therefore it must have come from the gods or from the nether demons. She was to be the agent by which all this came about. She looked again at Hormuze. He was staring at her, his eyes blacker than the night, deep and expectant, and there was something else there, a tenderness, a light of possessiveness, but no, that couldn't be right. How odd that she would think that. No, there was nothing there, nothing save prayer in an old man's eyes that his hide would remain on his aged body when the king remained a frail old man on the morrow.

The king nodded to Hormuze and the old man seated himself at their table. He clapped his hands. Young boys, all clad in white and silver, their hair braided in a dozen slender ropes, their feet bare, brought in silver and gold trays. There was wine from the land south of Kiev, the king told her, as he himself filled her silver goblet. There were grapes as green as her eyes, the king told her, as he insisted on feeding some to her.

The boys were well trained, silent, and all of them looked very foreign.

Hormuze dismissed them, finally. He seemed content to sit back in his chair, watch the king act like an old besotted fool with his young bride, and sip at his wine. Hormuze rose finally and poured the king another glass from a bottle beside him.

"I bid you drink this potion, sire. It will aid you in your dealings with this woman. It will begin your ascension."

The king laughed. He was giddy with his power, with the anticipation of what would soon be his. He looked at Mirana, then grabbed her, pulling her onto his lap. His hands found her breasts and began to knead them furiously. His mouth found hers, and again, it pleased him that she was quiescent. In truth, she wanted to kill him, but she knew she had to bide her time. She had to wait until they were alone. Then she would act. What she would do, she as yet had no idea. But it would be something. She wouldn't lie under this old fool like a lump, whimpering away her courage. She would kill him if she had to.

"Sire, you must drink."

Hormuze sounded to Mirana's ear to be impatient, nearly angry, but that was surely odd. She waited until the king was finished with her. She gave him a scared look that pleased him, she could see that it did, for he looked as proud as a new father.

He set her back into her chair. His hand skimmed over her breasts to her belly. She drew back, but he said, "Nay, stay still." He massaged her belly through her gown, then lowered his hand to cup over her. She wanted to scream at him, she wanted to fling herself at him, for she was the stronger, she knew it, and she could kill him with her own hands, but she held herself perfectly still. Not yet, not yet. Then the king raised the goblet and lifted it to her and then to Hormuze. "My old friend, all will continue. Your rewards will exceed your dreams."

"I pray it will be so, sire. Indeed, I am certain that it will be so."

He drank deep, his throat working, the flaccid skin folding and pleating with each swallow. When he finished the potion, he wiped his hand across his mouth and slammed the goblet onto the table.

"You said you had to prepare her, Hormuze. Do it now, for I do not wish to wait longer."

He turned to Mirana. "Go with him, my beautiful child. He will tell you what you will do. I wish you to wear the white gown, for it is pure, like you. Pure like you will render me. Hormuze, the gown is beyond, lying on the pillows. I put it there myself, just as you told me to."

Hormuze merely nodded. He stretched out his hand to Mirana. She looked at that hand, looked closely. There was an odd sort of smear all across the back of his right hand. He followed the line of her vision. He jerked back his hand, but said nothing.

"Come," he said, his left hand still there, waiting for her to take.

"Hurry," the king said. "Hurry."

Mirana didn't touch him. She rose quickly, and looked up. Hormuze was frowning at her. She quickly dropped her gaze. She followed him through a doorway hung with silk draperies. She stopped dead in her tracks.

The small chamber was like nothing she'd ever seen in her life, or imagined. All the walls were lined with red silk. The floor was covered with thick wool carpets, all patterned with deep reds and blues and creams. And there were thick soft pillows upon which to recline, all of vibrant colors. Upon which she would recline with the king, who believed he was her husband, but he wasn't.

Hormuze picked up the white gown and handed it to her. "Take off your clothes and put this on," he said.

She stared at him, then at the sheer white silk gown. "I will but you must leave."

He smiled, and not an old man's sour smile. No, there was a flair of triumph in his black eyes.

"I won't look at you, but I won't leave," he said. He sat down on one of the thick pillows. His motion was graceful and quick.

Mirana picked up the white gown and stepped as far away from him as she could.

"While you change, I will tell you what will happen," he said. Did his voice sound somehow deeper? She shook her head and quickly stripped off her clothes. The silk slithered over her head and down her body. It felt obscene against her cold flesh.

He turned and fell silent staring at her. "Loosen your hair," he said.

She unbraided the thick coils and smoothed her fingers through her hair, but the deep ripples remained.

"Aye," he said. "Just a bit of kohl at your eyes and you will look just like her. She was as soft and gentle as a summer rain that dampened the earth of the Lufta

Valley. She gave me all I ever wanted."

"What are you talking about?"

He rose gracefully to his feet. She knew then as sure as she knew herself. This was no old man who faced her, triumph gleaming in his black eyes.

"The king expects me to instruct you, to teach you how to arouse his old manhood, but I won't. He will never touch you, I swear it."

Suddenly there was a loud crash from the outer chamber.

"It is about time," Hormuze said, not moving. "He took long enough."

But then the silk hanging was ripped aside. The king stood there, weaving on his feet, his face red as blood, his eyes covered with an opaque white film, his throat working wildly for he couldn't breathe. "You," he said, staring toward Hormuze.

"Aye, sire," Hormuze said. "You are still standing. I gave you enough poison to send you on your way in but a moment. You have more strength than I thought you would. The years bred a strong will in you."

The king hovered between death and bafflement, and he knew it. "I trusted you. I took you in, listened to you, and made you powerful. Why do you kill me?"

"Kill you, sire? Ah, surely not. On the morrow, all will occur just as I told you it would, just as you told all your warriors it would. You will indeed appear before all your men, transformed into a young man as you once were. Behold yourself, sire."

Hormuze pulled off his beard, ripped open his tunic and unstrapped the padding from his waist. He stripped off all his clothes, then he rubbed at the cosmetics on his face.

Then he smiled, a beautiful smile, a foreign smile, for he had the look of a man not of the north. Ah, but he was a beautiful man. Lean, his body whipcord strong, his muscles strong within his man's prime.

"I resemble the man you once were, do I not? At least that is what I was told before I came to you, and when I came, sire, I knew even then what I would do, for I had seen her. She was very young, only fifteen as I recall, and she didn't see me. And I knew then what must be. Aye, look upon my man's body, young and vigorous, aye, sire, and I will breed sons off her, sons who will rule Ireland and beyond and into the future, just as I told you. Aye, look at me, for soon you will be dead. Since I was never a spoiled little princeling as you were, granted all I wanted with no restraint, no rules, I have no fat on my body, no arrogant moods to make those about me fear me, no belief in how I am more clever than any other man in the land. But I do look enough like you, sire. On the morrow, all will cheer and all will bless Hormuze, the advisor, truly a wizard, who, once he had accomplished your rebirth, he disappeared, perhaps to reappear again in the centuries to come in some other strange land where he will once again work his wondrous magic."

Sitric stared at him, at the young man who stood naked and proud before him. "I will kill you," he said, "I will whip you until you are naught but bone and blood at my feet." He worked his mouth, but there were no more words and no more breath. He fell to the floor, his hands clutching his neck, then his arms were falling away, curling at his sides.

Hormuze walked to him and knelt down. "He is dead. By all the gods, the old fool is finally dead."

He rose and turned to Mirana. "I know this shocks you. I know you don't as yet understand. Trust me, that is all I ask. You are pale and afraid, for all this is strange. I am sorry, I had hoped he would die silently, in the other chamber, alone, without you to see him."

Mirana looked at Hormuze and said calmly, "I am pale, it is true, but I am not frightened. The king is dead, not I. You have played a drama before me and now I understand some of it. But I ask you, Hormuze, why did you select me of all women? You say you saw me when I was very young and began your plans. Why me?"

He smiled at her, and the smile was filled with longing, soft and sweet, but it wasn't a smile that belonged to her, that belonged with her, in this chamber. It was a smile of long ago.

He said simply, "Because you are the image of my dead wife. Her name was Naphta and she served a great lady of our country. Aye, I speak of Egypt—" He said a word whose sound was utterly foreign to her ears. "She died because this lady was jealous of her, hated her because her lord husband wanted Naphta. She was sly, very sly. She stuck a *huza* knife—'tis a very small pointed blade—into the base of Naphta's neck, beneath her thick black hair, knowing no one would discover it. But I did. When I had my beautiful wife in my arms, I examined her and found the small prick and felt the stiff strands of bloody hair. Aye, the lady killed her, just as she had killed others who surpassed her in beauty. She killed my beautiful Naphta. I let it be known that I knew what she had done, even spoke of how she'd done it. I knew then that she would kill me too. I escaped just before her assassins came to kill me and my small daughter, Eze. I came here to the north to seek my fortune. And I found it."

Mirana just stared at him, unable to believe him, to comprehend his motives. "I look like your dead wife? All this planning, this elaborate scheme and the king's murder just because I look like another woman? By the gods, this is madness."

He looked at her with less softness now. "You do not sound like her, but you will soon enough with my tutelage. She never questioned me, never considered any wishes but mine. Her tongue was never sharp in disagreement with me, and you will change, Mirana, doubt it not.

"Aye, her image is preserved in my mind and before mine eyes every day of my life, for our daughter will grow into her image as well. There is already a great resemblance between you and my little Eze, not really in her physical features, but in moments when she is silent and looking off into her dreams. And when she smiles. Then I will have both of you to look upon. I will have my Naphta back with me. I will also have a kingdom and power and wealth. And I will share it with you, Mirana. You did wed with the king. I am now he. Behold your husband and your king. I am now Sitric."

# 30

SO MUCH WAS happening, too much, and she was reeling with all that he'd said, all that the king had said. She stared at him now, unable to accept his utter confidence in himself at what he'd done and what he expected others to do. He saw nothing save what he wanted to see, would accept nothing beyond what he had commanded.

"Surely you cannot believe that the people will affirm that you are the king. They would wish to believe it, for it is a magical thing, this rebirth you convinced the king to believe, but the people won't accept it, not once they look at you, not once they are standing close to you. You look foreign, different from us."

"Do you forget so quickly that you believed me an old man, that all those—including the king—have believed me an ancient relic, an advisor, some even saw me as some sort of priest? They will see and accept, for I will continue to disguise myself and each day I will use less and less disguise. Only you will see me as I truly am, each night, when we come together. Aye, they will become familiar with me, you will see. Soon, very soon, they will be shouting their enthusiasm that I am reborn and given back to them by that magician, Hormuze."

"No," she said. "No. The people aren't stupid. They won't believe you are truly Sitric reborn. It's best you face up to it and escape while you still can before they discover that you've murdered Sitric. His warriors have no love for him, but their loyalty is unquestioned. They will surely kill you."

He was frowning at her, completely unaware and uncaring that he was naked, standing there over the dead king's body as if it were naught but another pillow or a tray of food, something of no account at all. All his attention was on Mirana. He said slowly, "Naphta never questioned my judgment, my decisions. You will not either. She always bent to me, gracefully and naturally, as sweetly as a supplicant worships a god. You will as well."

"You were wedded to an idiot?"

He struck her hard across her cheek and she reeled sideways, trying to grab onto something to save herself, but there was nothing, only the soft pillows in piles at her feet, the slippery silk draperies beyond her reach, the lush carpets that were thick and deep but allowed no purchase. She sprawled onto her back on the pillows, hitting her elbow on a brazier and knocking it over. Chunks of cold coal fell onto the pillows, blackening the bright reds and golds and blues.

He came down on his knees beside her. He didn't touch her, but she smelled him, a musky odor that wasn't displeasing, only different, and it came from his flesh and from his man's sex as well, close to her, too close to her. She was frightened of him as she hadn't been of the old king, for he was young and strong, he had all the vigor he'd promised the king. He was angry, and she saw that he trembled with his anger, that it required all his will to control his anger. Einar wouldn't have even tried to control his fury. He would have struck out and maimed and killed, but not this man. This man had exquisite control over himself. She held very still. He said, his voice harsh, barely overlaid with a calm so naked that it chilled her, "Do not ever again speak ill of Naphta. You are not worthy to even say her name. You are nothing compared to her. She was my queen, the most beautiful woman in the world."

"I understand," she said. "Your wife was perfection and I bow to your memories of her. But that isn't the point now, Hormuze—"

"You will call me Sitric. Forget it not, Mirana."

"Very well, Sitric. But heed my words, please." Ah, she saw that the *please* suited him; he believed her already bending to his will. "I did not know, nor would I have ever realized that you and the old man you pretended to be were one and the same."

"But you did," he said slowly, looking down at the back of his hand, where some of the nut dye had smeared. And she'd seen it and wondered at it.

"Nay, I merely believed you had an illness of some kind, nothing more. But listen to me, Hor—Sitric, surely there are old men back at the court who well remember what the old Sitric looked like as a young man. They will denounce you."

He drew back, sitting on his haunches. He was too close to her, the smell of him was too close. He was smiling. He reached out and touched his fingertips to the red mark on her cheek. Even his fingers smelled of the heady musk scent and she wanted to draw back, but knew it would anger him if she did. She would bide her time.

He said, "I am sorry to bring you pain, but it was short-lived and necessary, you must realize that. You will not question me again, Mirana. However, what you just said is worthy of my listening and my response to you will prove my greatness. I am not a man who makes mistakes. Over the past two years I have cleansed the king's court of eleven old men, all his cronies since they were boys. I used different methods in all their deaths. All believed them natural deaths, for they were old, after all, that, or accidents. Now there are none left who remember him at my age, none. Three decades is a very long time. As for the men who know him now, why I will age and they will as well and none will remember, for time erases images. I will succeed, doubt it not."

There was pleasure and triumph in his dark eyes, and now something more, something that made her breath catch in her throat. He was suddenly looking at her with a man's lust. She didn't want to look, but she did. His man's rod was swelling from the thick black hair at his groin, jutting toward her. Odd how it was that the hair at his groin was thick and black and wiry, yet there was no hair on his chest and the hair on his head was as black and soft as the silk pillow beneath her hand.

"The king," she said, and shuddered.

He frowned at her, distracted from his purpose, and rose to stare down at the old man's body, drawn up tightly in his final spasms, the muscles of his face showing his agony at his death moment, his eyes filmed, and wide with shock and pain. "Even in death he offends me," Hormuze said. "You will remain there, Mirana, and I will move him. Do not move."

She watched him drag the king's body from the small chamber. She didn't doubt for an instant that he'd planned this for a very long time. Old Sitric's body would never be found, of that she was certain. She closed her eyes a moment. What would she do?

He was gone for a long time. When he came through the silken draperies, he wore a long robe of vivid green silk, belted at his waist. He was carrying a silver tray with two silver goblets on it, goblets of exquisite design.

"I have brought us wine that came from a land you have never learned of, Mirana. It will calm you and make the night pass pleasantly between us. You will not be afraid that I will savage you. I took three slave girls last night to drain my passion." He saw that she would question him, and added, "No, Mirana, I did not let them see me as I am now, for if I had, then I would have had to kill them, and I do not approve unnecessary death. They used their mouths on my rod and left me immediately after. I have told you to trust me, to know that I am a brilliant man. I will be careful not to hurt you overly. Here, Mirana. You are now my wife, my Naphta, and my queen. Drink to us. Drink to the king and queen."

She took the goblet and lifted it to her mouth. She smelled the deep cloying sweetness that rose to her nostrils like thick steam from the red liquid. There was a stench to it and she knew fear, deep grinding fear. She looked up at him. "I do not wish to drink this."

He tightened. Mirana saw it not only in the thin line of his mouth, but the long sinewy muscles of his body. Even his voice was taut and stiff and hard when he spoke. "You will do as I bid you. You are my wife now and you will never say nay to me. Do you understand me, Mirana?"

"I understand you very well, but I am myself, Hor—Sitric—not this woman you believe I resemble. I can never be her. You loved her, this Naphta. I am not she. You even said that I wasn't worthy of her. It is true. Please, look at me, listen to me."

"You are just as I wish you to be. All other things—those small movements with your hands, the way you will laugh, the way you will bow your head to me in pleasing submission, the way you will look at me when you wish to give me pleasure with your body—all these things I will teach you. You are an apt pupil. As for her spirit, I know you have it not nor will you ever have it, but you will become sufficient. You will obey me in all things. You will do just as I bid you. I have a daughter, Eze, who even now carries her mother's expressions—your expressions. You will care for her as if she were your own, and as she grows older, she will be more and more like her mother, as will you, and I will have both of you to remind me of my Naphta. That is all."

So he had a child to remind him continually of his dead wife. She knew there was nothing for it. He'd planned this for three years, and all had gone as he'd foreseen, except for one very important thing that hadn't been in his control. He'd trusted Einar. He hadn't realized what a vicious savage her half-brother could be, hadn't realized that he couldn't be believed or trusted in his word or his dealings. Also, he'd overlooked chance. Mirana looked at him straightly. She said, not unkindly, "I am already wed to Rorik Haraldsson. My half-brother, Einar, lied to the king. I was stolen from him and then returned, but I am not a virgin, Hormuze—aye, allow me to call you by your real name now—nor am I the king's wife or your wife. I am Rorik's wife. I love him. I owe him my loyalty and my loyalty is his forever, no other man's. Believe me, Hormuze, for I would not lie to you. He is my husband. He is looking for me even now, and he will find me. I am not the virgin you wanted. I am no maiden to fill your needs. I'm sorry, but I cannot change things to suit your pleasure."

"*No!* You lie!" He lurched to his feet, hurling the goblet away from him. The deep liquid arced in a stark clear red, then dissolved, splashing onto the pillows, staining the soft yellows and whites and golds with bloodred. He reached down and jerked her to her feet. Her silver goblet slipped from her fingers. She felt the wet of it on her bare feet.

He jerked her against him, and his long fingers were around her throat. "You lie," he said, then he kissed her hard. He was talking against her closed lips, cursing, for she knew the fury of the sound if not the meaning of his words. "You lie," he said again, louder now, and he was shaking her even as his mouth was devouring hers, as if he wanted to consume her and kill her as well and she was growing light-headed at the tightening of his long fingers around her neck.

Suddenly, he released her and shoved her hard away from him. She fell back onto the pillows. Her fingers massaged her sore throat. She didn't move, didn't speak, just waited to see what he would do.

He paced, the flap of his long robe opening, and she saw the black hair on his legs and his man's rod, limp now against the bush of black hair at his groin.

"I will kill Einar," he said. "But first I will know if he knew of this."

"He knew. I told him. He counseled me to suffer the old man's mauling and pretend to a virgin's pain to save myself. None of this was my doing, Hormuze. Einar only told me of his agreement with the king yesterday. I told him the truth but he wanted to be the king's brother-in-law. He wanted the power and the wealth."

"You swear to me that you are not a virgin? That you are truly wedded to this Rorik Haraldsson?"

"I swear it to you."

She wondered then if he would kill her. He could try, she thought. She would fight him until there was no more strength in her body.

But he hadn't moved to her. He was still pacing, and she knew he was thinking, plotting, trying to decide his best course of action.

She said, "Let me go, Hormuze. Return me to my husband. I belong with him, not with you nor with any other man. Only him. I love him. Please understand."

He turned then and stopped. He smiled down at her. "Oh no," he said. "I won't ever let you go."

"Aye, you will."

At the sound of Rorik's voice, Mirana cried out, unable to help herself. Hormuze whirled about to see one of those massive Viking warriors standing there, all golden and bronze and large, too large, just standing there, at his ease, confident and calm, ready to kill if called to, his eyes on Mirana—nay, on Naphta—and there was hunger in his eyes, more hunger than a man should ever have for a woman. Hormuze recognized it because he'd felt it himself for his beloved wife. It was then he heard a child's voice. It was then he heard Eze. He knew fear greater than he ever had in his life.

"Rorik," Mirana said. "You came. By all the gods, I prayed you would come. I prayed you would come for me."

"Of course I would come for you. I would search the earth to find you. You are my wife." He turned to Hormuze and looked silently at the other man for a very long time. Finally, he said over his shoulder, "Hafter, bring Eze."

Hormuze wanted to fling himself on the huge Viking, even though he would have no chance against such a man, but it didn't matter, the Viking had taken his Eze, he had to kill him, he had to.

Eze came into the chamber, her hand held by another one of those Vikings, this one more golden, less controlled, Hormuze knew, than the other man. He could tell simply from the way he held himself, the clenching of his muscles, the expression in his eyes, those damned blue eyes that most Vikings had, guileless eyes, beautifully light and clear, yet he knew these Vikings could kill as quickly and eagerly as they could love or laugh or drink their mead.

"Eze," he said, and held out his hand. The little girl would have gone to him but the Viking held her back, gently, Hormuze saw, but still he wanted to kill the man.

"I have brought your daughter to you, Hormuze," Rorik said. "I will make a simple trade with you. My wife for your daughter. Agreed?"

"Damn you, both of them are mine!" Hormuze wanted to hurl himself on the damned Viking, so calm he appeared, so sure of himself. He wanted to stick a dagger in his chest, deep and deeper still and twist it. He wanted to pour poison down his strong corded throat, and watch his muscles spasm and tighten until he was naught but a pitiful scrap, just like the king had been.

"Papa," Eze said, not trying to move from Hafter's side now, for she sensed the pain, the uncertainty, the rage of failure that filled her father. She said in a voice too old for a child her age, "Papa, Lord Rorik has told me what you have done and why. He realized that I have the look of his wife, Mirana, and that you wanted my mama back so badly you stole Mirana. But Papa, she isn't Mama. She belongs to Lord Rorik. She belongs on Hawkfell Island. Papa, please, let her go. Lord Rorik has no desire to harm you or me. Please, you don't prefer her to me, do you?"

Ah, Rorik thought, seeing the anguish distort Hormuze's face. A child's words could cut deeper than the sharpest knife. He held himself still and waited. He saw that Mirana was as silent as a shadow, her face pale, yet her eyes were bright and watchful. She was sitting up on those damned foreign pillows, looking like some sort of sacrifice to an alien god in that white gown that showed her breasts and her belly, so stark against her black hair.

"I have held contempt for most men I have met in this land," Hormuze said at last, speaking straightly to Rorik. "They are vain and greedy and would kill their brothers if it would bring them gain. But you are different." He turned to his daughter. "He hasn't hurt you?"

"Oh no, Papa. Lord Rorik and I spoke all the way here to Clontarf. He has been very unhappy without Mirana. Her half-brother stole her back and forced her to wed with the old king. Lord Rorik wants to kill Einar and he wants to have Mirana back with him. He kept telling me not to be afraid, that he knew you were a wise man, not a fool, and that you would quickly come to an agreement with him. You will, won't you, Papa?"

"Aye," Hormuze said, knowing there was no other answer for him. "Take your wife, Rorik Haraldsson. She is not an easy woman. She speaks the truth even when wiser counsel would be silence. She rejects being my queen and knowing ease and wealth throughout her life. I do not understand her fully. She speaks and questions when she should be silent, but she holds you in honor and she is loyal to you. That, I believe, is very important."

"I know. I heard what she said. It pleased me. I don't want an easy woman," he added, speaking to her now, watching her face. "I want a woman who will fight by my side, a woman who will love me until the day I leave this earth, a woman who will laugh with me or hit me when I treat her stupidly, a woman who will hold my honor as dear as she holds her own." Rorik turned to Hafter. "Let Eze go to her father."

The little girl didn't immediately run to Hormuze. She walked instead to Mirana and held out her hand. "I am glad you are all right," she said. "I don't think you look at all like me. I don't remember my mama so I can't speak about that. My eyes are dark like my papa's, and yours are very green. Lord Rorik hasn't been happy without you." She held Mirana's hand until they stood in front of Rorik. Eze gave Mirana's hand into Rorik's, then smiled up at both of them. "Do not worry. My father and I will survive. We always have. He is very smart and he won't let anything hurt me." She smiled at them, then turned to her father, running to him, hurling herself against him.

Hormuze gathered Eze against him, hugging her so tightly she squeaked. "I like you to look like you, Papa," she said, and he squeezed her again, then he laughed. "I don't like you to be old and fat and ugly. I hated that ugly scraggly beard. Please stay like you are now."

"I will try, Eze. I will try."

"I had no wish to kill you," Rorik said. "I am pleased that you are a reasonable man."

"I have no choice but reason," Hormuze said. He saw Mirana held close to the Viking's side, her head pressed against his chest. He felt something move deep within him. By all the Viking gods, she looked like Naphta. He watched her look up at her husband and remembered that look as well. It was the way Naphta had looked at him. He shook his head. It wasn't to be.

Hormuze said to Rorik, "You were lucky. I dismissed most of the king's warriors. I made it easy for you to board the barge. I have made everything very easy for you."

"I appreciate the result, though your motives were blacker than a Christian's sins. Aye, the warriors are within the fortress, drinking themselves sodden, I doubt not, so that you were able to kill the king with no witnesses, no interference from his vaunted Viking guard. Aye, I am grateful that Einar does not know I am here. I want Mirana safe before I take him. I assume you have already killed the king?"

"Poison. I would have preferred to kill him more slowly. He was a venomous man, old and rattled in his wits, but his greed was that of a younger man's."

"Sira is with Einar," Mirana said.

"I know. Hafter questioned one of Einar's guards. He didn't wish to die. He told us all we wished to know. We will take both of them. But first I would ask Hormuze what he will do now."

He shook his head. "I must flee, I suppose."

Mirana said, "Why? You will present yourself as the king on the morrow. Why must you change that?"

"You are not my queen," Hormuze said simply, finality in his voice, and acceptance of that finality.

Eze said, "Papa needs a queen so we don't have to flee."

Rorik stared at the child. Mirana said slowly, "Sira is a virgin. If we were to fetch her now, could you not bring yourself to wed her, Hormuze?"

Rorik laughed. "It is indeed a solution to Hormuze's problem, but Sira is a witch—vicious, heedless, beautiful, utterly without honor."

Hormuze straightened, belting his gown more tightly about his waist. "This Sira, she wants instruction?"

"What she wants is beating," Hafter said. "But she is beautiful, Rorik is right about that. She needs new direction. She needs to learn how to control herself. She wants taming."

"Discipline is important," Hormuze said, nodding.

Rorik said thoughtfully, "It is not that she is evil. I believe that my parents simply gave her no rules, no boundaries, and thus her wishes always took precedence. No one ever said nay to her. As to honor, I believe the concept foreign to her. She's had no reason for it and thus it doesn't yet exist for her. However, she isn't stupid and she is certainly passionate."

Hormuze stared at the fallen brazier, deep in thought.

"Papa, are you certain you want to have this woman?"

Hormuze stared down at his daughter with her too old voice and her too keen eyes. "I wish to survive," he said simply. "If I present myself as the king tomorrow with a queen at my side—the woman who was supposed to bring me back my youth and my vigor—why then, you will be a princess, my sweeting, and I will have a beautiful snake to tame."

Mirana laughed. "Do you believe it would work?"

Rorik shrugged. "There is only one way to find out. It would be a risk, Hormuze, but you must know that."

"Aye, I know the risk. I am willing."

Mirana said slowly, "Perhaps it would be best if Sira had hair as black as mine. You will change. Why not your queen as well?"

"She worships her beautiful hair," Rorik said. "She will howl to the moon. I should like to see how you deal with her rage. Aye, I like it."

"I do too," Eze said. "I should like to be a princess. My papa would be the best king in the world. This Sira, she will come to worship my papa."

"Aye," Hormuze said. "She will."

# 31

EINAR STOOD QUIETLY beside the sleeping woman. He was brooding and he didn't like it. There was no reason for it. He did as he pleased, always, and now he wanted her. His loins were tight and he ached and he wanted her now. It didn't matter that she was a virgin and that she was a cousin to the king of Norway. None of it mattered. She was a slave, his slave. He thought then of Lella, alone in the storage shed, unless some of his men had decided to rape him. Or some of his women, he thought, and smiled at the notion.

He stared down at that hair of hers. Hair so bleached of color that it was silver in the dim light, spilling over the sides of the box bed, nearly to the floor. She was beautiful, no doubt about that, and he did need sons, many sons. Even though he looked young and strong, he was gaining in his man's years. Aye, he needed a wife in order to have heirs. Why not wed her? He could control her, he didn't doubt it.

She was vicious. He liked that. He also liked that if he disliked any of it, he could strike her and see the viciousness turn to fear. Of him.

But first he would take her. It mattered not if she wished to keep her virginity safe until her wedding night. Her wishes mattered not at all. Aye, once he'd tested her, assured himself that she would please him, he would marry her and she would breed his heirs. He would continue to do just as he wished to. He would remove poor Lella from the storage shed on the morrow, a long enough time to punish the boy for his imprudence. He rather liked the notion of the two of them living together, each hating the other, each vying with the other for his attention and his affection. Of course there would be others in the future. He smiled.

He thought of Mirana and knew another surge of relief. He'd been worried, he admitted it to himself. Not frightened, no, not that, but concerned that she would not behave as he'd counseled her to. But it appeared that she'd chosen wisdom and life. She'd chosen to be a queen. She'd pretended to virginity. If she hadn't, if the old king had wondered at all about her vaunted purity, he would have raised an alarm, and both Einar and Mirana would be dead now. But there had been no alarm raised. Nothing. Mirana wasn't stupid, and Einar was profoundly grateful that she wasn't. He wished only that he'd had the chance to touch her, to know her as a woman before the old king had come to Clontarf. Einar shrugged. He was a man who didn't dwell on the past. It couldn't be changed or altered. Only the future was important. And thus this sleeping woman.

He leaned down to shake Sira awake.

In that instant, a thin rope went around his neck, digging into his flesh, breaking through the skin, tightening even as he struggled to get his hands beneath the rope to ease the awful pressure, even as he tried to yell, even as he tried to jerk about to face his assailant.

The rope tightened more, twisting and gouging in

very strong hands, unknown hands, and his flesh shredded and he felt the stickiness of his own blood. He felt the blackness coming closer now, so close that he knew he had just moments before he was unconscious, just moments beyond that before he was dead. Had the old king discovered the truth? Surely not. But who was trying to kill him?

He kicked back with all his strength, struggling as hard as he could against the blackness. He heard a grunt of pain but the rope merely pulled so taut that Einar would have screamed with the pain if he'd been able to. He wanted to give in to the blankness, to end the unbearable agony, and soon he did. He slumped back against the man who held him.

Rorik smiled as he eased Einar onto the ground. "Bind him securely," he said low to Hafter. "And stuff something in his mouth." Rorik then turned to Sira. He stopped, for Hormuze was bending over her, and he was touching her hair. He realized that Einar's struggle had been silent, utterly silent. He stared down at his hands. Einar's blood was on his palms.

Suddenly, Sira bolted upright. She stared into the face of a stranger, then saw Rorik standing behind him and opened her mouth to shriek, but Hormuze was faster. He smiled at her and struck her jaw with his fisted hand.

She sagged back onto the bed.

"She is beautiful," he said to Rorik. "Such hair I've never before seen and I have seen my share of Viking women. Ah, but her hair is splendid. It is like silver silk, an odd thing to say, but it's true. I will have her and that magnificent hair of hers will grow black overnight."

"Let us out of here then," Rorik said. "Gunleik, are we still clear?"

"Aye, Lord Rorik. The men are sodden and snoring loudly."

"You weren't asleep, Gunleik," Rorik said. "Nor sodden, and I thank the gods for that and your unexpected presence outside the fortress."

Gunleik shrugged. "I was worried about Mirana, yet there was nothing I could do. Einar isn't a fool. He knew the direction of my thoughts, knew that I was ready to go aboard that heathen barge, and thus stayed with me until just a few moments ago. He struck down Ivar to keep me here, and bound the lad. I thank you, Lord Rorik. Now, let us out of Clontarf before one of the warriors awakens."

Rorik smiled at Gunleik, a man he knew would be loyal to him and then to his sons and daughters. "Aye, let's away from here."

He hoisted a bound and gagged Einar over his shoulder. "He's heavy," he said. "The murdering savage." But there was joy in his voice, joy and triumph.

Hormuze had quickly bound and gagged Sira. However, she weighed just as much as he wished her to weigh. He was pleased at it. A pity about her hair. But he would allow her to return to her silver hair sometime in the future, if she obeyed him with grace and surrendered to him in all things. When she awoke, she would very likely shriek when she saw herself. But he would be there to explain everything to her, to tell her what she would do and how she would do it. Aye, unlike Mirana, this one would enjoy being a queen. She would enjoy having a man stronger than she. And he would beat her witless if she ever dared to set herself against him or his wishes.

Gunleik saw one of his men stagger to his feet and weave toward the closed doors of the longhouse. He was obviously going out to relieve himself. Gunleik waited, then quickly unbound Ivar and motioned him to follow. Gunleik quietly followed the man out, Ivar on his heels. He spoke to the man, then gently, as the man turned to away to relieve himself, he struck his left temple with his knife handle. He quickly turned back and motioned to Rorik to follow.

Mirana waited with Eze just outside the fortress walls in the deep shadows. She was furious with Rorik, but she understood some of what he felt, and had thus contained her ire. Had he not said that he wanted her to fight beside him? Ah, but not this fight. This, he'd said to her, was his fight, and his alone. Besides, she must stay with Eze and protect her. An afterthought, she knew, and had wanted to kick him.

When she saw him, she nearly cried out with relief. Then she saw Gunleik, and she smiled. Thank the gods he was still with Rorik. Without him, she wondered if Rorik would have succeeded in getting Einar and Sira out of the fortress. But there were both of them, unconscious and bound.

When Rorik had leapt out of the shadows and brought Gunleik down, his arm snaking out of the darkness to go around his neck, Mirana had stayed his arm and his strength. "It is Gunleik," she'd whispered. "He's coming for me. He's coming to the barge to save me."

Once Gunleik had regained his breath, Mirana hugged him and told him what had happened. Then she'd stepped back, saying little as Rorik and Gunleik had weighed each other and assessed the other's strengths. Then Gunleik had nodded. Now they were safe, thank the gods.

Mirana saw now that Ivar was on Gunleik's heels, looking a bit dazed, but nearly whole.

She stared toward Rorik, who was carrying an unconscious Einar over his shoulder. She'd known for so very long that Rorik must kill Einar, but when the moment had come, she'd known terror so deep she'd nearly choked on it. But she also knew that she couldn't dissuade him or attempt to use his love for her to stop him. She had no right to try to change his mind about her half-brother. He had to avenge his people, his wife, and his babes.

What would Rorik do now?

They left Eze and Hormuze—now King Sitric—with an unconscious Sira. She'd come awake and Hormuze had poured a liquid down her throat to make her sleep. He was now very calmly mixing a potion of nut meats and borla roots and a purple plant that Mirana couldn't identify. Soon he would dye her beautiful hair a dark, dark brown.

"I am unable to dye it precisely black," he'd said. "But this will be sufficient. 'Tis a pity she is so much larger than you, Mirana, but we will make do. Once she is conscious again, I will begin teaching her the responsibilities of my wife and my queen. If I succeed, you will doubtless hear about it. My rebirth is the stuff of legends and this one will be sung by your Viking scalds far and wide. If I fail, why, you will hear about that as well."

Rorik took one last look at Sira, and smiled. "I had worried about her," he said to no one in particular. "She was so ungoverned, her passions so very unbridled. But now, with Hormuze's assistance, she will become more reasonable, I doubt it not. My parents will be pleased that she is become a queen, despite her temper and her resentments."

"What of all Einar's people?" Gunleik said. "They know who she is. They won't be fooled." He had grasped what had happened and what they planned to have happen, but the shock of it was still writ clear on his face.

"Aye," Rorik said. "Those who chance to see her will surely wonder, but Einar will be gone. There will be disarray. There will be chaos. Sitric plans to remove himself and this barge and all his warriors quickly on the morrow."

Rorik hugged Eze good-bye, telling her that Sira was a witch but that her father would doubtless bring her to reason. Eze said in her too old child's voice, "I will help Papa. Between us, she will make a fine queen. Take care of your wife, Lord Rorik. I hope she is worthy of you."

Rorik looked over the child's head at Mirana. She was grinning at him. He felt his body tighten, and he felt remarkably fine. Then he looked over at the bound and gagged Einar. He was awake. There was hatred and venom and a goodly dose of fear in his eyes. He was staring at his half-sister.

Soon thereafter, Rorik guided the two longboats into the Irish Sea. The night was clear and warm, only a slight breeze ruffling the hair on Mirana's forehead. She stared at her husband, standing at the stern, his legs spread, his hands on his hips. He'd come for her. Not for Sira, no, he'd come for her.

She heard a muffled grunt over the smooth dipping of the oars and the conversation of Rorik's men. She looked down at Einar. He was at her feet.

She saw the hatred in his eyes and smiled at him. Slowly, deliberately, she lifted her foot and rested it on his neck.

"My wife has worried about you," Hafter said to her above the sound of his oars.

There was pride and some humor in his voice and

Mirana smiled. "I look forward to seeing Entti. I hope you have made her happy?"

"I had little time, for you were taken so quickly. However, she did not complain. We will see if she complains to you."

That had a sour sound to it and she laughed. Mirana realized in that moment that they were indeed going home—to Hawkfell Island. To her home. She stared toward her husband. At that moment, he turned. She saw all she needed to know when he looked at her.

Toward the following evening, Rorik put them ashore on a small island just off England's western coast. It was barren, save for a few scraggly sea shrubs, but the sand dunes curved one after the other, thick and deep and high, providing shelter and protection. There was no one around, no light, no dwellings, no other camp fires.

Rorik allowed Einar to relieve himself, then had Hafter bind him again. He kept him gagged. He didn't wish Einar to torment Mirana, and he knew he would try if allowed to. He left Mirana in charge of the camp whilst he and his men scouted the area. They'd already caught several large sea bass for their dinner.

Einar was fed, then bound again and left in charge of Gunleik and Ivar for the night. "Let him speak tonight if he wishes to," Rorik said, staring down at Einar. "Mirana won't be here to listen to him." In addition, all his men slept in a wider circle around Gunleik and Ivar.

"Watch him well," Rorik told them. "I have no respect for his honor but I have a great deal of respect for his skill."

"Aye," Hafter said, "but he isn't a magician. He can't fly away, Rorik."

Gunleik gently eased his knife blade across the pad of his thumb. "I should like him to move," he said. "I should like him to speak, perhaps give me orders, tell me how he will beat me bloodless if I don't release him. Aye, let him speak."

Einar remained motionless and silent.

Mirana felt shy and strangely nervous when she saw Rorik walking toward her like a conquering prince, two blankets over his left arm, and a look of hunger in his blue eyes.

"Come," he said only and reached out his hand to her. "We will seek some privacy."

She took his hand silently, following him, careful to watch where she stepped, for there were half-buried rocks in the deep shifting sand.

When Rorik was satisfied that their distance from the camp was sufficient, he spread out the blankets and eased down. He looked up at her and said without preamble, "I have never given you pleasure, yet you have suffered my demands on you. I would remedy that now, tonight. I want to come inside you, sweeting, and I want to place my hand over your mouth when you yell with the pleasure I will give you."

The last time he had forced her in the bathing hut. She remembered her terror, remembered the pain, certain he would kill her. She shook her head. That was in a past that didn't deserve memory. "What of your parents, Rorik? Will they accept me now?"

He shrugged and drew her down beside him. He made no move to touch her or bring her against him. He looked out over the gently roiling waves of the sea. It was calm under the brilliant half-moon. In the distance, she could hear the low voices of the men, muffled and deep. She could pick out Hafter and Gunleik and Raki.

"I bade them leave. I told my father and my brother that I didn't wish them to come here with me. They were thinking of Sira, you see, and I was thinking only of you. I told them I would rescue Sira for them and return her to Norway. I also told them that you were my wife, that you were the mistress of Hawkfell Island, and that I loved you. They left without saying what they felt, but they still wore their pain and their bitterness, I could see it in their eyes." He turned then and gently cupped her chin in his palm. "Heed me, Mirana, I love my parents and I listened to them. It was a grave mistake I made, for it led to but more pain, for both of us.

"But in the years to come, they will see what you mean to me and to our people. They will love our children and they will realize that they have been wrong to create a shrine of hatred. If they don't wish to join in our lives, then so be it. It is our life, not theirs. Come now, sweeting. I want to be inside you. I want to caress you. I want to *know* you."

"Will it hurt?"

He grinned at her. "Nay, not this time, for I will be as gentle as the waves creeping slowly onto the beach. Do you trust me?"

"With my life. I thank you, Rorik, for saving me. My situation wasn't hopeful."

"I believe that Hormuze—no matter how great he believes himself to be—would have found himself quickly at an impasse. You would have defeated him, Mirana. I just did it more quickly because I had Eze with me."

"But you found her and brought her to us. It was your plan and I thank you for thinking of it."

"It was my duty as your husband. It was also my pleasure as your lover."

He leaned over and lightly kissed her mouth. He didn't touch her, just continued to kiss her until slowly she parted her lips to him. She was tentative, uncertain. He'd momentarily forgotten her innocence, her inexperience. He wouldn't forget again. Her lips were soft and tasted of salt from the sea and of her, Mirana, his wife. He deepened the pressure and felt her lean toward him.

"Open your mouth wider, Mirana."

She did, with no hesitation. When his tongue touched her, feathery light, she eased and waited, no longer feeling as calm as she had just a few moments before, but knowing herself content to wait, to learn about him slowly, to let the warmth in her belly build and build. She would be what he wanted her to be and in opening to him, yielding completely to him, she knew she would be repaid tenfold. He was that kind of man.

Rorik smiled against her mouth. She felt it and opened her eyes. He drew back and said, "Feel my hand."

He lifted her breast in his hand. Then the other. He weighed them, caressed her nipples until he felt her heartbeat quicken and quicken even more. With no more words he brought her up onto her knees facing him, and unfastened the rich silver brooches at her shoulders, removed her tunic, then lifted her gown over her head. She wore only a shift, soft and virgin white, and it too was quickly gone.

"Are you cold?"

She wasn't cold but she was naked and he wasn't. Still she sat before him quietly, knowing he was looking at her, but she didn't move, just sat there, her palms open on her thighs, the moonlight spilling over her, making her white skin glisten. "No, but I would see you as naked as I am."

He laughed, then rose swiftly and pulled off his clothes. Never, she thought, looking at him, had she seen a more beautiful man. His size didn't frighten her or the thickness of his sex that was swelled with his need for her. It pleased her, this need of his, just as his strength gratified the deepest part of her.

"You will tell me what to do," she said, and held out her arms to him.

"Nay," he said, as he kissed her throat and her shoulders, "I will show you."

She felt him against her hip. She knew a man's lust drove him beyond his own best intentions, beyond thought, for she'd seen it in Einar and other men as well, and Rorik as well, although not this time. She wanted to touch his man's flesh, but when her fingers found him, and she drew in her breath at the wonder of how he felt, he gently pushed them away. "No, sweeting. Not this time. No, don't look uncertain. Your touch is miraculous and it moves me far too much. I am not content to wait for that pleasure, but I will."

He parted her thighs and eased himself between them, then rose to his knees, parting her legs impossibly wide, and wider still, placing them over his own thighs. She didn't pull back, either her mind or her body. She waited, relishing the pulsing warmth deep in her belly. He looked at her and there was hunger in his eyes and a knowledge that she knew he would give her and soon. When he still didn't come into her, she lifted her hips. He smiled as he lowered his mouth to her.

When she screamed her release, Rorik breathed in deeply, the clean sea air and her scent filling his nostrils. He continued to stroke her with his tongue, widen her with his fingers, and delve deep, feeling her smallness and how she accommodated to him. When he thrust into her, sinking high and deep, and she again lifted her hips to bring him deeper, he felt the tremors in her body and closed his eyes, feeling the power in her, the need, and that need was for him. He kissed her mouth and knew she tasted herself on him and he reveled in that too because he heard the soft keening from deep in her throat, felt the gentle spasms squeeze him, draw on him, pull him deeper into her, holding him so tightly he knew he couldn't bear it much longer. He heaved himself into her to his hilt and felt her soft flesh hold him tightly. When he felt his own release overtaking him, he eased his hand between them to find her.

He shouted his climax to the clean sky, his throat working madly, no thought in his mind to his men who probably heard his cries. All of it went upward, to the brilliant stars that studded the darkness, then he covered her mouth with his when she again came to pleasure.

"I pleased you," he said, a man's satisfaction deepening his voice, as he eased his weight off her. She tried to hold him, but he kissed her and pulled away. "I wish you to remain round and soft for me. If I continue to lie on you, you will become as flat as the blankets."

She laughed, her breath warm and soft against his shoulder. "I much enjoyed that, my lord. Aye, you satisfied me enough."

"Are you certain, Mirana? Do you swear you did not howl like a madwoman just to please me, that you did not feign your release with me, that you only pretended to enjoy my mouth on you?"

She hit his arm and felt the deep muscles flex beneath her palm. She looked away from him, her lashes hiding her eyes. She whispered, her voice meek and submissive. "Ah, 'tis the truth, Rorik. I didn't wish to disappoint you. I wanted you to feel proud of yourself and your prowess. I pretended and prayed it would be sufficient. Did I succeed?"

He laughed against her mouth, forcing her face upward to him. "I will never let you go. Never." And he kissed her again. When he entered her but moments later, she was surprised to feel the building warmth in her belly. She had felt so languid, so without any desire to move, but she welcomed him and his man's sex deep inside her, and moaned in his mouth even as he pressed himself against her belly. This time, it was she who found him and touched him, drawing him deeper into her, caressing him until he moaned and heaved over her.

"There is no other man like you," she said against his throat, licking his flesh, then lightly kissing him, then licking him again and again, tasting him, taking all of him into her body and her mind.

# 32

THEY WERE SO close to home, so very close, not more than a day away. Mirana stared at the gathering storm clouds, shivering from the sudden chill wind as she watched them roil overhead, gathering thicker and thicker, knitting the sky into blackness. The sun had been shining brightly just that morning, not more than two hours before, sparkling off the water in its brightness, the air warm, filled with the tangy sea salt and the scent of the dozen herring the men had caught.

She shivered again, drawing her cloak more closely around her. It was a queen's cloak and she hated it. She fingered the soft royal blue wool, and wished she could throw it over the side of the longboat. It was the only piece of clothing she had brought with her. Hormuze had wanted to give her much more, for, he'd said, the clothes had been made for her, and Sira was too large, after all, but Mirana hadn't wanted to wear any reminders of her time at Clontarf. She didn't want to be reminded of her few hours as the queen of Ireland, a position she prayed Sira would enjoy. She wondered how Sira had reacted when she'd awakened and seen Hormuze and her dark brown hair. Would she believe she looked coarse? That memory made her smile, but just for a moment.

The cloak, despite its black memories, felt quite warm. She would give it to Entti, she thought, once they'd returned home. To Hawkfell Island. She looked toward Rorik, who was speaking to each of his men, then shouting to Hafter, who was captaining the other longboat. He'd told her he'd brought the flat-bottomed longboats because he'd known he would need them to navigate on the shallow river Liffey. The warships were steeper, curving up higher on the sides, and sat deeper in the water. The warships would have fared much better in the storm that was surely coming.

All the men were readying the longboats and themselves for the storm, their movements efficient, no time wasted in talk.

She saw that Rorik was now frowning. He knew the storm would be bad. She wondered if he would take them ashore for the duration of it even as she remembered her own adventure with Entti when the storm had burst upon them. It seemed a lifetime ago. She said her question aloud to Gunleik.

"Nay," Gunleik said, shaking his head, even as he spat upon his finger and held it up into the wind. "This area is more dangerous than the storm. There are rocks just below the surface and dangerous currents. We cannot land here. We must ride out the storm just beyond the breakers. Rorik is pulling us closer right now, but he must take it slowly. It is a pity that we are here when the storm will strike, but the gods willed it so."

"I do not approve the gods' will in this case," Mirana said tartly. "I know of no evil we've committed."

Indeed, Mirana doubted the gods would waste their time on such a consideration as the exact location of two longboats, but she didn't remark upon it. She looked toward the other longboat, just to their stern, not ten feet away. Einar was still bound, doubtless still lying on the planking. She wondered, briefly, if he were frightened. With the storm, he might drown with the water flooding into the longboat, and he must realize that. She rather hoped he would. She knew and now accepted that Rorik would take Einar back to Norway, to his father, who would call together a meeting of the *thing,* and that would bring together all the *Thanes* and lesser nobles, even King Harald, and Einar would be judged. She knew too that Rorik would demand that he fight Einar to the death. And thus it would end. She wanted that ending more than anything.

Sometimes she wanted to strike her husband for his endless honor. She would have preferred sticking a knife in Einar's ribs. Rorik had said calmly, though Mirana had heard the banked rage in his voice, "I should prefer to kill him slowly, with my bare hands, but I should also like to see the man who killed so many of our family and our people stand before us and be judged. I will kill him, Mirana, but in a fight that will be fair."

"You speak of justice, Rorik, but it is a cold thing, many times a thing apart from men and women. It perhaps satisfies the mind, but never the soul. Thus, my lord, I believe you are really doing this for your father and mother, aren't you?"

He was surprised, his eyes narrowing on her face. "How can you know me so well?"

"I pray that I will come to know you in every way a woman can know a man. Can I not now know some of what is in your mind, in your heart even now? Aye, I believe you want to help your parents forget their hatred. You want them to look forward, to recognize and cherish what they still have, what they will have in the future. You want them to face their enemy and see that Einar is only a man, a cruel man, a man who deserves death for what he did, and he will get it."

"Aye," he said only, and kissed her.

"I would go with you to this meeting of all the *Thanes,*" she said, but he hadn't replied, merely kissed her again, and walked to the stern of the longboat to speak to Kron.

She raised her face now to the roiling black clouds overhead. A raindrop hit her forehead. She heard one of the men shout. It was beginning. She huddled in her cloak.

She heard Rorik's voice over the loud slamming waves against the sides of the longboats, calm and steady, and knew all the men responded to him and were calmed by him. But would it be enough?

All of them were soaked. She had spent the past hours scooping water out of the bottom of the longboat in a leather water pouch, little enough to do when all the men were nearly beyond exhaustion, their minds closed against the growing pain in their bodies. Gunleik had been seized with violent back spasms that morning and had soon run out his strength, and thus wasn't at the oars. He, like Mirana, was trying to scoop water out of the longboat before it swamped.

She felt her stomach rise in her throat when the longboat slammed down into a deep trough, burrowing deep and deeper still, sloughing through it, making it seem as if they would touch the bottom of the sea itself, yet staying intact, a miracle, Mirana thought, and briefly closed her eyes in prayer.

Again and again, the longboats were hurled to the bowels of the sea only to be thrown nearly straight up to catch the peaks of yet another wave, a wave many times as tall as an oak tree.

The sky was dark, but it couldn't yet be night. She heard a strangled yell, men's shouts and curses, and knew one of the men had fallen overboard.

She saw Rorik through a blur of rain hunkered over the side of the longboat, searching for his man, but there was nothing but the frigid water, frothing wildly, drawing back only to surge forward. It was then they had no choice. They needed another man at the oars. They released Einar and set him in the lost warrior's place. He was strong, she'd give him that, and he bent to the job, pulling and drawing with all his strength. She saw that Hafter had tied him loosely to the oar. Then she saw him no more for the other longboat was lost in a bank of fog and heavy rain.

Time passed. She continued to bail out the water from the bottom of the boat, her movements steady and rhythmic. Still the water covered her feet, and she wondered how much longer the longboats could hold together.

Through her thoughts and her fear, she heard Rorik's voice, never changing, always encouraging, steady, so very steady. She focused on his voice and continued her movements, filling up the water skin, lifting it, then dumping it over the side, only to have a wave of frigid water strike her hand and her face. It seemed for naught, but she had to do something.

Suddenly, it was over. From one moment to the next, the force of the winds died, the slashing rain became a sullen drizzle, and the longboats ceased their endless dipping and dragging.

It was over.

The late afternoon sun came through the quickly dispersing clouds. She heard the men shouting, cries of Odin All-Father and Thor and Frey on their lips.

She merely smiled, knowing that all but one of them had survived the storm. She saw Rorik as he spoke to each of the men, then heard him shout to Hafter in the other longboat, which was rapidly drawing close to theirs once again.

She saw Einar hunched over an oar, his head down.

"We will land," Rorik called out.

Gunleik, bowed forward from the pain in his back, looked up and nodded.

"Aye," he said to Mirana. "It is safe now. There are no treacherous shoals or half-buried rocks hereabouts to tear us apart. The storm pushed us farther east, beyond them. Thank the gods and your husband, we've survived."

"Aye," she said. "My husband is the best of men. As for you, Gunleik, I will try to find a spirl plant, 'twill help the spasms. It normally grows close to shore."

He patted her hand. "We're alive," he said. "What is a miserable little back pain?"

Both longboats headed toward the stretch of beach only some one hundred yards distant. It had trees growing close to the shore, and this worried Rorik, for trees meant cover for possible enemies, but he knew there was little choice. The men were exhausted, he felt himself as if he would fall over any moment, his muscles cramped from the hours at the oars, but the longboats had to be inspected for damage. He scanned the shore for any kind of movement. He saw nothing.

Suddenly, with no warning, Einar leapt from the longboat, the rope that had bound him loosely to the oar he was rowing now dangling from his wrist. He hit the water and disappeared from view.

Rorik turned to Mirana. "Can he swim?"

"Like an otter," she said, and jumped up to lean over the side.

As Rorik pulled off his boots and checked his knife at his wide leather belt, he shouted, "Hafter, keep watch! All of you, hold steady. We must wait until he shows himself!" Rorik held close to the side, preparing himself to jump.

Finally, Einar came to the surface a good twenty yards from the longboat, close to shore, far too close to shore. "After him," Rorik shouted, and the men bent to their oars.

The longboats were flat-bottomed and could slide through the most shallow water, but Rorik knew that once Einar broke the surf, he would disappear into those trees and he would never find him. He would slip away. Even though Einar had no weapon, even though if he did escape he would very probably be killed by animals or men, Rorik couldn't accept it and he knew he would never be able to accept it. Einar would always be there, alive, always alive, even if it were only in his mind. If he didn't see him die, he would be immortal. He had to catch him. He had to see him die.

He cursed his damned promise of justice. He should have killed the bastard, strangled him at Clontarf until the cord had cut through to the back of his neck. But he hadn't, no, he'd wanted to be a hero to his parents, to show them that he, their brave son, had succeeded, had brought back Einar as one would the lowliest slave.

He would fail, he smelled it, felt it in the deepest part of him. He watched Einar slough through the waves, no exhaustion showing in his arms as they sliced through the water smoothly and evenly, with great power.

He couldn't wait. He was stronger. He was the better swimmer, he had to be. Ah, but he was exhausted, his arms so tired, the muscles so knotted, occasionally seized with cramps, he wondered if he could lift them, much less set them to churning through the water. If only they'd set Einar to the oars at the beginning of the storm, if only . . . but he'd taken his place there for less than an hour. His strength had barely been tapped.

Rorik made up his mind in that instant. Even as drained as he was, he knew he could outswim the longboat, for the waves were high and the currents pulling strangely. He had to. There was no choice. He had to catch Einar.

He dove overboard. The last thing he heard before his head went underwater was Mirana's shout. He knew that Gunleik and Hafter would keep her safe, no matter the outcome.

"By all the gods, no!"

But Gunleik was too late. Mirana dove over the side, wearing only her shift. All attention had been on Einar and Rorik. He yelled and yelled, but she was gone from sight for several moments. When she surfaced, he was astounded that she was so very close to her husband and Einar.

He'd never before seen a woman swim as quickly and efficiently as she. Gunleik knew she could swim, her father had taught her, but he'd never imagined anything like this.

She was gaining on the men. To his further astonishment, he saw her swing away from them and make for shore at an angle. She beat the men by at least twenty yards. She struggled through the surf and onto the hard black sand. She didn't pause to rest, but ran to the nearest tree and began searching frantically.

She was looking for a weapon. Gunleik felt his back miraculously straighten, only to feel fear for her and for Rorik fill his throat, bringing up bile, thick and sour. By all the gods, did she realize what she was doing?

Mirana knew well what she was doing. She paid no attention to the men coming toward shore behind her. She finally found a thick maple branch, stout, but not too heavy. She swung the club, changed her grip, then whirled about to the beach.

Einar was on his hands and knees in the black sand, frothing water swirling around him, heaving, trying to regain his breath. Rorik was behind him, struggling to stand in the breaking surf, striding now slowly through the water, coming closer and closer. He yelled, "I will kill you now, you damned bastard!"

Einar was on his feet in an instant and running, but no longer at his full strength. He stumbled and went down, only to drag himself up again.

Rorik was breathing hard, but he was running fast, and soon he would catch Einar, she knew it. Mirana was amazed at Rorik's strength, his determination. But she wasn't at all surprised that she'd easily beaten them to shore. She hadn't been exhausted. She'd had her full strength. And she still had it now.

Einar whirled about to see how close his enemy was, then he heard a woman's laugh. He turned back and saw his half-sister standing in front of him. She had a stout club held in both hands. She was standing like a man, her legs apart, her arms firm, held in front of her, her wrists locked around that damned club.

"By all the gods, how did you get here?"

"I swam here quickly. Just for you, Einar, just for you. I won't allow you the chance to hurt Rorik. I won't allow you the chance to escape into the woods. Come here, brother, and let me kill you. Unlike you, I won't be your tormenter, I won't make you beg and plead. No, I will kill you quickly and cleanly and then it will be over and all your evil will die with you, and Rorik will be free of you forever."

Einar laughed. "You think you can kill me, you stupid bitch? I can break you in half with one hand. You are nothing, Mirana, nothing."

Rorik refused to believe what was right in front of him. No, it was impossible. No woman could have swum that distance so quickly, but she had and there she was, standing in front of Einar, just like a Valkyrie, a thick club in her hands, and he knew such fear he nearly choked on it.

"Mirana," he shouted. "Get away from him!"

He drew his knife and ran forward. He was nearly spent, he knew it. He was beyond spent, and that was the truth of it. His rage was the only thing that drove him now, and his fear for Mirana. The hours at the oars had drained him, and the wild swim to shore had nearly brought him to his knees. He felt exhaustion pulling on his legs, dragging down his arms, slowing his mind.

"Stay back, Rorik! Einar is a snake, I told you that. He has no honor. Stay back! I won't allow him to escape, to hide in the woods, to be free of what is due him, to leave you to wonder, always wonder if he lives or is dead. I will end it now."

"No! Mirana! No!"

Einar charged her, head down, his hands out and over his head to protect himself. Mirana struck him hard, but the blow struck his upper arms, doing him little damage. Kill him, ha, she'd barely bruised him.

Then he was on her, flinging her backward and he came down over her. She kicked upward, but he twisted her wrist viciously, and managed to jerk the club from her. He slammed his fist against her jaw, and sent his knee into her ribs. He was up in an instant, jumping away from her, whirling about readying himself to face Rorik.

She saw black, then shook her head violently to clear it. She felt no pain, nothing but a rage that burned hard and intense, fanning throughout her mind and her body. She saw Einar standing there with the club, waving it at Rorik. She saw him look quickly to the woods to his left and knew he was weighing his chances of escape without fighting.

Rorik ran at Einar, then jumped suddenly, his legs going out, and up high, striking him solidly in his chest. She stared, for she'd never seen a man move like that and so very quickly. It sent Rorik onto his back and he rolled gracefully, coming to his feet again. As for Einar, he was thrown backward, sprawled onto his back, his face turning blue because he couldn't draw breath into his lungs, but he was up quickly, and now he was running toward the woods.

He just might make it. He was more desperate than he'd ever been in his life. Aye, he just might make it.

She couldn't allow it. She was after him in an instant, and she was faster. She was filled with strength. Energy poured through her and she ran even faster. She would catch him. She had to catch him. She had to put a stop to this. It had to end, irrevocably. She could hear Rorik breathing heavily behind her, hear his footfalls in the fallen leaves.

She heard Rorik cursing and soon he was nearly beside her, and she veered away. He would stop her instead of catching Einar, because he was afraid for her and he wanted to hold her safe above all. She looked back at him, and knew she must be gaining on Einar.

Suddenly Einar's arm slammed around her throat, jerking her off her feet, tightening until she couldn't move, couldn't breathe, and he yanked her back against his body.

"I have you now, Mirana. Finally, I have you."

Her fear brought nausea into her throat, but she knew she had to control herself. She wouldn't let the fear control her. She felt tears sting her eyes, not tears of fear, but tears of rage and frustration, for now Einar had the advantage.

Rorik had stopped dead in his tracks, and there was a look of horror on his face. He didn't move.

"I have your bitch, Rorik Haraldsson," Einar called out, such pleasure in his voice that it made her flesh crawl. She held very still, waiting. The tears trickled down her cheeks, and she hoped Einar saw them and laughed and believed her afraid of him. She felt the heaviness of Einar's breathing against her back.

"Aye," Einar yelled out even louder now, for he was enjoying himself. He had the upper hand. "Aye, Rorik Haraldsson, she thought herself so above me in skill and cunning, but I know her, much better than you do. Aye, I will tell you something else, I had her before I had to give her over to the old king for the pathetic lecher to sweat over her and maul her. Aye, I stuck my fingers into her, for she'd claimed she wasn't a virgin, that she'd married you, but I didn't believe her. I had to make certain, and I felt her and she was ready for my finger, Viking, aye, more than ready. There was no maidenhead, she hadn't lied about that. She moaned and lifted herself for me. She begged me to take her, Viking, this faithless bitch of yours.

"You wonder why she's trying desperately to kill me, Rorik Haraldsson? It is because she knew I would tell you that I'd taken her, that she pleaded with me until I freed my rod and drove into her and she shrieked like a whore."

His arm loosened about her throat. She was ready. She closed her eyes a moment, drawing on what strength she had left. His arm tightened again as he shouted to Rorik, who'd remained obdurately silent, "Nay, don't come closer, Viking, or I'll twist off her skinny neck. You will remain here and I will take her with me. When I am tired of her scrawny body, why then, I might return her to you. I will survive, Rorik Haraldsson. I always have and I always will. Did I tell you that I finally remembered your precious wife? What a loud fishwife she was, yelling and screaming and trying to fight as my men held her down and jerked her arms and legs away from her body. But when I took her, she was just like your second wife here, she begged me, and pleaded with me and I took her, again and again, until she was quiet, very quiet. My men had enjoyment with her as well, but not all that much, for I killed her with joy."

She had to move and she had to do it now. She knew Einar. He would quickly realize that Rorik would not be taunted into foolish action and then he would take her away with him.

She jerked her head down and bit as hard as she could into Einar's forearm. He screamed, but she didn't let go. He tried to strangle her, but the pain was too great. He hit her head, but her teeth, strong as her will, went deeper into his flesh. She felt the bone in his arm. She tasted his blood and wanted to vomit. She knew he couldn't get enough leverage to strike her with the club. She hung on.

Then Rorik was on him and she released his arm. His blood filled her mouth and she spat it onto the ground. Einar no longer had his club, it had fallen on a pile of leaves. Mirana grabbed it up, readied it, and moved closer to the struggling men.

Einar was fighting for his life, and he knew it. He was crazed, striking Rorik at every chance, most of them glancing blows of little import, howling and groaning at the same time.

Mirana saw the *berserker* madness in Rorik's eyes, and knew the end was near.

Still, she moved closer, just in case he needed her, just in case he slipped or fell. She saw his large hands go around Einar's throat. She watched Rorik hook his foot around Einar's leg and whip him about to face him. She watched her husband's eyes grow calm and deadly even as he squeezed the life from the man who'd haunted him for far too long, squeezed even harder as he looked into his face and watched the life fade away. Einar fought it, fought it with all his might, but it wasn't enough.

Rorik said softly, his face but inches from Einar's, "This is for my sweet wife and for my two small babes and for all my people you brutalized and murdered. And it is for my parents as well so they will face the future without the horror of you still alive from the past."

Finally it was over. She watched Rorik release Einar and let him slide to the ground at his feet. He looked down at the man who'd killed so many of the people he'd loved. Then he looked up at her. He wasn't breathing hard. He looked strong and fit and ready for any number of battles. He looked neither triumphant nor brutal. He looked calm and, strangely, at peace.

He said only, "Thank you, Mirana."

"For what, my lord?"

He smiled then. "For allowing me to kill him."

They both looked about at Hafter's agonized shout.

MIRANA WATCHED ENTTI twirl around in her new royal blue woolen cloak in front of her besotted husband. It looked wonderful on her, her shining thick brown hair lying full over her shoulders, spilling over the swirling cloak.

"You look beautiful," Hafter said to his wife, grabbed her hand and pulled her tightly against him. "I missed you." He kissed her and laughed. "Aye, I missed you so very much I didn't allow you to sleep last night. I trust you've forgiven me for all my past sins—imagined sins most of them—but you're a sensitive woman, and thus I will beg your forgiveness yet again. Tell me you enjoy my man's body now, Entti."

Entti gave him a fathomless look, saying nothing, merely stroking her fingers over the soft blue wool. After a few moments, he began to fidget. Mirana looked down, trying not to laugh.

"I will suffer you, Hafter," she said at last. "I vowed to endure you, to care for you even as you become an old man, toothless and withered. And I will bear with you until your sons tell me I have no more need to, on the day they set your shriveled old body afloat on an equally aged longboat and set it afire."

"Sons? What mean you, sons?"

Entti kissed his chin. "If you continue as you have begun, I will give you more sons than you can count. Is it enough, you great lout?"

"Nay," he said, "for I would have an equal number of daughters with their mother's beauty but not her wicked tongue." Then he frowned down at her. "I do not wish to be toothless and withered."

"I have sworn to protect you, thus, if you do not wish it to happen, I will not allow it."

He kissed her again. Mirana laughed aloud, a laugh replete with happiness.

Amma and Old Alna stood behind her, Old Alna cackling as was her wont, about nothing in particular, just cackling, a marvelous sound. Amma, a baby in her arms, was rocking it and making soft cooing sounds. Erna was at the loom, humming softly, not yet smiling, it was too soon, far too soon. Utta was stirring porridge in the huge iron pot suspended over the fire pit. The men were gathering their weapons to hunt on the mainland. Rorik was sitting in his lord's chair, polishing his sword.

She heard one of the women laugh. She jerked around, joy stirring in her, but it wasn't Asta. Mirana shook away the sudden tears, and prepared to rise. She looked about, wondering where Gurd was. She'd seen little of him, she realized, since they'd come home the afternoon before.

Kerzog suddenly rose on his hind feet and put his large head on Mirana's lap. He woofed softly.

"Missed by my lord's dog," Mirana said. "It is the final pleasure in my life."

"Nay, I am your final pleasure," Rorik said, towering over her. "I am your first and final pleasure."

"You men," Entti said. " 'Tis all you can talk about and think about, your rod and your pleasure."

"Has Mirana not told you, Entti?"

"Told me what, Lord Rorik?"

"That she uses me, naught else, just uses me, milks me like a cow until it is she who has the pleasure. My pleasure is insignificant to her, of no importance at all. It is true. Tell her it is true, Mirana."

"I will continue to pat Kerzog until all of you have left the farmstead, then I will tell Entti the truth."

But Entti was no longer sharing the jest. She was shaking her head as she said to her husband, "I still cannot believe that Sira is a queen. Surely you could have buried her in a prison instead, Mirana. A queen! It quite terrifies me. She deserves to be beaten every day. If only you had shaved her head, even that would have pleased me enough."

"From my brief acquaintance with Hormuze," Mirana said, "I believe he will do whatever he believes is required." She unconsciously rubbed her cheek where he'd struck her, saying, "He is a man with very set views for women and what they should do and what they should say. I doubt he will change. Also, Sira no longer has her beautiful silver hair. It is an ugly dark brown from a mixture of nut meats, and thus, Hormuze will not be distracted. It is better than having her bald, Entti."

Rorik laughed. "You must understand that there is also a child, Eze, all of eleven years old and very wise in her years, much like little Utta here. She will assist Sira to become a reasonable woman, just as will her formidable father."

"I wonder when we will learn of their fate," Mirana said as she stroked Kerzog's head. The dog nuzzled against her palms and she scratched his head.

"By winter I think," Rorik said. "Hormuze is right. It is a story the skalds will sing of for years upon years to come, whether he succeeds or he fails."

Mirana said, "It is passing strange that no Viking holds the throne of Ireland, but rather a man from a foreign land very far south. He told me the name of it, but it was difficult, and I can't remember it."

Old Alna hobbled up and said, "My beautiful little Sira, such passion in her, and now she is tortured with ugly hair. She won't like that, my lord, aye, she'll rain shrieks and fists down upon this man's head, this man who will now be king."

"She will try," Rorik said, "but I doubt she will succeed."

"You brought back Mirana," Amma said, lightly touching her fingertips to Rorik's forearm. "We have missed her, my lord."

"I missed her as well, as did Kerzog. Hafter, leave your wife alone. 'Tis time for us to hunt."

And they were gone, talking and laughing, their jests ringing out as loud as their laughter.

Mirana continued to pat Kerzog, speaking to each of the women in turn, realizing that life here had carried on, the crops had continued to grow beneath the warm summer sun, the slaves had banged glittering silver pans to keep the birds away. The women had salted fish, had weaved and dyed cloth, had baked endless loaves of flatbread over the hot embers of the fire pit, but she, Mirana, wife of Rorik Haraldsson, had still been missed, her absence felt by those she'd left behind, for she was firmly a part of Hawkfell Island now. She belonged.

She looked over at Erna, silent now, her one good hand not moving on the loom. Raki, her husband, had been the warrior to fall overboard and drown. They'd not found his body. It was difficult for all of them to accept, and the grief was there stark and deep in everyone's thoughts. But it was Erna who had stood stiff and silent, her face white, her withered arm limp against her side, her eyes accepting yet filled with pain. She'd not cried in front of them. She'd not cried with her two sons either, and they'd held themselves just as stiff and proud as their mother, listening to Lord Rorik as he'd told them that he and all the other men of Hawkfell Island could never take Raki's place, for he had been the bravest of warriors, a man of great skill and cunning, but they would be there, acting in their father's place, now and forever. And Erna had been pleased and grateful. Mirana could only imagine her grief when she'd been alone.

Then Erna had seen Gunleik bent over with the pain in his back, and she'd tended him faithfully, feeding him panza root ground into a sweet pulp to relax the knotted muscles. Now he was better, sitting near to the fire pit, the lines of pain smoothed from his forehead. Erna had moved from the loom and was now sewing near him, her fingers working quickly, her head down, but Mirana knew she was aware of Gunleik, watchful that he was getting well again.

Gunleik rose then and stood over her. Slowly, she raised her head, her look stark and proud. He handed her a small piece of buttered flatbread. She accepted it with her good hand, and slowly ate it.

Gunleik patted her shoulder and left her alone.

Mirana rose at last to go about her duties. She oversaw the cooking, wrapped a cloth about her head and helped to pack down the earth near the tables in the longhouse, a seemingly endless and very dirty job that required water to be sprinkled on the loose dirt, then packed down by hand, then struck with the heel of the palm.

Her back hurt when it was at last finished. She

rose and stretched, patted Kerzog, who then grabbed her sleeve in his mouth and dragged her outside the longhouse. She laughed. Rorik and his men had just returned.

Gunleik smiled at her. "You're happy, Mirana, and it pleases me. Rorik is a good man. You've also more dirt on your face than this monster here."

Mirana looked at Kerzog, who was blissfully rolling about on the ground.

She laughed, kissed Gunleik on the cheek, and ran to the bathing hut. She heard Rorik calling her name behind her and knew he would be with her very soon and that they would bathe together and very probably they would do other things as well. She turned and waved to him.

"Where is Mirana?"

Entti looked up, frowning at Rorik's question. "Gunleik said she went to the fields to look at the barley and rye, but that was hours ago. I haven't seen her in a while, Rorik, but she should return soon for there is the evening meal to prepare."

Rorik merely nodded and went to the bathing hut. Two days in a row now they'd been very lucky at their hunt—killed a wild boar and six fat partridge. Three of his men were in the bathing hut, naked, shouting, throwing water on each other, insulting each other's prowess. They hadn't seen Mirana.

"Come bathe, Rorik!" Sculla yelled at him.

"Aye, you smell like overripe boar!" Kron made to throw a bucket of water on him, but Rorik held up his hand.

"Let me find my beautiful wife first, then I'll be back."

"Poor little girl," Sculla said, shaking his big head

mournfully, "soon she'll not be able to walk if Rorik has his way."

"Ha, he will have his way until she is so large with child he dare not continue."

Rorik didn't laugh, though he did smile at the thought of Mirána's belly filled with his child. It warmed him and he called out her name again and again. He went to the fields, but she wasn't there. He went to the cow byre, then to the small houses his warriors had built just beyond the fields.

He couldn't find her. He stood next to the palisade walls, breathing in the soft sweet air, looking over his island. Suddenly, he felt something cold and dark twisting deep within him, and it scared him witless.

He immediately raised the alarm. He set guards on the longboats immediately, not knowing why he felt it so important, just doing it.

Mirana was shivering. Her hair was still damp, tangled around her head and down her back. She wore only a wet shift, all that he'd allowed her when he'd taken her from the bathing hut several hours before.

He looked at her now, rocking back and forth on his heels. There was such rage in his eyes that she had to look away from him.

" 'Tis your fault," he said. "I vowed I would avenge my Asta if you returned. Aye, I prayed for your return, mistress, prayed you wouldn't die, prayed that I would be the one to kill you and avenge my Asta."

"But why would you want to hurt me, Gurd? I did nothing to Asta. I loved her as I would a dear sister."

"You let her eat your food, you murdering sly bitch!" He jumped to his feet and she thought he would kill her then, but he didn't, just kicked her ribs, sending her sprawling onto her back, her chest heaving with the pain.

"Why did you let her touch your food? You knew—I saw it in your eyes and I see it now—you wanted her to eat it. You knew she would die."

It was clear to her then, all very clear and very frightening. "You poisoned my food."

Gurd stared down at her, his hands fisted at his sides. "Aye, I did, but you didn't die, you let my Asta die instead, and you did it apurpose, and I swore I would make you pay for that. The gods sent you back to me so I could make you pay."

"You tried to poison me again but the taste was awful and thus I ate only a few bites. Sira was blamed for it."

"Aye, poor little Sira, a beautiful girl who didn't deserve your cruelty or Rorik's. Such lovely hair she had. I couldn't bear it when he whipped her. I wanted to strike him when he offered to let me whip her, too, believing I would want to hit her and force her to her knees for Asta's death. I left then, for her cries smote me, and that was your fault, too, for you convinced everyone that she was guilty."

She wanted to tell him that she hadn't done anything save lie in her bed and vomit until her face was blue, her throat so raw with pain that she couldn't talk, her belly so knotted with agony that she'd wanted to die more times than she could count. She said instead, "Why did you want to kill me? What did I ever do to you, Gurd?"

He came down next to her on his haunches. She didn't move, remained on her back, her arms covering her ribs as best she could. He raised his hand, then slowly lowered it as he said, "You dared to keep me from Entti. You made her change, made her sneer at us, made her refuse us, made her refuse *me*. I wanted her and I'd had her before you came, before you made yourself the mistress and gave your insolent orders and stuck your proud nose in the air, treating all of us like we were thralls.

"Aye, I wanted Entti, and I'd had her before you came and Asta knew and it pleased me that she knew, her anger and jealousy pleased me, but I had to show Asta that I was a man and that she couldn't have the ordering of me, ever. Always Asta laughed and I knew she laughed at me, even though she swore it was only her nature to laugh, to jest, that she loved me. But she changed and she taunted me and I knew it well. I needed Entti to prove to her that I was her master and she would never have a say in what I did."

"But that's madness," Mirana said, then instantly regretted the words, for he was on her, straddling her, leaning over her so close that she could smell the rage on his breath, see the wildness in his eyes, and he was locking his hands around her throat now, and she knew then that she would die. She'd come home, all right. Home to die.

Suddenly he leapt off her, panting hard, backing away from her as if he couldn't bear the sight of her, the feel of her. She sat up, rubbing her hands over her throat. The thick rope around her left wrist had rubbed it raw, but she no longer noticed the grinding pain of it, nor the pain in her ribs.

"No," he said, more to himself than to her. "No, you're not to die here, not like this. It must appear an accident so that none will suspect me."

"Asta loved you!"

"Aye, she did, and you killed her."

She could only stare at him.

"You killed Asta and you forbade Entti to come to me."

"Please Gurd, listen to me. It is Entti who refused to be the whore any longer. If you had taken Entti, it would have been rape, do you understand me? If you had forced her, she would have killed you herself. It is true, I swear it to you."

He was shaking his head even as he yelled, "Nay, 'tis a lie! Entti was mad for me! She begged me to take her, told me again and again that I was a better man than all the others on Hawkfell Island. But then you refused to let her to come to me. Then you killed my Asta."

Now it was her turn to yell and she did, so frustrated and afraid that she couldn't help herself. "But why would I want Asta to die? There is no sense in that! I loved her as a sister!"

He was silent a moment, his brow furrowed. "It matters not. You did it. You made her eat most of the food from your plate. I didn't realize what you were doing until it was too late. I had to watch her laugh and jest and knew that soon she would be dying because of what you did. You knew about the poison. You cajoled her. Perhaps it was jealousy of her that made you kill her, I know not. You are a woman and women are creatures beyond a man's understanding. You killed my wife and now I will avenge her."

"You fool! Do you think me stupid? Do you think I would chance killing myself as well as Asta? It makes no sense! I did not know the food was poisoned!"

His huge upper body tightened in his rage, but he forced himself to calm with a shrug, for he was the victor and knew it. "It matters not how you knew. I just know that you did. And my Asta is dead and Entti is wedded to Hafter. There is nothing here for me now."

What else was there to say? She lowered her head, the weight of hopelessness heavy on her, defeating her, numbing her mind. She felt beyond herself in those moments, and beyond Gurd, beyond the pain that would take her from life, and she knew it was because she was preparing herself to die, preparing herself to leave this earth, to leave Hawkfell Island, to leave Rorik.

She didn't want to leave Rorik.

She drew a deep steadying breath. She felt herself planted firmly within her own mind and body again. She would not die without a struggle. Gurd was the strongest man on Hawkfell Island, his years upon years as blacksmith making his chest and arms so powerful that few of the men ever wanted to wrestle with him, even in games. Rorik would laugh and say he had no wish for Gurd to break his back.

What could she do?

She could run. She looked about, careful to keep her head lowered so he couldn't see her eyes, guess at her intent. He was standing over her, breathing hard.

He'd brought her to the thick woods at the eastern end of the island, she recognized it now, for dunlin were flying low overhead, screeching and angry, for they nested here and were worried about their young. If she could run and hide in the deeper part of the woods, then she could sneak back toward the farmstead.

"Let us go," Gurd said. He grabbed her left arm and jerked her to her feet. He quickly untied the rope at her wrist. "You look like a witch."

Her damp hair was filled with twigs and leaves and dirt, her damp shift filthy from the ground. He held her there, his long thick fingers closing completely around her upper arm. He shook her, bringing her close to him.

"Aye, you're beautiful, Mirana, daughter of Audun, and you should have remained at Clontarf. You had your chance to wed with that damned foreigner who is now the king, but you didn't. You wanted to return here and make my life a misery, to brag about how you killed my Asta, to taunt me with your knowledge and how you'd succeeded in escaping punishment for what you did. And you've turned Entti against me."

"You won't escape, Gurd. You will die too."

He pulled her to him, kissed her hard, then his huge hand was rubbing over her breasts and down to her belly, then he dropped his hand and turned about. He was walking toward the cliff, dragging her now, for she knew his intent, and she had no intention of going quietly to her death. She screamed and yelled and grabbed at bushes and low-lying tree branches, but he just jerked at her and kept pulling her, her left arm shooting with pain now, and she wondered if he would wrench it from the socket. She dug in her heels, but that was useless.

They cleared the trees. The cliff edge was but twenty yards away. It was steepest here, the drop sheer, the bottom thick with tumbled black rocks, ancient and scarred with time, with surf striking against them hard, sending spumes of spray thirty feet into the air. She would die, for there was no ledge or outcropping of bushes to break her fall to those rocks.

She felt the black hopelessness curl through her, recognized it, and refused to accept it. She wasn't dead yet. She began cursing again, yelling again at the top of her lungs. "Rorik! Rorik! Help me, help me!"

Again and again she yelled. Gurd only laughed, shouting over his shoulder that she should scream herself voiceless for there were none to hear her, that the men still hadn't returned from the mainland, and when they did return she still wouldn't be missed for more hours. It would be a long time before they began to search for her. Perhaps, he said, screaming at her now, just perhaps the tide would wash her out into the sea and none would ever find her. Ah, and he would search for her as well, his face as downcast and worried as all the rest of them. Aye, he liked the thought of that, for she had pretended grief at Asta's death. He would pretend grief at hers.

Closer and closer he dragged her to the cliff edge. She yelled at him, "I will be found! I am wearing only my shift. Rorik will never believe I was out here in the woods wearing only my shift and fell to my death. He will not believe the sea could have pulled my clothes off me. He will find you out, Gurd."

He stopped in his tracks, whirled about and jerked her hard against him. "Aye, you're right," he said, and he grabbed her shift by the neck and ripped it off at her shoulder, a long single rent. "Now if your body is found, all will think the tides did rip your clothes off you, for they will see that even your shift is ripped. Mayhap even the fish will enjoy you."

Then he draped the ripped shift around her, fastening it securely over her left shoulder.

"Aye, that will suffice," he said.

Ten more yards, naught more, just ten more yards. He was jerking her and she was trying not to cry, trying to keep her wits about her, but it was difficult, so very difficult. Suddenly, she saw a loose rock just ahead of her. Without hesitation, she leaned down, grabbed up the rock and began again to yell Rorik's name.

So very close to the cliff edge now. She held the rock firmly, readying it and herself, and let him drag her just to his side. "Gurd," she said softly, and waited for him to turn.

Just as he did, she raised the rock and brought it down hard on his temple. It cracked loud against his head. He stared at her, just stood there, not releasing her left wrist, just staring at her, saying nothing.

"Let me go!" she yelled into his face. "I hit you! Die, damn you!"

He smiled at her then and dragged her another step toward the cliff. She cried out and brought the rock down on his head again. The rock cracked apart and this time blood spurted from his head. He slowed, he stood there quietly, gently weaving back and forth.

Finally, he dropped her wrist. But he didn't fall. He just stood there. Blood flowed over his forehead, into his eyes, dripped to his chest and to the ground, but he didn't seem to notice.

Mirana threw the two pieces of rock against his chest with all her strength, then turned and ran, her ripped shift flapping around her.

It was at that moment that Rorik, Hafter and Sculla behind him, burst through the line of woods. He saw his wife and he saw Gurd, standing there near the edge of the cliffs. He didn't understand, but it didn't matter.

"Mirana!"

He grabbed her to him, saw that she was all right, and quickly gave her to Hafter. He went in a dead run toward Gurd, who had now turned to the setting sun in the west, and he was still standing there, just staring off into the sky, so still he was, and the blood continued to stream down his face, dripping onto his feet and onto the ground.

"Gurd!"

He turned very slowly and watched Rorik run toward him.

"I'm sorry, Rorik, but I had to do it," Gurd said. "I had to kill her. She's below on the rocks. I wanted to strangle her, but it had to look an accident. Aye, Rorik, she's on the rocks below and she's dead. 'Tis justice, for she murdered my Asta. Aye, 'tis done now."

Rorik stared at the man he'd known all his life. He was standing there so quietly, his great hands limp and open at his sides.

"Gurd, this makes no sense."

Gurd raised his head and stared at Rorik. Then he looked beyond and saw Mirana. His eyes widened. "How is she there?" he said. "She is dead. I threw her over the cliff. I heard her scream. I heard her bones crush against those rocks."

Then Gurd yelled, a soul-curdling yell that filled the air. In the next instant, he ran at Rorik, his massive arms going around Rorik's chest, squeezing him, harder and harder yet, crushing him. He lifted Rorik, his face against Rorik's throat, for Rorik was the taller, but he hadn't Gurd's massive strength.

"Rorik!"

It was Hafter and Sculla who were on Gurd, each gripping an arm, pulling with all their strength. It did no good.

Rorik felt blackness filling him, felt it mask the awful pain from his ribs, knew his back would break, yet at the same time, he felt calm and detached from the man whose ribs were being crushed. He grabbed Gurd's head between his hands, gritted his teeth against the intense pain, and pressed with all his might. It did no good. Rorik drew back his hands, and with his last cogent thought, he fisted them, drew his arms back as far as he could, then drove fists against Gurd's ears.

Gurd screamed. His arms fell away and he staggered, yelling, crying now, and he took Hafter and

Sculla to the ground with him. Blood flowed from both ears, mingling wildly with the blood from his head. Rorik stood over him, his ribs on fire, light-headed from lack of breath. He heaved and groaned and stood there, staring down at the man who had very nearly killed Mirana and him.

He saw Mirana coming slowly toward him, her eyes on Gurd, who lay on the ground, howling and bawling like a child. Hafter and Sculla backed away from him, and it was in that instant that Gurd flung himself away from them, fell again to his knees, then forward onto his face, and rolled over the edge of the cliff.

He made no sound. They heard nothing over the crashing sound of the waves against the rocks below.

Rorik drew her against him. He kissed her and pulled her away.

# Epilogue

THE SKALD TAMAK, famous for his melodious *kennings* and his wondrous speaking voice, arrived at Hawkfell Island at the beginning of a winter storm, a storm that presaged such ferocity that Lord Rorik had ordered even the cows, sheep, chickens, and the three goats brought into the longhouse for safety after he'd looked at the roof of the stable. The longboats and two warships were dragged beyond the narrow beach to the higher ground and covered with thick oak branches.

The longhouse was filled with the warmth from the fire pit, a pale blue haze of smoke, and smelled of the rich hot flatbread just removed from the hot embers.

Tamak accepted a cup of rich mead from Entti, smiled at her too hopefully, bringing her husband, Hafter, closer, his eyes narrowed. Tamak, not a stupid man, then turned swiftly to the lord of Hawkfell Island, and said, "Lord Rorik, I am not here by happenstance. 'Tis the king himself who has sent me to recount to you all that has happened."

He saw the lord's wife grip her husband's hand and turned to smile down at her when she said, "Which king?"

Tamak shook his head, cleared his throat, drank more of the mead, regarded his audience for a long moment, preparing them and himself, then began to speak.

His voice filled the longhouse. He spoke of Magnificent Sitric, an old man barely clinging to life who defied death itself and all the gods of the afterlife and emerged the victor, renewing himself, claiming once again a young man's vigor and strength and shortened years. Aye, and this proud Sitric would rule now for more decades than could be comprehended by a mortal's mind. He had seen men as babes and he would watch them die as old men. And he would go on still.

The king was ably assisted in his miraculous renewal by his brave wizard, Hormuze, who himself had bargained with Odin All-Father, failed, then challenged Odin to a contest of logic. Hormuze had won, for Odin became tangled in the wizard's words and thus lost the skein of his thoughts, and old King Sitric thus wedded Mirana, daughter of Audun. She was also changed with him during the long magical hours of their wedding night, her name no longer Mirana, but Naphta, and she grew taller, it was said by some, but her beautiful black hair remained long and darkly glistening, covered with a soft veil of diaphanous silk. Her eyes had changed, too, it was said by some, from green to a vibrant blue, so clear and light they reflected the heavens and all the mysteries of the beyond.

'Twas said that the coming together of the old king and the one young virgin Hormuze had himself selected was the act that set the magic into motion, that the wizard Hormuze presided over them all during that night, and when the sun rose, and all the king's warriors were there waiting, the king came to them reborn and young again and wondrous handsome, but the resemblance was there to the old king, all recognized that, and they saw, too, that the old wizard Hormuze smiled upon the young king and queen and granted them long life, and he disappeared then, simply vanished into the pearl light of dawn, into the soft shadows that still clung to the earth before the harsh shining of the sun, melting into the clouds as if he were as insubstantial as they. And the warriors and the people were awed and silent, and then they all went forth to tell of the miracle that had occurred at Clontarf that night.

Tamak spoke briefly of the disappearance of the master of Clontarf, one Einar Thorsson, whose spirit, it was said by some, was seen in the reflection of the wizard Hormuze when he himself vanished that early morning.

Tamak then spoke at great length of the just and honorable king, wise in the ways of men far beyond his years, and of his queen, whose lustrous black hair changed yet again, becoming silver as the vivid lights of dawn as they lit the darkest corners of the earth, and that her silver hair was the king's pride and desire, hair so long and radiant that men were brought to tears by the sight of it.

He spoke of the queen's belly, now swelling with the first of the king's promised sons. He sang of the queen's soft voice and her gentle manner that made all love her, the king most of all, and a small girl who had been the daughter of the old wizard Hormuze, left in the care of the king and queen, and beloved by them.

He spoke reverently of Odin All-Father, content now that he had lost to the wizard Hormuze, and how he blessed this king and queen and all the sons who would be born of their magical union.

There was utter silence once Tamak had finished his tale. The rush lights were dim, casting long shadows against the walls of the longhouse. No one spoke for the longest time, then Rorik, the lord of Hawkfell Island, rose and stretched, and told Tamak that he would remain for so long as he wished. He thanked him, and gave to him a magnificent silver arm bracelet won on a raid many years before near Kiev by Lord Rorik's father. There was a smile in Lord Rorik's amazing blue eyes—as vibrant as the light blue of the queen's eyes, perhaps, which was surely odd—and a bigger smile on his mouth. He turned from Tamak then, kissed his wife's fingers, then bade good night to all his people. A huge mongrel followed the lord and lady from the outer hall.

Tamak drank more mead to soothe the burning in his throat. Even though the hours had passed quickly and the words had flown easily from his mouth, the *kennings* smooth and precise, just to his liking, there was pain now and many hours of rest needed to come.

He wondered as he fell into sleep, listening to the snuffling of the goats too close to his sleeve for his liking, what King Sitric had meant when he'd said to Tamak, "After you have recounted this miracle to the lord and lady of Hawkfell Island, I wish you to return and tell me exactly what they said."

They'd said nothing, Tamak thought, just thanked him, said nothing more. There had been that smile on the lord's mouth. The lady's eyes had been downcast. Had he seen amusement in the lord's eyes? Had he possibly heard the lady giggle? Surely not. There was no reason for her to giggle. He imagined he would never know what they'd thought of his miraculous tale, for the lord of Hawkfell Island did not seem a man to blurt out his thoughts or speak an incautious word.

Tamak fell asleep finally, his throat soothed from the sweet mead, dreaming of the beautiful silver hair of the queen, a beautiful lady, indeed, but one whose temper wasn't perhaps all that gracious and tranquil all the time, but no matter, and of the sweet smile of the woman Entti who'd given him the mead.

SPECIAL PREVIEW!

Turn the page for a look at
Catherine Coulter's historical romance,
*The Wyndham Legacy*, a novel of mystery,
humor, and unforgettable characters.

**Rosebud Cottage, Winchelsea**
**January 1813**

"I'M VERY SORRY to tell you this, Miss Cochrane, but there is more and it isn't good."

Mr. Jollis, her mother's solicitor, didn't sound sorry at all. He sounded unaccountably pleased, which was strange, surely, but she held silent, not only because of her grief over her mother's death but because she was used to holding herself silent. It was a habit of many years. Over time, she'd learned a lot about people by simply listening and watching them as they spoke. She realized in this moment, in Mr. Jollis's meaningful pause, that her father didn't yet know of her mother's death. She'd forgotten him in the suddenness of it, in the numbness it had instilled in her. Now there was no one else to tell him. She had to write to him herself. She could see him reading her words, see his disbelief, his bowing pain when he finally realized it was true. She closed her eyes a moment against the pain she knew he would feel. He would feel endless pain, for he loved her mother more than he loved any other human being. But her mother, alive and laughing one moment, was dead the next. Her death was so needless, so stupid really: a wrenched carriage accident, the shaft snapping for no apparent reason, sending the carriage hurtling off the winding road that ran too close above the chalk South Downs cliffs, near Ditchling Beacon. Those cliffs rose eight hundred and thirteen feet into the air, then plunged to the deserted beach below. Her mother was killed instantly, but her body was washed out with the tide and hadn't been recovered. At least it hadn't been recovered yet, and it had already been a day and a half. She looked up when Mr. Jollis cleared his throat, evidently prepared to finish his thought.

"As I said, Miss Cochrane," Mr. Jollis said, that smug tone coming more to the surface now, "I am very sorry about this but Rosebud Cottage is leased and the lessor is your, er, father, Lord Chase."

"I didn't know that." Indeed, she'd always assumed that her mother owned the cottage. But then again, perhaps that was the way of it when a man supported and kept a woman. All remained his, thus he retained his power and all his prerogatives. It was merely another unexpected blow that she didn't feel at the moment. She waited, silent, her body utterly still. His face changed then, and he was looking at her differently, not as a man feigning sympathy for a bereaved daughter, but as a man assessing a woman for his own uses.

She'd seen the look before, but not that many times on that many male faces. She'd been protected, but now, she realized, she was unprotected. Her father was in Yorkshire and she was here, quite alone, except for dear Badger.

"I must write my father," she said then, her voice curt, colder than it would normally be, but she wanted him to go away. "I imagine that since the lease will run out soon that I will have to go to Chase Park."

"There is another option, perhaps," Mr. Jollis said. He leaned toward her, like a hound on a scent, she thought as she eyed him with more hostility than she'd eyed anyone in her entire life.

"No there isn't," she said, her voice as cold as the ice shards hanging from the cottage eaves outside.

"Perhaps," he said, still leaning forward, his right hand outstretched toward her now, "just perhaps his lordship won't want you to live at Chase Park."

"His wife died seven months ago, just before my yearly visit. I cannot imagine that he wouldn't want me there. She was the only one who didn't care for my presence, and that, I suppose, is very understandable. She held him as her husband, but she didn't have his regard. I have long understood her bitterness. However, now she is dead."

"Ah, but now his lordship must be very careful, you understand, Miss Cochrane. His lordship is in mourning, very deep mourning. All his neighbors will be watching him closely, indeed, all of society, all those whose opinions are important to him, will be watching him closely."

"Why? Surely he won't wed again, at least not anytime soon. I am merely his bastard daughter. Who would care if I lived at Chase Park or not?"

"People would care and they would find out very quickly. It shows the ultimate disrespect for his dead wife, Miss Cochrane. You must believe me, for I know the ways of society and you do not."

She didn't believe him, but she didn't wish to argue with him anymore. "I do not believe men are watched all that closely, only women," she said, her voice remote. "Nor do I believe that men mourn anything that deeply for all that long a time." Her body became even more still, though she could feel herself shrinking back from his still outstretched hand.

She remembered when her father's wife had died. His reaction, she'd thought during her visit, when the countess had finally died birthing another babe, had been one of profound relief. When tears had wet his eyes, she knew it was from the death of the small infant boy, dead two hours after its birth, not from his wife's expiration.

"That is possible," he said. "But you have no one to look after you now, Miss Cochrane. Perhaps you should consider looking for someone well circumstanced who would protect you and keep you in this lovely little cottage."

She smiled at him. Mr. Jollis, like everyone who knew her for a long time, was startled at the smile. It was beautiful and it made him feel warm all the way to the bunions on his toes. She had two dimples and her teeth were small and white and as perfect as her smile. He could not recall ever seeing her smile before. "If I choose to remain here at the cottage, will you tell me who owns it?"

"It is Squire Archibald, but surely since you have so little money, you cannot consider keeping the lease, why it's absurd, it's—"

She rose, her hands at her sides. "I should like you to leave now, Mr. Jollis. If there is more I need to know, please write me a letter."

He rose then as well, for he had no choice, at least not at the moment, and stared down at her, her beautiful smile forgotten. "You think to be above yourself, Miss Cochrane. No matter, you're a bastard, nothing more, and that's what you will always be. You cannot remain here. The lease on the cottage ends on the fifteenth of next month and you will have no money to renew it. Squire Archibald is all of seventy and certainly not a candidate for your wiles. No, it is money he would require, not you warming his ancient bed. You will leave then. If your esteemed father wants you, then he will give you a home, but for how long? Don't forget, your beautiful mother is dead. Do you truly believe he ever wanted you? No, it was your mother he wanted, no other, certainly not you. I would consider becoming your protector, Miss Cochrane—"

Her face was very pale now, her eyes dulling in her rage, but he saw only the dullness, not the fury, for she just stared at him, then turned on her heel, and left the small drawing room without a word.

Mr. Jollis didn't know what to do. Would she consider his well-phrased proposal? He thought her uppity, arrogant, but that would change. He wondered if she was a virgin. He wasn't left to wonder anything then, for Badger, the servant who had stood as protector to both Mrs. Cochrane and the Duchess, appeared in the doorway. He was a large man, well-muscled, ugly as a fence post, his hair white and thick as a prophet's, and at this moment, there was blood in his eyes.

Mr. Jollis backed up a step.

"Sir," Badger said gently, too gently, "it is time to remove your carcass from the premises. If your carcass isn't absent within a very few number of seconds, I will have to see that his lordship learns of your most regrettable behavior. He won't be pleased."

"Ha," Mr. Jollis said, for he knew that this man didn't know what he was talking about. "His lordship would be glad to get the little bastard off his hands and no mistake about that. Soon, Badger, you will be without money yourself, for she has none to pay you. Then,

I dare say, you won't speak to your betters like this. It doesn't matter that you have more wits than you should, that you have excellent speech—who taught you to speak like a gentleman?—no matter, you're still here and you're nothing but a servant, of no account at all."

Badger, who smiled at him and shook his head, was on him in an instant, lifting him bodily, and tucking him under his mighty arm. He carried him to the front door, and dumped him out onto the frozen ground, that would, in five months, bloom wildly with the Duchess's red, yellow, and white roses. He turned back into the cottage, saw the Duchess, and grinned, showing a goodly sized space between his front teeth. "He'll rest a bit in the snow, but he's all right, don't you worry." He picked up her hand and made it into a fist. "No, Duchess, I've told you how to swing and strike and keep your thumb tucked under. Why didn't you knock him over the flower box?"

She tried to smile, she truly did, but her face seemed as frozen as the earth outside. "I just didn't want to see him anymore, Badger."

"No wonder," he said and gave her back her hand. "But don't forget now, if a fellow goes beyond the line, you shove his choppers down his throat, that or you slam your knee upward as hard as you can."

"I will. I promise. Thank you, Badger."

He grunted and took himself off to the kitchen to prepare the curry sauce for the chicken, currently roasting gently over the open grate. The cook and maid, Miss Priss, as Badger had always called her, had left for Welford-on-Avon to see her ailing auntie some two years before. Badger had taken over her duties. He was an excellent cook. He just wished the Duchess ate more of his wonderful concoctions.

Mrs. Cochrane had told him many years before that when the Duchess visited Chase Park, everyone pretended—at least outwardly—that she was some distant cousin from Holland or Italy, though her Dutch was nonexistent and her Italian was singularly bad. But no one ever said anything because she was, after all, the Duchess, and she was so very beautiful and so glorious in her pride and arrogance that all simply stood in awe of her, striving to please her, to make her give them one of her rare smiles. Mrs. Cochrane had smiled her beautiful smile at that, saying that she'd been positively terrified to let her go to Chase Park, and just look what had happened. She'd come back the Duchess and that was what she'd remained.

Badger heard the door to the drawing room close. He could see her going to the small writing desk, seating herself gracefully, her movements slow and elegant, and writing his lordship of their mutual loss.

The Earl of Chase read of her mother's death before she could write to him of it, and he informed her through his secretary, Mr. Crittaker, that she was to pack her things and be ready for the carriage that would bring her to Chase Park. She was to bring Badger along for protection. He gave her two weeks to comply with his wishes.

The two weeks came and passed. No one came to fetch her. She didn't know what to do. She stood by the window of the small parlor and waited. She wondered if she should write to her father and remind him of his instruction to her, but no, she couldn't bring herself to do that. It was too humiliating. She would wait. Four more days passed. She thought: *he grieves for my mother and he no longer wants me. He has forgotten me. I'm alone now. What will I do?*

Then she realized that she'd always dreaded going to Chase Park on her yearly jaunts. Just stepping into that impossibly grand Italianate entrance hall with all its half-millennium-old dark wainscotting and equally old paintings with their heavy gold-encrusted frames, and that huge, utterly overpowering central staircase with still more ancestral paintings climbing the wall, alone, made her freeze inside and gave her stomach cramps. She had walked through the great oak doors every year and immediately begun to count down the fourteen days she had to remain there, to pretend as though all these noble people and all the children of these noble people and all these servants of the noble people liked her and truly welcomed her, when they all wished she had never been conceived.

At least this year the Countess of Chase hadn't been there to shrivel her with her cold looks and the bitter disdain that radiated from her. The countess had died just the week before, and the mansion was draped with black crepe and every female wore a black gown and all the males wore black arm bands. She'd heard the servants whisper that the countess had been too old for childbearing and look what had come of it—the poor dear had died, cursing her husband, for he had forced her this final and last time, forced himself upon her until she conceived—at least that's what all the servants believed—forced her and forced her and look what had come of it. And, after all, she had managed to provide the earl with two healthy boys and twin girls, and it wasn't her fault that both boys had drowned in that boat race and left only the twins. All waited for the earl to take a new wife, a very young new wife who would breed a child every year until the earl was satisfied that no matter how many accidents occurred there would still be a boy left to succeed to the title and all the Wyndham lands. A man need only wait six months and it was past that time now. That's what she'd heard and then she'd repeated to Mr. Jollis, the miserable creature.

She frowned. Perhaps that's why he didn't want her now at Chase Park. He'd found his next countess and he didn't want to have his bastard there with his new wife. Yes, that was it. He naturally wanted to please a new wife and bringing a bastard into her new home and parading the bastard under her nose wouldn't accomplish pleasure, much less bring any harmony to the new union. But why didn't he simply write and tell her? She believed her father many things, but never a coward. It made no sense.

It began to rain, now just a drizzle, but the Duchess knew the signs. Before long, the drizzle would become sheets of slamming slate-gray water, driven against the windows by a fierce wind blowing off the Channel.

Even though he had deserted her now, she had to admit that her father had supported her mother and her for eighteen years, and her mother two years before she'd been born even. She had been like his wife, only, of course, she wasn't, she was just his mistress, with no legal rights, no recourse, nothing. But now that her mother was dead, she supposed she might as well be dead too, for he no longer felt any responsibility toward her, no longer had to pretend any liking toward her. He'd probably decided that since she was eighteen, it was now her responsibility to see to herself. But why had he bothered to lie to her? Why had he told her that she was coming to Chase Park? It had been a lie, buy why, she couldn't begin to imagine. All she knew was that she was utterly alone. Mama had no one, as far as she knew, at least there were never any letters, never any presents at Christmas from relatives of her mother's. She assumed they were Cochranes, surely that was her mother's name after all and not some tawdry made-up name. No, there couldn't be any brothers or sisters or aunts. It had always been just the two of them and the frequent visits from the earl.

The rain cascaded against the window. She wondered what she would do. Her mother's solicitor had told her in that sniggering way of his, for he knew well that her mother wasn't the widow she always pretended she was, but a nobleman's mistress, kept in this little love nest by the earl's man of business in London, and that the lease was ended on the fifteenth of the next month. The way he'd treated her made her feel dirty, but more than dirty, she'd felt incredible anger. He all but told her that she was no better than her mother, and pray, what was wrong with her loving beautiful mother? But she knew the answer to that, she simply shied away from it as she always did. At least she hadn't allowed him to make his insulting offer of another love nest, this one paid for by him.

She rose slowly, shivering in the sudden damp chill of the late afternoon. The fire was dying down. It was growing colder by the minute. She rose, carefully placed more logs on the fire, then began to pace the small room, lightly slapping her hands against her arms for warmth. She knew she had to do something, but what? She had no skills at governessing or being an old lady's companion or even creating a stylish bonnet. She'd been raised as a gentlewoman, thus her only talents lay in her ability to please a man, all with the goal of finding a husband who would overlook her unfortunate antecedents.

She paced and paced, feeling infinitely bitter, then wanting to cry, for her mother was dead, her beautiful mother who had loved the earl probably more than her mother had loved her, loved him even more than she'd hated the position in which he'd placed her.

Mr. Jollis had bragged how he knew society better than she. Her eyes narrowed now at that impertinence. She'd pored over the *London Times* and the *Gazette* since the age of ten, devouring all the goings-on of society, laughing at their seemingly endless foibles and acts of idiocy, their disregard for the most minimal restraints. Yes, she knew society and their ways, and as she thought about it, she realized that she did have one talent, but she'd never really considered it as a way to earn a living—she'd never had to.

She stopped in her tracks, staring unseeingly at the thick slabs of rain pounding against the drawing room window. Yes, she had a talent, an unusual talent, certainly a talent never recognized possible in a female. Was it possible? She would have to discuss it with Badger. If there was a way to make money at it, why then, he would know how it would be done.

As she walked up the charming but narrow stairway upstairs to her bedchamber, she smiled for the first time since her mother's death.

*　*　*